SKELMERSDALE

FICTION RESERVE STOCK
LL 60

The Four of Us

SCEPTRE

Also by Adrian Mourby

We Think the World of Him

The Four of Us

ADRIAN MOURBY

SCEPTRE

07012657

Copyright © 1997 Adrian Mourby

First published in 1997 by Hodder and Stoughton
A division of Hodder Headline PLC
A Sceptre Book

The right of Adrian Mourby to be identified as the Author of
the Work has been asserted by him in accordance with the
Copyright, Designs and Patents Act 1988.

10 9 8 7 6 5 4 3 2 1

British Library C.I.P.
A CIP catalogue record for this title is available
from the British Library

ISBN 0 340 64921 6

Typeset by Hewer Text Composition Services, Edinburgh
Printed and bound in Great Britain by
Mackays of Chatham PLC, Chatham, Kent

Hodder and Stoughton
A division of Hodder Headline PLC
338 Euston Road
London NW1 3BH

To my wife
Without Whose Help this book was begun
But Without Whose Help it would never have been finished

Acknowledgements ∫

My thanks to Norman Schwenk, Tim Jacob, Hilary Whitworth and to Jeremy Loeb for his inspiration.

Author's Note ∫

Much of this fiction takes place at the University of Wales which is in reality a fine, well-run and highly principled organisation which treats its staff with an exceptional degree of compassion and courtesy.

Introduction $\int$

'The problem with women,' said David Mosford, raising a glass in the candlelight, 'is that after children . . . they just change personality.'

'And the problem with men,' his wife replied from the other end of the table, 'is that they don't.'

And because the night was dark outside, and the Mosfords' dining room was warm and friendly, everybody laughed. And later on, as several couples walked home through the chill clear night, or fell into their double beds, there was a general view that Davy had been very much on form with that thing about women changing, and men staying the same, after the children are born.

Everyone had enjoyed dinner at the Mosfords. It was a big affair, five couples down that long dark table. So much noise, so much food! No-one could tell how nervous David had been. Nor could they have guessed that at 4pm Helena Mosford had sent her husband out to the shops, ostensibly for some missing ingredients, but really because if she didn't get him out of her sight she would have thrown – or said – something she might regret.

The Mosfords' home was a place where Truth was respected but the home truths that Helena might have flung at her husband were not the kind of thing that any sensible hostess airs four hours before a dinner party.

Unaware – or seemingly unaware – of this, Davy had had no problem enjoying himself right up until the moment their last guests bolted for the babysitter.

'Went very well,' he announced, returning from the front door and pulling off his jacket.

'Yes, very well,' replied Helena, collecting up the most valuable glasses.

'I didn't go on too much, did I?'

'Not too much.'

She was loading the trolley which had once belonged to Davy's parents and which still did excellent service bringing in and taking out.

'Just a *bit* too much?' he asked watching her bend over to secure something that wasn't.

Helena stood up.

'Just enough,' she admitted.

'I went on *just enough*?'

'You were very funny, darling. I'm just going up to check on Nick.' She gave him a little kiss.

'Linna,' Davy called after her as she went up the stairs. 'I thought you looked wonderful tonight!'

'So did you,' she called back.

Not entirely the worse for wear, he gazed at the tall mahogany overmantel where stood this short, stocky man with gold-rimmed glasses. If the truth be told, it was probably the clothes that did it. They definitely looked good, far more splendid than he. But then of course they were younger. David Mosford was something a little over forty but not yet forty-one. He had reached that stage in life when it was more important to look good for one's age than just to look good. Fortunately, having lost quite a lot of hair in his early twenties, Davy had never considered his large expanse of naked scalp the stigmata of middle age. That broad shining forehead was what he had always presented to the world. He looked like that as a baby, he looked pretty much like that as a postgraduate student. In fact, the brief period when Davy Mosford had hair on top of his head was really something of an aberration. To his more obstreperous students he argued that anyone who interpreted his baldness as a sign of ageing was overlooking the simple fact that it was one of the few bits of him that hadn't changed at all since he was twenty-two.

Helena came downstairs carrying her son's flask of night-time juice.

'He's breathing in that way again,' she told David and looked at him for guidance. 'That way' was how Nick had been the time he was so awfully sick in his sleep and Helena feared he might have choked to death.

'Nick's fine,' David replied. 'Mr Evans said that was nothing to worry about.' He put his arms around her. 'You should relax, Linna.'

Davy stroked her hair, hair which was as conspicuously present as his was absent. It had been magnificent hair when they had married, a living sculpture, so long and strong that it seemed to have a life of its own. She could twist and tug it into any number of styles and when she slept with it loose, it could take you a while to locate her face in the morning. But in recent years life had taken its toll on Helena's hair. Life had thinned the living sculpture so that if she put it up for the evening, its tenure was precarious. All evening that dark mane had stayed at its station, crowning her beauty. But now it was beginning to cascade down.

He lifted some of the strands away and moved just a little closer in the preliminaries to a kiss. Helena looked away, fingering her loose hair. 'I really think perhaps I ought to . . .' she said.

'Oh, yes,' said David, accepting the almost inevitable and feeling her melt away from him. The dinner party had been a definite success and, unbeknownst to the guests, it had also been something of a relaunch for the two of them. Davy always enjoyed an audience and Helena could shine in company if the atmosphere was right and this evening it had been. They had begun to feel very much like a couple. They had even made the same jokes that everyone else made about how wonderfully awful it was to be married with children. And when Davy wasn't entertaining everyone by talking about himself, Helena asked enough questions for the guests to start talking too. They seemed so well suited. But the slightest threat to her son took Helena back to a world of more primal concerns.

'I'll . . . see you later,' she said and absently kissed his cheek as she left their embrace. Helena Mosford was, quite easily, half an inch taller than her husband. As Davy liked his wife to wear heels on occasions like this, that kiss definitely came from somewhere above, bestowed like a blessing from a distracted goddess with other things on her mind.

'Yes,' said Davy. He looked down at the table, with its liberal splattering of wax from guttered candles, as if the furniture might be able to tell him what was supposed to happen next. Probably he would read something over a glass of something and make his way to bed in an hour or so, by which time Helena would be asleep on the temporary bed outside Nicky's room. These days, that bed was one of the most permanent features of their marriage.

The night was dark and Davy could hear the trees suddenly surge outside in the blackness. A dense tangle of conifers shielded the Mosfords' house from the winds that blew up the Taff Valley. He had been greatly looking forward to that dinner party but now that it was over the evening seemed like a small transient glimmer of light and noise, suddenly snuffed out. Winter had returned.

In the office he helped himself to a book on Poland, 1919–1939, and in the kitchen to a bottle of more recent vodka which was kept ready chilled in the deep freeze.

The consolation of being forty, Davy thought, was that winters did seem to be shorter. The disadvantage was, of course, that there were fewer of them to look forward to.

Other People's Wives

The woman in jeans was laughing with her daughter. David had noticed her as soon as he arrived in the Castle Park. Her laughter was like the birdsong. It sounded to him like the very essence of early summer. *Gaudy*, that's what it sounded like. Gaudy like the fruit trees in the park, outrageous in their blossom. May always affected him like that. After another winter of coats and caution, and leaving muddy boots outside, David Mosford invariably found himself longing for the easy sensuality of birdsong and spring.

And women who laughed like that.

He may have longed for easy sensuality but he doubted its existence. An *oxymoron* was, as any fool knows, a figure of speech that contained contradictory expressions. He knew that definition by heart because he had had to explain it to a first-year student who had taken exception to a criticism he had made of her long essay. 'Oxymoron is *not* a term of abuse,' Davy insisted to her, and to the head of department who had of course poked his nose in, and who wasn't just any fool but a very specific fool indeed. 'An oxymoron is a contradiction in terms: like *easy sensuality*.' For that was so. The sensuality did not come easily these days.

Of course he had not said that. Certainly not in the University. But he thought it this evening.

Yet to be able to take a walk at 6pm for the physical pleasure of a stroll was a delight. 'Let's go into the Castle,' he'd said to Emma on their way back.

'OK,' she'd said and run on ahead to the crumbling gatehouse. Where the pavement turned into the Castle Park Emma had turned to wave and given him a great big look of love and approval before she ran in. A seven-year-old daughter is a great delight, he thought. Why do only our daughters love us like that? Why do we end up marrying our wives?

Inside the Castle, Davy and his packet of sugar made for one of the many benches that had been donated in memory of someone who had loved this little park and whose memory was gradually being erased by young men with knives. He didn't look round for Emma. The park was really just a large lawn surrounded by ancient ramparts, the village to one side and the Taff down below. There was no exit other than the gatehouse. She would come back into view at any moment.

Davy breathed in and tried to smell the blossom. Last term, Dorkin had had some idiot come and lecture the department on stress. This well-intentioned Indian woman had got them all lying on the floor, trying to imagine they were walking by a beautiful stream and bending to smell wild flowers. In Davy's opinion the only sure fire way to alleviate departmental stress was to get rid of fools like Dorkin. He had tried imagining the great idiot falling headlong into this stream and floating away under a pile of dead, highly aromatic tulips. Then he had started to laugh in his corner of the carpet, and been viewed as disruptive.

But *this* now, this early summer evening, with just a hint of the warm Earth stirring again, this was indeed relaxing. Doubly so when you know that your daughter is a sensible sort of girl who won't climb anything or accept drugs from young calligraphers with their pen knives at the ready. Davy had genuinely, truly, almost completely relaxed and even forgot about the lamentable Professor Dorkin when he heard the sound of the woman and her daughter.

Laughter. What a rare sound it was, laughter like that. It spoke of pleasure in an accent few could resist. It entered the soul like music, confirming that there was indeed a point to everything.

Sex. Not a very profound point, admittedly, but one that had kept mankind going pretty well ever since mankind had started.

Not even the bubonic plague had destroyed our appetite for bodies and romance. Not in the way that parenthood did, anyway.

He could remember a piece of doggerel from his student days: *'The celibate and easily sated/May claim that sex is overrated.'*

He couldn't remember any more. Still, the lines that mattered had stuck in his mind. For he, David Mosford, was neither. Unfortunately.

He looked round and saw Her on a bench the other side of the lawn. Better still, he saw that the appearance of Her was as delightful as the laughter. She wasn't particularly good looking but she was casually dressed, even under-dressed for the time of year, and she was wearing an open necked denim shirt.

Davy invariably responded to women with that kind of neckline. He had wasted many hours of his life pondering this fact. He was, after all, an academic. It was his job to question the fundamentals of our existence but to this particular question he had never found an answer.

The heterosexual male, particularly the heterosexual male who has just passed forty, and particularly the one called Dr Mosford, will *invariably* be attracted to cleavage. Once, after one of Dorkin's interminable seminars on Unconscious Sexism in the Workplace, David, Glyn and Mike Hooper had locked themselves away and had a ten-minute plenary session full of self-denunciation and neat whisky. Glyn had admitted that, if he was going to be thrown out of the University, it would definitely have to be for Legs. Hooper's incorrectness was unfocused, much like his teaching, but David owned up immediately to being a Chest Man. This was an inexplicable constant of his existence. It wasn't necessarily a good thing, in fact on one particular occasion it proved disastrous, but Davy was not a moral philosopher. He was a humble Reader in History.

'Lovely evening,' he said in a casual way having crossed the lawn in an equally casual way.

The woman didn't reply immediately. She looked up at him and smiled as if she might burst out laughing at this sudden appearance of a man with fewer inches and less hair than was the norm. Then she looked around the park as if testing out the veracity of this assertion.

'Uhuh,' she said, looking directly at Davy now.

He suddenly felt terribly over-dressed in his maroon jacket and tie, his cream coloured trousers, his expensive gold-rimmed glasses. This woman wasn't glaring at him, she wasn't asking who he was, she had sat back on her bench and seemed to be eyeing him up, assessing him even.

'You Emma's dad, then?' The question came not from the woman but from her daughter nearby.

'Yes I am,' he replied, pleased to be able to develop the conversation. 'We live the other side of the green.'

'I'm Katrin,' the daughter said. 'Katrin Williams. Do you know your Emma's up on the wall?' She pointed over to where his child was indeed climbing gingerly down from a ruined battlement.

'O good lord,' said Davy.

'I'll get her!' volunteered Katrin Williams, happily self important, and off she ran across the lawn.

'She's never done that before,' Davy said, conscientiously watching his daughter being rescued. He was still standing six feet away from the cleavage of the woman who was the mother of the girl who seemed to know his daughter.

As social introductions go it had not got very far.

'I presume they're in the same class,' he added, turning back to the woman.

'Uhuh.' She looked up at him. 'You're David Mosford, aren't you?'

Davy was surprised.

'Aren't you on the telly?'

Now Davy was surprised and flattered. He had assumed that her quizzical gaze had been intended to keep him at a distance but in fact she had been trying to place him.

'I have been on once or twice,' he replied modestly but with secret satisfaction.

'I've never seen you but Katrin says your Emma's very proud.'

Now he was disappointed. He was not, after all, meeting one of his public but rather the mother of someone who had heard his Number One fan boasting in the playground. The woman suddenly laughed, presumably at his apparent loss of face. 'Don't worry, I'm never home,' she said standing up and offering her hand. 'You could be reading the news every night of the week for all I'd know about it. Millie Kemp.'

Millie, when she stood, was shorter than David expected. Not that he held that against her: so was he. But there was something very attractive about her proximity and physical ease. With Helena, you could tell if she felt comfortable or uncomfortable with someone by the distance she stood from them. Millie Kemp just occupied any space available. No problems.

The two girls were talking together on the other side of the lawn, developing a game.

'You a presenter then?' Millie asked with her eyes on the children. David could detect a strange mixture of Welsh and North London in her voice. He noticed it had a husky edge to it. This was an added attraction. Millie sounded as if she had been around. She could cope with strange men abandoning their daughters on some dodgy parapet in order to chat her up. As the girls began climbing an old apple tree that bent almost double to the lawn, Davy assured her he was by no means a TV regular. Modestly he admitted that he was occasionally asked on as an expert in certain aspects of twentieth-century history. Modesty, however, forbade him mentioning the fact that he spent quite a lot of time at the University ringing up producers and asking them to ask him on.

'It keeps the head of department off my back,' he explained lightly. More to the point, it gave Davy a certain valuable freedom. How long he could ignore Dorkin and get away with it depended very much on how good he was for the department's image and the research budget.

The conversation was easy but it came in small bursts punctuated by parental exhortations that Emma and Katrin might not damage any branches, or each other, or themselves. After a few minutes of discussing the Llandaff Usual – *How fortunate they were in having the late night Spar. How unfortunate in having so few places to park in these old streets* – David asked Millie what she did

'Me?' Millie replied, running a hand through her tousled hair. 'I design things. The rest of the time I'm a dreadful mother.' She laughed. Millie's hair was short and strong and copper-coloured. When hands ran through it, it bounced back into position straight

away. Helena's hair fell apart as soon as you touched it. Davy
wanted to touch Millie's hair, it had such vitality. But he'd made
that kind of mistake before. It was safer to keep talking.

'What kind of things do you design?'

'Pubs,' she said and turned from the girls to face him. She
wanted to see what he thought of that. David looked at Millie
Kemp looking at David Mosford and was caught by the playful-
ness in her eyes.

'You design pubs?' he repeated.

'Someone's got to,' she replied and they both laughed.

Davy took another look at the daughters who were now
swinging off branches and down on to the lawn.

'Well I'd very much like to see one of your pubs,' he told her,
still with a smile on his face.

'I'm sure you would,' she replied.

When David and Emma got back, Helena was helping Nick in
the kitchen with what passed these days for homework.

'Very dark in here,' said Davy, switching the lights on. Helena
and Nick winced. 'Sorry,' he said. Their home seemed unneces-
sarily cold this evening. Ty Escob was a tall gothic monster of
a house, bequeathed to them by Davy's parents, a good house
for the winter. It suited flickering log fires, heavy curtains and
dark shadows. It didn't suit the spring. Helena was being very
encouraging about Nick's dinosaur picture but Nick was staring
at his father.

'I've got eyes that see in the dark,' he remarked darkly in his
curious six-year-old way.

David felt reproached as he stood in the doorway. Specifically
and generally Davy felt reproached. That boy knows that I have
come back from chatting up a woman with a husky laugh,
generous cleavage and hair that I almost touched.

'Sugar,' he said, putting it decisively down on the table and
kissing the back of Helena's head.

On Friday morning Helena Mosford was walking Nick and Emma
to school across the green when a big dusty Citroën estate drove
past and beeped its horn. Somebody waved who was clearly
heading off towards the M4.

'Who was that?' asked Helena. She had been too busy keeping an eye on Nick to recognise who was on the other side of that grimy windscreen.

'Katrin's mum,' said Emma. 'She makes Daddy laugh.'

'Oh really?' asked Helena, checking the coast was clear.

'And he makes her laugh,' Emma added in all innocence.

'And when does all this hilarity go on?' Helena asked as they crossed the green and turned down the hill to school. She wasn't aware that David had a new friend but once in Heol Fair Emma ran on ahead and Helena thought it best not to bring the subject up again.

She used not to mind about these friendships but in the past he used to talk to her about them. These days his silence bothered her, for David had been silent ever since the one they never spoke about. And yet the *unspokenness* of it all was not the cause of their marital problems – it was only symptomatic. Nevertheless, as with a headache, the symptoms can end up hurting far worse than whatever it was that caused them. Helena wished she could talk to someone, even just about the headaches. She confided in few people: her father was one and (if truly he were a person) God was another. But with her father she was never specific. She just alluded to 'problems' and he nodded in a kind way that hid his embarrassment. God nodded too and seemed to be less easily embarrassed. In fact God didn't seem to mind how much she told him but she always sensed he was preoccupied. There was so much going on in the world and he had to be everywhere at once.

Then there was Sarah. Sarah had the time. And Sarah wasn't squeamish but she took a moral line. Neither Helena's father in Gloucestershire nor her father in Heaven did that. They just listened and these days that was what Helena preferred.

She didn't know if David had talked to anyone about their problems. Certainly he had hardly mentioned them to her, nor she to him. They should. They really should. She couldn't spend the rest of their lives sending him to the shops every time things got difficult. What did one do? Of course there was *one* thing. Helena's hand in the pocket of her waxed jacket touched the notebook that she took with her everywhere. For this day she had written

> Nick: – Hosp Appointment
> Cat food
> MOT?
> New gloves for Mrs Morgan
> Make Love to David!

That was something one should do, or try to do better.

The problem was that Helena could remember what it was like to be a sexual person but she didn't know how she was going to get back into *being* that person. The instinct had died when Nick was so ill and now that things with him were much more settled, Helena genuinely wanted to feel sexual again. But how do you reinvent passion?

Since February she had made a conscious decision to stop sleeping outside Nick's room and she'd often gone to bed hoping that Davy would soon join her. But he was a night owl. It was usually after midnight before he came up, a time when only the cries of her children could wake Helena. If they slept, so did she.

'We should talk about it,' she had told the dressing table mirror as she combed out her hair that morning. If at all possible Helena tried to avoid talking to inanimate objects. They were even less use than God. 'After all,' Helena reminded her reflection, 'you have a good-enough degree from a good-enough university. You ought to be able to think of something!'

But Oxford hadn't provided the kind of education that dealt with this kind of problem. In Helena's day the men outnumbered the girls by five to one and women students never had the time to learn how one initiated the subject of sex with men.

Helena saw her children into the school playground and picked up various bits of paper the cheerful secretary had kept for her. When Nick was well enough to start school she had had enormous battles with St Dyfrig's because they simply didn't understand the nature of his condition. A correct diagnosis had taken the hospital years but it sometimes seemed that educating the school over what could kill her son might take even longer.

'But no-one else in the class was sick,' said his reception-class teacher when they'd all been given birthday cake. Helena had been speechless at this woman's inability to understand the nature of digestive intolerance but even more outraged when the headmaster had suggested that perhaps Nick should be sent to a special school where his diet could be catered for.

'He is a normal boy with a small part of his intestine under-developed!' she shouted. 'There is nothing wrong with his brain!' Fortunately David had been some use at that particular impasse. He had written a firm and sensible letter. He was good at that kind of thing although Helena always suspected that really it was the prefix of *Dr* that intimidated St Dyfrig's. Wales was like that. But what did it matter? She got her own way in the end and Nick's dietary problems were recognised for what they were.

Since then she had made her peace by joining the Parents' Association. But this meant Helena now found herself stuck on various committees with full-time mums who found her insufficiently jolly and suspected she thought herself too good for them. Really she didn't. She didn't think anything of the kind. In fact she just wished she could find more in common with them. After all she had herself become a full-time mum but somehow Helena just couldn't get as excited by the headmaster's new suit, the Parents' Disco and *Isn't it wonderful about Miss Jones' baby*?

These days Helena no longer met Sarah in the playground. Sarah's children were on to the comprehensive now, so she pushed the notes and notices into another of her pockets and walked back through the village on her own. She could pick up some cat food and Mrs Morgan's gloves from the Spar. That would be a start on her list. Then she could think about how she might get the car and Davy serviced.

These days David Mosford was always in work early. At the moment he and Professor Dorkin had a thing going over who arrived first. It was childish but, in Davy's opinion, Dorkin started it. One departmental meeting the Fool had several times dropped into conversation the fact that his door was always open and that he was invariably in his office before 9.15. The man's self-sacrificing arrogance provoked David into making sure that he was in the next day by 9.05 and he had enjoyed calling out 'Morning, Peter' as Dorkin, in his lamentable cycling kit, wheezed slowly past five minutes later.

The next morning Dorkin was in earlier still. This had seemed a totally petty act to Davy but it hadn't stopped the duel escalating. Most of this week David Mosford had been at his desk by 8.45. The first day his victory had been no more than pyrrhic because it turned out that Dorkin had yet another of his hospital appointments that morning. Since then it had been mainly a draw but, by Friday, Davy had the definite satisfaction of having his feet up on the desk as Dorkin's measured and asthmatic footfall proceeded down the corridor.

'Ah David,' said the man stooped in Davy's doorway.

'Peter!' Davy greeted him cheerily but kept his feet on the desk.

'Bit of a puncture on the Boulevard de Nantes,' Dorkin explained. 'Just by the second set of traffic lights.'

'Nasty spot for a puncture,' Davy agreed.

'Left-hand filter lane,' Dorkin continued. The man had a positive mania for detail. Dorkin couldn't just have a puncture like any other idiot who insists on cycling to work through traffic fumes. Dorkin had to pinpoint the exact place and even the exact cause of the puncture. *One and a half inch nail, galvanised steel, manufactured in Taiwan.* Davy did wonder if the over-promoted idiot believed that by quoting enough specifics he would eventually put himself in the right. Or was he trying to draw attention to his personal sense of martyrdom by giving chapter and verse on each vicissitude endured?

'A word about Research Assessment Exercise, later?' Dorkin wheezed. 'If it's not too much trouble?'

' 'No problem,' Davy replied although he assumed that Dorkin was probably hoping to discover one, if he possibly could. The Great Martyr padded on cautiously down the corridor, not overdoing anything, taking good care of himself. Peter Dorkin was only forty-three but he deported himself like a brave old invalid, a man who, for the sake of the University and the general good of scholarship, rose above his infirmities. These were, of course, a useful tool for extracting sympathy from secretaries, for unreproached lateness at meetings and for keeping troublesome colleagues at bay. Dorkin wore his ill-health like a badge of privilege and, Davy suspected, intended to wear it for some considerable time yet. There were many things Davy disliked about this man: his pedantry, his veneer of concern for others, his hypocrisy, his ostentatious self-pity and his slavish political correctness which was born not out of passion but from a desperate desire to please anyone and everyone in authority. But worst of all was the fact that Dorkin was only three years older than David Mosford and most unlikely to vacate the professorial chair until his younger colleague was too old to slip into it.

Davy opened a drawer wherein he kept his publications file. It was labelled *Impact Factors*. In these absurdly competitive and ratings-conscious times excellence wasn't excellence unless it was measurable. University departments thrived or fell on the impact factor of academic publications infiltrated. The more points Davy could score for the department, the safer he was from Dorkin and the less effort he would have to make to accommodate him.

Fortunately the right journals, those which scored six or seven per article, were generally well disposed towards him. On a single sheet of A4 paper David could read off in his own neat handwriting an impressive list of pieces accepted for publication over the last two years. The only problem was that they weren't all in print yet. Davy had set himself a personal target of 20 points per annum. If he knew he'd already got that before the assessment exercise was done, Dorkin could whistle for any further cooperation. He could whistle for Dr Mosford turning up at all.

So what he needed was a publication date for the next piece. Dropping that into conversation ought to see off the Fool. Dorkin's own contribution to the departmental research tally was so low that he only crept on the list of returnable staff because he got to draw it up.

Davy switched on his computer and decided to browse what his rivals were up to.

Whirr, said the machine.

While the screen was welcoming him to the network, he paused for a moment to think about Helena. He didn't often think of her at work but they'd had another of those conversations last night. Helena suddenly, for no obvious reason, wanting to go away. She needed a break. Yes, he could see that, especially now that Nick was so much better she needed and she deserved a break. But when he agreed with her she had looked at him as if there was so much more that wasn't being said.

Beep, said the machine.

Davy thought of that Millie woman. Maybe she was the one. She had an attractive simplicity and directness about her. She was probably good in bed as well. It was a sad thought but he pondered such things more and more these days, not that it did him any good. Of course he never thought about his female students in that way. He daren't. Dorkin would have a field day if David even noticed the gender of those in his seminar group. But he did think about other people's wives.

Bing, said the machine. David engaged with the mouse and double-clicked.

Millie Kemp was in the West of England and, did Davy but know it, she wasn't somebody else's wife. Millie had lived with the father of her two children for so many years it sometimes felt like being married. Despite her parents' reproaches, she really saw no reason to make it feel any more like. Besides which, her parents' marriage was nothing to write home about and her brother and sister were both divorced. What was so good about getting married?

Millie was checking the pre-construction details on a conversion job near Taunton. The brewery called her a design consultant but really her role was ensuring that when one of their less appetising West and Welsh properties was turned into a Period Family Pub, the old building was made capable of accommodating the new fun factory design without actually falling down.

Millie was given a relatively free hand in the interior decor, selecting old prints that might look as if they reflected the locale 100 years ago and choosing the most suitable theme from a range approved by the company: *The Old Forge, The Barn, The Ship's Chandlery*. Instant fun and heritage she called it. Unfortunately she rarely got the opportunity to choose her team of carpenters, plasterers, plumbers and electricians and so less time was spent on fun and much more on the avoidance of cock-up.

It wasn't what she'd set out to do. She was going to be an actress. Her parents wanted her to be a teacher but her Dad had got her a design job with a Theatre In Education company that folded in the eighties. Pub design wasn't exactly art but it wasn't

Other People's Wives •

teaching either. However, on the Taunton job Millie thought herself blessed in her new foreman, a forceful ex-squaddie who treated her with great respect and told his team to *shut the fuck up swearing* when there was a lady present. Millie had become very fond of young Neville. His belligerent style of man management had meant that she could leave the boys to get on with stripping out for twenty-four hours and not return from Cardiff to find the one original feature she had managed to preserve reduced to a pile of rubble in the back of some skip.

At one o'clock sharp Neville's boys always stopped and sat on a wall in the car park for lunch, smoking sulkily. Nev wouldn't let them stray out of his sight and he didn't like them mixing with the dispossessed customers who would sometimes shuffle into the car park like refugees and ask what was happening to their old haunt.

'Mrs Kemp's got a difficult enough job to do without you lot mouthing off to the locals,' he would warn his crew.

'Oh call me *Millie*,' she'd remind him.

This particular day Neville was taking his sandwiches with Millie on one side of the car park while the boys exchanged monosyllables and cigarettes on the other.

'You married then, Mrs Kemp?' Neville asked. 'Only you don't wear no ring.'

'No, I'm not,' said Millie, lifting her face to the sun and squinting at its incipient glimmer. She liked being on site and always enjoyed watching the transformations taking place. She particularly luxuriated in calm moments like this when everyone took five. It was like the getting in and getting out with a touring company. Bodies, pleasurably spent by labour, taking time out. Roll up your trousers and get a tan on the knees. Great stuff.

'You got kids, though?' Neville knew that Millie liked to get back to Cardiff for at least one night during the week if she possibly could.

'Yes. Two.' She also sent them postcards, her large handwriting exploding merrily with jokes and exclamation marks across the page. Weekends with Millie usually began with presents from the service station and ended with stomach ache in Burger King.

'Your Mum looks after them?' Neville asked.

'No. I live with their Dad. In Cardiff.'

Neville took that on board but it wasn't what he had
expected.

'And he looks after you properly then?' Millie nodded. 'Only
my sister's got this kid and the bloke who done it, he wouldn't
marry her, right? So we took him out the back . . .'

Neville looked at Millie. Millie looked at Neville.

'Oh I don't think it has to come to that, Nev,' she said trying
not to smile.

'Only saying,' he replied. 'You're OK, Mrs Kemp. I don't like
to think of anyone mucking you about.'

At one o'clock David Mosford put in a call to Clare, one of the
first postgraduates he had supervised and now miraculously
transformed into the editor of *Radical History*. He knew this was
the time her secretary went for lunch and Clare Mankiewicz
was one of those people who couldn't let a ringing phone go
unanswered.

It had been a productive morning, mainly because neither
stray students nor Peter Dorkin had sought him out. Davy was
known to be a soft touch for students. During office hours his
patience and neat handwriting would deal in a measured way
with all their problems, real, imaginary and paranoid. Today,
however, he had finals to thank for the scarcity of unemployed
undergraduates looking for someone to bother and a benificent
deity to thank for the temporary disappearance of Dorkin.
However David did have a sneaking feeling the Fool was going
to try and nobble him before he padded off to the Faculty Meeting.
Once Dorkin was safely locked into an afternoon of procedural
and administrative tedium, Davy was safe. But, just in case the
man tracked him down over lunch, what was most desirable
now was to extract a definite publication date for one of the
Radical History six-pointers. Why Clare's little opus had taken
off so spectacularly and so quickly he really couldn't imagine
but what mattered more was the fact that people thought well
of *Rad Hist* and that its editor thought well of him. The phone
rang eight times before Clare gave in and picked it up.

'Hello?' It was odd to think this was the voice of an important
woman whose good opinion was sought by so many of Davy's

rivals. On the telephone she still sounded like the anxious postgraduate student who had arrived in his room sixteen years ago wearing a college scarf and leg warmers. Dr C.G. Mankiewicz, founder and – currently – still editor of *Rad Hist*, was the only postgraduate Davy had ever met who wore a college scarf. When he heard her on the telephone today he could still imagine that long floppy pullover, the tricolour scarf and knitted leg warmers.

'Clare, it's David Mosford,' he announced in a very warm and friendly tone.

There was a noise on the other end of the line which sounded like something falling over.

'David, hello,' she said equally friendly, but less confidently.

David asked her how she was and she asked him and then he asked about the health of *Radical History*.

'Very well,' she replied but giving nothing away.

'And what about *Welsh Nationalism and Its Links With Vichy France*?' David asked.

'Oh it's good. Very good,' Clare replied sounding a little warmer now but still not quite right.

'When do you think it's going to appear?'

She paused for a moment. She actually paused. Davy hated that pause. It was instantly significant.

'Well, it is rather similar to other things we've done recently.'

'What things?' he quizzed her, amicably but firm. After all, he ought to know if anything similar was being published in his field. There was another muffled crash as if Clare had failed to properly right the thing that went flying when she first picked up the phone.

'Well,' she began and David knew immediately that this was embarrassing for her. This was Dr Clare Mankiewicz, Founder and Editor of *Radical History* trying not to sound like Clare of the Leg Warmers, Clare of the Silly College Scarf, Clare who once sat in Davy's office in tears confessing that maybe research had been a big mistake.

'Well,' she said. 'I've asked a close colleague to have a look at it.'

He didn't like the sound of that. Clare had been very good so far refereeing all his stuff herself.

'Just in case it's too similar to your thing on Welsh Nationalism and Mussolini.'

'It's not "too similar". It's developing a theme,' Davy replied. Didn't academic study allow for that any more?

'Well,' said Clare,' I just wanted to be sure. It's just that the basis from which you're arguing is similar. Both pieces do explore the fascist tendency within the celtic diaspora.'

David was about to ask if she had any actual *criticism* of his article. She wasn't running the *Daily Mail* features page for goodness sake! But he held back. In truth, he had been allowed to explore Welsh Nationalism's connections with Mussolini, Hitler and Franco over the last two years. Perhaps Clare was getting stick from her editorial board.

'You must publish it when you think the time is fit,' he declared magnanimously but without real generosity.

With a certain amount of relief in her voice Clare promised she would try and find a space for it at the end of the year. She was sure it would get in soon. It was a first-class piece.

Goddammit, this woman had even asked him once if he thought men found her off-putting! There was a pause which neither of them could help.

'How are Helena and the girls?' she asked, trying to sound kind.

'One of them's a boy but apart from that fine.' Davy replied. Another crash. Oh for goodness sake, thought Davy, leave the girl alone.

They said their goodbyes and he put the phone down, feeling worse than ever now.

Helena was walking up the Cathedral steps that morning, her hands pushed into the pockets of her long waxed jacket. She had called in to see God and made a bit of a fool of herself.

The village of Llandaff was unusual, sitting as it did at the top of an escarpment with the architectural patchwork cathedral of Teilo, Dyfrig and Euddogwy nestling, in all its rampant eclecticism, down below. The Mosfords' house would have actually overlooked it but for some vast conifers that one Bishop of Llandaff had allowed to grow to preternatural height and no-one had cut down since. Nevertheless the proximity of the church to her home had meant that Helena had found it easy to turn back to God during all the scares they'd had with Nick. Now that he was, touch wood, so much better she still called in two or three times during the week to thank the Lord, just in case he'd been the one on call when she'd said those frantic prayers.

Helena Moreton had been brought up an Anglican so she found the physical attitude of prayer much easier than the spiritual. It had never been difficult to go into a church and simply kneel down but her relationship with the Almighty had not gone much further until Nick went on to solids and into a steep and terrible decline. They went through test after test but he continued to be thin and malnourished, vomiting in his sleep. Every night Helena listened with terror in case he choked to death and during the day she found herself increasingly drawn down the steps to that cathedral.

In her teens, good decent state education had turned Helena away from Christianity but an even better university had subsequently convinced her that belief was an emotional rather than intellectual leap. You could prove and disprove nothing. And, in any case, she was bright enough to recognise that her instincts regarding Nick were desperately pagan. One could believe in an underdeveloped cubic millimetre of digestive plumbing or a voodoo doll but it was *all* a stab in the dark unless it worked. Where did Truth lie if there was no cure? Truth was the cure.

All alone in those Winter afternoons she would bundle their sickly child into his pram and take him down the flight of thirty-three broad steps that led to the cathedral. And all the time her mind would be saying, over and over again, 'I don't know who you are, I don't know if I can believe in you, but you are more powerful than me and I can do nothing. Please save my baby.'

And then things changed. Big-hearted Sarah John put her on to the right man. A brilliant man. Or maybe he wasn't. The word on Malcolm Evans was that he was average. But even if he was a fool he was, in the end, a fool who didn't reject what worked. Mr Evans believed in evil trace elements that are to be found in wheat germ and he believed in propitiating these demons by excluding them from Nick's diet. Yet another stab in the darkness of desperation but it did stop the problem overnight. As simple as that. Finding the right food for Nick was a nightmare, of course, as was getting the school to give it him but these were routine horrors. The real nightmare, devouring and terrible, was over. But only just in time.

For the last eighteen months, nothing had gone wrong. Nick was a perfectly healthy boy, as far as anyone could tell. Yet still Helena touched wood when she looked at him and still she never sighted the unequal spires of Llandaff Cathedral, perpendicular and gothic revival respectively, without remembering to say thank you. Maybe she was just giving superstition its due but she couldn't help it.

Helena often talked to God these days. He was more on her intellectual level than many women on the Parents' Association committee.

'Does that make me a snob?' she asked, sitting in the Oudoceous Chapel. In the silence of the cathedral's vault the answer seemed to be that God loved all souls equally but even he found some more interesting than others. Helena said Amen to that and made her way across the nave to a metal votive table where candles could be lit for 10p. A wooden carving of the dying Mary lay in a recess behind the glass panel. Helena always called by here. The flame that she would cause to flicker was like a PS in the letter she was writing to the Almighty, a last-minute thought before sealing up. She rarely considered what it would be beforehand. Sometimes there wasn't any more to say and she had already given the Lord plenty to think about for that day but this morning when she watched her candle burn she found herself also asking 'Dear Lord, please let David and me enjoy having sex.'

Helena was a touch surprised. She glimpsed over her shoulder in case the Lord was looking in her direction and taking a dim view of this kind of intercession. She should try and focus on something more appropriate. The blackened carving showed a mediaeval figure in attendance on Mary. He had glasses. Apostles with spectacles, she thought. How odd. He had a little earnest face. Like David's when he had watched her struggling with Nick for all those awful years. For Nick was dying then and David, like this apostle, had been about as useful as a block of wood. She forgave him for being what he was but she was fearful. She was so fearful that she didn't love him enough.

It wasn't that they never made love now but it was obvious to both of them that it just didn't work somehow. 'You see it's not that I'm frigid,' she explained to God and to the row of little dancing flames. 'I don't *dislike* sex. If I did, that would make matters easier. It's just that I seem to have forgotten how to enjoy it and he knows that and so he doesn't enjoy it either.'

The candles lurched suddenly to one side, caught in a draught, but the Lord maintained his usual silence. Maybe he was shocked. 'I mean, good lord, you ordained sex for the procreation of children and avoidance of fornication!' Helena reminded him silently. 'What about all that mutual society we're supposed to enjoy? It's not as if I'm asking for something you don't approve of. I don't want your blessing on some wild affair. I just want to put things right between us and David doesn't know how to either. I've put him off, I know. But how do I encourage him? How do I help?'

Helena had rushed a bit ahead of herself. She sat herself down on the first row of chairs, just below the High Victorian lectern.

'Pretty sad, isn't it?' she asked the eagle of St John and stuck out her feet. Then she realised she'd actually voiced that bit out loud. She looked round to check that no-one had heard. A rotund and bearded tourist glimpsed across from where he was reading the Pitkin guide but he displayed no curiosity, a verger in a pony tail passed without comment. Helena walked to the aisle, bowed her head beneath the Majestas and put some money in the collecting box.

'Marital guidance.' she explained

What would she do now? Call in on Sarah who might be busy with her young mums and old dears? Or Pip who was only intermittently at work but invariably there when you wanted her to be at home? Helena missed her women friends and her cousins. They were in London and in Gloucestershire whereas she was in Wales.

'Dear Lord,' she concluded on her way up the Dean's thirty-three Steps. 'If you really wanted people like me to live in Wales, why did you create it so far away?'

*   *   *

David's answer was that Wales was created by the English who kept the best bits of Britain for themselves and shovelled the rest over the border.

'It's all my fault then?' she had asked him, staring at the humdrum horizon from their garden.

'No, I brought you here,' he conceded. 'It's my fault too.'

David Mosford had actually spent a very annoying day at work. The good news was that in the afternoon Dorkin had had to go and see the Head of School about a matter of no consequence whatsoever which meant that he and Davy never had their little chat about research funding. But the bad news was that Dorkin had therefore delegated one of his more mind-bendingly dull head of department tasks to a senior colleague: an hour and a half with the Cost-cutting Committee who had yet to get round to Davy's conclusion that they could most usefully start with themselves!

Unfortunately Dr Mosford, deputising for Professor Dorkin, had had his hands tied by the copious notes that the Great Fool had left for him. Being Dorkin's chosen deputy for the day was not a job to be enjoyed, or even undertaken if you could possibly avoid it, but unluckily David had been nabbed in the act of evasion by Megan, Dorkin's extraordinarily large and powerfully forbidding secretary.

'Dr Mosford!' she bawled as he headed for the lifts. 'Professor Dorkin's looking for you, Dr Mosford.' Megan was using the cheerful displeasure that sprang naturally into her voice.

'Then I'm sure he'll find me,' Davy replied and he continued out of the department. But Megan was used to dealing with him. In fact Megan could deal with most situations. She was a Butetown girl and one of those women who use their considerable size to even more considerable advantage. David and Glyn believed that Big Meg would be able to enforce departmental policy simply by leaning on the recalcitrants. Literally. Today she had come prepared with a pile of papers gripped in her great plump hand.

'Faculty Board, Invigilators' Reports and the University Costs Committee,' she explained. 'These are the Professor's notes. Can you cover?'

'What if I end up advocating we sack all the secretaries?' he teased, with his most winning smile, and knowing that he was bound to lose this one.

'Suits me,' said Megan and she turned and swung her enormous hips back down the corridor. Davy watched her go. She really was amazing, Big Meg. More like a giant fertility goddess than a minor administrative assistant. He was sure people had dug up statues to her at Sunbury Hill. Meg between the sheets would be somewhat akin to sex with a steamroller. Dr Mosford enjoyed the outrageous thrill of these thoughts for a moment, made all the more delectable by the thought that voicing even one of them would have meant serving himself up on a plate for Dorkin – and yet Dorkin had not an inkling!

So that was how the afternoon went. That was two and a half hours of what remained of David Mosford's allotted span well and truly wasted. Returning to his office at 4.30, he rather longed for the sight of a student, one of those listless things with problems (real or imaginary) who were the ostensible reason Dr Mosford actually went in to work. But the corridor was empty, as empty as his afternoon. David checked that no essays had been E-mailed in early by the overachievers and decided to telephone a few national newspapers. This was either a good time or a very bad time depending on whether they had just closed off or were in the last throes of wrestling the paper into shape.

Davy felt in need of some publicity. If he couldn't hasten on the academic press, surely he could get something in one of the broadsheets. His first two calls clearly arrived at the wrong time. One line was simply cut off before he could speak and on the other he heard a muffled voice shouting 'Will somebody please answer the bloody phone!' before it went dead. His third call, to the *Guardian*, got through to an assistant editor who was always affable and invariably willing to buy freelances lunch.

'How's the contentious business of History?' asked affable luncher.

'Fine,' Davy replied, 'I'm up in London next week.'

'Are you? Well, come and have lunch.'

'I think I may have something surprising to offer you,' David suggested.

'This about Welsh Nazis again?'

The voice at the other end of the phone was still sounding

very cheerful but David felt decidedly put out, not to say put down. Was he getting predictable?

'No, not at all,' he improvised. 'I think that one's been pretty well covered now.'

'I don't know,' mused the assistant who was enjoying a sudden flush of irresponsibility now his particular page had closed. 'I saw that piece you did in *Radical History* about old Himmler and the Taffy Blackshirts. Very good. What about Emil Hacha, have you thought of him? Or what about Scottish Nazis? We've got a few of them in this office, I can tell you.' David began to think he wasn't being taken seriously here. 'Have you thought about doing something more general? Street crime, that's very topical. *How good were the Good Old Days?*'

Davy ended the call with an arrangement for lunch but with his self-esteem definitely flagging. He wasn't going to get many impact factors out of tub-thumping on the law and order issue in a national daily. Time to go home.

For his fortieth birthday Helena had bought her husband a ridiculously expensive and flashy Japanese automobile which they both referred to as *that ridiculous car*. It was ostentatiously foreign and red and hugged the ground furtively as if waiting to pounce. It cost a fortune to run and had used up some savings that Helena's father had passed over to her when Nick got better. Old Mr Moreton had intended the money to give his daughter and son in law a really good holiday so they might all relax and recover. That was what he thought they needed and deserved but Helena had put the money into *that car* for her husband's fortieth birthday. She wanted to cheer him up and this was the only way she could think of doing it. After several months without so much as a connubial embrace, and insufficient joy once the embraces began again, Davy had considered this car something of a consolation prize but, even so, he couldn't help appreciating Helena's sacrifice and enjoying the beast for its own ridiculous sake.

It was yet another day when there didn't seem to be a point but at least David Mosford could slide through the Cardiff traffic in a car that turned heads. The students mocked and admired it. A rumour had even gone round that the car had been bought with the money Davy earned on TV. But that rumour was only current in circles that didn't know how little his kind of TV paid (and circles that didn't know David Mosford would have done it for free in any case.).

By the time he got home and tucked the ridiculous car away, Davy was feeling a lot happier. The car did that to him. Helena wasn't daft. Helena understood him. Helena knew what to do when she felt sorry for him. And Helena was beautiful. David wanted to find where she was and give her a kiss. She must get away and relax. Maybe everything would be better then.

But Helena was in the kitchen, her eyes streaming from onions. She was trying to cook Something Complicated from a book while her hair collapsed in all directions. He kissed her but the kiss missed because she didn't notice what he was doing until the last minute and, when she did lift her head to him, his lips hit her nose. They tried again and this time her nose dislodged his glasses. Where had this nose come from? In fifteen years of marriage it had never intruded so before. Had she been growing it over the last few months?

'I do love you,' he said nevertheless.

'This is Something Complicated,' Helena warned. 'Will you go and get salt?'

'Salt?'

'We're out of salt. Don't ask me why. And rubber gloves for Mrs Morgan.'

David prepared to go out again. 'I always suspected that Martha Morgan ate the gloves,' he mused. 'Never realised she liked them ready salted.'

Helena smiled because he'd made an effort to be funny.

'Oh and don't take Emma please, she's got to do some homework.'

Davy felt happier back out of the house. It was another bright evening and the sky was a resplendent blue over the castle grounds. He paused by an old statue of the Reverend Ridley, a Trollopian figure familar to him throughout his own childhood in Llandaff.

He hadn't asked Helena to cook Something Complicated! Why, in God's name, today?

If he'd waited for an answer God would have owned up. It was in fact all the Lord's fault. The unintentional request Helena had made for divine marriage guidance had resulted a few hours ago in the sudden idea of taking time over supper that Friday evening. Not a quick hot pot, nor a trip out to some Portuguese bistro where David would invite half the clientele to join them. A meal à deux. Maybe that way they could talk.

The shame of it was that the divine old duffer hadn't taken into account how long it could take to collect the children from school, and how long Sarah could keep people talking in the High Street, nor the effect of onions and steam on Helena's contact lenses. Helena knew all this. God didn't. Davy did, but he hadn't been consulted.

All David knew was that when he went to kiss his wife her nose got entangled in his spectacles. Nevertheless it was a beautiful evening. This was definitely going to be a good summer. He noticed someone, with a kit bag and padded parka jacket slung over her shoulder, emerging from the back lane that ran down behind the High Street. Undoubtedly, from the overtight jeans, sun tan, hair and everything else, this was the woman he'd met on Tuesday with Emma. The woman with the laugh who had assisted him in his long term research into the human cleavage.

Davy crossed the green to catch up with her. 'There's a coincidence,' he said. For a moment he thought Millie might not have recognised him.

'You're the man from the telly,' she said and her husky voice had a hint of that provocative laughter in it.

'That's right. I read the news every night.'

She laughed. Thank goodness she laughed. 'That's right. You're famous and I didn't know it. How're you doing?'

'I'm off to the Spar to buy some salt,' he explained. 'Last time it was sugar, this time it's salt.'

'Don't you have any cupboards in your house?' she replied. Millie hadn't stopped walking so they carried on round the corner into High Street together. She had a lazy way of teasing him which he liked. It went with the voice. Probably not particularly clever but the very sound of her voice made you hang on her words. This was the type, he thought. Maybe this was *the one*. Keeping pace he asked her what she was doing emerging from the back lane at this time of night. Millie explained that she parked the car down there, behind her house which was on the High Street.

'How's the conversion business then?' he asked.

'Just the same. How's history?'

'Changing day by day.'

Millie stopped outside a rather ramshackle eighteenth-century house that used to be a rectory many years ago and which would never recover its former grandeur given that it now adjoined the supermarket. Davy had no idea this was her place.

'Good lord. My friend Laurence Richards used to live here,' he explained, using what Helena referred to as his self-consciously boyish charm. 'You really live *here*?' He stood back to get a better view of the house and owner in context. Millie swung her bag down off her shoulder.

'Look, I'd invite you in,' she said, 'but I haven't seen the kids for a few days, or my chap.'

'What's his name?' Davy asked.

'Crispin.'

'Well you and Crispin must come round to dinner,' he told her.

'You don't hang about!' she laughed. That worldly rasp, that attractive catch in her throat yet again.

'I was forty last birthday, I can't afford to.'

Millie looked surprised. 'Christ, I'm older than you,' she said.

Davy was equally taken aback. 'Well, when I'm your age I hope I'll look as good,' he told her.

'Sod off!' She grinned at him and went back to her family.

Davy set off with a spring in his step. There were definite consolations in growing older.

It was a pleasant enough supper although Nick came down twice to demand drinks. And a student rang up for no good reason. At one point they talked about Truth vs History and about Dorkin vs Human Intelligence and David was quite funny about when on earth was the Great Fool going to be sacked, head-hunted or die. They hadn't really laughed for ages. But then Nick came down for a third time and after he went back up again the conversation turned to his problems and they seemed to stay facing in that direction, failing to linger at the table. So

David looked out his piece on Mussolini while Helena went up to bed.

'Will you be late?' she asked.

'I'm just going to see if this is any good,' he explained holding up the article.

'You'll be late,' she replied but Davy didn't hear her.

2

Nobody's Fault

Helena's friend Sarah John had been a great help during those difficult years with Nick. Sarah lived in part of the new, expensive, mock-ramshackle-Tudor development that sat at the top of the Green. Her children were older than the Mosford pair and two had already left home but Sarah always seemed to have gone through whatever Emma and Nick were currently inflicting on Helena. She would laugh and commiserate and get out the gin bottle.

Then as Nick became seriously ill, Sarah had been a real rock. One morning she had found Helena at the top of the steps down to Llandaff Cathedral with Nick in her arms and looking quite dreadful. Sarah had bundled both of them back to her warm modern kitchen and when Helena had started to cry it had been Sarah who held her. As a former nurse Sarah believed that illness had rational causes and possible cures and against that broad and bony chest Helena felt her superstitions melt. She no longer feared that Nick had, in some strange way, been cursed.

Yet even big jolly Sarah had been worried by the boy and she had spent some time on the kitchen telephone circumventing the National Health Service. For Helena the most comforting sounds that she had ever heard were the stentorian tones of her large friend telling a reluctant consultant at the Heath that she used to cover for him when he was just a houseman and he was not to try and fob her off with one of his registrars!

She owed a great deal to Sarah although these days they had less and less in common. That Saturday morning Sal had gathered up Helena and Emma outside Halls The Bookshop and borne them off for a natter.

Over coffee and Ribena the nattering had turned to the subject of Sarah's husband, Mostyn, a prosperous dentist whose leisure hours were spent restoring old vehicles. To avoid getting under his wife's feet, Mostyn John would spend most weekends lying flat on his back in the garage. It was a paradoxical arrangement that suited both partners well. Helena had just been going to ask how work was going on Mostyn's latest, a 1960s campervan, when his diminutive form entered their kitchen from the connecting garage door, wiping hands and smiling broadly.

'Do you know the nipples are still functioning!' he announced. 'I would have thought they'd rusted up by now but not a bit of it. Oh hello *Helena*!' Mostyn shook hands enthusiastically and very specifically. 'And hello little one.' he added, patting Emma's head. 'Sarah told you about the gear box? Tracked one down in Nottingham. Good, eh?! We're going to have her going this summer, I can tell you. Thought we'd do the Gower, a different bay each weekend, and then the Brecons. *Marvellous.*'

Helena could feel that she was wearing a fixed smile and that Emma was looking very serious. Any moment now Mostyn would be suggesting that she and Davy bring the kiddies down to West Wales for the weekend. Helena knew there was nothing in the world less likely to appeal to David than sitting round an open fire eating burnt meat and getting bitten by insects.

But Mostyn had more immediate plans.

'Why don't you come and have a look, eh Emily?' he announced, holding out a rolypoly hand.

'Emma,' Helena corrected, as her daughter dutifully accepted the invitation. Emma shot her mother an embarrassed look. She didn't like it when her parents argued and construed any disagreement – even ones relating to accuracy – as acrimonious.

'And how are Things?' asked Sarah with a smile as the door closed. It was an odd question which seemed to assume that hitherto not a single *Thing* had been discussed.

'Oh fine,' Helena replied. 'David's very busy.'

'Good,' said Sarah. It was Sarah's view that men should keep themselves busy.

'He's being *sensible* these days, is he?'

Helena sighed inwardly. She knew what lay behind that question. Now she knew why Sarah had raised the subject of Things. She even wondered if Mostyn had been detailed to come and distract Emma while we two girls had a proper chat. That beatific smile as the door closed was often Sarah's precursor to one of her 'proper chats'.

'Oh you know David,' Helena replied noncommittally.

'Yes . . .' said Sarah with significance. It was a *Yes* that hoped to speak volumes. Or to get Helena to.

Helena liked Sarah John but she had once made the mistake of telling her friend too much. In the days when things were bad with Nick, Helena used to complain about David and Sarah invariably took his part.

'Only a mum feels these things,' she'd explain. 'David will do what he can but men are *providers* at heart. They're not going to give you emotional support. He's very good really, David. He helps around the house doesn't he? He looks after Emma for you. He brings in the money, we shouldn't forget that. These are his ways of helping you. Taking the pressure off you so you can help Nick.'

'But he gets so uptight,' Helena replied. 'First he refused to believe there was anything wrong with Nick and now . . .' She sought around for a suitable description of David's eyes, avoiding hers whenever she was upset.

'Only a woman will understand,' Sarah reassured her. That, in Sarah's eyes, was how it was.

Yes, Sarah had been a very good friend during those times. She had helped Helena forgive David's inadequacy and happily provided the understanding and support she craved. But one day, only last year, her ready compassion had encouraged Helena to complain about this woman who kept ringing the house.

'Oh,' she had said before Helena had finished speaking. It was an *Oh* that conveyed the subject of David from one category to another. David Mosford was no longer a poor man doing the best he could, given that he was a man (and that therefore his best would never be that good). David was in all likelihood an adulterer.

When Sarah had questioned her for details, Helena insisted she really didn't know anything about it. This was the truth. What she did know was that after David had been on a routine-waste-of-time-symposium up north he had come back very morose and started following her around the house. It was as if he had something significant but unspeakable to speak about. She also knew that at about the same time this female voice had started ringing up at inconvenient moments. People often did but David didn't usually go into another room to take the call. Helena knew no more than that. And really she didn't want to know any more. That something might have happened when he was away in Leeds was most likely but Helena was feeling so emotionally overburdened at the time that she preferred to see it simply as yet another example of the way in which David lacked any understanding of her problems. But for Sarah this marked David out.

'Helena,' she said. 'I am a reasonable woman. I try never to judge. Don't forget I was a state registered nurse for fifteen years.'

But Sarah manifestly did judge and more than judge; she was quite hungry for specifics.

All this was disappointing to Helena. Realising that there were limits to the kind of emotional support Sarah could offer opened up a fissure between the two of them. She knew that Sarah now saw her as Poor Helena whose husband . . . *well we all know what goes on with these men* . . . Helena didn't mind that she and her friend placed different moral superstructures on the twentieth-century marriage but she did object to being characterised as Poor Helena, a woman wronged.

But the biggest problem now was that Sarah was tiresomely relentless in her attempts to get David and Helena back together, usually under the worst of all possible circumstances. She seemed to believe that what the Mosfords needed could only be found at parents' social evenings, family worship and barn dances.

'Or why don't you go away for the weekend?' Sarah asked. 'A hotel with some good walks?'

'David hates hotels,' said Helena. It was a way of avoiding the issue. Issues could be avoided but they never went away. Not once Sarah had adopted them.

'No, David's fine,' Helena replied, wishing that Emma would come back. 'Absolutely fine.'

'Oh good,' said Sarah but she did not sound convinced. Either she was disappointed to hear that Helena had no news with which to shock or maybe Sarah already knew that there was a woman in a Citroën who made Daddy laugh.

It was time to get back and think about lunch.

Over in the High Street Millie Kemp was admitting that it probably was day time after all. Crisp was a morning person and had already taken Jonathan, their eldest, for a swimming lesson. But Millie was holding on to the darker pleasures of night for as long as possible. When she did open an eye she could see Katrin sitting in the window seat, gazing down at the shoppers and tourists and wearing something that looked like one of Millie's old sweat-shirts over a pair of disco pants, for all the world like a younger version of her mother.

'Hello Rabbit,' Millie murmured. 'Do you want to get me a Coke?'

'OK,' said Katrin getting up but clambering over the bed en route. They exchanged a sort of hug. 'Mil, do you know it's the School Quiz Evening next week?' Katrin asked. Millie was stretching out beneath the duvet at the time and not quite up to complex questions like that.

'Will you go?'

'Uhuh,' said Millie shuddering with the pleasure of a long yawn finally completed. 'Sure I'll go. Fetch me that Coke will you, Bunny?'

'It's Tuesday night. I'm going to put it on the calendar, OK?'

'I'll be there,' said Millie who at that moment would have agreed to attend a revivalist prayer meeting if there was a drink in it. She could take tea, coffee or cola in the morning but she had to take something.

Katrin bounced off the bed and Millie slid back beneath the duvet. Not only would the chilled sugar and caffeine be very welcome but sending her daughter off downstairs guaranteed another few minutes sinking into the warm soft nothingness of bed.

'Mil,' said Katrin from the door.

'Mmuh?' mumbled Millie, just audible enough for Katrin to know she had been heard. Of late this precocious little seven-year-old had developed an annoying technique of asking supplementaries just when you thought the difficult questions were over.

'Don't you think you ought to wear something in bed?'

Millie was so thrown by the question that her tousled head appeared above the duvet again.

'What? What kind of thing, Bun?' she asked sitting up blearily and trying to focus.

'A nightie. Or pyjamas,' Katrin suggested. Millie looked at her in slow and total incomprehension.

'I was just thinking of Jonathan,' said Katrin. 'He's nearly ten you know.'

Millie really didn't understand this however many times she came at it.

'What if he walked in and saw you?' Katrin explained from the doorway.

'Well, if it's that bad a sight,' Millie replied, 'I guess he could just walk out again.'

What was it with Katrin? Jonathan had been a fat and happy baby and the easiest child a mother could have wished for but Katrin was thin like Crisp and always bugging her. They got on fine when Millie made her laugh or made her feel important but left to her own devices Katrin would start niggling. There were always ways in which her mother could be improved, streamlined, rationalised and generally tidied up.

'But then, I don't suppose you'll take any notice of me,' sang Katrin in a sing-song voice and off she bounced importantly down the stairs. Millie wondered how on earth Katrin had managed to pick up that irritating little phrase from her grandparents who lived one hundred miles away in mid Wales and were not frequently visited. Katrin was their favourite. Katrin sometimes seemed to be the embodiment of their values. All of which meant she wasn't easy to love. Even Millie, for whom love was a reflex action, recognised that.

* * *

On Sunday afternoon David was checking the retirement dates of professors within the UK when the telephone rang. He ignored it, assuming that Helena would pick the call up in the kitchen but he'd forgotten that after lunch she had taken the children out for a walk down to the river. Eventually Davy lifted the handset in his father's old billiard room which now served as the Mosford office. You could get a lot of computer hardware on the top of a full size billiard table.

'David Mosford.'

'Oh David, I'm so pleased you're there.' He had recognised the unwelcome squeaky voice, even before she had announced herself. 'David, it's *Wendy*.'

He would much rather have kept the relationship with his head of department's wife formal but Mrs Professor Dorkin did like to believe that she was on good terms with all Peter's staff. In fact, by the simple expedient of getting everyone to call her Wendy the woman seemed to have convinced herself that she had committed the entire department to the greater glorification of Peter as some major new force in Western scholarship.

David flinched and prayed she was not inviting them to dinner. Worse than Dorkin's subtle censure, worse even than the petty way he tried to submerge Davy with routine administrative nonsenses was the way he pretended that they were good friends and comrades in academic arms. 'This chair could have easily been yours as mine,' Dorkin had told him – with no tact whatsoever – soon after he took over. Then he had added 'I see this department as a partnership, you know.'

But really he wanted David Mosford out of it if he could possibly afford to lose him. Davy did not object to this hostility. He had always assumed that if he were as unimpressive a specimen as Dorkin he too would hate to have a colleague who stole the limelight. But what Davy disliked most was the way Dorkin pretended to be his friend and champion even. And undoubtedly one of the worst ways this vindictive fiction was inflicted was the dreaded annual dinner party when the Dorkins would parade their devotion to higher things by serving up badly cooked food in an underheated and undecorated house out in Rhiwbina.

But fortunately 'Call Me Wendy' wasn't threatening hospitality today. She was in a bit of a state, in fact.

'David! Peter's had a bit of a turn.' In moments of anxiety Wendy's voice could get quite shrill and precious. 'They've sent for an ambulance but he's very worried about next week. In fact I think he may be out for the rest of the term. Will you take up the head of department baton?'

David assured her he would do all he could. He had no argument with Wendy Dorkin despite her choice in food, decor and husbands.

'Oh bless you, David! Bless you. Peter's here now writing up notes on next week.' Bet he is, thought Davy.

'Will you come and collect them? I'd drop them off but I'm going in the ambulance with him, you see.'

'How soon's the ambulance coming?' Davy asked.

'Oh, it's here now,' said Wendy. 'They're just waiting for Peter to finish his list. I'l leave everything with the Very Nice Indian Couple next door.'

'I'll be there,' he assured her.

So the good news was that Dorkin might be away for as long as it took him to get on everyone's tits up at the Heath Hospital. But the bad news was that before the ambulance was allowed to set off with its precious cargo of Dorkin and spouse, the man would have written Davy a complete document of things to be done, minute by minute. Peter Dorkin was a cypher whose life's work was making sure Political History slavishly toed the university line. David dearly wanted to do something radical with that baton Wendy was passing to him – preferably to ram it right up the Great Hypochondriac's bottom.

Instead he got out his car and did what he was asked.

At supper time Davy and Emma were sent to the Spar again but the Castle Park was locked and there was even a bit of a wind blowing up from the river. On the pavement opposite a group of teenagers were hanging round the Great Wall Chinese Takeaway in the mistaken belief, common to many adolescents, that there was glamour to be had in eating chips al fresco. Sarah's daughter Katie was among them but her gaze wasn't directed towards the Spar so David didn't even chance a wave. On the way back they passed Millie's house.

'Why don't you invite Katrin to tea one day?' Davy asked because he rather fancied the idea of seeing Millie Kemp again.

'She says I'm boring,' Emma replied without any real sense of resentment. Well, it was a good enough reason not to have someone to play.

The wonderful thing about children is that they get all that hostility stuff out in the open, Davy thought. He said far worse about Dorkin to just about everyone he met but nothing to Dorkin's face and so the fiction of their partnership was, unfortunately, maintained. Oh, for a Katrin Williams to tell Dorkin that he was intellectually myopic and unjustifiably self-regarding! Oh for a Katrin who would tell Dorkin how much his silly little beard had irritated Davy on a daily basis for the last seven years.

'Is she new in your class?' he asked. The fact that he hadn't known Millie lived in that under-restored rectory on the High Street intrigued David.

'She came to school last September,' Emma replied dutifully. 'From London. I thought she was going to be my friend but she decided I was boring.'

How fond he felt of her. Emma was without guile. She had goodness stamped all over her. Davy just hoped that that would be the extent of this world's stamping over his daughter.

'She didn't find you boring last week in the park,' he pointed out.

'That's because there was no-one else to play with,' Emma replied simply. 'She hasn't played with me at school *at all.*'

Davy put his hand on to her shoulder and squeezed it. His poor child, she had made way for Nick so often in her life he wondered some times if she had a strong enough grasp on her own needs for survival.

That evening, over supper, he talked to Helena about Emma and suggested that they made more of an effort to support her, to help her gain confidence at school.

'There's this Parents' Association thing at the school,' Helena suggested. 'On Tuesday. A Quiz Evening. She's got her heart set on us winning it.'

'What?'

'Well you winning it. There's this enormous teddy the whole class is in love with. It's first prize.'

Davy must have looked completely vacant because Helena insisted that she had told him about it.

'I even asked you if you would come,' she reminded him. He had no memory of this. Absolutely none.

'What did I say?'

'Nothing,' she replied.

'Nothing?'

'Not a thing.'

'Well there you are, I probably didn't hear.'

'No the words went in. You just didn't listen to what they meant,' Helena explained.

'Oh. What a very tedious husband I must be,' he concluded. She did not reply.

'Am I a tedious husband?' he asked hoping to lighten the mood.

'It was your self knowledge that appealed to me before everything else.' Helena put down her fork in mild reproach.

'Not my hearing?'

'Not your *inattentiveness*, no.'

'Well I'll come,' he declared, crossing his knife and fork.

'Good,' she said, standing up suddenly and starting to clear away.

Late on Sunday evening Millie was packing her car for the next day. She knew from long experience that if she left anything, even finding clothes to wear, until the morning she wouldn't be out of the house until midday. On one occasion she had even gone to bed fully clothed so that all she had to do first thing was find the car, find first gear and drive.

Millie was not a morning person.

She and Crispin had a very old, very tall garage in the little service road, known as Back Lane, that ran down behind the High Street. It had been a stable mews in the days before the Spar's storage yard had blanked off the lane and created a cul de sac some time in the 1960s. That was the kind of thing that could happen in those days. With the lane cut in two Millie's was the last garage on the High Street side. Opposite ran a row of small cottages built for workmen who restored the cathedral in 1869. Although this little two-up two-down terraced street could have been fashionable and fun to live in, given that it was adjacent to the Cathedral Green and set back from the High Street, the lane was a focus for feuds. The problem was that each of the cottagers considered it a Briton's inalienable right to keep his or her car outside his or her house, and did, thus narrowing the lane considerably. Furthermore, unless cars were continually shunted up to make space, someone always came back at the end of the day to find that there was a five foot gap between two vehicles and a six footer between two others and, as a result, nowhere to put their nine-foot car.

But Millie Kemp regarded life as too short to worry about how big your parking space was. There were stars up there and when there are stars the night is always young.

Inside the house she checked the calendar to see what was happening next week and noticed that Katrin had written MILLIE BACK in big letters on Tuesday. That was right. Quiz Night. She'd be there. Millie tore a yellow sticky from the block and wrote herself a note *Tuesday. Drive back 5pm. Rabbit's Quiz.* She stuck it on her mobile phone and then spent fifteen minutes searching round for the charging unit. It was bound to be under something or other. It never bothered Millie that she lived in a mess although it sometimes bothered Crisp. Still, most of the time he only had her at weekends, poor old Baggy. The rest of the week the house could look like something of which her parents might be proud.

Crispin was in bed already and reading. There was nothing Millie found more tempting than Crispin in bed reading, unless it was Crispin in bed asleep. He took no notice of her as she set the alarm clock or as she pulled off her sweat shirt and T shirt, or indeed as she scattered the rest of her clothes. He tried not to take any notice as she got under the duvet either, or as she made her way slowly up his legs.

'*What* are you doing?' he laughed, lifting up the covers as if he didn't know.

'Just having a nibble,' she told him, pausing for breath. Crispin put his book down. There was no point in resisting and quite a certain amount of fun to be had from giving in. After a pleasurable while Millie clambered up and sat astride of Crispin, her tanned thighs either side of his nightshirt. He was breathing more rapidly now.

'You are a lucky bugger, you know,' she said appreciatively.

'Yes I am,' said Crispin. Millie leant forward so that her breasts were almost touching his mouth.

'Rabbit thinks I ought to wear pyjamas in bed,' she told Crispin as he began to kiss her. 'To save Jonathan's blushes. What do you think?'

Crisp was distracted for a while. It was reliably nice, this thing they called sex. Millie was getting distracted too.

'Not tonight,' he told her and then he went back to distracting them both.

On Tuesday evening Sarah's daughter Katie let herself in to babysit.

'Oh hi, David,' she said with her usual self confidence. Emma, who hero-worshipped Katie, rushed up for a hug.

'Hi Emma, don't you look smart?'

'Hi Katie,' said Emma with a studied nonchalance that suggested she'd been practising the phrase. Davy noticed his daughter was dressed in trousers and a sort of long waistcoat. It was an unusual outfit for Em but it did look a bit like something Katie might have worn.

'We're just going to this Do at the school,' he announced from the mirror where he was grappling with his bow-tie. 'Shouldn't be back late.'

'No problem,' said Katie.

'Nick's upstairs. He's had his bath.'

'No problem,' said Katie. David wondered why Nick having, or not having had, a bath might be considered by *anyone* to be a problem but he was off duty this evening. Somebody else would have to tax Katie John on the subject of misplaced commonplaces within the English language.

'Er, David, is it all right if my boyfriend calls round later?' Katie asked from where she was cuddling Emma. David looked up at her reflection in the hall mirror and he misthreaded his tie.

'Uh, have you spoken to Helena about this?' he asked in a friendly, noncommittal way.

'Oh yes,' said Katie's reflection smiling at Davy's. 'She doesn't mind.'

'Oh well, then,' he replied at something of a loss. 'No problem.'

On the walk down to school David asked Helena why Katie had asked him about the boyfriend if she'd already cleared it with her.

'She was being polite,' Helena suggested.

'Yes, but what if I'd said I did mind?'

'Then we'd have had to discuss it,' Helena replied reasonably. She could see that Davy was beginning to get steamed up about this.

'Yes, but *why* should I have to be involved in a discussion of Sarah John's daughter's sex life?'

'Well,' Helena replied. 'Because you're employing her.'

'We employ a cleaning lady. We don't discuss her sex life.'

'That's because she's sixty-four.'

Davy stopped them in the middle of Heol Fair. 'No, not because she's sixty-four, Linna. It's because if *Martha Morgan* has a sex life it takes place in her own time in her own place. What Katie is asking is can she conduct her sex life in our house while we're paying her!'

Helena was looking tolerantly and sadly at him. This didn't seem the moment to discuss such matters. But when was? David apologised. It was a pleasant evening in June and a man out walking his dog on the opposite pavement had stopped to watch, and presumably listen, and while he was so halted the dog had decided they must have arrived where they were going and begun to defecate. Helena took David's arm.

'We don't know that she's having sex anyway,' she said. 'They may just want to hold hands in front of the telly.'

'Then why can't they do that at home?'

'At Sarah's?' Helena asked and David began to laugh. Helena laughed too but she could understand the pressures of living with such a mother, one who believed that people should put all that silliness behind them as soon as possible. Sarah had had a sex life. She and Helena had discussed it once but Helena did get the feeling that Sarah had gone to bed with a few young doctors, in a kind but businesslike way, just to make sure she was through that phase. Mostyn John was the most undemanding of men. As such he suited Sarah's belief that the only things in this crazy world that never disappointed were a cup of tea and a good chinwag with the girls.

The Association *Do* was a jolly affair in the school hall but the Mosfords felt somewhat isolated as most of the parents stuck rigidly to their own social groupings. St Dyfrig's School drew on the villages of Llandaff and Llandaff North and its very proximity to the cathedral had made it a byword for high academic standards. It was as if the fallout from all that architectural godliness was bound to be learning. The parents who attended these evenings tended to polarise into two main camps: those who had faith in the school and those who just had faith. A third group of devoted helpers actively idolised the headmaster and congregated in corners to discuss him. At such events as these the teachers tended to polarise too, mainly towards each other and towards the bar. Only the headmaster and the school secretary, a cheery sort who always used such occasions to dress up in her clown's costume, circulated between the groups.

The Quiz turned out to be an event even less exciting than David had feared. Each pair of contestants only got three questions before passing on to the next round. It was a sudden death form of competition with most of the time wasted as mums and dads traipsed up and down the steps that led on to the stage. When it was their turn Helena whispered to Davy, 'Don't argue, whatever you do don't argue with them. Emma would die.'

He was rather put out by this suggestion that he might be a bad loser and initially failed to catch on to how the event was structured. Fortunately questions one and two were science and politics. Helena got the first right and the mother on the other side got in first with the second.

'Right, I think this one is just for the Dads, don't you?' the headmaster asked the assembly with a wink. It was salutary, David thought, to see how a man who is used to an attentive audience doesn't feel he has to work very hard to keep their interest and approval.

'Mr Mosford, Mr Parry, what was the result of the sinking of the Armada?'

David was about to answer when he suddenly doubted if he

knew at which level to pitch his reply. The short-term retreat of Catholicism, the growth of British naval hegemony, the stabilisation of the Tudor monarchy, the colonisation of America . . . Where did you stop?

'The death of Nelson,' said Mr Parry suddenly.

Thank Christ for that, thought Davy.

'Er, not exactly,' said the headmaster, in whose teaching standards David suddenly lost all confidence.

'The defeat of Spain and the continued reign of Elizabeth I,' Davy butted in, having found the right level at last. Ladybird book stuff, this was.

'Is the correct answer!' cried the headmaster. 'Which means that Mr and Mrs Mosford go through into round two.'

Brief applause ensued from the other parents who were obliged to stand around and watch all this. 'How many *Impact Factors* d'you reckon we get?' Davy asked Helena as they made way for the next Mum and Dad.

'Well done Mastermind,' said a voice with a laugh in it, somewhere in the crowd. He spun round to find Millie in a dress which looked as if it had been thrown on at the last moment, which indeed it had.

'I was going to shout *FIX* but you seemed to be struggling,' she joked.

'Not my period,' he replied. 'Linna, this is Millie . . .'

'Kemp,' said Millie turning to Helena.

'I knew that,' said David. Millie laughed. Helena thought, This is the new friend who makes David laugh.

'Hello,' she said.

'My daughter's Katrin Williams,' Millie explained shaking hands.' She's in the same class as your . . .'

'Emma,' said David.

'Will you stop that!' Millie dug him in the ribs.

Yes, thought Helena, I can see what he sees in you but what she said was 'Nice to meet you.'

'Crowded in here isn't it?' said Millie tugging at the top of her dress to let some more air in. 'Maybe it's just me.'

'When did you get back?' David asked, making the point that he knew she'd been away.

'An hour ago,' the woman told him. 'But we had a detour via

Burger King. Katrin actually had this dress and a can of coke out for me when I got back in. Isn't that sweet?'

Helena smiled and the smile stayed fixed on her face.

'Mind you, it's a bit tight!' said Millie.

Yes it is, thought Helena to herself. She could have agreed with that but she swallowed the thought. She didn't want to seem hostile. It wasn't Millie's fault that David was attracted to her. Nor was it David's fault that he was attracted to other women. He always had been and as far as she knew nothing ever came of these admirations. Until the one who used to ring up. The woman from the waste-of-time symposium. That one overstepped some mark that neither of them had actually drawn in the sand but that each half-recognised subsequently as having been transgressed. But it wasn't her fault, this woman from Leeds or Sheffield. It wasn't David's, or hers. It was, none of it, anybody's fault.

But what was going to happen with this one?

'She even asked me to wear a wedding ring!' Millie was telling David. 'Aren't I a rotten mother?'

'Is Crispin here?' David was asking, proving how much he knew of this woman's household.

'No. He's putting them to bed.'

'You've got more than one at the school?' Helena asked, finding her cue.

'Yes, it's usually my chap who brings them into school,' Millie explained to her with a great big smile. 'You probably know him. Crispin Williams? He's . . . um . . . Christ! . . . what does he look like?' She laughed. This is the woman who makes Daddy laugh, thought Helena.

The evening went quickly after that. The Mosfords won two more rounds but lost in the semi-final because their knowledge of pop music had stopped in the 1970s and not yet resumed, vicariously, through their children. They were given school mugs.

'No signed T-shirt of the headmaster?' Davy whispered as they came down the steps to a biggish round of applause.

When it was time to go Millie met Helena in the cloakroom where adult anoraks were dwarfing children's coat pegs for the evening.

'Do you and David want to come back to our place?' she asked in all friendliness.

'That's very kind,' said Helena. She was feeling better now. 'But I'm afraid we've got a babysitter.' She smiled.

'We're just up the High Street,' said Millie. 'Call in and give them a ring.'

Of course Davy was very pleased to be invited back to Millie's. He talked louder and faster, and was suddenly so much more *David* in her presence. From having set off in a dutiful and rather short tempered way he was now out for the evening. He had that dinner-party look about him, Helena thought.

Inside, the unpainted rectory was a lot tidier than one might have expected from Millie's description – but then Millie had only been back for a few minutes. Her kit bag and briefcase were waiting in the hall to trip people up but everything else was neatly piled on tables and packing cases.

'Crisp!' shouted Millie, switching on the lights. 'Sorry about the mess but we only moved in in August! Nine months. Gordon Bennett!'

A slight, thin man in a long old pullover, stretched almost thigh length, appeared from the kitchen. Helena felt sure she recognised him from somewhere. His hair wasn't long so much as uncut and he had a beard of such insubstantial proportions that she thought it might just be that he'd forgotten to shave for a few days.

'Crisp, this is David and Linna,' said Millie. David never called her that to other people. Interesting. So clearly he hadn't actually *mentioned* her name to Millie until they all met this evening. Helena saw Millie was making big gestures now. 'Dave's the TV guru who chats up strange women in the park and Linna's his long suffering wife.'

Crispin was rather a gaunt-looking character. His skin was white, his face was uneven with one side of his mouth twisted slightly and his cheeks were quite heavily lined. Yet when he shook hands with David and said 'Hello' Helena heard a voice of unexpected richness and softness. Very English, very gentle. And when he shook her hand and smiled all the crookedness about him seemed to vanish. Here was a man whose face only made sense when the muscles rearranged it into a smile.

'Hello, Linna,' he said. Normally she would have corrected him, pretended that he had misheard and denied David's diminutive for her but she liked him calling her that.

David used the hall phone to Katie who assured him that staying on till they got back was no problem. What a nice, helpful girl, thought Davy.

'There's some lager in the fridge if you and your boyfriend want one,' he added before putting the phone down.

He took the good news into the kitchen where Helena had already told Millie the story of her husband's outburst in Heol Fair.

'Honestly, Dave,' she said looking up at him. Millie had her hands on the back of Helena's chair where she'd been resting during the story. This meant that when he caught her eye he also looked directly down her neckline and caught her cleavage. Who was he to cast the first stone at other people's proclivities? Particularly in front of his wife.

'I'm not saying I wasn't unreasonable,' he admitted, sitting down.

'I mean this poor girl, how old is she?' Millie asked standing up.

'Sixteen.'

'OK this poor girl, living at home, *desperate* as we all were, her only chance the posh gits who pay her a pittance to babysit, while they are out having a high old time, she *even asks their permission for Christ's sake*!'

Millie let all this hang in the air. Grammatically it was not even a sentence but the meaning was conveyed.

'I could argue with you on a few factual points,' David began. 'Like the pittance and the posh gits and the high old time—'

He was about to say 'But I take your point' when Millie pretended to throttle him. Davy rocked to one side to avoid her hands and restrained her by the wrists. They touch easily, thought Helena. She wished she weren't making so much of this. She wished he'd told her that there was a woman who made Emma's Daddy laugh.

'I concede!' David was insisting. 'Would you like me to pop next door to the Spar and fork out for some condoms?'

'Actually it would be more use if you went to the cashpoint

and got some money to fork out *with*,' said Helena suddenly. There was no reason why she shouldn't be in this conversation but no-one seemed to hear.

'Crisp, d'you think I can take this dress off?' Millie asked, flapping at the neckline. 'There's no danger Rabbit's going to come down and check up on me is there?'

'She's asleep,' Crispin confirmed quietly from the distant sink.

'She does like me to at least look like a Mum,' said Millie with a fond smile. Then suddenly her attitude changed to exasperation. 'Crispin! What *are* you doing there?!'

'Making coffee,' he replied, lifting the kettle.

'Oh Gordon Bennett, Crissy. Get the wine out!' Millie ordered and she flung open the fridge door where several bottles clinked together alarmingly. Kissing him, she flapped her hand at where the glasses ought to be then went upstairs and dug around in the large pile of discarded clothing – which Crispin left unsorted on principle – until she'd found an old denim shirt and a pair of shorts. Millie looked at herself in a full-length mirror that was propped against the wardrobe door. The legs looked good but the shorts were too tight. She pulled up her shirt at the waist and let it balloon down out over the waistband to obscure her figure. Not bad.

When Millie came down Crispin and Helena were talking about the school and David was playing with his half empty glass. Millie topped him up and downed her own.

'Right,' she said as the alcohol hit. 'What say we send out for a pizza?'

'I've cooked,' said Crispin who was still standing in the corner, leaning against the sink. It was the place he'd been ever since Davy had entered the kitchen.

'Yes but there are *four* of us,' Millie told him with a mixture of scorn and affection.

'I've cooked for four.'

'*Why* did you cook for four, Crissyboo?' she asked as if one of them was thick.

'Because we have two children, Emmeline,' he explained slowly. Crispin's irony was so gentle it sounded as if he were simple. 'But as soon as you got back this evening you took them both off to Burger King. So we've got yours, and mine and two spare portions. Does everyone like lasagne?'

The evening was much more of a success than anyone expected and Helena decided that she really didn't mind about David and Millie – not that there was clearly anything much to mind about. Whenever David found a woman to admire, it rarely went beyond this simple stage of enjoying someone else's company more than hers. And that, in the view of her friend Sarah, was probably a jolly good thing. Millie was David's campervan. His latest toy, giving Helena time to concentrate on the things that mattered. That was the way Sarah used to reassure her anyway. Until, of course, David ceased to behave 'sensibly'. However this evening there was no doubt that David, very noisy and provocative, was nevertheless sensible. So that was fine.

Except it wasn't fine, was it? Helena didn't want to end up like Mostyn and Sarah. Helena didn't *want* David preferring someone else's company. And she certainly didn't want this Millie business ending up like the woman from Leeds. Increasingly she found that she was missing David. Missing him although he was there.

Fortunately Helena could see that Millie clearly had no designs on David. He was simply an oddball academic who chats up obvious women in the park. Besides which, she had Crispin who seemed to be one of life's listeners, who tidied up, looked after the children and cooked meals. Why on earth should she want David?!

Yet he could be amusing company when the company was right. David and Millie had got into a very noisy argument about her work which had enabled him to be outrageously rude about the packaging of pseudo-historical artefacts into a totally ersatz and acontextual impression of nineteenth-century Britain: barleycorn, ships-wheels and sepia-tone military memorabilia.

'It's a pub, not a fucking lecture!' Millie had shouted at him, feigning disbelief. Helena thought it wasn't entirely feigned. Maybe David had struck home without noticing. But he hadn't noticed. Not at all. David was delighted with the evening. Women didn't normally yell at him quite so early in their acquaintance. More than the gladiatorial fireworks, however, Millie had actually challenged him to come and look at one of the conversions she'd done and Davy had accepted. Excellent. Next Friday they were going to a place called Rock Point the other side of Newport where she had to check up on something. Better still, thought David, there really had been nothing underhanded about it. His wife and her husband had even been party to the arrangement.

Except Crispin wasn't her husband was he? He was her 'chap'. That was the word she used.

'Funny creature, that Crispin,' David remarked as they walked back.

'I rather liked him,' Helena replied.

'Very quiet.'

'Not particularly.' They walked in silence for a moment.

'Odd looking though,' David insisted. She had to concede that.

'Not as pretty as you, certainly,' said Helena.

He could never tell these days if she was joking or telling him off.

'You know what I mean,' said Davy. 'All that hair and the beard . . .'

'Yes, especially the hair.'

'All I'm saying is . . .' Davy didn't quite know what he was saying.

'What a pity she can't have you.'

David stopped on the pavement and looked at Helena, her eyes both sad and knowing, certainly knowing of him. And the corner of her mouth turning up, unable to resist a reproachful smile.

'Oh Linna,' he said, 'Am I so transparent?' He hugged her. This was how it used to be. They could speak of it now. They could actually speak of it now if she would say something. If *he* would say something. But they didn't. After a while she patted him on the back. She both forgave him and hated him for disappointing her. She blamed herself and blamed him and yet she forgave them all. It was nobody's fault.

When David came to bed Helena wanted them to make love and he wanted it too, it had been that kind of evening. They kissed facing each other and he stroked her long serious face, lifting away the strands of her hair each time they fell. After a while she kissed him on the mouth and put her hands on his waist as she had always done to move him on top of her.

'We haven't done this for ages,' said David kissing her throat.

'Mm . . .' Helena enjoyed the warmth and weight of his body.

'Do you think . . .' said David, fingering the lace on the neckline of her nightdress.

'What?' she asked.

'We could take this off?'

Helena was loth to interrupt the embrace so soon.

'Maybe in a minute,' she whispered in his ear.

'Why a minute?' he asked. What would be so different sixty seconds from now?

'Don't push me David.' He heard her words. They seemed harsh in the darkness.

'I'm not pushing. I just thought we were going to . . .' Words failed him as they often did on occasions like this. Helena didn't want to spoil the moment. 'Perhaps we *are*,' she told him.

But this remark, which was meant to reassure him, had the opposite effect.

'Does it have to be like roulette?' he asked. 'Why the uncertainty?'

'Why can't we just see what happens?' she whispered. She wanted him to know that she was loving him already. Anything else might happen but it didn't have to, did it?

David sighed, feeling that he was cast in the role of some predator. Insensitive, inconsiderate and in bed with a woman who had serious doubts about making love with him. He slipped on to his side. They were still lying together but only alongside each other now. Helena sat up.

'Oh all right,' she said fondly hitching up the long cotton dress over her knees.

'It doesn't matter,' said David.

'Why is it such a problem?' she asked, half-hitched.

'Look, don't,' he said, holding down her nightdress and trying not to sound too negative. 'It doesn't matter.'

He sighed again as Helena cuddled up to him.

'Perhaps if we have a sleep now. We might wake up in the night,' she suggested.

David flopped on to his back. 'Yes,' he said without conviction and stared at the distant architrave, high up in the darkness of their room. He was resentful and yet full of self reproach, aroused and yet deterred. The problem is, he thought, the male of the species is physically a very simple mechanism. Once primed for sex, sex has a very real presence in your existence. It takes a while for the body to forget that urge. It looms over you in the darkness of the bedroom. It makes sure you are very awake. If only the male of the species had emotions as simple as his physiology. If he had they would have done it by now instead of getting all steamed up about whether she really wanted to and whether he really wanted to and if she was only saying yes because she knew he wanted to and all that dreadful death-of-spontaneity stuff.

'It's no good,' he said getting out of bed and making for his dressing gown. 'I'm just too awake now. I'll . . . just, I'll just go and check on something.' He searched for his slippers. 'Interwar delinquency. Stupid Dorkin stuff,' he muttered. 'Usual bloody rubbish.'

'Yes,' she said, wanting him to stay and put his arms around her.

'I'll see you later,' he said, assuming it was best to go.

Millie was pleasantly drunk and had been washing the same glass under the hot tap for five minutes. Crispin took it off her gently and placed it in the dishwasher.

'You are wonderful Crisp,' she told him.' Great lasagne.'

He patted her copper-coloured hair, feeling it rise and fall beneath his finger tips. Crispin could see which strands had taken the henna dye and which ones needed it. Millie was not one for make-up and artefacts. Shampoo and a hairbrush was about all she ever carried round with her but Crispin liked these little touches of artifice. The dyed hair, the way she had started wearing her clothes loose at the waist; he wished she would wear make-up.

She took his hand from her head and kissed it, knuckle by knuckle.

'Great lasagne,' she muttered again and started to snigger. 'You're my pasta masta, Chrissy-boo!'

'And you've got to drive back to Taunton first thing,' he reminded her. 'Come on.'

He turned them both towards the stairs. Millie didn't want to go to bed.

'Kiss me,' she said. Which he decorously did. Then she kissed him hard on the lips and hugged him tight to her.

'Oooh sometimes I just want to eat you, Baggy,' she warned, forcing up his pullover and gripping his pale skin with her finger nails. 'Eat you all up.'

'Well I'm very tired old meat tonight,' he reminded her and yet he obligingly unbuttoned her denim shirt.

'Come on,' she said, moving them towards the kitchen table.

'No,' he said.' Not down here.'

'Why?'

'Things always get broken.'

'So?'

Crispin sighed. 'So I'm the one who has to sweep the bits up in the morning and go into town to buy a new one and write to the insurance company and think of a good story about how yet more things have got smashed in our kitchen. Do you realise that this room is virtually uninsurable?'

'God, I love you when you're anal,' said Millie.

Emma Mosford was in her parents' room early that morning but finding her father not there she checked downstairs. Davy had actually fallen asleep on the chaise in his office and was just waking uncomfortably up to that very fact when Emma came in. She didn't think it strange, her parents not sleeping together. Her mind was on other things.

'I had a look upstairs and in the kitchen,' she began. Davy's heart missed a beat. He had forgotten all about the Parents' Quiz.

'I'm ever so sorry, Em,' he said. Please don't look brave about this he prayed.

'Oh,' she said.

'We did the best we could—'

'It's all right,' said Emma. 'It doesn't matter.'

He felt a bad father for failing to win the teddy and then forgetting, but far worse a father for having been lying down half asleep when she came in. If only he'd been pacing about, unable to have slept with the disappointment.

'Yes, it does matter,' he said and he held out his arms to her. She came over.

'Did someone in my class win it?' He didn't know, they'd been talking to Millie at the time.

'I don't think so.'

'As long as it wasn't Sophie.'

'I don't think it was Sophie,' he lied. He had no idea.

'She said her Dad was much cleverer than you and you're never on the telly anyway.'

Emma leant her head into his shoulder. Oh dear, this was getting unbearably sad.

'Look,' he said. 'We did very well. We got to the semi-final so I think that entitles us to a runner's up prize, don't you?' He wondered how much big teddies cost. 'What if we say . . . ten pounds. You could use that to buy your own Big Ted couldn't you?'

'It's not the same.' She was suddenly sulky.

'You could still take it in to show everyone.'

Emma wasn't mollified. He stroked her head; her hair was thin, wispy, it would never be like Helena's was.

'Cheer up Em.'

'Could I use the money to buy some rollerblades?' she asked. That hardly seemed to be the point if it was Big Ted that she had been in love with but he agreed, of course she could.

'Oh great!' said Emma and she rushed off to tell Nicholas.

David was alarmed. This wasn't quite how he expected to save his daughter from heartbreak. He nipped upstairs quickly to find Helena. She was almost dressed and slowly combing out the dark folds of her hair. He explained what had happened.

'Don't disillusion her, whatever you do, OK?'

'I don't think you should have done that,' said Helena putting her brush down on the dressing table.

'Why for God's sake?'

'For a start, it's not true.'

'What?'

'It'll give her a false idea of competitive games. She'll think she'll always get a prize if we treat her like that.'

David was angry. He felt a real surge of annoyance as Helena deliberately gathered up her hair into a leather buckle and secured it with a pin.

'Linna, she's seven. She was . . . heartbroken,' he reasoned. 'You said yourself she'd set her heart on it and we've let her down.'

'We didn't let her down! It was a game. It was so shambolic it was virtually a raffle!' Helena glanced up at him from the stool. 'You're just giving her ten pounds because you don't want her to stop thinking there's nothing her Daddy can't do. That's what you don't want me to disillusion her about!'

David was staggered by his wife's words. At first he didn't know what to say and then when he did know he knew he didn't want to say anything at all. He took a deep breath and walked out to the dressing room-cum-bathroom where he got dressed silently and noisily. What had got into her?

Mainly what had got into Helena was her husband not bothering to come back to their bed last night but it was all mixed up with meeting Millie and with feeling premenstrual. But the real irritant was all this fuss that David made over Emma just because she adored him. And not just Emma but all these silly noisy women and really anyone but her. She stood up and looked at herself in the wardrobe mirror. There was no doubt that in her white blouse and pearls, in her long skirt and boots, and with her hair fastened back, she looked like all her county cousins over in Gloucestershire and the Thames Valley, but *her eyes*.

Did their eyes ever look so red and angry?

Millie was in Taunton by the time Crispin had deposited Katrin and Jonathan at school. Helena saw him making his way back up the High Street and calling into Halls The Bookshop. *That* was where she had seen him before! He was the rather scruffy looking one who sometimes helped out Peter and his mother. That must be what he did while the children were at school. She was tempted to go in and say hello, to thank him for the lasagne even, but she was feeling rather out of sorts at the moment. She really didn't like the way she had behaved with David. She didn't like the fact that she had been short with Nick and Emma because they dawdled on the way to school. She didn't like the sight of herself reflected in the windows of the Cathedral Cleaners and the Banc National Westminster.

Helena headed back home, forgetting once again about Mrs Morgan's kitchen gloves. As she crossed the Green she looked at the mismatched spires of Llandaff Cathedral and reminded God that Friday's meal hadn't worked. Neither had Crispin's lasagne for that matter.

'Maybe food isn't the answer,' she told the statue of Archdeacon Ridley as she passed. 'Maybe we should stop all the eating and talking and just—!'

She held her tongue. Helena had no wish to be characterised as the mad woman of Llandaff Green who muttered obscenities in front of the statuary. Besides God was clear on this one. She and David could talk. They *did* talk. And it was good. Sometimes she even seemed to understand the essence of History better than he. At Millie and Crispin's they had even laughed at the same things when Millie and Crispin hadn't. So what went wrong in bed? Surely it wasn't the shock of meeting the woman who made Emma's Daddy happy?

Her friend Pippa had once described meeting her husband's secretary and feeling devastated because Anders had never told her how beautiful this woman was. But Pippa was only thirty and recently married and seemed to live on a different marital planet. Pippa swore she would die if Anders even so much as looked at another woman but only after killing him first. Oh to be thirty. If only life were that simple! 'Go forth and procreate,' the Bible said. That was all very well but when you've gone forth and done so, and the fruit of your loins are on an even keel at last . . . well what then? Are the loins redundant?

God did not reply. She was sure she'd shocked him this time.

David Mosford was in at 9.30 that morning. 9.30 exactly. On Monday he'd done his usual race out of the house just after eight only to remember that Dorkin wasn't competing this week. Or even for the rest of the term. So on Tuesday he had resolved to be in late but then remembered he had a nine o'clock seminar on Tuesdays, a particularly nasty little irrritant Dorkin's timetable had managed to inflict on him. So it wasn't until Wednesday that he got to trundle pleasantly in at 9.30. The only problem was that all the parking spaces were taken by then. He hadn't thought of that. Davy had been coming in so early for so long that he had forgotten how quickly the University's multi-storey clogged up with big, lumbering, sensible, *'take the family down to Cornwall'* estate cars. It took him fifteen minutes to find a space into which the ridiculous car could be snuck.

'Professor Dorkin's *always* in by 9.30,' Megan sang out robustly as Davy passed through her office into Dorkin's somewhat after 9.45. David had long realised that Megan Oporto's racial origins (white mother, black father) combined with her gender (female) made her a protected species in Dorkin's domain. Meg, by dint of the dual oppression she had suffered at the hands of David's forebears, was licensed to be as rude as she liked to him.

'I bet you've been waiting all week to say that,' he replied. He aimed at batting the ball back with the same degree of challenge, the same illusion of banter.

'Well, I didn't have to wait long!' Meg replied and she roared with laughter. Maybe he had got her wrong. Maybe this was her humour.

'There's a fax for you,' she said and brought it over to him.

'It's from Professor Dorkin.'

'File it,' David replied.

'Dr Mosford,' she growled and wagged a finger. He reluctantly accepted the handwritten notes about a forthcoming examiners' meeting which had been faxed through from Heath Hospital. Clearly some overburdened administrator had recognised it was easier to give in to Dorkin's demands than try and lead a normal life. Screeds and screeds of paras, and sub paras. Davy looked at the sprawling black ink. Was this to be the shape of the rest of the term—? Dorkin deluging him with crinkly paper and Big Meg happily haranguing him at every turn? Did he actually need this?

Helena was cleaning with Martha Morgan when the second post came. She had rung Pip and, finding her at home, invited her for coffee. But suddenly Helena had felt the house to be very scruffy. Some housewives clean, some housewives let their cleaners clean. On the days when she recognised herself of the genus *housewife* at all, Helena Mosford definitely belonged to the second camp. The delegator. In truth she relied heavily on Mrs Morgan and would happily have paid for her to do through on a daily basis were Martha not in demand elsewhere. However, occasionally Helena would join in because suddenly she had the desire to batter the floor with a brush or beat a carpet to within an inch of its life. Today was one of those angry days.

'Post's come,' said Mrs Morgan pausing for breath and nodding at the letter box. It was her preference to clean at her own pace and she welcomed any opportunity to distract Helena who was wielding a mean and exhausting mop that morning.

There was a postcard for David from a campaign run by three mad historians who wanted supporters for their campaign against a Marxist vice chancellor, and something about an international conference which David would want to join, given its salubrious setting, but most of his post went direct to the University. There was also a newsletter from one of the support groups Helena had joined when Nick was so ill and a postcard from Gareth who was travelling via New Mexico. Or rather Gareth who was writing to say he was spending the long vacation in London and could they all meet up some time. 'Will give you a ring' he signed off 'Lots of Love Gareth'

Helena was both pleased and bothered. It was a day for being bothered. Of course she always liked hearing from Gareth. She never minded that he invariably forgot Vermont was five hours behind the UK and that the wonderful news he wanted to share had occasionally been phoned through at one o'clock in the morning. Or that when he sent her a book he rarely managed to pay the correct postage. The real problem here was that David didn't like Gareth ringing, or sending books or even writing books in the first place. And David really wouldn't like the fact that Gareth was going to be in Britain over the summer. He claimed that he couldn't care less about *Professor* Gareth Box but David always put his title in italics and when Gareth wrote 'all meet up in London' he must have had little expectation of David being a part of the *all*. Gareth's *all* was one group he didn't want to join.

Helena wondered what to do with the card. She wasn't going to hide it, for goodness sake, yet David would only get grumpy if he found it lying around or Nick drawing on it. Nor was she in any mood to throw away a perfectly friendly communication just because David and Gareth had this feud. She crossed to the lobby and, pulling her notebook out of her jacket, tucked it in.

At the University Davy was looking through Peter Dorkin's timetable which he could access on the computer. There did seem to be an awful lot of meetings. He was actually quite surprised. Davy knew, as everyone else did, that Dorkin was one of the few professors who actually seemed to relish administration. He also knew that Dorkin claimed he only had time to teach his speciality (the Corn Laws, a subject on which he had published once, and then most unremarkably) but now, to be honest, Davy couldn't even see where he fitted that in.

'Are all these meetings really necessary?' he asked Meg who was filing letters, banging filing cabinets alarmingly back and forth as she hurled their contents in.

Meg shrugged. Davy was not to be put off.

'Come on, how do I decide which ones I need to go to?'

The phone began to ring next door.

'Ask Professor Dorkin,' she told him.

'Yes, but he goes to them all.'

'Then maybe they're all necessary!'

With that Big Meg slammed the last cabinet drawer shut and waltzed out with a laugh, one gigantic buttock rolling sideways after the other. Davy sat back and double clicked the computer mouse on a key that illuminated allocated time within the schedule. As he watched, the screen seemed to fill with hours already designated. What a totally bleak prospect. No research time. Virtually no student contact. Just hours and hours of unbroken bureaucracy. Dorkin's chair was endowed. Why on earth had he agreed to be head of department as well? Did he actually *enjoy* this kind of thing?

Megan appeared at the doorway without knocking and just remained there. He could feel her over his shoulder. Really, if David was going to do this job for any length of time Meg had got to stop treating the place as her own and start working round the departmental needs.

'Professor Dorkin,' she said.

'Not again,' Davy replied, presuming now that the Great Fool was now ringing in from his bedside.

'He died this morning,' said Megan. David looked up at her large blank face but she was looking over his head, gazing at the wall.

'I told him,' she said. 'I told him if he carried on like this!' And with those words she left.

Peter Dorkin was dead.

David had sounded strange on the telephone, almost as if he were going to talk to her. Except Helena knew they rarely talked on the telephone. The phone was for information and arrangements. Some evenings he would gossip away happily on the phone in his office but he never did to her. Their relationship didn't include gossip.

'We're not going out are we?' he asked, meaning could they spend the evening discussing the implications of this news?

'No.'

'How are the children?' Meaning he was feeling worried.

'Fine.'

'Can you record Paisley at six if I'm not back.' Meaning not so worried that he he'd forget one of his rivals was on television that evening.

They sat in the dining room. Not at either end of David's father's table but half way down on opposite sides. Helena had cooked something substantial that Davy could keep dipping into. There were times for meals with twelve separate dishes, when selecting and arranging the right combination of bits was half the pleasure, and there were times for hot pot, lasagne and macaroni cheese. Crisis food she called it. David ate and talked.

'The thing is, will they advertise the two as one post? If they do, do I want it? Do I really want to be head of department? And even if I do, *should* I? Isn't it foolish to throw away my chances of a personal chair? But, then again, if I don't go for it . . .'

'Who else will get it?'

'Precisely.' He chewed the idea and the macaroni around.

'He's blocked me for so long, I'm going to hate myself for saying this I know, but I just can't believe he's gone.'

'Have you spoken to Wendy?' Helena asked. His agenda was political but hers also took in the plight of a woman whose life's work had been her husband. A husband who was now dead. Davy explained that he had left a message on the Dorkin answer machine offering to be ready to talk as soon as she wanted.

'Of course it's nothing to do with her,' he added. 'Her claim on the college, which was tenuous to say the least, is now ended.'

Helena didn't like him for saying that.

'But on the other hand she has nothing now. Absolutely nothing. The least I can do is listen to her.'

David stopped eating and came at this another way. 'I mean, you'd have the children, wouldn't you? If it had been me.'

'I *do* have the children,' replied Helena. She didn't add she had them virtually all the time.

'The thing is . . .' he began again referring to his forthcoming conversation with the Head of School. 'You see the thing is I could tell her, Stella I mean, I could offer to take on the departmental duties short term as a *quid pro quo* for getting Dorkin's chair later on. But I could be making myself too useful. What d'you think? It keeps me to the fore but maybe they're really keen to make me professor and are willing to agree to split the job anyway. Maybe Stella is *looking* to split. It's way overdue. On the other hand she could keep costs down by keeping the two in harness and if I go in on Monday, beefing about how you can't combine the chair and the headship, and then Stella decides to keep both in harness . . .'

'You've talked yourself out of a job,' Helena agreed.

'So? What do I do?'

'Well,' said Helena, pouring herself a glass of water. 'If the University is only half as badly managed as you claim, I'd imagine they're all running around like headless chickens at the moment. And in circumstances like that you need to be invaluable. Offer yourself as the solution to their problems.'

'But what if Stella talks about the long term?' David asked, dipping directly into the macaroni pot with his fork.

'Remain noncommittal. Say it's too soon for you to tell if the two jobs can work in tandem.'

David smiled. 'You are brilliant,' he told her.

'I'm just suggesting you tell her the truth, David. It *is* too soon for you to be sure.'

'Oh, I'm sure all right. Combining the two jobs in Dorkin was way out of date and a total disaster.'

Helena cleared her plate suddenly to one side without saying anything. This was the kind of thing she did when he suddenly annoyed her. She didn't like him speaking ill of Peter Dorkin. David could feel her censoring him for that remark.

'I know it sounds harsh,' he began.

'No it doesn't,' she replied, as if nothing was bothering her.

'But I can't help being excited.' He leaned across the table. 'I am genuinely sorry for Dorkin and for Call Me Wendy, but this is, to be honest, just what *We* need.'

Helena took his plate. 'You're not pleased, though?' he asked.

'I'm pleased for you,' she told him honestly. 'If this is going to make you happier in your work I'm pleased for you.'

'Us,' he told her. 'It could make things better for all of us.'

Helena stood up abruptly. Another of these movements. Like a horse bolting, like a gazelle in flight, like the way she had suddenly joined Mrs Morgan and punished the mop. David was thrown by the force of her reaction. Recently there seemed to be more and more of these bursts of sudden irritation. Helena walked into the kitchen angry with herself and with him. This was not the answer to *her* problems.

Not surprisingly David worked late that night. When he came to bed Helena didn't seem to notice and when she turned over angrily in her sleep he didn't seem to notice either.

3

David and Millie

The large brown envelope disgorged flow charts on to David's desk. Or rather on to the desk that was once Dorkin's and which was currently his. At least until he had been briefed by the Head of HISAR.

Davy gazed at the mass of coloured paperwork. Someone somewhere in the University claimed to believe that the School of History and Archaeology could radically increase its throughput and to prove her point lots of diagrams had been generated on computer. As far as Davy could tell from this technicolour visual verbiage, a person or persons called Deputy Director (S Pers) seemed to think the answer lay in maximising student input *qualitatively* and close targeting all teaching functions. This last, he discovered in a footnote, meant *relating the syllabus more closely to the means of final assessment.*

The comments of all professorial staff and each head of department were invited.

'In other words,' Davy wrote in a margin, 'bring in only the best students and then tell them which questions you are setting for finals. This should reduce the *throughput period* from three years to about ten weeks.'

Or twenty, given the department's usual intake, he thought. Then he reached for the correcting fluid. That was the kind of thing David Mosford would write. What did the acting Head of

Political History write? Particularly when he had set his sights on the Chair of Political History and might have to take one with the other. Did he *really* want Dorkin's chalice if this was the kind of mind-numbing poison it contained?

The inner door of Dorkin's office opened and it was Hooper looking somewhat stunned. Hooper wore a leather jacket and jeans. He always did. Davy knew that the consensus among students was that Hooper regurgitated his own undergraduate notes mercilessly, and occupied the time, thus saved, by fancying himself something rotten. But not this morning.

'Er, I've just heard,' said Hooper.

'Yes,' said Davy standing up in a fraternal way.

'Bit of a, well you know . . . Phew.'

'Yes,' said Davy.

Hooper was having difficulty articulating this one. Presumably nothing he had prepared fifteen years ago could help him now.

'I mean, Christ Almighty,' said Hooper.

'Yes, look, do you want to sit down?' David asked.

Hooper declined. He had to invigilate in ten minutes' time.

'I mean . . .' said Hooper, still in the doorway, 'Well. Dorkin eh?' And then he was struck by a new thought. 'You're taking over, are you?'

'Short term,' David told him.' I'm seeing Stella this afternoon.'

'Christ Almighty,' said Hooper, shaking his head, and then he was gone.

Davy hoped that it was Dorkin's death, rather than his stepping into this particular breach, that had driven Hooper to such inarticulate misery. The telephone buzzed before Davy could get back to defacing the college post.

'There's a personal call for you on line two,' boomed Megan with just the level of reproach that David might have expected from Peter Dorkin's secretary when having to do something as unwelcome as putting a call through to him.

'Which is line two?' he asked, refusing to apologise for the call.

'*This* is line one,' came the flat reply. David picked up the other hand set on Dorkin's desk.

'David Mosford.'

'Is that the man from the telly?' asked a voice. It was Millie. Her voice sounded very clear.

'Where are you?' he asked.

'Sodding London. Wasting time. Listen, about tonight.'

He liked that. He liked women with that kind of laugh ringing him up and saying 'about tonight'. He rather wished some of his more blasé students could hear this conversation.

'I'm having trouble getting away.'

Then again he was quite pleased they couldn't hear if he was being stood up.

'That's a shame.'

'So can I meet you there? At seven?'

'Fine.'

'Tell George you're a friend of mine. He might let you have a packet of nuts on the house.'

Before he could say good-bye properly, Meg buzzed through on the other phone.

'Head of School on line one,' she said. Davy was feeling quite chirpy having been reminded that there was life outside the University. 'Is it always this busy?' he asked.

'Poor Professor Dorkin never took personal calls,' Megan informed him. Again that bluff response. Was this badinage or sheer bloody rudeness?

In fact it wasn't Stella but her secretary who just wanted to know if she could move their meeting back till Monday. After putting the phone down David walked through to the outer office and asked Megan if she couldn't have fielded that call for him.

'I don't have your diary,' she replied as if that was an end to the matter.

'Well, if the Dean asks me to caretake till the end of term, I suggest I *give* you my diary.'

'Fine by me.' Megan was staring at her own screen. Really she was getting worse. Or he was making her worse? David decided to take Dorkin's post back to his own office for a while but then he noticed the outer door frame filled, if filled were possible, by the diminutive form of Alun Taylor.

'David, this is *terrible*. Can I have a word?' he asked. David was not tall but Alun Taylor was probably a good two inches shorter than him and, like many small men, he was prone to seize the initiative before any big guys muscled in. Once in Dorkin's office, Alun immediately started pacing and running his hands through those few strands of long dank hair he had retained (and which were so despised by the studentry).

'What was Dorkin *playing at* cycling to work at his age?'

David agreed.

'It's a complete disaster for the department.' David couldn't agree with that but he tried not to show it.

'I mean they're going to want me to take over, aren't they?' Alun was clearly sweating.

'D'you think so?' Davy asked.

'Bound to. I've got eight conferences over the summer and a chapter to get out by October. I mean, I hate to say it about the man, David, but Dorkin should have been more responsible! His job was to keep the pressures off people like me – and you of course – and to be fair he did do that. But if they ask me to step in what happens to Bismarck and the Dual Alliance?'

This great project had been so long in the writing up there were rumours Count Otto himself had helped Alun with the preliminary drafts.

'It would be a disaster if I missed that October deadline!'

'I'm seeing Head of School Monday morning,' said Davy in the hope that this would calm his colleague down.

'Are you really?' Little Alun looked relieved. 'Oh thank you, David. They must be going to ask you to take over *pro tem*. That would be an enormous help. I don't suppose I'll escape beyond September but if you could just hold the fort, over the vacation say, I may be in a better state by the time they put me on the spot.'

Packing his briefcase with Dorkin's post, David reflected that if he *were* offered the chair Little Alun Taylor was going to be another problem. Alun wouldn't mind if Davy took over as head of department. No-one with a serious interest in research really wanted to spend their time ploughing through all this tedious stuff but Alun was senior reader and nearly fifty. He had already had his request for a personal chair turned down. His clear assumption was that Dorkin's death would mean that he would now inherit the Professorship of Political History, as his due. There might be all these unwelcome departmental duties thrown in, of course. That was the problem of not getting a personal chair. You did have to *work* if you were head of department. But a chair was a chair after all, and this was clearly Alun's, at least in Alun's view.

Back in his own office David shut the door and put out two filing trays amid all the marking. On the plastic label of one he wrote 'Crap' and on the other 'Complete Crap' and then went back to dealing with Dorkin's post.

Helena had told herself to read a book. It was a decision she had taken independently of God but she was sure he would approve. It was a long time since she had done so and although David's office in the billiard room had shelf loads of the things she had decided to go out and buy a new one. It didn't have to be a new publication but she did like the feel of pages that hadn't been opened before. On her way down to Halls The Bookshop she checked her list. Only the recently added imperative *Dad's Present* and the aide memoire relating to David's marital requirements seemed not to have been fulfilled. She tore that sheet off and looked for a bin to throw it into. There wasn't one. Helena Mosford walked the length of the High Street conspicuously unable to find any way of dispensing with a piece of paper that said on it *'Make Love to David'*. Outside the Banc National Westminster there was a little slot where unwanted receipts from the cash point machine could be stuffed but she felt anxious about their personal account manager getting his hands on this information. Not that it was information per se unless you deduced from the instruction Mrs Mosford had given herself that Dr Mosford wasn't getting his quota at the moment.

Which was of course just the kind of deduction that personal account managers do make! It helps the nosey creatures build up the customer profile. But it wasn't as if she hadn't tried. Helena was half tempted to go into the bank, borrow a biro and write 'He Gave Up!' at the bottom of the sheet and pay it directly into her account.

No she wasn't. She just felt silly standing there, conspicuous on the pavement, a small piece of paper in hand as if trying to give out leaflets. She crossed the road to Halls the Bookshop, opened the door and came face to face with Crispin.

'Hello,' he said from behind the till.

'Hello,' she replied screwing the piece of paper up even tighter in her hand.

'Have, have you got a bin?'

Crispin said he'd have a look. While he was ducked beneath the counter, Helena told him that she'd realised after the lasagne night that she'd recognised him from the shop.

'Um, yes,' said Crispin, resurfacing with a waste paper basket. 'Do you come in often?'

'With the children,' she replied, dropping the red hot paper into the basket and immediately worrying if she had screwed it up tightly enough. Did this man go through the bins when Halls was quiet? Did he try to divine local gossip from laying out flat all the bits and pieces tossed away by unsuspecting customers? Was it possible she was going over the top about this?

'There's a good Children's Section here,' Crispin agreed.

'That was a *very good* lasagne!' she told him with sudden and undue enthusiasm for the courtesies. He thanked her and returned the bin to the floor, displaying no obvious interest in its contents.

'Is there anything I can help you with?'

There was something seductively quiet and gentle about Crispin. David thought there wasn't anything much to him but to Helena his ascetic appearance contrasted interestingly with that honeyed voice.

'You don't do books on tape, do you?' Helena asked. 'I don't mean you personally,' she added and then laughed to cover her embarrassment. How nice it would be to have Crispin Williams reading a book to you.

'I'm afraid not.'

'It's not for me,' she explained speaking too quickly. 'It's for my father. He's eighty. Well he will be.' Before she could stop herself she added 'He was quite old when I was born.'

What was she saying? All this silly, silly stuff:

'I'm thirty-seven,' she told him unable to stop herself. And then she burst out laughing. 'I'm sorry, I don't know what's the matter with me. I suddenly didn't want you thinking that because my father is eighty next month—'

Crispin laughed too. Or at least he smiled widely. His eyes didn't change. But he shared the moment with her.

'Look, would you like to come round to dinner,' Helena asked. She was thirty-seven after all, not seventeen. She could say things like that if she wanted to particularly to the man whose common-law wife her husband fancied. 'How about Saturday?'

'Um, well, thank you,' he said. 'Er, yes. That would be nice. It . . . it all depends on Millie . . . on how long she'll be back. She hasn't told me yet.'

'She's very lucky to have you,' said Helena thinking how very tolerant he was.

'Yes,' he replied. 'I keep telling her that but it doesn't always sink in.'

At three o'clock David remembered to ring home and to say that he was going straight from work to Rock Point.

'Millie said to meet her there. Is that OK?'

Helena said she was sure it was OK. She hadn't started cooking yet. Was he eating with Millie?

'I don't think so, I'm just looking at this pub.'

'And having a drink.'

'Yes,' he agreed. 'Looking and drinking.'

'But not eating?'

'Looking, drinking but probably not eating,' he agreed. It was one of these conversations he got into with Helena sometimes. It was at a tangent. But a tangent to what?

'And talking,' she added. 'I imagine you'll be talking too.'

'Yes.'

'Well, have a nice time.'

David replayed the conversation in his mind as he drove out of Cardiff. Were these jokes or jibes? Sometimes he couldn't gauge her. Never could. So often Helena's feelings just left him behind. In the past that hadn't mattered so much but now every silence, every misunderstanding seemed like a reproach. Was it him, was it her? Was it guilt?

What it definitely was, however, was a splendid early summer evening on the narrow roads that wove down to Rock Point. So bright and golden, in fact, that there was an illusion of heat. Davy flicked a switch to lower the windows and immediately flicked it back to staunch the ensuing gale. It wasn't that warm. He could remember June evenings like this when he was a student. Hints of summer, tantalising while revising. And the summer term itself, that heady mix of celibacy during finals and, if you were lucky, something that wasn't celibacy afterwards.

He remembered Helena's finals too. That summer of sudden rain and bitter winds. By that time he had left London and was doing research at Oxford and there was some doubt about whether this tall, really very English girl was going to get the degree she deserved. '3B' David had noted against her college address when they first met. Definitely a 3B. (Thank God he'd thrown his old address book away.) 'Breasts, Brains and Beauty' The order of priority fluctuated.

And to think that 3B was now his wife. Helena had coped badly with Schools and afterwards, when she was referred for a viva. That Summer was a time of dreadful tension. The two of them would walk unhappily up and down the towpath while tourists punted and pretended to be students. Helena felt desperate for letting herself down in the exams and would spend days in her bedroom with the curtains drawn. It was ironic that he'd come to Oxford in the hope of a long hot 3B summer romance. Ironic, given that the beautiful undergraduate he'd found and fallen in love with wanted to do nothing in bed but curse her own stupidity. She had felt so inadequate and he had felt inadequate too for not being able to help her. God, he had spent so much of his life feeling that!

The pub at Rock Point was actually an old farmhouse on which the River Severn had encroached so completely that the rivers authority now hid it from sporadic floodwaters behind a tall earth and concrete embankment. When David parked he could see that there were tables and chairs actually set up on the flood barrier. Steps were cut into the turf so that drinkers could make their unsteady way up to view the estuary and stagger back down again to the bar.

To his surprise Millie was already sitting at a table on top of the embankment and she waved, shielding her eyes against the sun. Davy shouted up and asked if she wanted a drink but Millie had already got her own.

'Tell George you're with me!' she reminded him as he went inside.

The bar was dark and low-ceilinged and for a moment Davy forgot that Millie had converted it to what it was. Only the flagstone-effect carpet, the tassels on the curtains and the brass lights over inconsequential pictures alerted him. The place didn't seem particularly busy and the burly Scotsman behind the bar was very welcoming.

'Yes, sirrr!!' he announced with a flourish.

David asked if there were any real ales.

'No sirrr, but we do a few very good imaginary ones!!' A *wit* thought Davy, and he ordered Felinfoel. 'Millie Kemp said to say I'm with her.'

'Ah, then there'll be no charge for that, sir!' said the man with an exaggerated gesture of his enormous fist.

Davy thanked him and then waited for the pint glass to be filled. It took a while.

'Nice place,' he said, realising that he was going to be standing there for some time.

'Locals hate it,' replied the silver-haired Scot.

'Really?'

'Ever since the brewery did that conversion job. Just can't get them in.'

'Oh yes?' Davy was intrigued.

'They find it phoney, that's what they say.' With a flourish the big man brought Davy's glass to the counter. '*Ersatz*. I think that's what they call it. And *acontextual*. Hey now, haven't I seen you on the telly somewhere?'

It was at that moment that Davy realised he had been set up. He smiled about it all the way back up to the embankment.

'Nice one,' he said bending down to kiss her on the cheek

By eight o'clock the Mosford children were finally in bed, and Helena was just wondering when David might return, when the telephone rang. She assumed this meant later rather than sooner but the voice wasn't his.

'Helena?' asked a man who sounded full of concern.

'Yes.' But then who else would it be? This was her. It always had been.

'*Helena. It's Gareth.*'

Gareth. Of course! This wasn't a voice redolent with concern for her, this was a voice that liked to sound concerned. An easy mistake to make with Gareth Box. She'd made it herself when young.

'Gareth! Where are you?'

'London. Did you get my card?'

Gareth Box. Professor Box of the University of Moosejaw, Saskatchewan, as David insisted on calling it. Gareth Box who sent them postcards of a place called Vermont. Gareth who had been her first 'boyfriend' at University. All these years later, no-one pronounced her Christian name quite as he did and yet it always took her a moment to recognise his voice on the telephone. There were only three syllables involved in the business of saying 'Helena' but Gareth did something with them that nobody else did. Something she couldn't describe but that was distinctly him. Perhaps it was just that his was the first voice she had heard saying her name in a darkened room at three o'clock in the morning . . . But that was all a long time ago.

'When are you coming up to Town next?' he asked.

One thing that never changed was Gareth's effortless egocentricity.

'Which town were you thinking of?' she goaded him.

'I have to talk to you.' This was a man who walked out of her life when she was twenty-one. Sixteen years ago. Sixteen years – one husband, two children and a misjudged move back to Wales – ago.

'Gareth, I'm a housewife and mother, living in Llandaff,' she pointed out. 'Trips to London are not part of my daily routine.'

'You're more than a mother to me,' he reminded her. 'Can you make it next week?'

'No,' she said virtually on principle.

'The week after?' He was trying to slide under her skin.

'I can *probably* manage then,' she conceded. 'Perhaps towards the end of that week?'

'Monday,' he replied. Helena knew she should have been outraged.

'Oh all right,' she agreed. 'Are you going to buy me lunch?'

'I thought we'd go to the Tate—'

'No,' she replied. Of that she was sure.

'You used to like exhibitions,' he reminded her. Of course. Of course he *would* remember that. Husbands forgot things like that, Gareths didn't.

'I've got flat feet, Gareth. Exhibitions are a pain in the spine these days.'

'How about lunch at the Hayward, then?'

'Fortnum's,' said Helena. She found his enthusiasm for the visual infectious but two pregnancies had left her unable to stand and gaze at paintings like she used to. And in any case she would be travelling four hours in a train and making contingency arrangements for Nick and Emma just so Gareth Box had someone to talk to. The least he could do was let her listen in comfort.

'You're a remarkable woman, Helena,' Gareth conceded. She was used to this.

'How many more of us remarkable women are you ringing today?' she asked him. There was a moment's pause.

'I'd forgotten how well you know me,' he conceded. Well, after all this time she certainly understood the agony of being as brilliant and misjudged as Gareth Box. She'd had a lot of practice.

Davy and Millie were getting cold on the embankment but neither had mentioned it yet because the conversation had turned to Dorkin. Half way down his second pint David had been struck by the vague profundities relating to Dorkin's death.

'He was such a pedantic, *political* man. So much of this world, riding its fads and fashions. I just can't imagine him having any spiritual dimension at all. And yet if there is a God, he now knows that God. If there is an afterlife he is there. I just cannot conceive of Peter in a world without petty bureaucracy.'

'Maybe he'll be glad to be shot of all that,' said Millie. She was keen to get inside but she had rather taken to this maudlin side of David. It reminded her of Crispin. How often men like this needed to be lifted out of themselves, and how easily it could be done, if only they would try.

'You mean if the soul can be divorced from the personality?' he asked her.

'Do I?' Millie laughed. 'God, that's a bit big for me. Crisp's the one to ask about that. He's all churchy.'

'What are you then?' Davy was interested in her answer but he kept his eyes on the setting sun which was just about to be submerged in the distant Bristol Channel. Suddenly it dipped, or rather it seemed to extinguish itself in the horizon. He waited to hear the cosmic sizzle.

'You've only got one chance, I reckon,' said Millie. 'The thing is to enjoy yourself now.'

Davy agreed. 'And do you?' he asked.

'Sure,' she replied. 'Don't you?'

'Sometimes.' He couldn't be more positive than that.

'And you a media star!' she mocked. 'Come on. The brewery will buy you another pint, I reckon.'

At eleven o'clock Helena rang Crispin. It wasn't difficult to find his number from the directory although she wasted a lot of time looking up the many Williamses in Cardiff before finding the number under Kemp, E.K., High Street, Llandaff. *E.K.*? Millie must be short for Emily, she supposed. And that's why Crispin called her Emmeline sometimes. And she called him Boo.

Crispin was already in bed but Helena didn't know this. She was too concerned about David to picture the person to whom she was talking.

'Have you heard from Millie?' she asked.

'Um, no. No. I haven't,' Crispin admitted. His voice was wonderfully calm. 'Is it late?'

Helena could hear him putting down a book and looking at the clock.

'Oh dear, she can be stupid like this,' he explained, without any malice or even weariness in his voice. 'I'll try her mobile. Let me ring you back.'

Millie and Davy had had a good evening. First of all they'd had pie and chips – 'The Ferryman's Supper' as it was called on the menu. Then they'd got into an argument about instant heritage at the bar which George had umpired. Then Millie had challenged

Davy to a game of bar billiards and he had accepted, warning her, as he took off his jacket, that he had a full-size table at home. Millie wasn't impressed and when she eventually won the game and claimed her drink she reminded him 'Size isn't everything, Dave.'

The bar was pretty full by this time but George took time off from his ostling duties to adjudicate the question of whether Millie or Davy was best fit to drive back.

'If you want my opinion you're both over the limit and this was a nice quiet pub before you two came in.'

'Well, I can't risk my licence,' said Millie. 'I need that car for my work.'

'And I daren't risk any trouble at the moment,' David added. Dorkin or no Dorkin, he had a particular need to keep his nose clean at the University these days.

'We'll get a taxi,' said Millie.

'At this time on a Friday night?' said George. 'Out here?' Which was when Millie realised the time and also when her mobile phone went off.

'Oh Cris, I'm so sorry, what a stupid, stupid cow. Oh Boo Boo, I *know*! We were playing billiards.' Davy left Millie to her fulsome apologies and went to look for a call box and the gents. When he got to the phone he found Helena engaged so he returned to the bar.

'All done,' Millie announced.

'What's all done?'

'George says we can go back with this hen party from Whitchurch. They've got a driver and some spaces in the minibus. And Crisp's ringing Helena.'

Davy felt very guilty at how the evening had fled without his even telephoning home. Why did he do these things? But if Millie felt any guilt it didn't show because off she went to find the hen party to give her fulsome thanks for their forthcoming lift. Left on his own, Davy felt suddenly morose. Alcohol could do that to him. He caught sight of himself in a brass-framed nautical mirror. Over it an enamel plate declaimed SEVERN RIVER PILOTAGE with a bogus list of crossing rates, presumably dreamed up by Millie. And there beneath it was the reflection of this round-faced, red-faced academic with gold-rimmed glasses and expensive shirt, abandoned in a sea of other people's conviviality. He went outside where the air was clear and the urban glow from Newport's street lighting was distant enough to let the stars shine out of the dark night sky.

Davy felt a sudden and very primitive instinct that Dorkin was up there. It was an absurd notion to think that there was a little celestial constellation above wherein the soul of Peter Dorkin revolved and sang praises to his Creator. Dorkin couldn't sing a Eurovision Song Contest entry, let alone a perpetuity of Hosannas. Yet if Peter Dorkin was looking down on this material world, how frustrated he must feel at this very moment to have finally before him the ocular evidence of what he had always suspected: Dr Mosford's gross moral turpitude. Reader in Social History driven by lust to a dodgy pub on the Severn estuary!

On an impulse of sheer physical delight, Davy ran up the steps to the top of the embankment. He was suffused by the realisation that *he* was still of this world. To be alive, to exist in bodily form meant that there was still hope. While we were still here there was still Time. And Time meant that things could happen, things could improve, things could be resolved.

He reached the crest of the rise, somewhat out of breath, and wanted to shout. What? What did he want to shout? 'I'm alive!' that's what he wanted to shout. But he didn't. Partly because he was out of breath, partly because he wasn't really drunk and partly because the tide had risen whilst he and Millie were inside and the sudden shock of this great, black, slow-moving wall of water, only four feet below the embankment gave him his second visceral moment of the evening. Primitive Mosford face to face with the great dark river of life and a bit frightened of tipping over into it.

'What you doing up there?' cried a voice from below. It was Millie. She'd got her parka on now and had a bottle in her hand.

'Making a fool of myself!' he shouted back.

'But there aren't any cameras around,' she replied coming up the slope after him. Really this media star joke was beginning to wear a bit thin.

'I was suddenly struck by the preternatural enormity of nature,' he told her in all honesty and gestured at the river. But Millie hadn't heard.

'Look,' she said, joining him at the top of the embankment and holding up what was, on closer inspection, a half drunk bottle of sparkling wine. 'One of the girls gave me this and I thought, seeing as we're both getting a lift back, we may as well get pissed.'

'Absolutely,' said David, kissing her on the lips. The way he felt at that moment, had she suggested they plunged into the chill River Severn he might have gone along with it. Life was for seizing the moment. Then he realised what he had just done. He had kissed her. But she seemed not to be making anything of it.

Well, perhaps he hadn't then.

Millie had two half-pint beer glasses which she put down on the table in front of them and into both she was pouring a generous draught of the ready opened, and lamentably cheap, fizzy wine.

'Italian,' said David in disgust.

'Didn't know they made champagne,' Millie observed as she passed his glass.

'They don't,' he replied. '*Can't* in fact. Neither technically, chemically nor geographically is this champagne.' Fortunately it didn't taste too bad.

Had he kissed her? He'd kissed her to say hello when they met, to say 'well done' at setting George up to make fun of him, but that was on the cheek, that was a public kiss. What had happened just now? Privately and on the lips?

'Cheers,' said Millie taking a draught herself. He hardly recognised her, wearing that bulky old anorak. She looked older without cleavage.

Maybe nothing had happened. Perhaps he only *thought* he'd kissed her. Maybe the impulse had completely bypassed the act and become instant memory. What a waste of perfectly good lust.

'What are we drinking to?' he asked, suddenly feeling the cold. It was 11.30 at night, it was May and they were in an unheated part of South Wales.

'Absent partners,' she said. 'Your wife, my chap. Are you going to get it in the neck tomorrow?'

That might be the case but it wasn't really fair of her to mention it.

'Helena's very tolerant of me,' he told her. 'Like Crispin is of you.'

'Crisp is gorgeous,' she announced.

'So's Helena,' he replied.

'Absent partners,' Millie proposed again and she took another generous swig of that thing which was not champagne.

'Absolutely.' But Davy had another toast in mind. 'To only coming here once.'

'What, Rock Point?' Millie asked in surprise.

'No. The thing you said. That we've only got one chance to enjoy ourselves.'

'Oh that,' she remembered. 'Sure.'

On Saturday morning Crispin was due to help out at Halls. He had reminded Millie of this when she came to bed in an amorous state some time after midnight. Having spent a fun-evening with David Mosford, and a riotous journey in the back of the minibus with those hens still capable of lewd behaviour, Millie was in a mood for even more fun with Crispin but he was peeved with her for being so irresponsible and said so.

'Helena Mosford was genuinely worried,' he insisted as Millie pulled her top off. 'Emily, will you stop dropping your clothes everywhere.'

Millie stood up and regarded him from the bottom of their bed. 'Crisp, Helena Mosford is Dave's responsibility and you are *whingeing*.'

'No I'm not.'

'You are. You're always the same if I've been out for a drink.' She could see her reflection in the full length mirror, propped against the wardrobe. Millie linked her arms above her head, Salome-style. It was an angle that showed her off to best effect.

'Very nice,' muttered Crispin returning to his book.

'You are a very lucky bugger,' Millie reminded them both. She wasn't vain but she did know that the more she stretched the better she looked. It compensated, impressively.

Millie ducked down and lifted up the duvet from around Crispin's feet.

'I'm working tomorrow morning,' Crispin pointed out from the top of the bedclothes.

'So?' said Millie.

'So you'll be in charge first thing,' he told her as she began to make her way up his legs. 'Millie, why can't you get into bed like anybody else?!' he asked as the duvet went everywhere yet again.

David's return was in a less jovial frame of mind. He found the prospect of a journey in the back of the hen night's minibus about as appetising as his wife would have found the invitation to join the tail end of a stag night. As soon as they got inside he pretended to fall fast asleep and succeeded in ignoring a few stray remarks about the legendary virility of bald men.

When the long-suffering driver dropped Davy off on the Green he made his way cautiously inside Ty Escob. But no, there was no note on the settle informing him of his wife's decision to camp outside Nick's room tonight. She was in their bed and asleep. By the light cast from the landing he could see her hair spread across the pillow, her shoulders encased in another of those long Edwardian nightdresses that so frustrated him.

In the dressing room he thought of Millie and the fact that we have seventy years or so to enjoy ourselves until the lights were turned off forever. So why didn't he? Millie seemed to have the answer. But did that mean he had to have Millie? Was she the one? Should he seize the sexual moment? And what about the fact that she had met Helena? Didn't that alter everything? David, in the dressing room, shuddered. He had memories of anguish in distant railway stations. He really didn't want to go through all that again.

When he had put on his pyjamas and returned to the bedroom he found Helena was watching him. He couldn't see her eyes but he could tell that her head was turned towards him.

'I'm sorry,' he said getting into bed. 'I should have rung.'

'I always said you didn't have to tell me,' she replied quietly, talking of wider issues. That had been what she had said two years ago. 'But listen David, there's Crispin to consider—'

'We were playing *billiards*,' he interrupted, resenting the implication.

'And talking?' she asked.

'Yes talking,' he agreed. 'Talking and eating. And playing billiards.'

There was a silence between them. They weren't actually touching. After a while Helena sighed artfully.

'Oh well, I hope you haven't run out of things to say. They're coming to dinner tomorrow.'

'What?' David didn't like impromptu dinner parties.

'Just the two of them, the four of us. I arranged it with Crispin.'

David was annoyed

'I thought you liked Millie,' she mumbled happily into her pillow.

'I do.'

'And I like Crispin.'

'But you know I hate little bourgeois dinner parties,' he reminded her.

'Yes,' she replied. 'But I don't.'

And with that they turned in opposite directions and went to sleep.

At ten o'clock the next morning Millie was awoken by Katrin who was holding a can of Coke only a few inches from the pillow.

'Hello, Bunny,' she smiled, ready for a cuddle but quite happy to be left in peace.

'Crisp's at the bookshop. He says you're in charge.'

Millie, under attack, slid down beneath the duvet.

'*And*, listen Mil, he says if you've got a hangover it's all your own fault.' Katrin held the can closer to Millie who could actually feel it pressing against her head from inside the bedclothes.

'And that David Mosford is here to pick up the cars. He's brought Emma and his son. They're downstairs.'

However much she loved her children, at that moment Millie

simply wished Katrin would bugger off. There ought to be a law against daughters *in loco parentis.*

'Oh and I've got you some clothes that don't fit too tightly.'

Millie put her head up above the bedspread.

'Thank you Rabbit,' she conceded as nicely as she could manage.

When Davy and Millie got to compare notes it transpired that Crispin and Helena had spent some time on the telephone last night. While Millie and David were up on the embankment with that spare bottle of Italian fizz, their partners were deciding it would serve them right to be put in sole charge of the children on Saturday morning. Helena was going to try and spend a relaxing day cooking and Crispin was helping out at the bookshop which meant David and Millie would have to work out how you got two abandoned cars back from Rock Point using only Helena's battered estate. To make matters worse all four, probably very resentful, children would be deposited in the back of the estate and David and Millie would have to be responsible for them as well.

'Gordon Bennett,' muttered Millie as she sighted Katrin and Emma, little Nick Mosford and her great big son Jonathan all sitting round the kitchen table with various signs of dissatisfaction on their faces. 'Hiya kids!' she added but no-one was convinced by her bonhomie. It was going to be a long trip to Newport. To make matters worse, Emma had brought a selection of singalong tapes in a plastic carrying case and the four children argued all the way to Rock Point over which to listen to, plumping, as they turned on to the A48, for something truly nauseous.

'I never realised what a malicious person my wife was,' said Davy over the engine and cassette noise. Millie tried to pretend none of it was happening, particularly when the children started on some absurd game of guessing who everybody's girlfriend was. All too soon they got through all the people they knew in common and started on animals.

'Who's that pig's girlfriend?!' shouted Katrin as they left the main road.

'Oink, oink!' said Jonathan.

'Who's that *tree's* girlfriend?!' shouted Nick Mosford who

seemed not to have grasped the essence of this game. Everyone in the back hooted with laughter.

'I have misjudged Crispin,' Millie grumbled. 'All these years. Really he is a total English bastard.' She then used a choice phrase in Welsh which had been handed down from medieval times for just such occasions.

'Where're you from then?' Davy asked, turning down the cassette. He'd been meaning to ask Millie about her origins for some time. The name didn't sound Welsh but she pronounced her daughter's as though Cymric born and bred.

'Montgomery' said Millie. 'Till I escaped.'

'Ah, Powys,' said Davy referring to the county.

'Not if you're from there,' Millie corrected him.

'*Montgomeryshire*,' he agreed. 'My dad knew the doctor.'

'Humphreys,' she said. It was a typical exercise in Welsh networking. Within five minutes they'd established whose aunties knew whom and were almost related.

'So your Dad was University bursar?' Millie asked. 'That must have helped.'

David told her they hadn't come back until his father had retired although old Mr Mosford had always wanted to see him Professor of History.

'What's with the name then?' David asked after a pause.

'*Emily Katrin*,' said Millie in a very exaggerated accent that made Davy laugh. 'What would you have done with that, eh? Welsh names weren't that fashionable when I was young.'

'What are we going to do about tonight?' he asked. With Millie it was easy to switch subjects like that. She usually returned any topic very much to where she'd found it and easily moved on to another.

'What's the problem? Is Linna going to be resentful all evening?' Millie seemed to feel no inhibition about discussing his wife in this way but any criticism made David feel uncomfortable. Maybe this was her style and not at all significant. Maybe not.

'No, she'll be very nice, I'm sure. Much nicer than me. It's just that I hate little boring dinner parties. Particularly two couples. So safe and middle class. Eight or ten is good but not the four of us!'

Millie shrugged. 'I don't mind either way.'

'Maybe it's me,' David conceded taking the turn for Rock Point.

'Yes. Maybe you just like a bigger audience, Dave.'

Just before lunch time Helena passed Halls and called in to give Crispin a progress report. One car was back although it seemed Millie hadn't been able to get her Citroën across the garage doors because of the way someone had parked in the lane.

'I saw them all getting back into my car for Trip Two,' said Helena. Crispin smiled. He had a fair idea how his son and daughter would take to spending their Saturday morning commuting between Cardiff and Rock Point and although he was sorry for Jonathan and Katrin he wasn't at all sorry for Millie. Helena would have enjoyed sharing the joke for longer but a thin student-looking girl was waiting for his attention and making it fairly obvious.

'See you tonight,' said Crispin. 'Yes *Susan*?'

But it was a better evening than David had expected. With the children off her hands most of the day Helena had cooked Something Complicated to the kind of standard she felt it deserved. She'd also laid the table, which was so often a point of unspoken contention between them. Far too often he laid it as his family might and she corrected it as her family did.

'We are living in a pluralistic and meritocratic society!' Davy often ended up shouting on such occasions. But not that Saturday. When Helena laid the table she got knives where she wanted knives and forks of the right size were where such forks should be.

Furthermore that Saturday was the day that Emma and Katrin struck up a great friendship and spent the entire afternoon in Emma's bedroom which meant that after finishing his marking David finally got to spend some time with Nick. He had wanted to do this because he was guiltily aware that he hardly knew the person that his son had become. Emma was his angel but Nick was a mystery. He was also Helena's, had been ever since she began to protect him from the incompetence of the medical world, the ignorance of his school and the seeming indifference of God. All that wasn't healthy.

Father and son they walked down to the thirty-three steps to the cathedral. It was such an easy route from Ty Escob. Then, from the cathedral, they followed the path as it fell away gradually into the swampy graveyard that lay towards the Taff. Another easy route. Here amid the cracked and broken vaults Nick wanted to be chased. Davy lost him at one point and, although it was a bright, warm afternoon, he found himself alarmed to have lost his son in such a place. He found the boy sitting on an eighteenth-century flat-topped tomb, the sun in his hair.

'I nearly died when I was young,' Nick announced.

'Yes,' said Davy. This story was well known in the family.

'*Dad*, why did God make me sick?'

'God didn't make you sick,' David replied, ruffling his hair.

'Who made me sick?' Nick demanded. 'Was it you and Mum made me sick? Or was it Emma?'

Davy wanted to get off the subject but it was a story he told later over dinner.

'He's not like other children,' he concluded, more proud than worried now. Crispin looked thoughtful.

'Neither is Jonathan,' said Millie who was sitting next to Davy and tucking in with enthusiasm.

'Jonathan's like you,' Crispin observed.

'What? Big and bloody noisy?' Millie made a joke of it.

'He likes to get his own way.'

Helena, who was sitting next to Crispin, and on a diagonal from Millie, noticed that Crispin was placing these statements without any colouring. His voice – which she found so difficult to ignore – had a neutral tone as if he couldn't help reproaching her and really took no pleasure in the act. She wondered if Millie always recognised his rebukes for what they were.

Crispin and Millie had arrived altogether in a strange mood. David hadn't noticed because he was only noticing how Millie noticed him but Helena could tell. Having a husband like David helped you observe things about other people because while he was talking, and they were listening, she could watch.

Millie made a great enthusiastic noise about everything David said as he showed her around.

'Christ, Dave, do you own all this?' she asked, awestruck.

'No, the house is split in two. It was like that when my father bought it. Fortunately we got the garden. The other half just has a patio where the stables used to be.'

But Millie didn't pass any of this back to Crispin. She didn't say 'Look at the garden, Crisp!' or 'We could do with a place this big, Crisp!' Or anything intended for his hearing. She just assumed her chap was being entertained elsewhere. So Crispin followed Millie and David mutely from room to room, functionless but attached to the main party, like the consort of some head of state. Helena joined him once the food was ready. She found him looking on from a corner, rather as he had that night in their kitchen. Significant, that. David always walked into the middle of a room and occupied it. Crispin kept to the shadows.

So Helena and Crispin trailed behind their spouses in companionable silence and stood there foolishly on the office threshold while Millie raved about the billiard table which David was pointing out.

'Let me show you,' David offered and he'd stood to one side to lift the large melamine lid. At this point, Helena thought, someone like Millie would have normally said 'Come on Crisp, lend a hand'. Except that she very obviously didn't on this occasion and it was David who had to ask Crispin.

'They're not talking to each other,' Helena said to herself. This intriuged her. David had hinted his approval of the very easy relaxed way Millie and Crispin got on. She was supposed to take note of that wasn't she? To learn the lessons. Well, maybe things weren't as simple as that. They rarely were.

Millie and Crispin thawed out during the meal. They did so via little digs at each other. Helena found the process quite absorbing to watch – it was quite unlike the way in which she and David argued. But she didn't once stop to wonder why the guests had arrived on such bad terms. David, being of a gossipy nature, would have been fascinated to know what had happened between them but Helena was much more interested to know what was *going* to happen.

What *had* actually happened was not something either David or Helena or even Millie would have predicted. After lunch Crispin had come back from dropping Jonathan at his friend Maxy's to find that he couldn't park Millie's car across the garage door as per norm because half a mini had edged into the space in front of their garage. He tried twice to back in and then gave up and left the car wedged in at an angle with its wing sticking out uncomfortably into the lane.

Back in the kitchen he had started tidying away the salami and bread that Millie had left out from her lunch when the thought struck him, or rather the impulse struck him, that Millie was in their bed upstairs and both Jonathan and Katrin were away for a few hours yet. It was a rare moment of daylight opportunity that rekindled his instincts. Millie was very responsive to Crispin's hand beneath the duvet but after a few moments of rolling round and purring like the great big sensual cat she was Millie had taken the initiative, climbed over on top of Crispin and begun to loosen his clothing.

'Millie,' said Crispin. 'Can't I make love to *you*, just once?'

'Oh shut up, you Bone Bag!' said Millie who was simultaneously aroused and frustrated by the battle she was having with Crispin's trousers. Suddenly there was a persistent ring on the front door bell. Crispin got up and looked down from the window seat.

'It's one of those little men from the lane,' he said.

'Well you're the one who's dressed,' Millie pointed out pulling the duvet around her. The bell went again and Crispin went downstairs.

The little man from the lane was in a state because his daughter had been visiting him but now she couldn't get her Mini out unless she reversed and she didn't like reversing and it was Crispin's car that was making her reverse because its off side wing was in the way of her going forward.

'Oh, um, yes,' said Crispin thoughtfully. 'I see. I'm afraid it's only parked like that because your daughter's car was stopping me getting in front of our garage.' He felt he should put this reasonably. This man was a neighbour after all. 'I did try to get in parallel with our doors but I'm afraid your daughter was parked ever so slightly over them.'

'Don't you get on your high horse with me,' said the little old man abrasively.

'I'm not getting on my anything,' said Crispin, somewhat taken aback. 'I'm just trying to explain—'

'Well I don't want you to!' said the man who had come to make a statement, not to discuss.

'Oh? What do you want, then?' Crispin asked.

'Don't you ask me what I want!' spluttered the enraged father, goaded by what he took to be Crispin's condescension to him.

'Well . . . why don't you just *tell* me then?' asked Crispin, out of his depth and trying to get back in.

'Why should I tell you?!' came the outraged reply of one who was angrier than he had intended to be. In no uncertain terms he told Crispin that they didn't like his sort in Back Lane. Furthermore it was about time he started putting their car in the garage and leaving a bit more space for everyone else who lived there.

'You know you have a point there,' Crispin agreed.

'Don't you tell me I've got a point!' the old man shouted.

'No, really, you have. In the meantime I'll go and get my car keys.'

When Crispin got back from moving their car, under the reproachful gaze of several silent neighbours, Millie was sitting at the top of the stairs in an outsize T-shirt which she'd tucked between her legs. Stretched down the staircase those legs did indeed look as elegant as Millie thought them to be but Crispin wasn't interested any more.

'Oh poor Crisp,' said Millie. It was a salutation to which he didn't reply.

'Bloody neighbours,' she added and held out a compassionate hand to him. Crispin hung up his keys on a hook by the door where they were supposed to be kept.

'Come on back to bed and I'll let you take the initiative. I'll surrender myself to you *entirely*, I promise.'

Crispin looked up at Millie. 'We are going to talk about getting things done around here!' he announced.

'What d'you mean?'

'Like emptying that garage tomorrow and starting to keep your car in there,' he told her.

Millie looked up in surprise. 'But I'm away most of the week—' she protested.

'Yes and when you come back everyone thinks how selfish you are blocking off several extra feet of the lane by not keeping our car inside the garage because the garage is full of stuff that you won't sort out!'

It was in a frame of mind that was an inheritor to this argument that Millie and Crispin turned up to dinner. And it was partly in this mood that Millie had chosen her dress for the evening. The blue one was a bit tight these days but mainly in the right places. It did wonders, if wonders needed doing, for her chest. Whenever Millie felt the need to go on the offensive that offensive was often sexual. It was not the desire to seduce that made her choose the blue dress but the need to assert.

For Davy the blue dress made playing billiards with Millie after the meal particularly difficult. They had cleared the office table and set about a game which ought to have been his revenge but Davy got distracted every time Millie bent to the table. She, however, was more interested in talking about his wife.

'I don't know how she coped with all the problems you've had with Nick. Y'know, with doctors and the school.'

'Women are remarkable things,' he replied, lining up his shot.

'Not all of us.' said Millie from where she was tucking her feet up on the chaise longue.

'Aren't you remarkable?' he asked.

'Me? No. I'm very straightforward.'

'That's remarkable,' David replied. 'In a woman.'

His shot ricocheted well off the cushion but not quite well enough. Millie got up to continue the game.

'You're not exactly a *New Man* are you, Dave?'

'I was joking,' he told her.

'Uhuh.' She picked up her cue. 'The thing is, I've had a very easy life.' It was an unusual thing to say. Millie bent low to the table. 'I mean nothing's really ever gone wrong for me. Not really.' She saw David looking at her. 'I mean, I can't help that, can I?'

'No,' he replied. It was true. And as if to prove her point she effortlessly potted a red. For her next shot Millie had to walk round the table and as she passed by she tapped him on the nose with her finger.

'And you'd play a lot better if you stopped looking at my tits,' she said.

'We pass this way but once,' he reminded her, laughing.

'How's that?' she asked, not recognising the allusion.

'At Rock Point you said something to that effect.' He tried to remember what it was exactly that she had said. 'That we only get one chance,' he recalled.

'You're not even getting one chance, Dave,' Millie told him with a broad smile. 'Go and take a shower.'

David was aware that he was behaving ridiculously but there was no harm in it, surely? Helena knew he was just enjoying Millie's company. She was used to him. Surely? And as for Crispin, well, he must be used to Millie. What an odd fellow he was: so dry, so lifeless, so scruffy, so quiet. Fortunately Helena was well practised in good works.

Fortunately, too, Helena found Crispin interesting, amusing and compassionate, which view hardly coincided with her husband's. After they'd moved into the drawing room for coffee, David and Millie had gone into his office to be noisy and she and Crispin had continued their conversation about the social life of young children and what a parent should do and shouldn't do about it. At what point our children should be allowed to have friends like Jonathan's Maxy. And at what point they should be *forced* to have unsuitable friends, as Helena put it. Then Helena had found herself talking about her day and the *emptiness* of her day. That wasn't what she'd started talking about. Crispin had simply asked her if she often went into Halls the Bookshop. It was the kind of question that could be construed as small talk. It certainly wasn't a 'tell me what's wrong with your married life' question of the kind that Helena found herself answering.

She had started explaining about the job she didn't want to go back to and about how she often went into shops to buy things and didn't.

'I think I'm a kind of passive kleptomaniac,' she joked but she meant it too. 'The impulse to pick things off the shelves is there but in my case I go in and *don't* take something without paying for it, do you see what I mean?'

'Oh yes,' said Crispin thoughtfully. 'I think it finally accounts for all those books we've discovered not missing from the shelves.'

And this time there was a real smile that was in his eyes as well as in his face.

'The thing is,' said Helena, 'I can't settle to anything. I keep waiting for something to go wrong with Nick. And nothing does.' She touched wood despite herself. 'But I can't do anything in the meantime. Does that sound terribly stupid to you?'

Crispin shook his head. 'No, it doesn't sound stupid. You haven't got enough to do.' For a moment Helena felt stung by that remark. Lazy, middle-class housewife lives off husband and pays others to look after children and house. But Crispin wasn't saying that.

'You'd like to do more but you're keeping yourself in readiness in case. The problem is it's very wearing being in a state of readiness for something that doesn't happen and it's very depressing not having enough to do.'

'I'm in Limbo, aren't I?' Helena asked. 'What kind of options does that give me?'

'Heaven or hell,' he replied. 'Theologically speaking.'

The party broke up just after 12.30 although Crispin had been trying to get Millie away since quarter to twelve. He had had difficulty finding a sitter and they had only managed it by promising to be back by midnight.

'It is entirely my fault,' said Crispin, kissing Helena good-night.

'Yes it is, Boo Boo,' said Millie as she gave Helena a glancing kiss. Crispin was already outside on the gravel. 'Couldn't you have organised a proper grown-up teenager!'

'Good-night, Millie,' said David, kissing her as she passed through the lobby.

'That's the third time,' Millie pointed out. 'He thinks I'm not counting,' she told Helena. 'But don't worry, he's safe with me.'

'That's the only reason I kiss you,' David joked but his mind was running on the 1–2–3. So he had, last night. And, more to the point, she had noticed.

To his surprise, and hers, David and Helena felt attracted towards each other once the door was closed. It wasn't usually something they both felt at the same time, nor that they were that good at recognising in each other these days.

Davy took off his jacket and put it over a chair.

'Very good evening,' he said, returning from the door and expecting to see Helena stacking things away. 'I stand corrected.'

But for once she wasn't stacking. She was watching him.

'What is it?' he asked. Helena came across the dining room as if to kiss him. Then she seemed to change her mind. And then she did indeed kiss him although his glasses got in the way again, so definite and indecorous was the kiss. He removed them in the hope of more.

'That's one,' said Helena. It took Davy a while to catch up, during which time he had put his hands round her waist and during which time she had slipped gracefully, elusively, out of the embrace.

'You mean Millie's ahead by two?' he asked.

'I'll see you upstairs,' said Helena, moving to the kitchen.

'We don't have to stop at three you know,' he pointed out. 'There's a lot to be said for four and five.'

'I'm just getting Nick's juice,' she promised.

Please Nick, Davy thought, please don't be ill, don't wake up or want a drink. Not tonight. But when he went upstairs all was quiet on the landing. He went into their bedroom and started taking his clothes off in the dressing room, several buttons simultaneously. By the time he heard Helena come in next door he was searching round for his father's shoe horn which was nowhere to be found. Davy wrenched off his shoes and kicked them away. The stretcher bars could wait till morning.

Millie and Crispin wandered back quite fondly across the Green. It had been a good evening for them too. Certainly it had ended up better than either had expected. But when they got back to 27 High Street Crispin was surprised to find all the lights on and a woman who was not young Siân Cooper but Siân Cooper's far from young and far from happy mother standing in the kitchen, her hands digging hard into the pockets of her cardigan.

'Do you know what time it is?' this woman demanded without preamble.

'A quarter to one,' Crispin conceded looking at the clock. *'I am sorry*, we had difficulty getting away. Has Siân—'

'Siân's got GCSEs!' Mrs Cooper announced in violent irritation.

'What? Now?' asked Crispin. Somewhere behind him Millie sniggered.

'This month,' Mrs Cooper explained. 'And she was worried that if she wasn't back by midnight she might fall behind with her revision.'

'Oh dear,' said Crispin. *'I* really am sorry. We had difficulty getting away. You must let me make it up to her,' he said reaching in his pocket.

'Siân doesn't want your money,' the woman told him.

'Oh, um, I think she does,' said Crispin, not wishing to argue but very clear in his memory of the rate this serious-minded teenager had negotiated with him for that evening.

'Her father and I will make it up to her!' Siân's mother declared imperiously. 'She shan't be sitting here again.' And with that she walked out, casting a very censorious glance at Millie's dress.

After she had gone Crispin, as was his habit, locked and bolted the door for the night. Then he turned to hear the sounds of Millie laughing on the stairs.

'Oh poor Crisp. Two outraged parents in a day!'

Crispin was seething as he hung up the keys. 'If you had come when I asked— ' he began.

'What?'

'I said "If you'd come— "' he repeated.

'Oh don't start blaming me again!' Millie interrupted sulkily. 'I didn't book little Cinderella. That was your mistake.'

'No,' said Crispin. 'My mistake was believing that you'd understood when I said we had to get back for twelve. My mistake was trusting you. Really, Millie, things have got to change. You are just so irresponsible!'

Millie who was half way through pulling off her tights, looked at him in disbelief. 'Gordon Bennett, Crisp, you really do take the biscuit! You park the car in the wrong place and it's my fault. You book the wrong babysitter and it's my fault. Well, well . . . fuck off!'

And with that Millie returned to the bathroom, swearing in two languages. And Crispin made his way wretchedly to bed and, not surprisingly, he was not a lucky bugger that night.

4

Crispin and Helena

When David arrived at the School of History and Archeaology that bright and summery Monday morning he refused to be distracted by the nice little girl who greeted him. True, she did smile as if his arrival had made her day and, when he agreed to a cup of coffee, every impression was given that fetching it might prove the high point of her week. But nice little girls like that were the same age as his students and Davy never fancied his students. This was not some moral, husbandly stance on his part. After all he fancied women of a certain age, like Millie. He fancied women under a certain age too, like Helena's friend Pip. He had even allowed himself to fancy postgraduates from other Universities (once quite disastrously) but never students. Or anyone of student age even, just in case they turned out to be plain clothes undergraduates set by Dorkin to spring a turpitude trap.

But the nice little girl didn't just restrict herself to satisfying his needs for refreshment. When Davy agreed with her that the weather *was* remarkably good for Cardiff she gave a merry little laughed and wrinkled up her nose as if it were some extraordinary witticism. And when she traipsed into the Head of School's office with him, and actually sat down next to Stella Price, she gave a great big smile as if it was so nice for the three of them to be here together. What was going on?

'Well,' she said, this girl, and then she waited for Stella to put her coffee cup down. 'Well, the death of Professor Dorkin is a great loss to the University and of course to the School itself.'

David felt himself completely thrown. Who *was* this? Might she be the Head of School's oft-denounced teenage daughter brought in to read Stella Price's words because the august lady had lost her voice? Was she some promising sixth former employed on a job creation scheme to deliver eulogies when members of the teaching staff departed this life? What was going on?

'And I'm grateful to Stella' (here she bobbed her head with mannered significance at David's colleague) grateful to Stella, for bringing me in at this early stage.'

Yes, but who are you? Davy wanted to ask.

'You do know Carys?' Stella asked, picking up her cup again and seemingly happy to let the school leaver in question continue running their meeting.

Well, he thought. I know she fetches a mean cup of coffee.

'Carys Rees is deputy director of senior personnel,' Stella observed for his information. Stella clearly thought David ought to be aware of this. Ah, thought David, I bet you're the person who uses coloured diagrams to increase my throughput.

'And while you're deputising as Head of Department I'll be your actual direct link with Management,' Carys told him and she bobbed her head from side to side in a friendly way.

'Management?' David asked. 'I didn't know we had Management.' Carys laughed her merry little laugh which was more like a squeaky exhalation of air. It sounded as if she had a special '*Oh yes Dr Mosford is known for his wit*' noise which she was going to use each time he spoke. This could be tedious. There is nothing worse than people with no sense of humour who are frightened of yours.

Carys continued talking and David's mind began to wander but he refused to let it think about sex. Not in here. Wasn't she very young to be deputy head of whatever it was? Still, what Carys seemed to be outlining were the procedures, responsibilities and other tedia that would be his during the interregnum. David was catching up. This made some sense at last. However, what was not so good was that Carys clearly wasn't dealing with extra responsibility payments nor with his chances of holding out for the chair itself. In short the things he'd actually come to discuss.

'Before we go any further,' David interjected at a point when Carys had paused between paragraphs and sub paragraphs, and when her bobbing head was briefly still, 'before we go any further I would like to discuss the long-term advisability of appointing a departmental administrator for Political History. Or of splitting the roles of professor and departmental head.'

He was pleased to see that this demand had rather taken the wind out of Carys Rees' sails. She smiled at Davy and then at Stella Price. Then she smiled at Davy again but she didn't laugh. Stella screwed up her mouth and chewed the corner of it, a habit that was becoming more pronounced as she grew older, had fewer teeth and more to think about.

'That's for another conversation,' she said.

'Why not now?' Davy asked. He was quite happy for Carys to leave the room so the grown ups could discuss what was of real significance.

'That decision will have to be taken before the chair is advertised,' said Stella. 'I'm talking to the VC.'

She had stopped munching on her mouth. Whatever it was that had been caught between her teeth had now become dislodged. Or maybe it had been his future that she had been chewing over and now she had decided to spit him out. It was something of a shock for David to realise that there was going to be no indication today of whether or not it was in the bag. Nevertheless he rallied quickly.

'You mean that you're asking me to shoulder the running of the department with no guarantee that I will be offered the chair.' Best to go on the offensive. Best to sound as if this was quite outrageous.

'Yes,' said Stella. Clearly he hadn't sounded outraged enough. 'But if your current research commitments are too great, I'm willing to ask someone else to take over in the short term.'

And who would that be? David wondered. Should he bluff this out? Make them worried about losing him? Make them really worried at the idea of a department being run by little Alun Taylor, the only man of Davy's acquaintance who suffered premenstrual tension. That would be truly worrying for all concerned.

'When will you decide on splitting the jobs?' he asked. 'I think I have to consider my position if you take that option.'

Stella smiled from the opposite corner of her mouth. 'Carys is doing some work on the available field. I'll make my recommendations on the basis of what she comes up with.'

'It's very interesting demographically,' Carys confirmed with tactless enthusiasm. 'A large band of academics were recruited fifteen to twenty years ago, many of whom have now reached the sub professorial ceiling of senior lecturer/reader/etcetera.' David hated people who actually said 'etcetera.'

Stella was nodding. Ah, thought David, so this is why Friday's meeting was put back. The tiresome deputy head of senior things had memoed HISAR and suggested they shouldn't just be looking for a new departmental head. Clearly she thought they could do better than Mosford.

'I think you mean,' he said, 'that there are a lot of us about.'

Carys smiled, unsure whether she should laugh. Davy stood up, assuming that the meeting could usefully end here.

'Well, if that is everything,' he said and made to leave.

'Come and see me this evening, why don't you?' Stella threw in as he reached the door. Davy turned and inclined his head to acknowledge the olive branch.

'SCR or here?' he asked. He preferred the Senior Common Room as they would both speak more freely.

'We'll have sherry here. I'm working late,' Stella replied. 'In the meantime, any problems speak to Carys.'

She wasn't letting him off was she? She was assuming he'd keep drinking from the Dorkin chalice in the hope it would be worth grasping.

'Of course.'

David left the humanities building feeling distinctly undervalued and disenchanted. He had failed to get any undertaking that he might get the chair, he had failed to make Stella anxious about keeping him, he hadn't even managed to mount his high horse and stalk out, had he?

Right, well if they were going to treat him like some academic administrator he would apply for a personal chair and if he didn't get that he would resign.

He slammed the glass doors behind him – or slammed them as best he could given that the University had fitted impact-resistant pistons. The doors hissed slowly and calmly together.

Resign? What would he do? What did people like him do when they couldn't get any further up the academic pole? Try journalism? Become a TV star? Sulk? Certainly there were few openings for door-to-door historians these days. But was his only option to stay in post, fester and go a bit mad like Alun Taylor?

He decided to ring Helena. After that sherry with Stella they would need to talk. He must check the Mosfords weren't going out that evening.

Helena was in Halls the Bookshop that morning. She still hadn't bought Dad's present. After breakfast she had started a new list on the pad in her pocket and put her father's eightieth at the top. She didn't write MAKE LOVE TO DAVID! this time because that had been mentally crossed off after Saturday night. Or rather physically crossed off. Or just crossed off. Maybe they should just cross sex off again. Maybe it was too soon.

Crispin didn't seem to be in.

Towards the back of Halls Helena found herself browsing the guides to personal relationships which were kept discreetly on the top shelf. These were probably not the ideal gift for her ancient father but Helena had lost track of her primary purpose now. She was having a mental conversation. And it was one to which God was not a party. She had to have some secrets even from him.

The guides were all photographed in attractive colour. However erudite their content, they did seem to be pitched at people who believed that the human relationship was an art form conducted by naked models lying in front of a roaring log fire. The models inclined fondly towards each other thus obscuring bodily hair and saggy bits. They seemed to be nuzzling like horses rather than attempting what she and David had been doing on Saturday night. Saturday night had been unfortunate. Saturday night had started well but David would keep urging her to let herself go.

She wished he hadn't. There was nothing more inhibiting. And certainly a woman's desire to ask her partner to shut up does diminish the divine moment. That was Helena's view, although she couldn't bring herself to express it to David. God's view, she was sure, was that sex was part of a relationship not the test of it. Helena and God agreed on this although God wasn't supposed to be in this conversation. In any case it was all right for God. He wasn't married to David who needed perfect sex every time, Heaven knows why. Was David trying to maximise the number of impact factors each time they did it?

If only they could get rid of the sex thing for a while and concentrate on other ways of being happy together. That was what she'd thought before, wasn't it? When things were so bad with Nick.

'As long as it's no-one I know.' That's what she'd told him and that was when the woman from Leeds happened, wasn't it? Well that hadn't resolved anything, had it? Anything but.

She wished she could go and see her friend Pip but Pip was working that day. In any case Pip was very silly about sex. Mind you, was anyone sensible about it? Sarah claimed to be. Sarah behaved as if we all ought to be happily past it by now. So was that really how you got it in proportion? By getting it out of your system?

Helena felt depressed. She put the guide to relationships back. Crispin was definitely not in the shop that morning.

He had told her his hours were variable depending on when Peter and his mum needed extra cover. The rest of the time he worked at home but he hadn't told her at what. Perhaps he was just a househusband in the way that she was just a housewife. Which was *not all that much*. Helena did the meals and worried about the children. Mrs Morgan did the rest, except on those days when Helena joined in and frightened the appliances.

She decided that she was not going into Cardiff to buy a talking book for her father. He was going to have a Read It Yourself, just like his grandson. She looked to see if there was a WAR section in Halls. You couldn't go far wrong with WAR. Mr Moreton had spent six of his formative years trying not to be killed in various parts of the world and like so many of his contemporaries he seemed to actually enjoy reliving that experience. Helena selected a very big book that told the story through the eyes of the people who were there. As opposed to the people who made it all up, she thought as she paid.

'Is Crispin Williams in today?' asked a female voice from behind Helena, and from mid-Wales too, by the sound of it. It was an accent that stood out in Cardiff, stronger, more obviously Welsh and clearly less at home in the English language. And, as with most people speaking in a foreign language, the speaker seemed very abrupt, aggrieved even. She was certainly speaking before Helena had finished paying for her purchase.

Mrs Hall blinked as she put Helena's book into its paper bag and explained that he wouldn't be in till lunch.

'Oh,' said the speaker who turned out to be a young woman and more than somewhat put out. Stepping back to let her cross examine Mrs Hall further, Helena noticed that this was the same angular girl who had been queuing up to speak to Crispin on Saturday morning. Clearly he had his fans.

Millie was in Taunton where Neville and the boys were tramping mud everywhere. This was an essential part of the process. It was rare for mortar not to generate mud and when it didn't that was usually a sign that conditions were so dry the stuff would flake off before it had time to set.

Normally at this stage she would expect to be told to start pricing up where she was going next. Which was the next lucky pub from Wales and the West Country to be totally transformed by Fun? Indeed that morning Millie had been on the phone to Harry, the man who employed her on behalf of the brewery. She'd spent all day last Friday waiting to talk to him in Chiswick. Now she was waiting for him to phone back in Taunton.

When the phone went Millie was trying to explain to one of Nev's boys how a particular brick plinth would run all the way round the main bar. Neville had told Dan where to build it but not why and Dan was confused that floor levels across the bar were going to be different. Millie had started the conversation believing that some intelligent man management might be worthwhile here, particularly as she'd be moving on soon and this might be the last time Nev's boys could be privy to her ideas. But five minutes into the conversation she was coming round to the decision that Neville's 'because I bloody say so' was perhaps, after all, the best answer to Dan's questions.

The call from Chiswick was a great relief.

'Millie Kemp!' she announced, taking the receiver from where it lay on the remains of the bar.

'Millie, it's Harry,' said Harry in his usual dry metropolitan monotone. 'You're going to hate me for this but the people in Bristol are playing up.' Bristol was the job after this one. 'Seems there's some kind of preservation order on the place. Don't know how it wasn't picked up when the company bought in but Selwyn's screaming for blood.'

At first Millie was rather amused to imagine the scene in Chiswick. She could see Selwyn's fist going through the little cardboard model she'd rigged up for the brewery.

'I want this fucker fucking built!' That was how Selwyn would probably deal with a sensitive conservation issue. 'We reopen in three months with a fun fucking factory or some fucker round here is going to be out of a fucking job. Do I make myself clear?'

'So what's next?' she asked, swinging her legs up on a cement encrusted bar stool. Harry was Millie's Kismet blowing her hither and thither, up and down the M5. But Harry was himself blown, or rather blasted, by Selwyn and Selwyn's moods.

'Well that's just it,' said Harry. 'We've got a bit of a bottleneck now. Nothing's really ready and Selwyn doesn't want to start you off on something else.'

'What?' said Millie.

'So I think we're going to have to stand you down for a few weeks.'

Millie was shocked. She sat better to listen better. Millie hadn't been without work since she'd started and that was a long time ago. Millie had always worked.

'Course we'll pay you,' Harry reminded her.

'Uhuh,' said Millie.

'Look at it as a holiday.'

Millie was silent.

'You OK?' Harry asked.

'Sure,' said Millie. 'Speak to you later.' She hated that phrase. Why did he have to suggest she looked on it as a *holiday*? God, it took her back. Over twenty years. Phew. Strange how things come out of the past to blast you like that. Emily Katrin Kemp, twenty-two years old, out of drama school and cheerfully out of work. She'd hung around in London for a few months and lived with two lovely fellahs, one of whom was now dead, but then the money ran out and they'd needed her share of the rent. She'd had to go home then. Back to Montgomery. Back to Montgomery when she had been going to be something. Of course she could wear outrageous clothes and talk about casual sex but she was *back*, wasn't she? Back in town when hers had been the best leaving party ever inflicted on the eardrums of Broad Street. 'Look on it as a holiday,' her Dad had said. Poor, poor man. A holiday? Millie shuddered. Never again. That was what she had vowed twenty years ago. Gordon Bennett, what a downer.

That night David and Helena talked over hot pot and Millie and Crispin talked on the phone. The dilemma for both could have been worse. Both still had jobs. Both still had an income but both were frustrated to say the least. Fortunately Millie had completely forgotten her weekend quarrels with Crispin. She was not one to hold long term resentment. Instead she just blurted out everything as soon as he answered her call.

'It sounds like just what we need,' said Crispin who was tidying the bedroom and noticing that Millie's mountain of unsorted underwear had not diminished. Sitting where he was on the window seat, it seemed to Crispin that Millie's clothing loomed very large indeed in the glow of the yellow street lamp.

Millie could not understand him.

'We could spend some time together, do some work on the house, get the garage cleared out and working, finish the bedroom,' he suggested.

'Sure,' replied Millie, just hoping to hell he wouldn't suggest she looked on it as a holiday.

'You could spend some time with the children,' Crispin added.

'Oh that's true.' The idea of taking Jonathan and Katrin out did appeal to her. 'We could have a day out at Barry Island,' she decided.

'Don't forget they're in school at the moment.'

'Oh, that's a drag.'

'It's also the Law,' he reminded her. Nevertheless Millie felt really cheered by the idea of spending some time with her son and daughter.

'Thanks Chrissybag, you are a love. I'd better get off now. Got to talk to Nev. Give the kids a big hug from me will you?'

'They're in bed. It's ten o'clock.'

'Oh, well give them one in the morning.'

On Wednesday morning Helena was visited by her young friend Pip. Pippa Arnstein was thirty but she lived in a house without children and this made her different from Helena. As did the fact that Pippa had a sort of career, talked about her cats, was self consciously devoted to her beast of a husband and bothered about which car they ought to get next. All of which made her seem not so much a different generation from Helena but sometimes a different species.

She and David had much more in common with Katie John who although only sixteen knew all about schools, rows, family holidays and even bouts of financial insecurity.

Pip had very belatedly brought round the tickets for Saturday's Glamorganshire cricket do and over coffee she brought up the question of what Helena was going to be wearing because they would be on the same table.

'I wondered if I dared wear the Green again?' Pip asked with a look.

'Now which is your green?' Helena asked, making it sound as if she knew her friend's wardrobe in such detail she couldn't quite distinguish the green from the turquoise, the sage and the emerald. There was one dress that David had liked which he said gave a very good view of Pippa's shoes but which was that? And, come to think of it, what did he mean? Shoes?

'You *know*,' said Pip with the look again. 'I wore it at your Christmas party.'

Oh dear, this was clearly a very bad day. Helena had no memory of giving a Christmas party unless, oh yes, they did have some people round for coffee and mince pies just before the midnight service on Christmas Eve and Pip had turned up dressed for cocktails. And virtually shrieked with embarrassment. And kept asking Helena if she had a scarf she could use to cover up her decolletage until absolutely every man in the room had noticed. And Anders was glowering darkly. And David had said that thing about admiring Pip's shoes. Oh, yes, of course.

'Oh yes, wear the green,' Helena assured her. It was after all what Pip wanted to hear and no doubt it would make the Friends of Glamorganshire Cricket even more friendly.

That afternoon Helena met Crispin at the school gate. They didn't often coincide because Jonathan Williams often brought his sister home the three hundred yards up Llandaff High Street but today Jonboy was going off on the school bus which was taking him and Maxy back to the depths of Canton.

'How's Millie?' Helena asked, as Nick handed over something that he had done to some pieces of coloured paper.

'Worried,' Crispin replied, looking to see if Emma and Katrin would ever come out.

'I can't imagine Millie being worried,' said Helena charitably.

'She's either up or down or asleep,' Crispin explained. 'Bit like a yoyo. With a duvet.'

'Can we go home?' asked Nick.

'We've got to wait for Emma, darling.'

'Why?'

'Because she's your sister,' Helena explained.

'*Why*?' Nick demanded with all the logic of a six-year-old.

'And how's David?' asked Crispin thinking he'd recognised some daughter in the crush who might be his.

David had actually settled, after a fashion, to the day to day running of his new workload but that sherry with Stella Price had done little to cheer him about his professional prospects. So on Wednesday evening the Mosfords had yet more hot pot.

'What gets me,' he began, coming at this from yet another angle, or rather from an angle that had not been essayed for the last twenty-four hours, 'is that she was as good as warning me not to push too soon. Reminding me that readers are supposed to put in three years before applying for a personal chair. I know that, she knows I know that, so why's she telling me?'

He looked at Helena for the answer.

'She's saying I can't expect to be treated differently from anybody else. Isn't she? That I'm not remarkable.'

'Yes,' Helena agreed.

'So I'm not remarkable?' he asked.

'No I think you're remarkable,' she replied. 'But I assume Stella is saying the University doesn't think so.'

'Bloody cheek.'

'They're quite wrong,' said Helena. 'But then they often are. You know that. You tell me every day how much they've got wrong. You can't really expect them to get this, of all things, right. Can you?'

There was a moment's silence of the kind that would allow them to change the subject or start on it all over again.

'Pip called round today,' Helena announced, guessing that little would be achieved by mulling the iniquities of the University of Wales over yet again.

'Oh good,' said David. David liked Pip. Helena liked Pip. This was agreed common territory. Helena and David probably liked Pip for quite different reasons but they could talk about her without having to acknowledge that critical ambiguity.

'And how is *Anders*?' David asked. He found the man curious company but the name inherently funny. Helena smiled.

'Still looking at other women, I gather.'

'Ah, well,' said David feeling his way towards a lightening of the mood. 'There *are* a lot of them about. I looked at two today. And Big Meg. I suppose that counts as three and a half altogether.'

'Do you say that kind of thing at work?' Helena asked.

'Certainly not,' said Davy. 'But I am thinking that if I get the Chair I shall inaugurate a Political Incorrectness Room, just next to the Smoking Room, where Hooper and Alun and Gwyn and me can lock ourselves away and make lots of sexist remarks. Get it out of our systems.'

'You'll never get it out of your system,' she told him. 'None of you. Especially now that Peter's gone. You paid lip service to it, nothing more.'

The telephone rang. She looked at him. He looked pathetically at her. 'Will you get it?' he asked, handing over the plates. Some nights David got a real high out of answering calls. If he had surplus social energy then the office phone could be a very useful device down which it could be hurled. But at the moment he hadn't lifted quite far enough out of the slough of professional despond to be jovial.

Helena took things through to the kitchen and used the wall-mounted receiver to answer. She had a fair idea who it was.

'If that's Stella Price I'm out!' David shouted from the dining room.

'Helena? It's Gareth.'

'And if it's Alun Taylor or Carys Bloody Rees I've emigrated,' he continued, booming in the distance.

'Gareth, hello' said Helena, finding that she had a *this is not a good time* timbre to her voice.

'Is this a bad time to talk?' Gareth asked. It was quite remarkable that, for someone who had spent so little time with her during the last seventeen years, Gareth could read the signals she put out so well. David couldn't. At all. Or maybe it was just that all the women Gareth rang were now married to men who hated him and so he checked up as a matter of course.

'Not ideal,' she said but she was uncomfortable saying even this. Helena felt she ought to be tactful about speaking to Gareth in David's presence but at the same time she didn't want that tact to railroad her into entering some kind of conspiracy with him.

'Morning's are better,' she explained. 'We're putting the children to bed at the moment.'

Now she had lied but at least she had stopped Gareth thinking that she was uncomfortable talking to him just because her husband was around.

God, however, was not impressed. God foresaw two lies coming home to roost. One to her former lover, one to her husband. Helena didn't like it when God put things like that. In her opinion, the Lord took a very simplistic view of bearing false witness, a view which, as she had pointed out before, was only possible because God was not married to David.

'I'll ring you tomorrow,' he said and his voice went quieter still, more intimate, as if helping her with the deception.

'Stop whispering, Gareth,' said Helena and put the phone down. She put the kettle on for coffee and went back to tell David that she had done so. When he was depressed he stopped helping round the house completely. It would be very good for his morale to make some coffee.

'I've put the kettle on!' she announced then noticed that David hadn't even cleared away the place mats. He always did that.

'Who was on the phone?' he asked. Honestly he could at least have *started* to clear them away. The world is full of career-stalled men who nevertheless manage to put a few melamine table mats in a drawer, for goodness sake.

'Gareth,' she said point blank. She felt angry.

'Which Gareth?' There were a lot of Gareths if you lived in Cardiff.

'*That* Gareth,' she replied feeling increasingly irritated with him. Why should she compromise herself to protect the feelings of a man who could not even put four tablemats into a box and stick them away in the sideboard?

'The bastard!' said David in sudden amazement. He turned to look at Helena with what was almost an accusatory glare. 'He's heard!'

'Heard what?'

'About the chair.'

'He can't have,' Helena reasoned. 'Stella hasn't even seen the VC.'

'Someone's tipped him off!' David was genuinely appalled.

'Well don't look at me,' she replied. '*I* haven't told him.'

'Well don't.' David was pale and angry now. 'Don't even say it's up for grabs. OK?'

'It's Peter's funeral tomorrow,' Helena pointed out. 'Am I suppose not to have noticed that?'

David was breathing heavily. 'If he gets it I'll quit, you know.'

'*Coffee*,' she replied.

Crispin had, for several years now, been doing some research for a man in America who was sponsoring a TV series for reasons that were connected with altruism, christian fundamentalism and tax evasion. The germ of the idea was a small mediaeval christian sect that had been viciously extirpated for failing to move with the times. Just as the Middle Ages were really getting underway, these simple French men and women had refused to drop certain passages from their Bible. Unremarkable passages of little obvious consequence but passages that were worth a grisly martyrdom. Passages for which the misguided martyrs incinerated their own children, rather than let them be taken into care in the mediaeval community and re-educated. This world had a pretty vicious track record when you came down to it. That was Crispin's opinion.

But what intrigued Crispin, and what had now captured the imagination of his curious sponsor, was not the detail of this persecution, which was well known, but the mentality of martyrdom. What self justification could a father offer his wife for burning her children to death? In his study, a tiny tidy former walk-in cupboard taller than it was wide, Crispin often pondered this cruel conundrum as he went about his early morning work. Most nights of the week Crispin slept alone, which suited him. He would get up at five, choose the next book out of the five hundred that had been assembled over the past few years and check the cross reference that he was building up while the shooting script was being written. Sometimes he would write his anonymous employer a brief monograph on an aspect of *The Contagion of Hatred, The Anatomy of Martyrdom* or *The Choice To Suffer* as these thoughts clarified in his own mind. He always received a prompt acknowledgement for such essays but never a comment.

Millie never went into Crispin's study. She couldn't see the point of dwelling on so much unhappiness which was one reason why the room remained so tidy.

But Crispin liked his study. There were no windows in this room. No heating, just one lamp. The austerity suited him and he had always been more at ease with a chill in the air. These summer mornings bothered him. Waking up to find the world outside their bedroom trying so hard to be young and beautiful bothered him. There was a cruelty inherent in that hope which Nature persists in engendering in us.

That cruelty bothered Crispin even more now that Millie had returned for the foreseeable future. Waking up to find her round tanned body face down in the mess of bedclothes was distracting. It spoke of transient pleasures. Waking to find Millie's leg over his spoke even more persistently of transient pleasures. That Thursday morning he had very nearly been tempted to give The Anatomy of Martyrdom a complete miss for the anatomy of Millie

Kemp but, in the end, he did not succumb. Crispin put in his two hours, choosing to prepare a few paragraphs on *Procreation as an Act of Hope*. Millie didn't surface for another five.

At breakfast time Jonathan was taciturn while Katrin was relentlessly full of herself.

'He's afraid people will think I'm his *girlfriend*!' she announced when Jonathan was reluctant to take her into school.

'I don't think anyone would make *that* mistake,' Crispin observed keeping an eye on his son.

'Pig,' said Katrin.

'I'm worried about Jon,' said Crispin to the lump in the duvet that was his common-law wife. It was now ten o'clock. Millie stuck out a hand and Crispin passed her a can of Coke. Feeling the welcome chill of its clammy metal in her grasp Millie surfaced.

'Thanks, Boo Boo.'

Millie loved her family but if there was one thing that she would change about Crispin and Katrin it was their tendency to come and talk to her when she was just waking up. Millie could take a good two hours to wake and she did it much better if people weren't bringing problems to her bed. Jonathan knew better. Jonathan was great. Fat but great.

'Jon's fine,' she replied sitting up.

'He's got some very odd friends,' Crispin reminded her.

'Kids do. I spent my entire adolescence looking for odd friends.' She took a generous gulp of cola. 'Wasn't easy in Montgomery, I can tell you.'

'We really should talk about this,' Crispin argued, pulling at a hole in his jumper. 'Jonathan's only ten.'

'He seems fine to me.'

'All he ever says is Orright!'

'Maybe he's happy.' Millie hated this idea of bringing people down if they were happy. She'd had enough of that at home. Her father had been happy once. They hadn't let that last, had they?

Crispin was still playing with the ragged threads of his pullover.

'I think we should, um, well give Jon more attention. He doesn't talk to me. Will you . . .'

'OK,' said Millie.

'. . . talk to him.'

'Uhuh.'

'Now you're home, you know.' Crispin kept playing with the idea like he played with the hole in his jumper.

'Sure,' said Millie. 'There's that place with all the video machines on Newport Road.'

'No. I don't mean take him out. I mean I want you to *talk* to him.' Now he was being all pofaced.

'Don't be daft. We can talk *and* have fun. It's what Jon and me do best.' Millie took a deep draught of Coke. 'What do I talk to him about?' Crispin wasn't sure.

'Well, you're his mother,' he replied.

'You want me to talk to him about *that*?'

Crispin smiled instead of laughing. 'I am serious, Millie. He may talk to you.'

'You never talked to your mother,' she reminded him.

'That was self preservation.'

'Well don't worry. I'll do it. I think he's fine but I'll do it. Will you run me a bath please?'

Helena was tidying Nick's room when Gareth phoned. David had been complaining about the dismembered toys that were underfoot everywhere. She ought to sort them out. Then the phone went. She just knew it was him. *That* was the sound the Mosfords' phone made when Gareth Box was on the other end of it. How on earth did he manage to make it ring so distinctly?

Helena had very mixed feelings about this bond that was between them but she couldn't deny it was there. Many years ago Gareth had told her that he had to leave her. Or more to the point, as she was in his rooms at the time, that she had to leave him. To be fair to the man, on that occasion he had been quite ruthless and left her with absolutely no crumb of hope. But for the next three days Helena hadn't eaten or slept in her misery. By the end of that time she had reconciled herself to the fact that she would never be Gareth's wife. She would not be the thing she thought herself intended by Nature to be. She had had to make herself believe it. She had broken her own heart deliberately in those terrible three nights so that it would eventually mend and it had. Subsequently she had plunged into misery from time to time but she never wanted him back. These days she was quite relaxed about being in his presence or talking to him on the phone but she still had these intuitive moments. Helena could recognise a postcard from Gareth, lying on the doormat, from the other end of the hallway. She sometimes even guessed when he was in the country. And she certainly recognised when he was making their telephone ring. There was a curious umbilical cord between them, but it was one-way. She was sure it was one-way. After all Gareth could not have a psychic connection with every Oxford virgin he had seduced. That would leave him no time to earn a living or write these books that David grumbled about.

'Helena . . . It's Gareth.' Of course it was. He didn't have to tell her that.

'What do you want?' she asked more abrupt than she intended. Yes what *did* he want? She wasn't meeting him till next week and he couldn't be ringing to cancel. Gareth only cancelled the morning in question. Or after you'd travelled two hours in the train to see him. So he had to be after something.

'I've just heard about Peter Dorkin.' So he *was* after something. 'Is David standing in?'

'Yes.'

'Oh good. He's absolutely right for the job. I'm sure they'll give him the chair.' Gareth paused to see if Helena said 'Oh no, he's very pessimistic,' or 'Oh no, he's told them he doesn't want it' or 'Oh no, he'd be a *disaster*'. Getting no reply, Gareth continued: 'Or are they splitting the headship?'

'I've no idea,' Helena lied and both God and David applauded her. God seemed to have no problem with that little fib.

'Poor old Peter Dorkin,' said Gareth with what sounded like genuine feeling. Helena was sure she had no recollection of their ever meeting. 'You know he had sounded me out about taking a sabbatical with the department?'

'No I didn't.'

'David didn't mention it?' Well she could be sure of that. Had David known he would have mentioned it and had David mentioned it she would certainly have remembered, fireworks, depression and all. Then again Gareth might just be spinning her a line. She was very fond of Gareth and his little lies but if he started seriously underestimating her intelligence she would have to take him to task. There was a ring from the doorbell.

'I'll have to go, there's someone at the door,' Helena blurted. Why did she feel guilty that the doorbell had caught her talking to the telephone, just because Gareth Box was on the other end of it?

'Helena, don't forget Monday,' he urged her with great significance.

'I won't.'

The bell went again.

'You know how much I'm looking forward to it.'

'Gareth,' she said. 'I am hardly likely to forget Monday, given that I have had to rearrange David, the children and the cleaning lady all around you.' And with that she put the phone down, aware of course that he would have enjoyed that rebuke. It seemed to place him in the centre of the Universe yet again.

The bell went a third time and it was Pip in pale blue leggings, new hair and tears.

'What's the matter?' asked Helena, preparing to prepare the inevitable coffee.

'Don't you just hate this?' Pip asked. It had to be the hair. 'I know what Anders is going to say. Whenever they cut it like this he says I look like a schoolboy.'

No-one had ever said that about Helena. Even when her hair went thin and she had it cut back. Helena was unmistakably female. Even when, as during the Nick experience, she had been through her most unattractive phase, Helena had remained female in her unattractiveness.

'All I can say is Thank God Saturday's off,' said Pip with a sniff.

'Off?'

'The Glamorganshire Cricket thing.'

'It's off?'

'*Yes*,' said Pip as if Helena was being more than a bit slow today.

'But I thought—'

'They cancelled it yesterday. Not enough of the players were willing to sit at the sponsors' tables without being paid. I *did* tell you.' Pip was full of pathetic indignation. She was also totally wrong. Either that or Helena was going mad.

'Did you ring?' she asked.

Pip tried to remember and, being unable to remember, she sniffed pathetically at this cross questioning. 'Well, it might have been earlier in the week, I don't know. Anders didn't tell me till last night. That's all I know.'

Click went the kettle.

Click went Helena's mind as she poured water into the cafetière. It was not the kind of thing that men like Anders forget to tell wives like Pip. Unless men like Anders have their minds on Other Things. Helena knew about men having their minds on Other Things and about what Other Things can do to a marriage. But Pip was only just thirty. Pip was in her prime. Pip wasn't distracted and desiccated by children. Pip had a body that stayed in place on its own. The wife of Anders Arnstein was a woman who could make a whole room of men, bent on the midnight Eucharist, turn away from the paths of righteousness with just one tinkling laugh. No, it was people like her and David who were supposed to go haywire as forty approached, revisiting the illusion of youth before they were too old to recognise it any more. Helena decided she was wrong. For Pip's sake she would be wrong.

'Well,' she said. 'David will be disappointed.'

On Thursday afternoon Millie met Jonathan and Katrin from school.

'Hello Bunny!' she cried gleefully, holding out her arms. Katrin Williams looked at her mother as if she had trodden in something.

'Mum!!' she gasped in acute embarrassment.

Millie had more success meeting Jonathan.

'Hiya Jon, fancy going somewhere?'

'Orright,' said Jon lumpishly. 'Can Maxy come?'

'Who's Maxy?'

Maxy turned out to be a certain kind of Cardiff boy: one possessed of very little height and very mixed racial origins. Millie guessed straight away that, wherever Maxy lived now, his family originated in the docks. Only in that once heady mixture of race and hard-fought commerce were such families blended. Maxy had genes from all four corners of the globe but he had an accent from the capital of Wales.

'Me and Jon was going down the P*aark*,' he announced defensively, as if Millie was trying to spoil their fun.

'We could all go down the park,' Millie replied, minimising the breadth of the Cardiff vowels. It was a strange, good-natured accent, full of worldly weariness but not one she felt at home in.

'Why for?' asked Maxy.

'Well, I could buy you ice creams.'

'Yesss!!' shouted Katrin who had waited ungraciously for Jonathan and felt she deserved some reward.

'Oh orright,' said Maxy generously. 'Come on, Jon.'

'Great,' said Millie 'But what about your Mam?'

'Oh she can't come. My Mam works,' Maxy insisted

It sounded odd, that phrase. Odd to Millie's ears. Odd to think that if someone had asked how they could get the agreement of Jonathan Williams' mother to such a jaunt he might have replied, 'Oh my Mam *works*.' Millie didn't often look at herself from the outside, except in mirrors.

That afternoon between 3.30 and 7pm she took all three children to two different parks, two ice cream vans, Techniquest where they ran wild and frightened the exhibits and finally to a dingy takeaway burger outlet that was owned by a friend of Maxy's Mum. When Max was finally dropped off on the corner of his street he waved happily but Crispin was in a complete state when they got back.

'Have you had Maxy with you?' he asked at the door.

'Yes we have,' said Millie, giving him a kiss and a hug.

'Maxy's crazy!' roared Jonathan happily. 'Oink, oink!'

'You're the one who's crazy,' grumbled Katrin, who had entered upon a huff as soon as they reached home. 'Those boys shouted *all the time*.'

'What's the matter?' Millie asked with her arm round Crispin's waist.

'I've had Maxy's mother's boyfriend round here looking for him,' Crispin announced in quietly controlled outrage. 'When Maxy wasn't on the school bus they virtually sent out a search party.'

'But he said his Mum was working,' Millie explained.

'Yes but even working mothers have people who pick their children up from school. Or hadn't that occurred to you, Emily?'

Millie had to admit, even to herself, that she should have tried a bit harder to divine Maxy's domestic arrangements.

'Sorry,' she said with the embarrassed shrug of a child who has finally owned up.

'Have you seen the *size* of Maxy's mother's boyfriend?' Crispin asked.

'Oh, Boo Boo! I am a stupid cow, aren't I?'

'Yes, Millie,' said Crispin. 'I'm afraid you are.'

On Friday morning Helena and her two met Crispin and his at the school crossing.

'How's yours today?' asked Crispin.

'Up and down. How's Millie?'

'I think she's in need of domestication,' he replied. The lollipop man waved them over. The two girls had already teamed up when they reached the other side of the road and were chatting away while Big Jon was watching Nick with interest.

'David's depressed because we were going out on Saturday and now we're not,' Helena announced as they walked up the school drive.

'That depresses him?' Crispin asked. It seemed to Crispin a novel cause for depression. He was not a man for restaurants and night clubs.

'Well, at the moment he's liable to go that way,' Helena explained. 'Professional frustrations, I'm afraid. What's wrong with Millie?'

'Oh she's . . . um . . .' the curious lines across Crispin's face furrowed. He didn't quite know where you started when describing Millie. 'She's not *house-trained*. I suppose that's what I mean. I sometimes feel she isn't quite at home in a family. She ought to be, she grew up in one, which is more than I did.' He smiled despite himself and then continued. For Crispin he was being very chatty that morning.

'I think she needs a project, you see. She's used to a challenge. She doesn't quite function without one.'

They had reached the playground now. 'Bye Dad!' shouted Katrin. Emma waved.

'She wouldn't like to take on David, would she? Cheer him up?'

'What had you in mind?' Crispin asked. 'More abandoned cars by the River Severn?'

Helena laughed. She had to take Nick round to his class now and he was pulling her away.

'Bye,' she said.

'Why don't you come round to dinner tomorrow?' Crispin shouted across the gap that had opened up between them.

'What?' said Helena, walking backwards as Nick pulled forwards.

'Come to dinner tomorrow night!' Crispin shouted. Big Jonathan looked blankly at his father.

'But you came to us last week!' Helena shouted back unable to halt her son.

'So? It's our turn!' Crispin yelled. 'Unless you've got anything else arranged. At least David would be going out!'

'I'LL RING YOU!' was all Helena could manage.

Nick had stopped pulling as they reached the Infants. 'Is that your boyfriend?' he asked.

'No,' said Helena stroking her son's head.' He lives with Daddy's friend.'

Back at the house Helena discovered the post had come early. Deliveries to Ty Escob fluctuated markedly, as if the postman forgot them entirely one day and made up for it the next, dropping by first thing with as many letters as he could justifiably stuff through the Mosford letter box. A second invitation to a conference somewhere that just wasn't warm enough, a postcard from one of Helena's cousins who had had lunch with somebody funny who wanted to be remembered to her. And a padded envelope that was, unmistakably, from Gareth. It was odd that she'd actually picked it up without recognising the feel of a parcel from Gareth. There it was though, replete with his exaggerated script, and there within a catalogue of some exhibition she would have enjoyed at the Hayward Gallery had her back been up to it. So he'd been without her. And he'd thought about her while she wasn't there and then he'd sent her the catalogue. There was no note, no letter, no inscription. It was a gesture eloquent in itself. What a *very* good job she was immune to all this kind of attention. Helena decided to save this up for later. She put the catalogue down on a coffee table in the drawing room. After all, David could have no cause to object to a simple catalogue with no inscription. Besides, he'd never even notice it.

5

Other Women, Other Men

Saturday was absurdly bright and beautiful. David woke early to a riot of birdsong and blue skies and went into the garden in his dressing gown. At about the same time, Crispin detached himself from Millie's warm embrace and wandered down to his study with a pullover over his nightshirt. Light seemed to be breaking in on every damn side of the house on High Street; through windows, past curtains and under doors. Crispin scowled at the day and locked himself away with his books.

It was a beautiful day, the kind of day that Nature lays on in the hope of generating good nostalgia. David loved the past. He was a historian by training but a sentimentalist at heart. Looking around the garden he could remember summers from his teenage years like this, his father always doing something with the lawn, his mother forever bringing out tea trays. Memory is like a series of time loops, he thought, and the people we love are recorded, repeating forever, gestures and actions that the mind has randomly chosen as their emblemata. And people we don't love too. Dorkin laying his hand with great pride on some papers that Megan had filed and telling everyone that the department couldn't cope without her. That image had been constantly in David's mind since yesterday's funeral.

As was Stella Price, in black, damnably chewing the corner of her mouth.

But this morning he could remember deeper loops in time too. His father getting up and extending his hand in greeting to Helena. Getting up from whatever gardens needed in the summer. And offering his hand. It must have been fifteen years ago that she had finally agreed to meet his parents. And in the tape loop of Davy's memory old Mr Mosford had lifted his hat decorously to Helena. But that wasn't true. He didn't wear a hat. He certainly wouldn't have worn a hat to garden in but he was a Welshman of the kind who carried a metaphorical trilby for just such occasions.

Memory had supplied the hat.

How tall she had seemed in that garden. Like one of the Bishop's conifers. Tall and dark and still a bit unsure. Not of herself, she had the physical confidence of her Anglo-Norman forebears, but she was unsure of him, of them. He'd taken her down to the river after tea. That was in the days before the Taff embankment was built. The fields below the cathedral were often flooded but not that summer. They'd sat on the scorched brown grass behind some heavy foliage and Helena had told him that despite her degree, which was good enough, she definitely didn't want to do research anymore. And he had asked her again to marry him and she said why couldn't they just have sex. And he'd said 'What, now?' and she'd laughed and said 'Why not?' He was twenty-five and he wasn't used to nice girls like her saying things like that.

How odd, thought David, looking round his parents' garden now. Fifteen years ago his wife had all but suggested having sex down there on the river bank. Fifteen years ago they all but had. He went back through the house, up the stairs and down the creaking landing and would indeed have got cautiously into bed but the children had beaten him to it.

Crispin was putting out things for breakfast when Katrin announced that she was going 'Over Emma's' that morning.

'Have you checked with Millie?' Crispin asked.

'No,' Katrin replied in surprise. One didn't check that kind of thing with Millie. Mil had her faults but she never stood in the way of a girl enjoying herself.

'She might have something arranged,' he suggested.

'Mum?!' Katrin laughed.

Millie was right, Crispin thought, Katrin could sound just like her maternal grandmother. That little laugh which was jovial in the execution but entirely censorious in its intent.

But Millie had nothing planned for the morning other than a long bath and her usual can of Coca Cola. She came downstairs to raid the fridge and make a marmalade sandwich. It was Millie's habit to eat in the bedroom, bathroom, car and garden. In fact anywhere but the kitchen.

'Don't forget we have David and Helena coming for dinner tonight,' Crispin reminded her as he cleared away last night's debris.

'Am I cooking?' Millie asked.

'Certainly not. I want to be sure something is on the table when they arrive.'

Millie let that pass. 'You know Harry really is a bastard,' she said, half to him but mainly to herself.

'And you haven't rung your parents for two weeks,' Crispin reminded her.

'I'm the best they've got, Crisp. Really I am.'

'Yes you are,' he agreed.

'And Selwyn's a ponce,' Millie grumbled as she went back up the stairs. 'A total ponce.' They had had a number of conversations like this since Millie returned from Taunton, although not all of them dwelt so exclusively on the shortcomings of her employers. Some centred on what Millie might have done with her life instead and was it all too late? Others dwelt on Harry's lack of balls.

'I don't think they were even cut off,' Millie had decided last night.' I think he was just born without.' After they opened a second bottle she had claimed to be determined on mailing two ping pong balls to Harry first thing Saturday morning, as a damning indictment of his managerial style, but this morning she seemed not to have remembered that intention.

'Will you come and talk to me in the bath?' Millie asked from the staircase.

'I've got a lot to do.'

'Make it worth your while,' she offered. Crispin pretended not to hear that.

'You know, you could make a start on the garage,' he suggested, turning round and facing her across the kitchen. Millie held out a hand to him.

'Millie . . . sex isn't everything,' he told her. 'It's a lot I know but it isn't everything. We have *got* to try and get some order in our lives. This house is a mess. Katrin's virtually bringing herself up and Jonathan, well I really don't know about Jonathan. His entire conversation these days seems to consist of the word *"Orright".'*

'He's *happy*,' Millie replied as she disappeared upstairs. 'Jonathan is capable of just *being*. He has *fun* and he doesn't fret around as if someone's stuck a broom handle up his arse!'

'I'm going to the Spar,' Crispin called after her. 'Try not to have too much fun while I'm out.'

The supermarket had recently annoyed Crispin by changing all its shelves around but when he finally located the new dairy counter he was cheered by the sight of Helena and Nick Mosford.

'Have you still got my daughter?' he asked.

'They're helping David with the garden,' Helena replied. 'Both of them. David was trying to explain about pollination but they've got him cornered in some discussion about whether plants have willies.'

'Horrible thought,' muttered Crispin.

'Stamens?' she asked.

'No, having Emma and Katrin lecturing you about sex.'

Nick diverted Helena away at this point but when they met up again by the cereals, Crispin seemed in a better mood. 'I see you haven't actually managed to steal anything yet,' he observed, pointing to Helena's empty basket

'Summoning up the strength,' she replied with a smile. 'Once I get going there'll be no stopping me. Though actually,' she added, as if plucking up the courage, 'I'm glad I've seen you. We're having trouble with babysitters. After the Cricket Thing I stood our girl down and she's working for someone else now. Do you know anyone?'

'Er, no,' Crispin replied hopelessly. 'Um, I'm afraid we may have been blacklisted.'

The light from the Spar's glass doorway was suddenly darkened by the bulk of Jonathan Williams in clothes a touch too small for him.

'Mum wants me to help her in the garage,' Jonathan complained.

'Say hello to Mrs Mosford,' Crispin interjected.

'Why?'

'Because you're ten.'

'I was ten in March,' Jonathan argued.

'Fair point I suppose,' Crispin agreed. 'But that's no reason not to start being civilised now.'

'Hello Jonathan,' said Helena to help matters along.

'Hello,' said Jonathan.

'Hello Jonathan,' chorused little Nick.

'*Orright* Nick?' said Jonathan.

Jonathan and Nick got on so well while their parents were queuing up, talking and ignoring them, that Helena took both boys back to play in Ty Escob so that Crispin could get on with the food.

By lunch time it was very hot for June and Nick had taken all his clothes off on the lawn.

'Should he be doing that?' Helena asked David. 'What if the girls join in?' Their garden was fairly private but should they be sanctioning under-age nudity? David was more concerned that Jonathan looked too hot in his Welsh International Rugby shirt and vest. So while Nick was taken inside to be dressed again, David had a word with Big Jon who was playing with Nick's cars in the undergrowth.

'Bit hot John?'

'Yeah,' came the reply.

'Why don't you take your shirt off?' Jonathan laughed as if this was a trick question. 'Don't want you boiling over.'

'No way,' laughed Jonathan and he went back to making car noises.

Millie had worked up a considerable thirst in the low attic above their garage. Summer sunshine made for a particularly dry heat up there. When Crispin came over from the house with some cans of lunchtime lager, she called him up the fixed wooden ladder and demonstrated gleefully what had been achieved. The hot dark space reminded Crispin disturbingly of the attic in Loudon where the martyr Urbain Grandier, maddened by the baking heat and unable to stand, had been kept before being put to The Question. Back in the twentieth century, however, he had to admit that as a result of a great deal of rubble landing in the back garden there was now a considerable amount of new storage space created in the low-ceilinged loft. Millie had also found a heavy duty pulley that must have been used in the days when getting things in and out of the old stable block was a regular event. More to the point, she knew how to get it working.

'I'm impressed,' said Crispin easing his stiff legs into a sitting position on the bare boards.

'Particularly when it's so hot.'

Millie opened a can of lager appreciatively, sighed and leant back against some sacks . . .

'God I'm sweating!' she laughed, feeling the shock of cold wetness down the back of her T-shirt and tugging it over her head. Crispin watched as she wiped her brow and unshaven underarms with the discarded top.

'How're the kids?' she asked.

'Won't be back for ages, I imagine,' said Crispin. Millie looked up to check his face. She knew that hungry look. She threw her T-shirt at him.

'Oh yes, Baggyboo? I thought sex wasn't supposed to be everything.'

Crispin picked up her shirt and pressed it to his lips.

'I sometimes think it is for us,' he admitted ruefully and high on the aroma of her armpits.

The noise that was heard in the back lane caused some eyebrows to be raised. It never occurred to Millie and Crispin that the wooden loft actually enhanced the audibility of their lovemaking. Several silent people came out and looked at the tall stone building as if their visible censure would diminish the noises issuing from it. The stable block continued to groan and shout, however.

Later, when Crispin actually got the ground floor doors opened and actually backed Millie's car inside for the first time ever, he felt very pleased with himself and smiled at the pair of neighbours who were watching this manoeuvre. The fact that they turned away in disapproval left him staggered. What was it with the Welsh? He didn't let it bother him, however. He was still savouring that particular sense of well being that could occasionally result from sex with Millie.

What did bother him was realising that the loft interlude had caused something he was preparing to set sooner than it should and so the food for that evening was in danger of not being ready in time.

'Damn and blast!' said Crispin, gazing at the sink.

'Don't look at me,' said Millie who had just emerged from yet another bath. 'I am but a simple Welsh country girl who was seduced by the wicked squire.' She squeezed Crispin's bottom appreciatively. 'In a loft t'was too, he didn't even take me to his bed.'

'Millie, will you bugger off and let me work out what I'm doing!' Crispin growled. His mind was now, of pressing necessity, on other things

'Only just in time, too.' Millie leaned forward and put her hands round his waist

'The one thing about your life that runs to schedule,' Crispin replied washing out the bowl. 'I'm glad to say.'

'I am the best, aren't I?'

Crispin turned to face her. 'How you manage to satisfy me, Selwyn and Harry never ceases to amaze, Emmeline, but we also live in the real world.'

'Can I do anything to help?' she asked.

'Do you mean that?'

'Course.'

Crispin sighed. 'Well,' he said. 'Could you go and see David and Helena, find out if they've got a sitter. And if they *are* coming tonight ask them to make it 8.30, not 8. Oh and you ought to bring ours back, I suppose. The children I mean.'

'Aye, aye, Cap'n!'

Millie walked across the Green in a very good mood and a tight pair of shorts. All was well in the world. Her kids were great kids. She and Crisp had great sex and she'd definitely be back in work soon. She knew she would. Harry might have no balls but he wouldn't let her down. Men like Harry didn't let you down. Not in the end.

Millie found the front door of Ty Escob open and wandered through into the garden. Nobody seemed to be about although the radio was relaying a cricket commentary. Then in the deck-chair she noticed David asleep. He had been protecting his scalp with a panama hat that had fallen over his face.

Millie sat down in the chair next to him and squeezed his knee.

'What have you done with my kids, Dave?'

He awoke in some confusion, switched off the radio and apologised for falling asleep. 'Helena's taken them down to the river. The boys wanted to throw stones.'

'Meanwhile you're taking it easy?'

'I've been playing chase with Emma and Katrin. That, one glass of wine and the burdens of high office – however temporary – seem to have finished me off.'

Millie laughed. After a moment she pointed at the absurd trees that obscured everything in sight and told him that it was, otherwise, a very nice view. Then they fell into a silence that was strangely companionable. David was going to explain about the bishop planting those poplars and no-one ever trimming them back but somehow he couldn't be bothered or maybe it didn't seem necessary. He had not imagined you could sit quietly in a garden with Millie. But then he didn't know Millie was a sun worshipper. The warmth on her face and knees had left her settled and centred.

'D'you want a drink?' David asked after a few moments. Millie shook her head.

They sat a bit longer. The silence was comfortable. And yet he didn't quite feel comfortable feeling so comfortable in her presence.

'I'm afraid we're still waiting for news on a sitter for tonight.' Millie didn't reply. 'I hope Crispin isn't going to any trouble.'

David already knew from Helena, had he not guessed, that it would be Crispin who would be cooking for that evening.

'Poor old Crisp is flapping about like a blue-arsed fly,' said Millie. 'We took advantage of the house being empty earlier on and now he's behind with all his preparations.'

David didn't understand what Millie meant until she smirked at him.

'Oh,' he said. 'Oh I see. Good for you.' He felt a bit foolish saying that but then quite what was the form when your hostess tells you she has spent lunchtime having sex with your host?

'Tell you what,' said Millie. 'Why don't you send your two over to us this evening? Emma and Katrin can share her room and if Nick's happy he can have the room next to Jonathan. Then you don't need to get a sitter.'

'Oh,' said David for the second time. It did seem like a good idea. 'Are you sure?'

'Uhuh,' said Millie. 'I mean it's only fair. You've had mine all day. What if I take them back at five? I'll give them tea somewhere. That'll give you three hours.'

'Well thank you,' said David.

'Then you can take advantage of the house being empty too,' said Millie. David tried not to look embarrassed when the woman he fancied suggested he had preprandial sex with his wife. Millie, in this relaxed postcoital state, was even more provocative than Millie noisy. 'After all,' she said. 'You are married, aren't you?'

'Yes,' said David. 'But it doesn't always follow.'

Millie didn't understand at first. He hadn't been looking at her when he spoke those words. He was looking down to the river.

'Oh,' she said cottoning on. 'That's a shame.'

'Yes,' David agreed, 'It is a shame. It's, er, sort of connected with Nick's problems.'

'But he's fine now?'

David felt he couldn't say more without telling more, and the more he might tell would definitely be far more than his wife would want another person to know. Last Saturday had been the nearest thing to sex that they'd managed for almost a month and yet it went wrong. Why? Why had she become so tense? Why afterwards did she look away like that? She had cut off from him.

At that point Helena came up the lawn with four children in tow.

'Linna!' said David. 'Millie's just made a most moral suggestion.'

*　　*　　*

When the Mosfords turned up for dinner with Millie and Crispin, the food was ready but nothing else was. Unsurprisingly, and unfortunately for Crispin, rampant lust in the Mosford household had not materialised, quite possibly because once Millie had gone Helena did not take the hint any further. All of which meant that the guests turned up at precisely 8.30 to find Katrin and Emma upstairs in the bath together, Jonathan in the front room watching a video and Nick asleep on the landing, having chosen that as the place where his sleeping bag would lie. Millie could be heard getting dressed somewhere and shouting at the girls.

'Lovely to see you,' said Crispin, kissing Helena. 'Lovely to see anyone rather than this lot.'

'Have they been very bad?' asked Davy handing over a bottle of wine.

'Temper tantrums, screaming, throwing things, sulking, you name it.'

'Oh dear,' said Helena

'But fortunately the children have been fine,' Crispin added.

He led them down towards the kitchen.

'Jonathan, can we come in and switch off the television?' he called out provocatively as they passed the front room door. Jon threw a cushion in reply. Helena looked at David. What had they let their two into? Emma and Katrin appeared at the top of the kitchen stairs dressed in towels, waved and ran back upstairs laughing.

'Strange things, girls,' said David as Crispin passed them both a glass of wine. Helena decided she should leave hers and take a look 'at Nick which left the two men together, Crispin in his usual position leaning against the sink, David at the table.

'Er . . . how's work?' asked Crispin.

'Tedious. I'm waiting to see if they're going to split my boss's old job.'

'This is the Chair?'

'Of Politcal History, yes. He was also Head of Department.'

'And that's the job you don't want?'

'Not if I can help it.'

'Ah,' said Crispin. David felt that Millie was missing from this conversation. Crispin was a nice enough fellow but talking with him was like a very slow game of tennis.

'How's the bookshop?' Davy watched as that one travelled over the net.

'I gather we're waiting for people to – um – to buy their holiday reading.'

'Of course,' said David. Crispin to serve.

'Have you been on telly lately?'

'Course he hasn't! He'd be telling us all about if if he had. Wouldn't you, Dave?'

Thank goodness for Millie, thought David. And so did Crispin. Millie gave them both a kiss.

'Isn't he marvellous?' she announced, her arm around Crispin's waist. 'I haven't done a single thing you know.'

'It never occurred to me that you would,' David replied. Millie gave him his usual nudge.

'She did lay the table, scrub the potatoes and do the washing up,' Crisp admitted.

'That's more than David would have done,' said Helena joining them and reaching for her glass.

By nine o'clock the meal was going well, by ten it was very noisy indeed with David giving a very animated and grossly caricatured re-enactment of his meeting with Stella Price. Millie was of course defending Carys Rees and giving him a hard time.

'You just don't like powerful women!'

'I have nothing against powerful women,' he replied. 'And anyway, Carys Rees is not a "powerful woman," she is a pretty little thing who has been handed more power than she deserves just because some middle-aged fool fancies her.'

'How on earth can you justify saying that?' Helena asked.

'Yes come on, Dave,' Millie added. 'Prove it!'

David paused for a moment. 'Well I fancy her and I'm middle-aged of course.'

'So you *fancy* her!' Millie shouted. 'Now we come to it don't we? You don't like being pushed around by someone you fancy.'

'No I do,' David replied. 'Really I do. But not on university premises.'

'How *do* you get away with being such a dreadful old letch?' Millie asked, leaning forward.

'Practice,' he replied. Helena frowned. The door bell went. Helena was wondering about the woman who used to ring them from the north of England but there was no point in dwelling on that. The bell went again and this time Crispin got up.

'Christ almighty, who's that now?' asked Millie and she started to tell the story of Crispin and the neighbours. David watched Millie He couldn't help but enjoy her energy, her conviction that everything would be OK in the end, and probably quite soon. He was never that sure. He wanted to touch Millie, not for all the usual reasons he wanted to touch Millie but because he wanted some of that conviction to rub off on him.

Helena watched David watching Millie but only until Crispin returned to the room with a very thin looking young woman whom Helena was sure she recognised. To David this stranger was completely alien except that she looked like a student. She was of that age, and her sensible clothing and censorious demeanour confirmed the impression. Oh dear. David Mosford liked students but only between certain hours and never at weekends.

'Er, everybody. This is Sue,' said Crispin. Sue gave a half smile.

'Hi! Come and sit down and have a drink,' said Millie, determined not to have the atmosphere spoiled by the stranger's obvious discomfort.

'I've just come to borrow a book. I won't stop, thank you,' said Sue. Try as she might to smile, Sue did give every impression that stopping would be a very unpleasant experience for one of her obvious sensibilities. Crispin took Sue up the kitchen stairs. Millie leaned forward.

'Crisp's study group,' she explained. 'Do you understand kids like her?'

Because Millie was wearing a dress of reasonable restraint this evening, David had no trouble concentrating on her question.

'Students are like that these days,' he replied.

'God, in my day we never refused a drink,' said Millie.

'Alcohol isn't what it was,' David replied.

'Could have fooled me,' said Millie taking a generous gulp.

After dinner David and Millie wanted to play billiards again but this was not possible without a billiard table. Even they admitted that.

'We could turn that loft into a billiard room,' Millie announced. They were all four of them in the front room by now, thanks to Big Jon having finally gone to bed. Crispin and Helena were ensconced by the fireplace. 'I may as well be talking to myself!' she grumbled.

'What loft?' asked Davy who was begining to realise that brandy had been a bad idea.

'Come on! I'll show you.' Millie got to her feet and took him by the wrist.

'Where are we going?' David asked.

'I'm showing Dave the loft, Crisp!' Millie informed the room. 'The *loft*.'

Crispin looked up from the hearth. 'You be careful, Emily,' he said.

'What's he mean?' David asked but, getting no reply, he simply repeated to Helena that he was going to look at the loft and dutifully went with Millie.

Millie's garden was strewn with things she had ejected that afternoon from the loft and that Crispin had pulled out of the garage last week. In the moonlight the scattered rubbish looked quite white and beautiful but even June is cold at midnight. David found the garden distinctly chill after Millie's front room.

'Come on!' she urged him already at the stable door.

'I thought you said we were going to the loft?' David asked. A swirl of white dust and old straw eddied round as she tugged the side door open.

'*This* loft!' said Millie and she started to climb the wooden ladder. My God, this used to be Laurence Richards' garage, thought David as he watched Millie's bottom disappearing into the dark. His dad kept their car here and we were never allowed in. Then his mind suddenly caught up with him. He was going into a dark and secret place with a woman he found attractive. And at midnight. David steadied himself and did his best on the ladder. Thank God the cooler air had cleared his head.

'Well, what do you think?' Millie asked as he got to the top.

The room was only lit from a window in the eaves so it took him a moment to adjust to the dark.

'Very nice,' he said keeping his head down. 'Long as we play with luminous balls.'

Millie nudged him. 'Have you no soul. Dave? Look here's the table,' she stepped it out. 'And here's the rack for cues and here,' she sat down on some old sacking. 'Here is . . .'

'The chaise longue?' David suggested recalling their last game at Ty Escob.

'Yeah, if you like,' she said and she swung her legs up into a reclining position. 'What d'you think?' Millie asked of the pose but she didn't laugh. It was silly of her not to laugh.

'Very nice,' said David, a full four feet away. It was a significant distance physically and emotionally to cross. Millie was about to get up. Game over. Time to go home. Davy stepped forward as she stood up. The distance that was four feet had suddenly become two and was now nothing at all. David and Millie kissed. Just like that. This was it, David thought. Yes, this was losing yourself. This was melting, one person into the other. Millie, as he had always known, kissed wonderfully. Not deliberately as Helena did, nor intensely as Helena could, but effortlessly and seemingly forever.

Eventually they stopped.

'Yeah, very nice,' said Millie with a wry smile. 'I suppose I saw that coming.' She tapped his nose affectionately with her finger. 'Come on. You've seen the loft now.'

'I'm sure there's more,' said David, trying to manipulate the innuendo.

'Oh yes, much more,' said Millie. 'You've no idea.'

'I think I have,' said David as he tried to kiss her again.

'Dave,' said Millie. 'Three things you should know: I'm happy with Crispin. I like Helena and I've got my period.'

'Ah,' said David. Then after a moment he added. 'Helena's not a problem, you know.'

'No?'

'It, er it takes a bit of explaining,' he began to explain. This wasn't quite true, was it? Some explanation *might* help convince Millie – but Helena?

'Well, you don't need to explain,' Millie replied. 'Not to me.'

'You're not married to Crispin,' David pointed out. He knew already that he was losing this one, but the allure of Millie was so strong at the moment that he couldn't just go down that ladder as if nothing had happened. He had to go down fighting.

'I don't have to be,' said Millie. 'Look, I'm sorry if I led you on a bit but that's me. You know what I'm like.' She could see him looking unhappy about this. Millie was fond of David. She enjoyed the attention she got from him. Of course she had had no idea about things being bad between him and Helena. Or that Helena was not a problem – whatever that meant. To be honest, she half wondered if that might be a line he was spinning. But, to be even more honest, she and Crisp had no hard and fast rules. Rules were for people who needed them and Millie Kemp didn't. But the fact of the matter was that she just didn't want to. Mind, it was nice to be asked.

'Oh come on,' she said, putting her arms around him. 'You and me are friends.'

'Yes,' he said looking all of six years old. She kissed him on the cheek but felt him pursuing the kiss.

'Downstairs,' she said.

Millie wasn't aware that at some time gone midnight she was seen clambering in and clambering out of the loft with a man who was not her husband by a woman two doors down who was putting out her cat – and who told Mrs Tom next door who in turn told some people in the lane, one of whom had heard the sounds from the stable block that Saturday lunchtime. Millie Kemp was about to be the thing of gossip. Long had there been suspicions about goings-on. People from London were notorious for goings-on. But now there was evidence.

The dinner party broke up in strange circumstances. As the Mosford children were already asleep, Crispin suggested that the parents stayed over too but David was quite sure they should get back home. Discussion arose over whether to leave Nick and Emma or carry them back. Both ideas had opponents. At one point Helena offered to stay on her own so she would be there in case either child needed her. It was a proposal that elicited a glare from David.

In the end Crispin and David carried Nick and Emma, respectively, over to Ty Escob. By the time Crispin got back, locked up and checked some stuff in his office, Millie was already half asleep.

'David fancies me,' Millie told Crispin as he got into bed.

'Of course he does,' said Crispin. 'That's why he's round here all the time.'

Millie was surprised that Crispin had guessed this already.

'You'd better watch out, hadn't you?' she giggled and promptly fell asleep.

David stared at the ceiling in a mixture of frustration and anticipation. Part of him was still physically uncomfortable with the rejection. Yet part of him was replaying the scene, remembering the warm moistness of Millie's mouth, the pressure of her body on his. She may have said No but she had enjoyed that kiss, he knew it.

Helena came to bed and curled up against him in that particular way that told him what she wanted him to know. And what he had wanted to know for some months now. David was as capable of appreciating irony as the next man but it went beyond irony for Helena to be finally aroused just when he had set his mind and body on the body of another woman. She was lying on his flank, almost on top of him in fact, her head above his. He stroked her hair gently and felt it fall down into his face. Why can't you *do* something with your hair, David thought.

'That's nice,' said Helena.

'You get on well with Crispin,' David said. He had stopped stroking her head but an evening talking to Crispin always had a good effect on Helena. She felt very relaxed and relaxing seemed to make sex feel both desirable and possible. She rubbed her head against his hand and he, being her husband, did not feel he could withdraw it.

'That's nice,' said Helena again and David started to stroke her head once more. Helena responded to his touch and rolled over on to her back, trying to pull him on top of her. David, on the other hand, felt anything but relaxed. He felt confused. Part of him definitely wanted to make love. But the part of him that did was a part that really didn't care to whom. The rest of him, however, felt uncertain about having sex with Helena when he was still aroused by Millie.

Helena was asking him to unbutton the front of her long white nightdress. She could indicate this request without using any words. He felt sad at the slackness of her breasts since children. Physical imperfection in women had always bothered him but there was a distinct sense in which Nature was saying apropos of Helena *this woman's body has served its purpose now, try and impregnate a younger one, one where all the bits are where they're supposed to be.*

Nevertheless as he bent to her familiar nipple he found himself gaining in enthusiasm. And in his enthusiasm he found himself losing those uncertainties until a familiar sound penetrated the night.

'Mum-mee.' Oh no.

'Mum-mee.' Nick. In his room. But awake.

'Mum-meeee!'

God was never much in evidence in Llandaff on a Sunday morning. He tended to avoid the Cathedral at these times. Helena was quite sure that bad singing and noisy children and all that getting up and kneeling down put him off. It certainly put her off at times. And as for parish breakfast in the Prebendial House! No chance of bumping into him there. But she was very much in need of his advice that morning so down all thirty-three steps she went with Nick in tow, just in case the old fellow put in an appearance.

David spent Sunday feeling very confused for quite different reasons and very keen to buy things from the Spar, just in case he could catch sight of Millie. Every time Helena couldn't find something Davy offered to go and fetch it. And he turned Millie's words incessantly over in his mind. His timing was bad, she had no wish to hurt Helena, she was happy with Crispin. None of these was actually a total, incontrovertible *no*.

On Monday life was back to normal, except that Helena went to London to see Gareth Box. That wasn't normal, in David's opinion. That was annoying. That was an occasional stray irritant in his life. Fortunately, however, his concentration was soon taken up with the regular daily irritants of a working life. By 9.30 he had reappraised himself of the fact that the University was tedious, Megan was tedious and Stella still hadn't informed him of her decision about the chair of Political History. Only the ridiculous car was a consolation.

Arriving at the office he dealt with the multi-faceted tedia of Dorkin's post and found he now received two copies of *Radical History*. His own and the department's and, worse, on the cover of each was a name he did not wish to see. *Professor Gareth Box.*

Professor Box was a boyish handsome man in his mid to late forties with an engaging lock of hair that invariably fell forward. Catching sight of him in the foyer, Helena was struck by the fact that she had been taller than both of the men in her life. Did that say something about her or about them? But Gareth and David were not alike. Her husband dressed well for effect and from habit. By contrast the man who had asked her to sleep with him after their first tutorial affected a casual style. His tie was never quite to the neck. His sleeves were always rolled up. He looked like the hero of a film about crusading newspaper men. Small newspaper men who compensated with huge circulations.

'Helena,' said Gareth standing up and taking her hand in a very slow and deliberate way.

'Right first time,' she replied.

'You are good to me,' he told her, with genuine satisfaction at the sight of her.

'And you're paying,' she reminded him.

They had arranged to meet in the lobby of the Royal Academy because at Fortnum's there was nowhere to sit and be sufficiently conspicuous whilst waiting. Helena had been surprised to find Gareth already there. Of inveterate habit he chose to arrive slightly late, covering himself in profuse apologies. The dynamics of Gareth's relationship with most women were those of transgression and forgiveness. He would start off apologising for arriving late and be forgiven. Then he would progress to ordering champagne and asking forgiveness for plying his guest with too much, then for the presumption of having booked a room in a hotel round the corner, finally he would apologise for having to get back to work so soon afterwards.

This was pretty much what had happened between Helena and Gareth seventeen years ago. She had resisted him at college but agreed to meet him in London during the vacation. That meeting, that champagne, that really rather nice hotel room in Jermyn Street had been her undoing. Not in a sexual sense. She had more than half a mind to give in to Gareth. It felt like time she gave in to someone. But it was being sucked into supporting Gareth's ego that all but undid her. Funny to look at him now, and look at her now, and think that once they were going to be Mr and Mrs Academic High Flyer. He destroyed that. Whether he did so deliberately or not she still didn't know but it no longer mattered.

When Helena sat down to lunch she was quite confident that Gareth had not booked a room in Jermyn Street for that afternoon. Or that if he had it was not for her. She always felt that nothing Gareth did would surprise her. In fact the fact that it soon transpired he *had* just come from a hotel room in Jermyn Street didn't surprise her. Not really.

But what *did* surprise her was that he had left the latest young woman in question, an American, reading magazines in bed. At twelve o'clock he had gone out and bought her every glossy he could get his hands on.

'Gareth, you can't do that,' Helena exclaimed, putting down her cutlery. The Fountains Restaurant was noisy with tourists and babies that lunchtime.

'I had to get away to talk to you,' Gareth insisted simply.

'Did you tell her where you were going?'

He sighed as if this was a professional difficulty he would have to handle carefully. 'I told her I was meeting a former colleague for lunch.'

'She must've guessed.'

'She's not as bright as you, Helena.'

'Gareth, one doesn't have to be bright to know when you're lying!'

This was the opportunity Gareth needed to tell Helena all about his latest. He usually did on these occasions but it was rare for the woman herself to be lying in bed 200 yards away.

'She's so young,' said Gareth, as if he had had no choice in the matter.

'How old?'

'Twenty, I think. You were twenty,' he added.

Helena smiled and looked away. Gareth stopped spooning his hollandaise sauce, he wanted to know why she was smiling.

'Just thinking,' said Helena, trying not to laugh. 'She was *three* when we met.' As if to make her point, a toddler at a nearby table started crying.

'Young women,' Gareth explained pitifully. 'There's nothing to them.'

'There's sufficient to get you into bed with them.'

'I'm regretting it already,' he admitted. 'I do wish I'd stop doing it. It's ridiculous in someone my age.' Helena smiled again, remembering Gareth's total lack of irony. In David such a statement would have been outrageous posturing. Gareth meant it.

'Gar, you are quite capable of dropping someone,' Helena told him. 'Or do you want me to remind you how it's done?'

He looked hurt. 'Do you know something? That was the biggest mistake of my life.'

'Yes,' said Helena flatly, attending to her food.

'You don't believe me?' he asked.

'No, I believe you. I believe it was a mistake for you but it was a lucky escape for me.'

Again Gareth looked hurt. He looked good when he looked hurt. And it encouraged whoever was sitting opposite him to say more.

'But listen, Gareth,' Helena said, saying more than she had intended. 'Listen, however much you feel that now, I don't think you'll be feeling it when you go back to your hotel room, when you see Miss America again. I think you'll have forgotten all about me.'

Gareth tried to interrupt.

'And so you should,' Helena informed him. 'You should have the decency to keep your mind on the person you're making love to.'

Gareth sat back and regarded her. 'You know me so well,' he remarked as if he admired this faculty in her above all others.

'It's really not difficult,' she replied.

David also felt he knew Gareth well. Too well, in fact, and particularly on the printed page. Open before him on Dorkin's desk were two copies of an article by *Professor* Box of the Something Not Very Impressive Institute, University of Vermont. Not just an article but a four-page article. With a photograph of some Prussians in spiky helmets. Clare had let *him* have a photograph for his first piece in *Radical History*, but not last time. Last time David had even lost part of a column for a conference advert! But there were no adverts, errata or cutaway coupons intruding into Gareth's article. And the byline *Gareth Box* did loom very large indeed. Ridiculously so. Davy checked two other articles to make sure. Surprisingly the typeface for *Gareth Box* was no bigger than for anybody else. It just looked bigger. Really Clare, out of fairness, ought to have set Gareth's name in smaller print. That way it might have come over on the page about the same size as everyone else's. Whichever way you looked at it, the name *Gareth Box* just had an intrinsically large look about it.

He wanted to ring Clare to complain that she had deliberately taken an article by Gareth over his Welsh Nationalism and Vichy France in order to spite him, or worse, to diminish his chances of getting the chair. What had he ever done to make her so hostile to him? Gareth seduced all his postgraduates as a matter of form, whereas he had never laid a finger on Clare. Or any of them. No that wasn't true. But she was more of a colleague . . . Oh, he was getting off the point!

David tried to keep calm. He was being hugely irrational, he knew that. As a fellow academic, in the circumstances, the only sensible, responsible and mature thing to do was to read this thing of Professor Box's through, giving due attention to detail and argument, and then blast it out of the water with an article or letter that Clare would be obliged to publish.

Unfortunately though this wasn't Davy's area. Gareth had always made a speciality of high profile nonsense. Flash-in-the-pan stuff intended to get him on to television. David knew nothing about German foreign policy 1914–18 and there was no time to set one of his postgraduates to do a rottweiler on this. On the other hand . . . Davy picked up the internal phone and dialled.

'Alun!' he said as the fractious voice of Dr Alun Taylor came on the line.

'I've got some first years with me at the moment, David.'

But Davy ploughed on.

'Have you read this nonsense in this morning's *Rad Hist*?'

'No, should I?' Alun asked, forgetting instantly that he had a room full of students preparing their summer reading lists. One of the good things about little Alun Taylor was that he was quite paranoid that someone was going to steal a march on him. Mind you, this was a reasonable fear, given that Alun's own march towards publication had been at snail's pace, to put it kindly to Alun. And not very kindly to the average mollusc.

'This Box fellow is making some pretty sweeping assertions about German foreign policy in the post-Bismarck era.'

'Oh my God,' said Alun.

'And I'm told he wants to trace the influence back.'

There was silence from the other end of the phone.

'The editor's a former student of mine,' David explained. Then he lied. 'She tells me Box has another piece in with her already.'

'Then, then I insist on refereeing it,' said Alun, his voice quavering.

'It's already been sent out.'

'Fuck!' exclaimed Alun. Hearing Alun swear David knew this must be hitting home, particularly given the list of asperities Dorkin had proscribed for use in front of undergraduates. Following an informal plenary session, during which Glyn had taken Peter deliberately and gleefully through every possible swear word, Dorkin had ruled that graduates could be expected to tolerate the odd profanity, particularly those graduates whose course of study extended two years and upwards, but the *f* word was most definitely forbidden, and so was *the other one,* even in front of those conducting postdoctoral research.

'Look, I'm not just thinking of you,' said David finding it remarkably easy to lie. 'I'm thinking of the department, Alun. We've got a lot riding on that book of yours.'

'I know.' David could virtually hear the sweat dripping off him.

'So I want you to go for it. Give him no quarter. Blast him out the water, Alun. That way Clare won't dare touch anything else he's written.'

'Absolutely,' said Alun.

'Good man,' said David.

'He's a good man, David,' said Gareth at just about the same time, although he was probably even less sincere. They were sitting on one of the benches outside the Royal Academy, looking up at the statue of Sir Joshua Reynolds, palate ostentatiously in hand and seemingly intent on waltzing with it.

'Won't you be expected back?' Helena asked with a smile. She had been amused to find that Gareth's latest, when she wasn't waiting for Gareth to return, was majoring in History and Gymnastics. It had seemed so very Gareth, that combination: History and Gymnastics. She daren't tell David. But Gareth seemed in no hurry. He displayed no fear that he might be spotted by his interdisciplinary paramour, should she have grown tired of just reading about glossy sex and come looking for it in Piccadilly. Instead he sighed significantly.

'What is it then?' Helena asked. Lunches in the past tended to fall into two categories. Matey or poignant. This was definitely the latter. The matey kind put 'all that' happily in the past whilst admitting, of course, that it had been very important. The poignant spoke of lost opportunity, of Gareth saddled with yet another brainless beauty and of his professional frustrations. The poignant also spoke of losing Helena as the biggest mistake Gareth had ever made but she was sure he had similar conversations elsewhere. She couldn't be the only biggest mistake of his life.

'Well, what's it all about?'

'You know me well,' he began admiringly.

'Oh come on, Gar. Is it Peter Dorkin?'

She was forcing the issue here, not playing by his rules, nor Davy's for that matter. Gareth's preferred method would be to seduce the information from her, tease it out by flattery and earnest looks. Helena felt damned if she was going to go through that kind of charade.

'Well, yes. That is one thing.' Gareth's eyes followed a flight of pigeons that arched across the roofing. 'I had heard a rumour that they're divorcing the chair from the headship. Of course, it would make the post more attractive to someone like David,' he suggested disingenuously.

Helena had already thought what she was going to say to this.

'I'll tell you what I know, providing you tell me if you're applying.'

'I haven't decided,' said Gareth, almost looking at her.

'And I haven't heard anything,' said Helena.

She couldn't help but mischievously enjoy the anti-climax.

'But I may,' Gareth added with significance. 'And, if I do, I need to know if David's putting in for it.'

Helena wanted to ask him why but she was instinctively wary of his answer.

'How did you get to hear about it?' she asked.

'Some friends,' he said. 'In the University. They're quite keen to have me back.'

She was unsure how true this was. 'But you've never worked in Cardiff.'

'In Wales,' he said 'And I want to come back. Back home to Wales.' Helena hadn't been intending to look at Gareth but she did turn round at that point. She had been listening to the traffic's roar on Piccadilly but when she heard it fade into the distance she looked up at him. She could not believe he would say such things. Not Gareth. And she was sure she would know if he was lying. But no, he was looking at her and looking sincere. Slighty foolish too. Gareth pretending to be sincere was a handsome sight. He gave it everything an actor might give because, amongst the many talents that he had squandered, Gareth was an actor. But no, this was real. This was *hiraeth*, the longing for the homeland.

David said it was the Welsh equivalent of mid-life crisis. Suddenly, in middle age, all those boys who have done their damnedest to get away feel the pull of home. They come back and build bungalows near where they were born and then wonder what on earth they've done.

'I've let too many things go that mean a lot to me, Helena.' She felt a bit unnerved by that for the first time in sixteen years. This wasn't his 'biggest mistake of my life' speech. This was real. Helena didn't like it.

'But why are you bothered about David? You've been a Professor for years.'

'But in America.'

'Well, Cardiff will love that. David's just the local candidate.'

'It's important to me. They're going to ask him for his opinion. The departmental morale. Bound to. Helena, you must understand that if I go for it I'm going to give it everything I've got.' He was looking her in the eye.

'Look,' said Helena, suddenly uncomfortable. 'I'm on David's side. I'm married to him.'

'Yes,' said Gareth looking foolishly sincere again. 'The biggest mistake we ever made.'

Helena travelled back on the 125 in a state of some concern. She thought she knew how to handle Gareth but he had got under her guard. She knew he had got under her guard because she was worried now. Up until today she had had absolutely no problem with Gareth. She could even have contemplated his coming to live next door without it upsetting her equilibrium. But now she felt, and strongly she felt it, that she did not want him back. Not in Wales, not in Cardiff and not at the University. The reason for this was simple: she didn't want him back in her life. Up until now there was no chance, not while he was the old Gareth. She'd never let *him* back. But this Gareth, the one with the silly earnest expression on his face, he was worrying.

David met her at the station in the ridiculous red car. Helena was expecting the children too but they were at Crispin and Millie's again.

'Bloody Gareth!' said Davy showing her a rolled up copy of *Radical History*.

'Yes, bloody bloody Gareth,' she agreed.

Millie was in the garden and opening a bottle of wine when the Mosford parents arrived to pick up the Mosford children. It was 7.15, one hour and a quarter after the sun was supposed to have dipped over the whatsit, so why was Crispin looking so censorious?

'So far this week you have opened a bottle of wine every evening,' he had told her. Millie was finding that being at home with Crispin could be a bit of a drag. Millie liked a drink every evening. A drink, not a lot, not a specified amount, but a drink.

'Are you like this at work?' he asked from the kitchen doorway. 'They think so well of you.'

'That's 'cos I'm good at my job,' Millie explained from the patio. 'That's all they care about. They don't care if I'm completely paralytic in the evenings. Which, in case you're going to ask, I'm not.'

Fortunately David and Helena arrived before anything like argument ensued.

'You can come in as long as you're drinking!' was Millie's greeting at the front door.

David had been pleased to find that her attitude to him was unchanged since Saturday night. When he'd arrived at St Dyfrig's to collect Nick and Emma that afternoon she had made a point of coming over and teasing him for sporting his panama on such a domestic occasion. She had even offered to have all four of them to play at her house as he looked so ridiculously out of place collecting children from the school gate. 'You go back and seduce some students,' she'd joked. It was a risqué remark in the circumstances but Millie did seem to behave as if on Saturday night he had paid her a nice but unnecessary compliment. Which in some ways he supposed he had, although that certainly hadn't been his intention.

Nick was watching a video with Jonathan in the front room and Katrin and Emma were having a low-key argument upstairs. It looked as if neither Mosford was going to be ready for a while so the four adults made their way into the garden and three of them took their usual places round the plastic table while Crispin, unable to lean against the kitchen sink, leant against a raised flowerbed.

'Saturday evening was very good,' David told him.

'Thank you,' said Crispin nursing his wine glass.

'You must come to us,' said David.

'Yes, soon,' added Helena but wanting to avoid the next weekend.

'How about next Saturday then?' asked Millie.

'Millie!' Crispin exclaimed as if she had no shame.

'Suits me,' said David.

'We've got that thing on Saturday,' said Helena, embarrassed about mentioning it.

'What thing?' he asked.

'Hooper and Glyn, the CADW man . . .'

'Oh God, yes,' said David. 'Sort of office party thing. Well you must come as well.'

'Is this one of your mammoths?' Millie asked Helena who nodded.

'No we can't gatecrash something you've arranged with colleagues!' said Crispin from the wild geraniums.

'We are not gatecrashing. We are *invited*, Crisp.'

'You'd liven it all up a bit,' David declared.

'How many are coming, Helena?' Crispin asked.

'Ten.'

'Well that's settled. You can't have twelve of us.'

'It is not settled!' Millie put her wine glass down with a bang and a look of annoyance.

'I think we should have this discussion later,' said Crispin quietly.

'And I think we should go,' Davy announced. 'Give you two a chance to fall out properly.'

'You're very welcome to come,' Helena added meekly as they all went back in.

That night David and Helena talked about Gareth while Millie and Crispin talked about David and Helena.

'We don't have to spend every Saturday night with them,' Crispin said.

'Are you jealous?' Millie asked him.

'No.'

'Then why are you being such a pain? Why does everything have to be so safe and dull and *limited*? So bloody cautious, Crisp! So many reasons for not doing things.'

'Emmeline!' said Crispin as if talking to a recalcitrant child. 'You've only been back six days.'

'And already I can see we need a social life. And that's what David and Helena are. They are fun!'

'All right,' said Crispin. 'You go.'

'Me?'

'You go on your own. You want to have fun and I'm a pain in the arse. You go on your own and I'll stay here and then everyone will have a good time.'

Now Millie looked at Crispin as if he was the wayward child. 'Oh Crisp,' she said and she held out her hands to him. 'Don't let's fall out over Dave and Helena.' Crispin took one of her hot warm hands in his and gave her a kiss on the cheek.

'What's happening to us?' he asked with an arm around her shoulder.

Millie put her arms around his waist and gave his ribs a squeeze. 'It's just me. Me and work. Give me a pub to bash about a bit and I'm happy.'

'Mm,' said Crispin looking over her head. 'What a pity we can't have sex.'

'Uh-huh,' said Millie. What a pity it was.

Later that night David and Helena lay wrapped together in bed, sharing an anxious equilibrium. Their arms around each other confirmed an act of solidarity against the threat of Gareth, or rather the two threats of Gareth. What danger he posed to each of them, individually and together.

'I think I like Millie,' said Helena apropos of nothing. 'She's not going to be a great friend of mine but I do like her.'

'Hm,' said David who had had another unproductive sherry with Stella that evening

'She likes you,' Helena added. 'Millie.'

'Mm,' he replied. 'Not that much.'

They could speak of it then.

'No,' said Helena after much thought. 'No, probably not that much. No.' She sighed and turned over. 'Probably a good thing.'

6

Life is Complicated

Tuesday was not a good day. It rained, for a start. Just when everyone was starting to talk of a long hot summer, the Welsh skies opened. Millie stayed in bed till nearly twelve. Davy threw *Guardian Education* in the bin and Crispin got ridiculously wet walking from the school to the bookshop.

Helena bumped into Sue the student in the Llandaff Pharmacy where she was sheltering from the rain and wondering if now was the time to buy sun tan oil for Nick and Emma. The chemists was a small shop divided into two congested aisles by a central display shelf on which hung shower caps, loofahs and plastic sandals. Anything that one might actually want was down the other end which was where Sue and Helena found themselves squeezed together on the narrow apron in front of the till. It wasn't eye contact but the security camera that told Helena she was standing next to Crispin's surprise guest of Saturday night. The black and white monitor, centrally displayed to deter any clandestine loofah-thief, showed Helena this great long mass of dark hair and waxed coating which surrounded a pale white face that was looking abstracted. That was Helena Mosford, she guessed. And next to her a young woman. You could see the difference in age. A young woman with a long thin nose in a cheap but respectable coat trying to edge back a bit and with every shuffle impaling herself even more on the toothbrush display.

'Hello,' said Helena before it had occurred that she might be the very thing from which Sue was trying to edge.

'Oh hello,' said Sue with an awkward smile. She was clutching something in her hand, presumably something to buy, and clutching it more tightly still now. Oh dear, thought Helena, I'm embarrassing her. But why? After giving birth to two children nothing ever seems quite so private ever again. Really she ought to think of something to say.

'Have you known Crispin long?' she asked. Sue smiled back as if Helena had said something that didn't actually require a reply, something bland like 'Rotten day' or 'That's a nice coat, given how little you must have paid for it.' Assuming that her first question had not been properly understood, Helena was about to summon up another from her repertoire of bland things to enquire of young people when the old lady in front backed her plastic mac abruptly from the till and made a space for Helena to move forward.

'After you,' said Helena because she hadn't really decided about sun tan oil.

'Oh no,' said Sue, very anxious that Helena went first.

Poor girl, though Helena. Whatever is it that I mustn't see her buy? What on earth can be *so* embarrassing? And what a relief to be thirty-seven.

David Mosford was in the bad mood that he had known he was going to be in since Monday night's sherry. He had woken up on Tuesday morning knowing he was going to be in it. He had gone to bed on Monday night knowing he was going to be in it. And now he was most definitely in it. In the office, *Megan*. In on time, *Megan*. And most definitely in a *mood*. Knowing the mood was booked for this morning had been no help. He had still thrown *Guardian Education* in the bin at home and would have done the same with Dorkin's copy were it not for the fact that Mrs Oporto already had it open on her desk as he arrived. She had actually got her bloody scissors out and was cutting round the advert as he walked in the bloody door.

Stella's bloody advert for Dorkin's bloody job which should be his bloody job which he was bloody well certain Gareth Box was now applying for. Gareth would never have taken the chair if it meant running the department. Gareth was too bloody selfish to do that but now that Stella had decided to float the professorship free of all administrative responsibility . . . oh, Gareth would certainly go for that.

Stella had told him of her decision last night over sherry.

'We need to get someone in place soon,' she had warned him. 'For the good of the department. But I want to do a wide sweep of the available field.'

'Of course,' he'd replied, trying not to sound terse but hoping she didn't have him in mind as the new Professor's chief factotum.

'I thought you'd be pleased,' she added chasing something briefly round her mouth.

'I am.'

'After all, you yourself said Political History should split the chair and departmental headship. Who knows, you may be the one we're looking for.' Whatever it was Stella had been pursuing round her mouth she now impaled on her tongue – like a chameleon, thought David. And my career is the fly. He very much wanted to tell the Head of School that she could stick her job, that he had decided to take up the chair at Harvard that had been his for the asking several years running. But on the whole it seemed more sensible not to, given that this was total fantasy on his part.

'I shall want your views on all the applicants,' Stella reminded him. 'Whoever comes in will have to take over a first-class department and keep up morale.'

This business about a first-class department was news to David. So was the stuff about departmental morale, something that had, in his opinion, been relentlessly undermined by Dorkin and seriously dented by a young lecturer in mediaeval Welsh who had last year run affairs simultaneously with Hooper and Michael Morgan and brought out the worst in both.

But the Head of HISAR was talking corporate speak here. This was Cardiff University PLC, the best and most profitable institution of higher education in the market place. Well, he would do his best, David had decided, as he drove that car of his home. The more impressive his behaviour now, the more chance he got later, not only at interview but also when the applications came in. He could do a subtle job recommending those who didn't stand a chance. Stella would know that was what he was up to but he would know she would know, so it was up to him to be political and subtle. And political he would be, Megan. And subtle, Megan. Oh yes, subtle he would be. But not with Megan herself. Not first thing Tuesday morning.

'Oh, collecting coupons are you, Meg?' She didn't look up from the paper. 'Or is it air miles today?'

'Professor Dorkin's job,' said Megan with dignity. 'They are advertising Professor Dorkin's job.'

'Yes, I know,' said David resisting the temptation to say he'd been told last night. It would sound so petty to point out to the departmental secretary that he knew before she knew.

'He was a good man,' said Megan.

David didn't feel inclined to disagree. That obviously came from deep inside Big Meg. Whatever Dorkin's faults he had touched the heart and soul of Megan Oporto. 'Oh, Alun Taylor says he wants to see you,' she added casually as if it was no concern of hers who might want to consult Dorkin's temporary replacement. And then she went back to snipping out the advert.

As David walked down the corridor to Alun's room he revolved again in his head the arguments for getting rid of Megan. The problem was, he told himself, that the department had been moulded around the personality of Dorkin and Meg was part of the Dorkin legacy. Any professor who wasn't Dorkin-shaped would have to adapt to her way of doing things. Any professor apart from Gareth Box, of course, who would have Big Meg eating out of his hand within hours. But then that was Gareth. He would go to any lengths. He lacked even the integrity to be irritated by Megan.

David reached Alun's room and prepared his eyes for the darkness inside. Being a furtive creature of the night, Alun Taylor had many years ago fixed heavy drapes to the windows of his little modern office. Every time there was a fire inspector's report they were removed but were usually back up in a week.

In answer to David's knock Alun opened the door half an inch or so and let him in.

'Ah, David. I'm having terrible trouble with this Box piece,' said Alun launching straight in as was his practice. 'Factually there's nothing obvious and the methodology is sound. His conclusions, though unremarkable, are of interest. I really don't know. Are we committed to demolishing him?'

'Bad for the department if we don't,' David admitted. He was sitting on the edge of Alun's desk while the little man paced angrily up and down.

'I mean I hate to attack a fellow historian *ad hominem* but if, as you say, he's got his sights on Bismarck . . .'

'I don't think there's any doubt about it,' David lied. Lying about Gareth was something he found worryingly easy. It was almost as if *Gareth lies* were not lies. Anything was possible with Gareth Box, *ergo* anything one said about him might be true.

'Well, the only thing I can suggest is the amount of unacknowledged material.'

'What do you mean?'

'Well it's petty,' said Alun. Yes, *go on*, thought David. This was no time for Alun Taylor to get scruples about being petty. A man who had built his entire academic career on mean-minded pedantry should not baulk now just when it might finally be of some use.

'Well, I'm almost certain he's failing to acknowledge work that I've read last year. Not claiming it as his own but letting it by as common knowledge. You know the kind of thing. We all do a bit. It's just insufficient footnoting really. The problem is, I'm sure I could pull him up on it but it would make me look a pedantic little fart.'

David hoped that his face gave the impression that this would be a grave, unprecedented and wholly unjustified slur on Dr Alun Taylor.

'On the other hand if this man is seriously setting his sights on the Prince, then we've got to knee-cap him.'

'Absolutely.'

Alun suddenly stopped his ridiculous pacing. 'I've got a thought, you know. I'm sure there's a cove I met in Naples last year. New York man. I could ring him up, sound him about this Box fellow. See if there's anything else. It's a pretty mean trick mind . . .'

David slid off the desk. 'Go to it, that's what I'd say. We've

got a lot riding on your book, Alun. This is not the time to give
any quarter.'

'Right,' said Alun as David moved towards the door. 'Oh, have
you seen the advert?' he asked out of the blue.

'Yes,' said David.

'Haven't had a dekko myself!' Alun laughed. 'But I gather
Stella's finally decided to ditch the admin load. She mentioned
it to me last night.'

David felt his stomach muscles knot.

'One of Stella's chats over sherry?' he asked with phoney
bonhomie.

'In the SCR,' said Alun, blithely unaware of David's mounting
concern. 'Wanted to remind me that I could be the one they're
looking for. Nice of her, wasn't it?'

What was that woman playing at?

When Crispin came back for lunch he was surprised to find that
there *was* lunch. In the kitchen and on the table in fact. And
not just lunch. He was also surprised to find a shelf had been
put up in the very place where a shelf had been going be up
since last November.

'Surprise!' said Millie, holding her electric drill aloft and
indicating the salad that she had personally unwrapped from
several plastic bags. When Crispin had got over his alarm at being
greeted at the door with a power tool, he was genuinely delighted
and down they sat to eat. There were even paper napkins and a
bottle of Ty Nant spring water on the table.

'Is it my birthday?' he asked, as Millie outlined how she
intended to use the rest of the day to put up enough shelves
to store all those kitchen utensils currently growing mould in
the tea chest.

'No,' she replied. 'I'm trying to get round you.'

'As long as you're not planning to convert *this place* into a
fun factory.' Crispin knew Millie was still grumbling about not
having any work to do.

'No. I want to go to David and Helena's on Saturday.'

'Oh,' said Crispin. 'Why?'

'Because it's Fun, Boo.'

'But we've already said No,' Crispin told her.

'No, you've already said No,' she told him back. 'And because I was being a good little wifey I didn't argue in front of them but I want to go.'

'This isn't anything to do with the fact that David kissed you in the loft?' Crispin asked.

'How do you know David kissed me in the loft?'

'You looked kissed,' he replied. 'And David looked very uncomfortable.'

'That's only because I turned him down,' Millie explained, digging, with engaging candour, into the salad. Crispin put down his paper napkin and smoothed it out patiently.

'Emily, isn't this all rather silly?'

'Well, no. I don't think so,' she argued. 'I think it's fun.'

'Look,' said Crispin with a sigh. 'If it's fun you're after, why don't *we* go out on Saturday evening?'

'What?' Millie asked. 'To a restaurant?'

'Yes.'

'You don't like Cardiff restaurants.'

'I don't like gate-crashing the Mosfords' departmental dinner party either.'

Millie leant across the table and planted a great big kiss on Crispin's forehead.

'I love you, you sexy old skeleton,' she told him. 'But *I* choose where we go. No looking sniffy at the wine list, no sneaking a look at your watch half way through and no complaining about the muzak.'

'I shall avert mine ears,' Crispin promised.

Helena was supposed to be helping Emma with her project but Pip had called round for a chat and a little cry about Anders being beastly when she'd rung him at work. Helena felt she should be kind to Pip in the way Sarah had always been kind to her. And taking herself quite literally, Helena therefore looked out the gin bottle. Pip, still in a state, downed hers in one so Helena topped her up and had some more herself, and Pip downed that one almost as fast. All of which meant that when David came home his wife and her pixie friend were no longer entirely sober.

They met in the hallway as Helena took one step towards him

and then another diagonally into the wall. 'Are you all right?' he asked.

'Pip's here. And she's very upset,' said Helena staring, with slow sententiousness, at the frame of an oil painting which was currently two inches from her nose.

'Why's she upset?' David asked, hanging his jacket on the coat stand and still unsure of what was going on.

'Anders is horrible,' whispered Helena.

'We all know that.' David hadn't meant to be joking – he was just confused. But Helena giggled in a most uncharacteristic way. This was all most unlike her.

'I mean,' she said. 'Anders is *being* horrible. Do you know, I think I've got to lie down.'

And with that his wife weaved her way to the stairs. David was just about to try and work out what on earth was happening when Emma ran in from the garden and hugged him.

'Will you go and see how your mother is?' David asked. Packing his daughter off upstairs, he went into the kitchen. Pip was indeed there at the table and looking more normal than Helena although she wasn't her useful chirpy self.

'Hello David,' she said. He noticed the gin bottle on the table in front of her and finally worked out that the rules of the known Universe hadn't changed. They had just shifted sideways, as they are wont to do under the influence of alcohol.

'How are things?' he asked.

'He can be so nice sometimes,' said Pip.

'Well, yes,' said David in the vaguest of all possible agreements. Pip stared at her glass.

'But sometimes it's as if everything I do is wrong. Do you find that?'

David, not entirely sure what he was being asked, stalled.

'It's difficult to say,' he admitted. The funny thing about walking in on this kind of inebriated scene was that although *his* brain was the one that was working properly, he actually felt excluded from a level of profundity which Pip believed she had reached, and which *he* believed she had reached, but which she clearly hadn't.

'He says he loves me.'

'Well I'm sure he does.'

'But men do say that, don't they?'

'Er, yes.' Well it was true they do, David thought. He had said it himself on occasions.

'But he hates Noggin,' said Pip with a sniff.

'Really?' David asked. What a waste. If he had been married to Pip, *Noggin* would certainly have been one of the main attractions. She was a bit of a silly little thing but Noggin, morning, noon and night, would do very nicely. Pip started to cry. 'He doesn't like *any* of the cats.'

Later that evening Helena emerged from a deep slumber to find the children asleep and David banging round in the kitchen. Her husband used a kitchen with all the subtlety of an orangutan reversing a Rolls Royce. However streamlined the machine itself, the current operator was incapable of producing anything out of it more than a few sudden jolts and some very loud thumping noises.

'I'm very sorry,' she said putting her head round the kitchen door. 'I really don't think I have a head for it anymore.'

'I took them for some chips,' David announced, 'Nick and Emma. From the Chinese. Then I gave them a bath. Then I put them to bed.'

'Yes I've just checked.' Helena made her way to where the aspirin were kept.

'I also rang Anders who came and picked up Pip.'

'Thank you,' said Helena.

'And now I've defrosted supper.'

'I won't have anything, thank you,' said Helena cautiously.

'Oh right,' said David in controlled surprise and re-opening the microwave noisily.

'Could you stop banging about?' Helena asked as inoffensively as possible.

'I am not banging about,' he replied pedantically. 'I am doing *Everything*. Or haven't you noticed?'

'Yes, I've noticed,' said Helena pouring herself a glass of very noisy water. 'I'm sorry.'

'No need to apologise,' said David. 'It's just that I have had a busy day.'

'You always have a busy day,' said Helena. Some women have busy days, come home and put the children to bed, she thought.

Some women even cook supper instead of just putting a frozen cottage pie in the microwave and failing to remove it from the cardboard box. Some women do all that every day and yet they don't parade around the kitchen as if they expect a medal. But she didn't say it.

'I had hoped we could discuss Stella Price's advert,' David continued but before he could reproach her further the telephone rang. Helena winced at its raucous noise. David picked it up.

'David Mosford.'

'Er, David . . .!' said a delighted voice. 'David, hello, it's Gareth.'

He stared at the receiver in distaste and then handed it pointedly to Helena.

'It's for you, I think,' he said and marched out. As Davy retired to his office the last words he heard were Helena speaking quietly into the receiver. 'No, not really convenient at the moment.'

On Saturday morning Millie met David outside the Bishop's Tea Rooms. It wasn't surprising. Sooner or later the whole of Llandaff was bound to meet David because Helena kept finding things she hadn't bought for their mammoth dinner party and, since Tuesday's outburst over Gareth, David had been very solicitous about Helena's needs. All of which meant that he had virtually worn his own furrow to and from the High Street that morning. When he and Millie coincided at half past eleven she found him emerging from the deli with a packet of After Dinner Blend and a plastic bag of carbonated water.

'Course you've got this bloody great dinner party tonight, haven't you?' Millie asked when she heard the bottles clink together. 'How's it going?'

They were walking up past the pharmacy.

'One couple have cancelled,' David replied. 'So we're down to ten in total.'

'Oh, that's manageable.'

'You could come instead if you like,' he suggested.

'No thanks. We're going out. Crisp is taking me to a restaurant.'

'Anywhere interesting?'

'I haven't decided yet.' Millie already knew that David had clear ideas about which restaurants were worth going to in Cardiff and she had no wish to be swayed. 'But I was thinking we might try Le Monde – now don't you say anything, Dave.'

'Nothing wrong with Le Monde,' he insisted. 'It's a bit tarty, that's all.'

'Suits me,' said Millie.

'And noisy of course,' he added.

Millie nudged him to shut up. 'You're such a snob, Dave.' They were back on those terms now.

'What about next weekend?' he asked. 'Your turn to come to us?'

'Great,' she replied.

'No problems with Crispin?'

'If Helena's still standing after tonight, we'll be there!'

They parted amicably at Millie's gate.

'Don't forget they do a very reasonable Muscadet sur Lie,' he reminded her. 'But make sure it's sur Lie.'

'Fuck off,' she replied kindly. 'This is me and my chap going out to dinner. You're not going to be there, Dave, even in spirit.'

Walking back across the Green David found himself brooding on Gareth Box. Last night Helena and he had ended up holding on to each other in bed. The need had come upon both of them suddenly. And when his face pressed close to her hair Helena had told him something of her meeting with Gareth in London. Not much, no more than he asked and no more than she felt would reassure him that she was still on his side. But enough for him to be worried. Deep down he had wanted to ask her if she still loved Gareth. It was a simple question. But it had been difficult enough to articulate over the last fifteen years. Why should last night have been any different?

Fifteen years ago he was twenty-five. He had been the young man who had brought Helena Moreton to meet his father in the garden and the old boy had stood up and lifted his metaphorical hat in good decent Welsh gallantry. Fifteen years ago Helena had been twenty-two and very loth to commit herself, even to meeting his parents, after all that had happened. 'Why can't we just have sex?' she had asked by the riverbank. But Davy didn't find it easy to just have sex. He never had. He was in love with her then. He had been in love with her since some time before her finals. Probably he had been in love with her since Gareth introduced them.

It seemed odd to think that once he thought Gareth his friend, was pleased to be recruited by this rising Welsh star of the academic scene.

'You and me, David. You and me,' Gareth would say. 'We'll take the place by storm.'

David shuddered. Surely no-one believed anything Gareth said? Not then, not now. But no-one challenged him either. That was the problem. He found himself back on the Green, not far from good old Archdeacon Ridley. It was the *presumption* of Gareth Box that angered him so. The presumption that this rookie Welsh graduate, arriving in Oxford after London University, would automatically seek the support of Gareth Box.

David didn't mind that Gareth claimed academic precedence because he was in the final year of a senior scholarship. It was his presumption of moral superiority that was so galling, just because his father had been a miner and died from 'the dust' whilst Davy was from middle class Llandaff stock. So Gareth was born with a silver cliché in his mouth but it shouldn't somehow make David less Welsh for having had a pleasant, happy childhood surrounded by books, and people who read them. Why should that exclude him from the moral vanguard when it was time to storm those English citadels? To be Welsh could be a useful disadvantage politically. But Gareth clearly felt he had the advantage of greater disadvantages still. He was Welsh and *poor*. Welsh and *nonconformist*. Welsh and *Labour party, General Strike, father dead of silicosis*. All that stuff. And he made no secret of it. Secret? He promulgated the fact. It was virtually his chat up line.

'You'll like Oxford,' Gareth had said, 'if you like women.'

'Oh, we had some of those in London,' David had replied. This was on the occasion of their first meeting and however much he'd taken to this fellow Jesus man, he was determined not to be his foil.

'But the English girls *here*. They believe anything you say,' Gareth had laughed. 'And I mean anything.' And he was right.

You are talking about *my wife*, David thought. He had been standing still for some time and was feeling all the old angers

rise, primitive, black and violent. Then across the green he saw
the statuesque figure of Sarah John giving her garden gate a
hearty slam to.

Entrapment by Sarah could take several hours off your life.

*'Now, never mind about all these dinner parties, David, what about
you two having a break? I know a nice B&B in Carmarthen with twin
beds and community hymn-singing in the park.'*

As Sarah John set off in search of old dears David Mosford
diverted his eyes and made his escape.

When he arrived in the kitchen Helena was on the phone.
David's hackles rose but he said nothing. Helena shook her
head so that he'd know. She could tell, by the way his bag of
bottles went down on the table, what her husband suspected:
Gareth.

There was no point his getting in a state just because Hooper's
wife was cancelling.

'What?' said David as Helena came off the phone.

'That's Mike Hooper, Pat and the Glyns now.'

'What the hell's wrong with Hoop?' David looked angry.
Helena began to say it sounded like a sort of flu but he wasn't
listening. 'Why can't he do something useful, like be ill when
he's supposed to be teaching? Do us all a favour!'

Helena looked at him the way she did when he had one of
these outbursts.

'Sorry,' he said. 'How many are we down to?'

'Six still coming so that's eight of us all together.'

'Dangerously close to cosy,' said David.

'Well, do you want to invite anyone else?' Helena asked
hopelessly. 'There's plenty of food.'

David sat down.

'Penny and John, I suppose, but they've got a baby now.'

'They could bring the baby,' she suggested.

David shook his head. 'It'll wake up,' he explained.

'Not necessarily while you're talking.'

'Pippa and *Anders*?' David suggested. 'She's always good
fun.'

'Well, I don't know,' said Helena. 'I don't think they're getting
on at the moment.'

But David was warming to the idea of Pippa.

'No, my understanding was that this whole tearful business was just a result of him kicking Crumpet.'

'Who?'

'The cat. They call it Crumpet.'

'Noggin,' Helena pointed out. But David was already on the phone. Pippa Arnstein worked hard at making it clear that she and Anders had been going out with some friends that evening but something had come up and now they weren't and so, in principle, it was possible but she'd have to check. However once Pippa had found Anders the news came straight back that they'd be delighted.

'Right,' said David to Helena. 'Seating plan!' Things were definitely looking up.

Katie John was at Millie's house early that night which meant that Millie and Crispin were at Le Monde ahead of themselves. On such a bright sunny evening the place was virtually empty. Its black and silver decor sparkled and echoed for all the world like the site of some bacchanalia for which the pagans had been unavoidably delayed.

'Is it always like this?' Millie asked Simon, the manager. He squinted, unperturbed, at the sunshine, still visible beyond the black shutters. 'Give them another hour I'd say. It's always late when the sun's out.'

'Got the place to ourselves, then,' said Millie to Crispin as they sat down. Crispin was wearing a cord jacket and he seemed to find it difficult to move his arms inside such an unfamiliar item of clothing. She laughed fondly to see how he kept checking that his sleeve wasn't lying in anything. Crispin looked up.

'Um, you look very nice,' he said with a little smile, rather as if he felt he should make such a rejoinder from time to time. As it happened, Millie did feel she looked good. She had spent the afternoon in Pontcanna with Katrin and they had been very girly trying things on. What was purchased was something in black which wasn't really Millie's colour but it hid everything that should be hidden wonderfully and even emphasised a few things she'd forgotten she had. Katrin had been disappointed by lack of frills, lace and complete absence of pink but Millie felt that she was perfectly packaged. She could take on the world in a dress like this.

Back in Ty Escob, Helena's choice of clothes was not making her at all happy. The only thing that seemed suitable and not hugely overfamiliar was a classic Laura Ashley dress that David had considered matronly.

Well thirty-seven is a matronly age, thought Helena and she glared at him for that remark. After another ten minutes in the dressing room she emerged in a blouse and skirt combination about which David said nothing, nothing at all, because it was very sensible attire. But not much else.

Pippa was not dressed sensibly although she had eschewed her Green in favour of something that did more than justice to her legs. David accepted a kiss from her and a bottle from Anders and then followed her legs down the hallway, exchanging words with Anders very much on automatic pilot.

Everyone who hadn't gone down with something dreadful had just about arrived, been offered drinks and given a view of Pip's legs in the drawing room, when the telephone rang. Helena looked at David who looked at Helena. The phone was becoming a matter of some contention between them at the moment.

'We are having dinner,' said David pointedly as he got up to it.

Closing the door on Pippa's laugh he was preparing himself to kill dead that tone of phoney bonhomie in Gareth's voice when he found himself being addressed in Welsh. David spoke enough for social occasions but once he agreed he was indeed 'Dr Mosford is it?' he shifted the conversation to English.

The woman at the other end of the telephone sounded less comfortable in that language but she persevered. She was sorry to ring at such short notice but a discussion programme that was being made on Sunday had just lost one of its speakers with this dreadful lurgi that was going round, wasn't it? And his name had been suggested. Did he know anything about Wales and Socialism between the Wars? From anyone but an independent TV company David would not have taken that at all well but probably this earnest girl had only that afternoon come off shooting a twelve-part Welsh language children's drama and now she was landed with setting up and directing tomorrow's studio discussion. The television scene in Cardiff had become so busy since the inception of a Welsh Fourth Channel that many people went straight from college to writing and producing their own TV series and hardly paused to draw breath thereafter.

'Yes I do know quite a bit about the period,' said Davy, 'but I'm afraid I don't broadcast in Welsh.' Then he went, tactfully, into Welsh to explain that his grasp of the language was insufficient to make his points with professional clarity.

'Oh well,' said the woman who still hadn't divulged her name. 'Oh well, it's an English language programme, you see now. We're making it for the BBC in London. Independently.'

'It's going out on national television?' David asked, suddenly much more interested.

'Oh yes, next Friday.'

David wished Millie could be there to tease him about his total volte-face. He went back into the drawing room as happy as if she had been.

In Le Monde things were hotting up with an influx of underdressed, overtanned young people and Crispin was having difficulty hearing himself think, let alone talk. Millie was enjoying herself in all the noise and she'd ordered another bottle of the Muscadet. *Sur* or off the *lie*, she didn't care. Crispin had made his two glasses last. He'd also spent the quieter part of their evening talking to Millie about provisions for Jonathan and Katrin, Parental Responsibility Agreements and wills.

'We don't need wills, do we?' Millie had asked, gazing at the happy melee of new arrivals and listening to the beat. 'I mean what's mine is yours and theirs.'

'It's not that simple if we're not married,' Crispin had insisted. Millie turned back to look at him.

'In the event of our splitting up the house is legally equally mine, you know. Because we're not married. If we're married the courts would apportion it according to how much we've each contributed.'

Millie was surprised.

'Oh *that's* why you won't marry me!' she laughed.

Crispin furrowed his brow and Millie stopped laughing. Didn't he know she was joking?

'I *asked* you, Millie. On two occasions. Once when you were pregnant with Jon. Once after Katrin was born.'

'Well,' said Millie, trying to lighten the atmosphere, 'if I ever change my mind I'll let you know.'

'Have you?' Crispin asked. For him it was not a joking matter. 'Have you changed your mind?'

Millie didn't reply. 'You are going to wear me out,' she said leaning forward and stroking his beard. 'Eventually. You worry so much.' Crispin was about to say that life had a habit of getting complicated if you didn't worry a bit but Millie wasn't listening. 'You're free,' said Millie. 'I'm free.'

'There are the children,' he reminded her.

'Oh Christ, Crisp!' she entreated him. 'My parents stayed together *for the children*. My Dad gave up happiness *for the children*. It's no reason.'

'Not that I'd ever act on that,' he assured her, solemnly pursuing his own agenda.

'On what?'

'On the letter of the law.' He looked so serious. 'I wouldn't want to see you have to sell up and dispossess the children just to pay me off.' Millie felt very fond of Crispin at that moment and she leaned across to stroke his cheek again.

'Oh Crisp, it isn't going to come to that,' she assured him.

Crispin was silent. Then he smiled and told Millie, once again, how nice she looked.

David was enjoying dinner. Anders was no substitute for Glyn so the badinage was not all it could be but Pippa was certainly a good substitute for Glyn's wife, who at the age of forty-seven was doing an open university degree and very keen to talk to lecturers. Glyn, not surprisingly, was having nothing to do with this and consequently she often made a bee-line for David. Relieved not to be talking shop after all, David was letting Anders Arnstein and Stephen Lucey tease him about his forthcoming TV appearance.

'Three minutes of fame,' said Anders rhetorically. 'What can you do except draw attention to yourself and leave the subject matter totally obscured?'

'That's not true,' Helena put in but Anders was an ocean liner when it came to conversation. It took him hours to get going and took even longer to stop.

'Tell me one historical truth that can be communicated in three minutes, David.'

'Well, Japan surrendered in 1945,' said David. 'That took about three seconds I think.'

'That is not a historical truth,' Anders insisted waving a slow finger. 'That is a fact.'

Helena tried again. 'Yes, but how can we build up an impression of the truth if we don't allow for the role of facts?' Anders continued to ignore her.

'You are telling me, David, that *Japan surrendered in 1945* is actually worth saying?' he asked.

'It's certainly worth saying if you're on a South Pacific island and some old soldier comes out of the jungle whirling a bloody big yataghan at you,' David replied. 'And it's generally worth saying if no-one has heard it said before. And if we don't say these things eventually they won't get heard. Not every true thing has to be profound.'

'But Truth *itself* is profound,' Anders contended for all the room to hear. From where she was sitting Helena reckoned this was so much posturing on his part.

'It can be both simple and profound, yes,' said David.

'And can you really communicate a profound truth in three minutes? And *really* do justice to it?'

David was aware that people were looking at him.

'No,' he said taking a gulp from his wine glass. 'But I can raise a bloody good question in three minutes and then they can come to Cardiff for three years to find out the answer.'

'Advertising!' said Anders grandly. 'So what you are doing really is advertising the University when you appear on television.'

'And himself,' chimed in Stephen.

'But also *ideas*,' David replied. 'I'm advertising the possibility that there are ideas to discuss.'

'Now advertising I can understand!' Anders laughed and he

turned to the rest of the table as if a great and salient point had been made.

'Dessert,' said Helena helpfully.

What a strange man, David thought, and what a curious alliance to be married to Pippa. He had been watching her purring at all the attention she was getting from an Arts Council bore. Pippa Arnstein responded to men rather as cats sometimes do, rubbing her metaphorical head against their metaphorical legs. Whilst she was chatting to David she had expressed delight at most things that he said and her green eyes had positively glistened. Earlier in the evening she had given the CADW man every reason to believe that marketing Welsh ruins was the sexiest job ever and she had positively glowed with interest when her partner at the table turned out to have a hand in the Welsh Arts Council's accounts.

'Oh you're so lucky!' Pippa trilled.

David enjoyed watching her at work. Pippa did something in finance herself but really she should have sold, or run a dating agency. She would make every male client feel he was the best thing to have ever walked in off the street. How on earth did she come to be married to the prematurely middle-aged Finn who, having made his contribution from the other side of the table, had now fallen back into a characteristic, brooding silence? Earlier in the evening Anders had let Helena try to bring him out, but he had only emerged in little unconnected pieces. Fragments of conversation emerged sluggishly as Anders kept one eye on Pippa. But anyone would have to work hard to assemble these gobbets into anything resembling a discourse.

They were now on to dessert, an opportunity for David to palm her away from the audit man.

'Pippa, what is it *exactly* that you do?' he asked. She turned to him with the same delight in her dark green eyes that had greeted him at the door and had not diminished all evening.

'Do?' she asked.

'Apart from looking wonderful, of course.'

David enjoyed saying that. There weren't too many women of his acquaintance who would let him get away with such dubious chivalry. Certainly not at work, not in the land of the midnight Dork. Pippa's eyes sparkled. She had told him several times before but her relationship to men didn't run as far as censure and so she told him again without rebuke.

'I work for Seattle Credit.'

'And what do you do with them?'

'Oh,' she said, as if she thought he really didn't want to know this but she would tell him again because she always aimed to please. 'Oh I suppose I run checks on creditworthiness.'

'Really?' It did sound a very grown up job for fluffy little Pip.

'And make reports, that kind of thing.'

'What, on people or companies?'

'Both.'

'Over here or in . . .' Davy was begining to formulate a thought. 'In Ver—?'

'Sorry?

'In Ver—. *Virtually Anywhere*,' he stumbled, 'say America, for instance?'

'Oh. Anywhere in the world,' said Pippa as if it was fun.

'And can anyone check through you? I mean if say the University was appointing a new *Head of School* for example. They could check to make sure she hasn't run up debts outside Britain.'

'Oh yes.' Now this *did* sound fun. 'We mainly work for big organisations, and for our parent company, but no, anyone can do it,' she smiled. 'Even you.'

David laughed. 'Sounds *great* fun,' he said.

'But it is expensive.'

David poured Pip another glass of Beaumes de Venise. 'How much would it cost, say I was going to recommend this facility to the University, how much would it cost to run checks on, say, eight candidates?'

'UK or non resident?'

'Well,' David was cautious here, 'let's say, for sake of argument, UK and USA.'

'I think it would work out expensive,' said Pippa, looking earnest, looking so very very nice but also looking evasive.

'I tell you what,' said David. 'Can you give me a demonstration some time and then I can go back to the college and talk to them about it properly.'

'A demonstration?' Pippa seemed to be wondering whether he was just spinning her a line here. She was quite ready to laugh but uncertain whether she should.

'Just one check so we can see how it works. We can use me as the guinea pig if you like.' He threw that in hoping to lead her off the scent.

'Oh, I don't know. I'd rather not run something on you and Helena,' said Pippa, looking ravishingly compromised.

'OK,' said David. 'There's a colleague of mine, Gareth. I'll check he doesn't mind.'

'Well . . .' Pippa did look tempted, not because there was anything in it for her but because here was a man who very much wanted something, and it was in her power to give that something, and it came naturally to her to want to please such men. 'Well, I suppose if it was in the lunch-time, I could show you how it's done. Show you what comes up. I couldn't write up a report.'

'But I'd get an idea of how detailed the search is. I mean if Gareth owed thousands in Hong Kong or Alaska – which I'm sure he doesn't – but you'd spot it?'

'Oh yes,' said Pippa happily.

'Splendid. What day shall we say?'

Pippa shrugged. She was a little thrown by his enthusiasm but happy to be of service. 'Monday?' she asked.

'Monday it is.' He took a sip from his glass. 'Now tell me, how *are* all those cats?'

When Millie and Crispin got back at one in the morning Katie was asleep on their sofa and someone who must be the boyfriend was sitting in a chair opposite, watching her from the depths of his hooded anorak.

'I am um – most frightfully sorry,' said Crispin, trying to find some money.

'It's OK, no problem,' he replied, standing blearily.

'Oh Christ! You should've gone to bed!' Millie announced from where she was hanging up her jacket. 'There's plenty of spare rooms up there. We wouldn't have minded.'

Crispin gave Millie a look which was intended to signify that they shouldn't intrude on such personal arrangements.

It was the kind of subtle gesture that she was quite incapable of recognising.

'You shouldn't have stayed up,' she repeated to poor Katie who was now waking and looking terribly, terribly young.

'Oh it's no problem,' said Katie in a little voice that was hardly her own. Crispin dug out two five pound notes.

'You should have gone to bed!' Millie ploughed on. 'We really wouldn't have minded.'

'Oh,' said Katie, looking as if she wasn't really at all embarrassed. 'It's OK. No problem.'

Crispin added a third fiver to the money he was offering Katie in the hope that it might cover all the sexual harassment she was getting from Millie.

'Oh, some lady dropped this in,' said the boyfriend, picking up a package. Millie looked at it.

'It's Sue for you,' she said to Crispin, handing over something book-shaped with neat writing on the envelope.

'Oh yes,' he said. 'I'll, um, take it up.'

'Goodnight,' said Katie and the boyfriend.

Crispin was a while in his blessed study. In fact so long that Millie not only got undressed but actually put her clothes away for a change. Bending down to the chest of drawers, she was struck by the sight of her bottom in the full length mirror opposite. Millie normally only saw herself in that mirror by design as she took her clothes off. That great slab of tanned and untanned bottom did loom very big in the mirror. In fact it looked horribly like her mother's bottom. It was a disturbing sight that bottom. It even put Millie off a bit. *Diet*, she thought. *Diet Cola* from now on.

'Went rather well,' said David, taking off his jacket. Helena was looking at the trolley in a distracted sort of way.

'Went rather well,' he repeated.

'Yes . . .' she agreed. David crossed the room and put his arms round Helena's waist. He had begun to hope that a pattern might emerge for their Saturday nights. It was certainly the evening that Helena tended to be most interested in sex.

'I'll just go and check on Nick,' she told him. David looked into her face. Check on Nick? Nick was fine. What did she mean?

'See if he's all right.'

'What's the matter?' he asked and holding her tighter. She must know that an evening spent with Pippa would quicken anyone's enthusiasm for sex. Mind you, Helena had spent an evening with Anders which could well have the opposite effect.

'I just want to check on Nick,' she replied.

'Nick's fine,' he told her. 'What's the matter?'

Helena broke away from the embrace. 'I'm sorry,' she said. David felt confused.

'You were keen last weekend,' he reminded her.

'Yes,' she said. 'Well that was then.'

'Well then, what is it? Is it because Crispin wasn't here tonight? Or because I spent too long talking to Pip?'

She really didn't want to pursue this conversation. This was territory they didn't discuss.

'Is it Gareth?' he asked casually.

Helena felt stung by that. She didn't know if it was Gareth but Gareth was linked. She had found herself thinking about him during the meal. That phone call David had had from the TV-company had been the start of it. She had thought it was Gareth and was relieved to find her instinct palpably no longer worked. But the things that he'd said at their last meeting had started to invade her thoughts. During the meal she hadn't been able to get him out of her mind.

'It *is* Gareth?' David asked. He felt stung by the significance of her silence. It would have been funny if Helena seemed to need the stimulus of a chat with Crispin to get into bed these days, funny if she was jealous, finally, of Pip after all the silly women he'd paid court to harmlessly over the years. But this wasn't funny. Not Gareth.

'No, not like that,' said Helena. 'I'm just bothered about him coming into our lives again.'

'Me too,' said David moving towards her and kissing her neck in a gesture of sexual solidarity. 'But is that any reason—?'

'There doesn't have to be a reason!'

This was Helena's view. Her refutation of Freud. Sex was to do with feeling. Reason didn't apply. You cannot argue someone into bed with you. You cannot persuade them to be relaxed. It was an old point of contention between Helena and Sigmund, Helena and David. Once uttered her assertion re-established an old gulf between them.

'OK. All right,' said David stepping back from her, and from the brink. They were both silent for a while and then Helena began stacking the most valuable glasses on the trolley.

'I'll do that,' David sighed. 'You go and check on Nick.'

She thanked him and went quickly upstairs. David stared at the table with its empty glasses and guttered wax. Gareth Box. This had to be settled by *any* means. He wasn't going to have Gareth walk in after all these years and spoil everyone's lives. They were worth more than that. Maybe he would have to find out how much Gareth was worth after all.

7

Career Developments

Sunday morning broke with every promise of yet another hot day. David was up ridiculously early. Despite last night there seemed to be such a *point* to everything. He was actually dressed and walking round the garden by seven o'clock. This morning, he thought to himself, I am going to be on television. He could imagine his father over there on the lawn glowing with fondness and pride. Well, why not? As Millie says, we only pass this way once. Why not enjoy it? Why not put on your best clothes and drive down in the ridiculous car and be made to feel extremely important by people who have no idea who you are? It was silly, it was fun and it couldn't have come at a better time as regards nabbing the Chair of Political History.

But while you're at it, he thought, why not go and do the washing up from last night so that Helena isn't left at the kitchen sink all day? David hung his jacket on a coatstand in the hall, found an apron, rolled up his sleeves and set about being Wonderful. After a while Nick teetered past the kitchen door, drinking from his beaker cup and going in search of television programmes.

David's 'Morning Nick!' drew no response other than a baleful look. By this time six cut-glass red wine goblets had been washed and left polished on the drainer. Before David had done all ten, Emma came swooping in like a little bird, her dressing gown fluttering like feathers.

'Is it true you're going to be on telly?' she asked excitedly. David agreed it was.

'When?'

'Most of today,' he replied.

'All day?!' Emma's eyes widened. This was *wonderful* news.

'No,' said David laughing. 'It'll take all day to record. It usually does. I won't actually be on till next Friday.'

'Can I come?' she asked, all aglow. 'Please?'

'It's very boring,' said David. Emma said she wouldn't mind and promised that she'd be ever so good and not make a sound. David felt torn so he agreed they'd ask Helena. Helena wasn't sure. 'Is it a good idea?' she asked, drinking the tea that David and Emma had brought up on a tray.

'Oh, *please*,' said Emma again.

'Won't the production company mind?'

David shook his head. 'This director woman said that if childcare was a problem . . .'

'It isn't a *problem*,' Helena pointed out. 'I do it all the time.'

'Please,' Emma asked doing a little dance. Helena looked at her daughter.

'You might be terribly bored, sweetheart. It is boring, isn't it?' she asked David.

'Very boring,' he agreed. 'Apart from the thirty seconds I'm on.'

David and Helena looked at each other, undecided.

'*Please*,' said Emma. 'I'll let Nick play with my Barbies.'

So Emma won the day and she went down to the docks in David's little red car and tried to help him find the studio which used to be in one place but had relocated to a giant shed on East Moors. It wasn't an auspicious start to the day but they did make it in time for the enormous continental breakfast which was laid out on trestles all down one side of the studio. Nobody seemed to be particularly interested in who David was, or who Emma was for that matter, and the only person who actually recognised him was Bernie the caterer.

'*Hello again*,' he said warmly. 'Don't tell me, last time wasn't it that chat show you know, you and the other bald guy from the Poly? Not that I'm one to talk!'

Big Bernie ran a hand over his shaven scalp. He was beginning to place David now.

'And the girl interviewing you was ... you know, the ginger-haired one who had that affair with the pop star.'

'Ah yes,' said David. He remembered now. *Wales, the Future of Its History: part of a millennial discussion on the concept of nationhood.* Or as it was known to the public, Two Bald Gits and The Guitarist's Girlfriend.

'Dr Mosford,' said an extremely tall blonde English woman who was clearly in a hurry. 'I'm Jane. Can I take you to make-up?' Emma nearly dropped her croissant.

'All part of the fun,' said Davy.

Breakfast in the Kemp/Williams household was usually a staggered affair at weekends. Crispin had his immediately after emerging from his study, but with no appetite for grilled anything after the accounts of immolation, branding and mutilation he had just been revisiting. Millie had hers three hours later in front of the TV. In between Jonathan came downstairs, just long enough to grab a box of cereal, a spoon and return upstairs to his bedroom, and Katrin came down to wander round the kitchen complaining that her favourite Weetos were missing. Crispin and his daughter were supposed to be talking that morning about why some people married and others didn't but Katrin was now much more concerned with the missing cereal and she stalked upstairs in order to kick Jonathan's door.

By 11.30, when Millie finally emerged into the garden wearing Crispin's dressing gown, he had done a very good job bagging up all the rubbish from the garden and loft. Millie was talking on the portable phone to Chiswick Harry who seemed to have some news for her.

'Course I could do it,' she said. 'Don't *worry*. If you'd let me choose my own team I could have the decorators in in three weeks.' By this time Millie had wandered over to where Crispin was taking a rest and started stroking his head. He hoped this meant work. Millie needed work to be happy. And Crispin needed Millie to be happy. 'Let me have a look at it,' said Millie squinting up at the sun which was clearly limbering up for a really hot Summer after all. 'OK. No problem. See you.'

She put down the aerial and in reply to Crispin's question agreed that it did sound like good news. There was a pub in London that they might be able to pull forward and the guy who usually did south of the Thames was on a month's holiday. 'Harry's panicking,' said Millie. 'And that means he needs Me. I may have to go up. Is that OK? D'you think there's anywhere round here I could sunbathe?'

This was all rather a lot for Crispin to catch up on.

'Um, well. We're south-facing, aren't we?' He checked the sky. 'I thought you'd get the sun all day.'

'I thought I might give the neighbours a shock,' Millie joked.

'Emmeline, this is Llandaff,' Crispin warned her. 'Not the South of France.'

'Tell you what,' said Millie. 'You go and get me a nice long drink and I'll see if I can rig up something discreet out here.' Rigging up was Millie's term for a barricade of deckchairs and windbreaks which meant that she didn't have to, as she put it, sunbathe with her vest on.

Crispin looked dubious.

'It's not just the neighbours, you know. You've got to think of Jonathan. He is ten.'

'Uhuh,' said Millie, idly pulling the head off a rather promising flower. 'So everyone keeps telling me. Hey, how about that trip to Barry?'

'Barry Island?' Crispin's face couldn't help but remind Millie that he didn't think much of funfairs.

'It's the day for it,' said Millie suddenly enthusiastic and looking up at the empty sky. 'OK. All right. How about *I* take the kids? Give you an afternoon off. You can sit inside and read some of your horrible books. What d'you think?'

'Very kind of you,' said Cripsin.

'Uhuh,' said Millie picking up a sun-bleached deckchair. 'Ah sure am!'

Crispin went inside. He was pleased to see that Millie had got a new toy and some of her old friends to play with again.

By lunch time Emma was very bored and about to show it. Twice now David had seen the video clips they were going to be discussing: retired miners talking about the rise of fascism, fighting Franco and the betrayal of the left. The director, whose name he still hadn't gleaned, came in and explained to him that she was keen to have someone who would challenge the left-wing consensus in the valleys.

'And that's my role?' David asked.

'Balance, isn't it, you know,' said the director looking at her watch. They had been there three hours now and nothing had really happened, mainly because the executive producer's train was stuck in the Severn Tunnel. David overheard a camera man muttering that London ought to let them get on and make the show on their own.

Poor little Emma sat on the floor having read all the children's Sunday sections and eaten all the chocolate biscuits that had come round at coffee time.

'Dad, I'm bored,' she finally said. David picked her up and put her on his lap.

'You're not the only one.'

Suddenly the big metal doors swung open with an alarming flash of summer sunshine. The entire studio looked up hopefully into the light. But it was only Bernie.

'Lunch is ready when you are!' he called cheerily.

That afternoon Helena took Nick for a walk to the Castle grounds where it was too hot to sit comfortably. Nick asked if he could go to Scallywags, the inflatable children's fun complex which lived permanently in the Memorial Hall these days. Helena felt she should indulge him as Emma was off having fun at the TV studio, although she feared Emma might demand reparations if Nick turned out to have had more fun than her. It was the first day of the year on which she had not worn tights. The air on her legs was very welcome, so was the Sunday stillness of Llandaff High Street. Half way down they bumped into Sue the student who looked no more happy to see Helena today than she had in the chemists.

'Hello!' said Helena nevertheless.

'Oh hello,' Sue replied without enthusiasm.

'Visiting Crispin?' Helena asked.

'No,' said Sue. She seemed to be taking the view that Helena was accusing her of something.

'Lovely day!' Helena replied in the hope of ending this conversation on a pleasant note.

'Yes,' agreed Sue with what was almost a smile, but not quite.

'Can we go?' demanded Nick, to Helena's great relief.

At about one-thirty in the afternoon, the Severn Tunnel – which had been clinging on vindictively to a very important BBC producer from London (and two hundred other passengers) – finally decided to let him go on with his journey. The man arrived just over half an hour later in a very bad mood and could barely find time to shake hands.

'We've got to get on,' he announced to the director as if she were at fault for not having personally dug him out three hours earlier. He then sat at the back of the darkened control room drinking orange juice by the carton and grumbling about not having the budget to over-run.

The presenter was, fortunately, flawless and after one rehearsal everyone was ready to record his introduction and go into the first clip.

'Thank Christ for bloody professionals,' muttered the producer whose name seemed to be Keith. From his position by the monitors David could see that the director hadn't taken that remark at all well and that she was building up to have a real go at him. He was quite pleased to be ushered out into the studio itself.

'Hello *David*,' said the presenter. 'We're going to have to get a bit of a ding dong going here. All right if I give you a hard time?'

'I haven't said anything yet!' David joked. He looked around for Emma but she had been given a video screen to play on in the little office and was now far too happy drawing pictures to actually turn up and watch her father in the studio.

When Millie and the children got back, later that afternoon, Crispin was setting tea on the kitchen table. 'You are wonderful,' she said giving him a kiss and some horrible cuddly thing that they'd won.

'Your mother phoned,' he told her. 'To remind you—'

Millie pulled a face.

'To remind you that they're coming down next Friday.'

'Oh no!' Mille exclaimed.

'It is on the calendar,' Crispin pointed out.

'Well they can't,' said Millie. 'We're going out to David and Helena's next Saturday.'

'Emmeline . . .' said Crispin.

'Yes we are.'

'Well you ring them and explain,' Crispin insisted with a sigh.

'Oh please, Crisp, you know how they bring me down,' Millie moaned.

'*I'll* ring Gran,' Katrin interjected, happy to be important.

'Oh bless you Bunny,' said Millie heading for the stairs.

'Can I ring Gran?' Katrin asked.

'No,' said Crispin. He really did feel Millie's family should be her responsibility but she had already disappeared.

'Doesn't Mum like Gran?' asked Jonathan, surprising everyone by being in the same conversation.

'Mum likes Gran,' Crispin explained. 'She just likes David and Helena better.'

'Why?'

'Ah well,' said Crispin. That was a long story.

David and Emma didn't get back till 7pm. Helena was going to ask how it all went but Emma was immediately sick, a result of the nausea induced by staring for too long at a VDU screen and of the indigestion arising from several seafood sandwiches and a whole packet of chocolate biscuits, at least.

David was in quite a good mood however.

'I think I was on the longest,' he told Helena as she wiped her daughter's mouth. 'Difficult to tell but the cameras were on me more than anyone, apart from Vincent, of course. Mind you, you never know how they're going to edit these things down.'

Helena was trying to get Emma to sit on the lavatory.

'The producer was very nice afterwards,' David continued from where he was standing in the hall. 'Thinks I should be on TV more. Said I should go and see him in London.'

Seated on the lavatory Emma started to heave again.

'He's doing a thing on right- and left-wing historians and would like me in it.'

Helena just got her daughter to the sink in time.

'Oh, this one isn't going out on Friday after all. I thought that was a bit tight.' David paused at the sound of violent retching. 'Is everything all right in there?'

Later that evening upstairs Helena got the full story. How Keith the producer had seen an opening in Continuing Education's output and was trying to pull together a discussion on contemporary perspectives in history.

'He reckons I'm the only half sane academic he's met who could put the right-wing perspective,' said David as he watched Helena pull back the covers.

She looked at him sceptically.

'Well, I think it's really good news,' David insisted. '*Oh come on*! I could be on telly two weeks running if I'm lucky.'

'But as a right-wing historian.'

'Yes.'

'Which you're not.'

'I am by Cardiff standards.'

Helena began stripping the bed. 'But David, the television audience aren't going to be judging you by Peter Dorkin's yardstick. They'll see you as an apologist for all those people who claim that Hitler was misunderstood.'

He didn't like it when Helena got all hard-line and unnecessary like this. The telephone rang in the kitchen below.

'I thought you'd be pleased,' he muttered. The telephone rang louder. It seemed to ring in a very Gareth Box kind of way. David saw Helena stop and her eyes move in its direction.

'Is that him?' he asked.

'I don't know,' she replied.

'Perhaps you should answer it,' David suggested, feeling doubly hard done by now. Helena refused to be made to feel guilty for answering the telephone.

'Do you object to me speaking to Gareth?' she asked.

'No.'

Helena picked up the washing basket. 'Right then,' she said.

'I just object to your *arranging* to speak to him,' David added.

This pedantry was pointless and petty but she had started. Helena put down the basket.

'I do not arrange to speak to him. I have not *arranged* to speak to him.'

'When he rings, you tell him when he should ring back.'

'When he rings, if he rings, and you're being impossible – I ask him to ring back at a time when you're not being impossible,' she explained. 'Or when it's *possible* you're not being impossible!' The telephone was still ringing away downstairs. They were at an impasse.

'Do you object to my speaking to Gareth?' she reiterated.

'No,' he repeated.

'Right then!' Helena picked up the basket. The telephone stopped.

Sadly the telephone call which David and Helena never received would not have been from Gareth at all but from Millie Kemp who had just come off the phone from Harry of Chiswick. It seemed that Selwyn wanted Millie in London next weekend to get this fucking stupid pub fucker underway.

'Emergency conference, all day Sunday,' said Harry wearily. 'Selwyn says, can you give it the once-over beforehand?'

Millie was delighted. 'I'll go up back end of the week,' she offered.

'No, don't.' Harry was very definite. 'Don't. They've no idea we've got anything planned at the moment. There's some delicate talking to be done. Selwyn's going to take care of that during the week.'

Millie twiddled the flex and laughed quietly at that idea. She loved the image of Selwyn talking delicately to anyone. 'Can I go in on Saturday evening then? Have a nose?' she asked.

'Sure,' said Harry. 'Saturday evening's fine.'

Crispin said Saturday should be fine too. He could have the children all weekend if Millie had to go up to London Saturday afternoon. And Saturday really suited Millie, particularly because it meant her parents couldn't come down and make her thoroughly depressed.

'I could take the kids if you like,' she offered.

'And fill them up with junk food? And lose them in Oxford

Street?' Crispin felt that a weekend in London with an easily distracted working mother could prove disastrous for his children.

'We could all go?' she suggested.

'Millie, if I'm going to be looking after the children while you work I'd rather do it here. You go and stay with Gail.'

Millie had liked that idea. She hadn't stayed with Gail for ages. The only sadness was going to be missing dinner at David and Helena's. But there you go.

'They're out,' she said finally putting the phone down. 'Never mind, Boo. This could all be very good news.'

Yes, indeed, thought Crispin but he couldn't help asking when they might finish the kitchen and convert the garage.

'Oh we can do that any time,' Millie explained. Which was in fact exactly what she said ten months ago when they moved in. Back to normal, thought Crispin.

Helena's friend Pip was something of a paradox for David. Arriving in Oxford after London he had been surprised to find so many silly, apparently brainless, girls whose whole three-year raison d'être was boys. For David, who had not applied to Oxford or Cambridge, it was galling to see how flappers, like Pip, and charlatans, like Gareth, were everywhere, happily wasting their time and talents. But eventually he had come to realise that most of these girls had had a good enough brain when they arrived. And that when most of them left to marry someone in the city – or a prospective Tory MP – that brain was still intact, if not exactly overextended. What was odd was that eighteen months ago the Mosfords had found themselves contacted by one of these girls in Cardiff. Pippa had got Helena's name through the Oxford Society and was delighted to track down a fellow emigrée. But girls like Pippa did not end up in South Wales. Girls like Pippa did not marry men like Anders for that matter.

Surely not.

Although David Mosford mounted the steps to Seattle Credit in a spirit of true enquiry, he was not seeking to discover the real Mrs Arnstein beneath the fluff. He had his sights on the dodgy truth about Professor Box.

It was a hot day on St Mary's Street and taking the lift would have been a better idea but Davy was impatient and so he jogged up the last three flights of narrow stairs. This was not a sensible thing to do. He was still red-faced and perspiring when the receptionist ushered him into Pippa's office where she sat spraying perfume on her wrist. This action he noticed even before he took in her eyes (green and sparkling still) her jumper (fluffy) (still) and the poster on the wall (three of the sweetest, most enormous, kittens). Pippa gave every impression of being delighted to see David and closed the door discreetly behind him.

'Oh David,' she said. 'Thank you for a lovely evening on Saturday.'

David told her that it had been their pleasure.

'This is for Helena,' said Pip, passing over an expensive-looking card with a smile. David thanked her as he settled himself down in an expensive leather chair. Behind Pippa he could see two TV screens with rows and rows of compound numbers in coded jumble. Both displays were meaningless but maybe amongst all those figures was the number of the beast himself. David wondered whether he would be able to recognise the evil that was Gareth Box just by looking at them.

'And this is for you,' said Pippa. She slid across the desk another envelope, this time emblazoned with the logo Seattle Credit. Pippa didn't withdraw her hand from the envelope. It rested there, small and fragrant.

'Have you run the check already?' David asked, finding himself reluctant to actually touch the envelope wherein might lurk the dark soul of Professor Box.

'Better,' said Pip. 'I went to see Myron, our director, this morning and he gave me this for you.'

'What is it?' David asked.

'It's something we give all prospective clients,' Pippa explained and she pushed it further towards him. 'It's beautifully illustrated and it gives you an example of every kind of query we can answer. Myron thought it would be of much more use than running a sample check.'

'Oh,' said David. Did this mean Myron had said no to a freebie?

He made a show of opening the envelope and browsing the large booklet within.

'Very interesting,' he said for want of something better.

'Yes,' said Pippa with a smile.

'I would like to see though – I mean if it's not too much trouble.'

At this point some tea arrived in two mugs decorated with kitten motifs. Pippa was effusively grateful to the secretary and before David could make his request again, her face became ashenfaced and serious.

'Do you want to know what happened here this morning?' she asked, holding her mug before her. 'One of my colleagues was investigating an account in one of the Arab countries and she came across sundry debits enforced by the state.'

'Oh really?' said David, wondering where this was leading. 'Fines?'

'You might think so,' said Pippa looking devastatingly serious. In fact she seemed to have lost her fluffiness entirely. 'Actually they were hospital bills. Debts enforced by the state to cover the cost of amputation. Now the kind of thing that *I* have to calculate,' she explained and not giving him time to digest this information, 'is whether, given the regime, whether that amputation – be it hand, ear, nose or foot – was for financial irregularity or dissident activity.'

David felt rather sick. 'You mean that while running a credit check you can discover that someone had had their hand or ear chopped off?'

'Oh yes,' Pippa nodded. 'And the nature of the crime affects their credit rating, you see.' She smiled. 'That's my job. To assess that.'

'Good God,' said David and he put down his mug of tea. He had imagined this clean little office in the centre of lovely scruffy Cardiff might give him an insight into the wickedness of Gareth Box, not a hotline into hell.

'One of my colleagues actually did some work for the American Government,' Pippa continued with that same look of exaggerated concern which she might extend to a pussy with furballs. 'He was able to discover that one of their top local men had been executed. Certain countries charge for the bullets, you see.'

'And some of that gets on to computer?' David asked. Pippa nodded again. He was losing his enthusiasm for this game. On a scale of one to ten, what Gareth Box was doing to the Mosford family didn't really register when you thought about what went on elsewhere in the world.

'And I think today,' Pippa told him, 'if it's all right with you, I think that we haven't really got time today to do the kind of demonstration you were hoping for.'

'No, no I don't suppose you have.'

'But do read the brochure,' she insisted, taking a serious sip from her kitten mug. 'It's beautifully illustrated and it covers just about everything you need to know but if there are any questions . . .' she smiled at him. 'Do come back to me.'

David left Seattle Credit far less resolved than when he went in and not feeling too happy about himself either. He felt rebuked. Had Pippa seen through him? There was something worryingly implacable underneath all that fluff.

Later that afternoon, when David was passing Alun Taylor's office, the little man leapt out and grabbed him.

'I think we've got it!'

David had absolutely no idea what Alun was talking about. The Award for Least Offensive Male Dominated Department Within The University? The opportunity to bid for a postage stamp that Bismarck had once licked and whose prestigious spittle was currently on sale to all interested academic institutions.

'Box!' said Alun, beckoning Davy inside the darkened pit of his office. 'On *two* occasions last year editors of journals he contributed to in the States had to publish corrections.' As ever Alun was launching straight in, leaving David both to try and pick up the threads and to find himself a chair in all this stygian gloom. 'On one occasion he had failed to use some term like Native Americans of Hispanic descent, you know the kind of thing.' Now Alun was pacing excitedly. 'But on the *other* he had misattributed or omitted the footnotes for source material. Do you see?'

'So what are you suggesting?' David asked.

'I have written this.' Alun brandished a letter on departmental paper. Davy looked at it, as best he could under the Anglepoise lamp. What he saw was Professor Box being taken to task for two minor misattributions and one complete omission in his recent lengthy piece about German Foreign Policy (1898–1914).

Furthermore, the author of this letter considered that *Radical History* should beware of using scholars who have a track record of making such lamentable errors and omissions. The author then quoted Box corrections that had had to be published on two occasions in recent American publications. Finally, beneath the strange signature of Alun B. Taylor, read the explicit statement, spelt out in harsh capital letters, that this letter was FOR PUBLICATION.

Well, they were the kind of mistakes that anyone could make. And did. Mistakes that did no-one any harm. But the letter was a much graver kind of mistake. This was the kind of letter that did no-one any favours. Not Box, not Taylor nor the institution from which Dr Taylor would be sending it. It was the kind of letter that David, as temporary acting head of department, should strongly advise Alun not to send. And it was certainly the kind of letter that Alun would never normally have written had not David, *as* acting temporary head of department, wound him up to such a pitch of precious indignation. David thought about debits for amputation in a far-off land.

'Very good,' he said but he handed it back without enthusiasm.

It was also the kind of letter over which Stella Price would, quite legitimately, hit the roof. It would harm Alun's chances greatly. His own somewhat. But, *and this had to be taken into consideration*, it would also have a devastating effect on Gareth. Not only would Professor Box be seen as an unreliable beacon when it came to attracting much-needed attention to the department, but that department had already shown that his arrival would be the occasion for a lot of bad feeling. In both directions.

'So do you think I should send it? I mean do I come out of it all right?' Alun asked. David wondered about that. He also wondered about the Gareth Box who misattributed references and research. That was forgivable. What was less forgivable was misattributing other people's jobs and misappropriating their wives. But did he deserve this? The Gareth Box who told David Oxford girls were easy, the Box who kicked Helena out three weeks before her finals, the Box who told David that Helena had always liked him when it wasn't true, who rang Helena up the night before their wedding and told her it was all a mistake and asked her to marry him instead. Did he deserve this?

'Send it,' said David. 'Think of The Prince. Bismarck is what matters.'

He went back to Dorkin's office, feeling a complete and utter heel. Fortunately Megan wasn't there. After two minutes checking the timetable to make sure he wasn't due anywhere important, and Dorkin's diary to check that Dorkin's deputy wasn't due anywhere stupid, David decided to take some marking home. He had had enough of this. Then half way home he decided to call in on Millie instead. Maybe she was there . . . maybe he could do with cheering up.

Millie had had a good morning. By the time she had surfaced the post had brought plans of the pub in South London. She could have some fun playing with these. There was also a panicky note from Harry which just reiterated everything he had told her on the phone but asking her to ring him as soon as the plans were actually in front of her. This she had done for ten minutes, lying in the bath with the portable phone.

'What's that noise?' asked Harry. 'It sounds like water.'

'It is water,' she replied.

'Oh.'

'I'm having a bath,' Millie explained, trying not to giggle. She just knew how Harry would feel about that.

'This is *serious* Millie,' Harry warned her.

'I can be serious in the bath,' she replied.

Millie then went on to tell Harry all that he wanted to know about the current state of the building and its likely potential. From time to time she leaned over the edge to check a detail on the bathmat but mostly she was fluent. She could almost hear Harry realising with relief that she had taken it all in after all.

That conversation was enough for Millie to be able to leave Harry happy for the rest of his difficult day. The norm was that people enjoyed Millie's relaxed approach to work until they started to worry that she hadn't grasped the enormity of the problem. Then they usually challenged her. And that was when they found that she really had taken it all in. That was when Millie's relaxed approach really came into its own.

There was nothing that Harry liked better than knowing that Millie was on top of a problem that scared the shit out of him.

After the bath Millie had borrowed Crispin's old paisley dressing gown and taken her breakfast into the back garden. Then she read a few bits of the newspaper and soon it was time for lunch. Crisp was working over at Halls again so there was no point in getting lunch properly.

She helped herself to an apple and a tub of ice cream from the freezer. The apple was officially her diet. Millie could only diet by adding to her menu. Subtraction was just too unpleasant and made the whole business of eating a bore.

After lunch Crispin called by to say that he wanted to go to the University Library so would Millie collect the children at 3.30?

'Uhuh,' she said from the depths of the hammock in which he'd found her. Crispin went inside and came back with an alarm clock which he set for 3.15 and put on the coffee table below.

'It's not that I don't trust you,' he said.

By two o'clock the sun was very hot and Millie decided to do some serious sunbathing. Her tanning oils were still out from Sunday and it wasn't difficult to reconstruct the barrier of tables, chairs and windbreaks. As she crawled inside and discarded Crispin's dressing gown Millie felt for all the world as though she was sunbathing inside a defensive corral of Zulu shields and was about as relaxed. She took a while rubbing in the sun tan oil then pulled on her sun-glasses and settled down. She lay on her back for a while but Crispin had so got to her with his fear of the neighbours that she turned over on to her front. If some guy in the lane with a periscope caught sight of her bum that was his fault for standing tip-toe on the garden wall. Millie refused to think of the size of the bum in question that would greet any Welsh Peeping Tomos. Maybe her bottom was bigger than it ought to be but very soon it was going to be very, very brown.

In her mind Millie was still turning over the drawings that Harry had sent her when she heard a noise. It was little more than a stirring in the air but it was the kind of imprecise, semi-silent rustle that betokens a footfall. Someone had moved in the vicinity.

For David Mosford, standing in what he thought was an empty

garden, it was a shock to see Millie poke her head up over the windbreak. But not so much of a shock as realising that the tanned cleavage just coming into view was not *just* a cleavage but as yet undisclosed inches of unrestrained flesh.

'Oh hello!' said Millie and then she gathered Crispin's dressing gown around her in a deliberate way. She didn't fall to the ground and thrash about in embarrassment until she'd somehow penetrated every fold and recess. She just sat there and dressed. The result of which was that David had a very clear sensation of the woman he fancied, sitting not twelve feet away, unclothed, behind a very makeshift screen. And not caring a damn about it. Her physical ease with being unclothed in the same garden as him (albeit on an occasion when he was clothed and she was behind the garden furniture) had a significant impact on David Mosford.

Up until that moment he had been balancing several difficult concerns in his mind. He was still coming to terms with the death of Dorkin, he was worried about getting the chair for himself, and worried that Gareth might seize it from him. He was also worried about Helena – for very good reasons – about the children for no particular reason and he was feeling pretty bad about leading little Alun Taylor down the paths of vituperation. Furthermore he was still musing on Helena's anger over the ethics of adopting a deliberate right-wing stance for BBC Television. But the moment that Millie sat up and David realised there was only an ancient mildewed deckchair between his loins and her nakedness he was converted, totally, to lust. Bereavement in all its complex forms, professional anxiety, marital problems, Truth and the ethics of popularisation, even a father's routine concern for his own offspring, and a husband's deep sense of his own unworthiness, all these things went completely by the board. If *his* hands could touch *her* skin and explore the wondrous curves in which that skin was formed he would be completely happy and if he couldn't there would be no point. To anything.

From Millie's point of view David was taking this whole *potentially extremely embarrassing to the likes of Crispin* thing very much in his stride. But then she was used to working on a building site. If men were not actually whistling they were probably not aroused.

'Hi,' said David in a voice that came from nowhere. It didn't sound like him. But then this was the first word spoken by the new Mosford. The new streamlined version, the version who only had one thought on his mind, and that a purely biological one. No wonder he sounded a bit different.

Millie laughed, pulled the dressing gown round her and got up.

'Like some tea?' she asked walking over in a matey sort of way. David did the best grunt he could manage, given that he was recovering from a recent, and pretty fundamental, sea change. For today a new and very basic imperative had come into effect. Nature had decided Dr Mosford must have full sexual intercourse with this woman as soon as possible. But if that wasn't possible, perhaps after tea and biscuits.

They sat in the kitchen talking but David found his mind kept wandering. To the folds of her dressing gown, to the freckles he could detect on her wrist, to the creases around her eyes (which, though deeper than Helena's, were somehow easier to forgive). Millie was being very sensible, very much like a normal person. She wasn't teasing him or flirting. That afternoon it was very much one Llandaff parent talking to another over a cup of tea, except that one of them was all but naked and the other bent on penetration.

David noticed her fingers. They were short and the nails were flat like a man's. The skin on the side of one nail was cracked and open for half an inch. He wanted to kiss it that cracked skin and then he wanted that finger to run all the way down his back and then . . .

'Sorry?' he replied to something Millie said.

'Oh, I was just saying that we won't be able to come to you on Saturday after all. I'm up in London.'

'Oh, that's a shame,' said David, realising that his plan to take Millie into the garden late at night and ravish her in amongst his father's rhododendrons would have to be postponed. It wasn't a plan he had hitherto formulated. In fact he wasn't sure they actually *had* rhododendrons. The scenario had sprung into his mind perversely at the moment that he discovered it would not be possible.

'I'll probably be stuck in some bog-awful London pub all

evening on my own!' Millie joked. 'I suppose you could have Crispin round. No reason why you three shouldn't enjoy yourselves.'

'*I'm* in London . . . on Saturday,' said David out of the blue. It wasn't easy for him to articulate complex sentences like that with Millie sitting opposite but he had to try.

'Really?' Millie asked.

'I'm seeing this producer, from the TV. About a TV programme . . . He's er . . . He's the producer of it . . .'

God, it was difficult to talk when the thing you most want in the world is just arm's length away, wrapped in a tatty old dressing gown and every time she moves you think of what's underneath. David realised Millie was looking at him in a slightly disbelieving way.

'Same programme as last week?'

'No,' said David. 'Different programme. But same producer. Keith Something. He said to go and see him next time I was in London.'

'Which is Saturday?'

'Well Friday. But I've got some work at the British Library Saturday morning.'

'I thought we were coming to dinner Saturday?'

'Well yes, I was coming back then. After, you know.'

David had thought he was doing rather well, inventing the work, planning how he would turn up in Bloomsbury and spend a few useful hours there marking and filling in his expenses before tracking down Millie and her pub.

'I . . . um . . . thought we could, y'know . . .' He detested the habit of saying *y'know* when clearly one doesn't have the foggiest. Had he been brought to this? And so quickly.

'I mean I could hang on, help you with your research, chaperone you or whatever you need in London pubs these days.'

'I can handle myself,' said Millie. But she said it with a smile and the smile was sympathetic.

'Oh I'm sure you can,' said David. 'I think I thought you could look after me actually.' Joking seemed to be the best way to extricate himself out of this one. Millie laughed. It was a kind kind of laugh.

'OK. If you want to.'

'I think it would be very interesting to, er, see one of your pubs beforehand,' David explained. 'I can compare and contrast at a later stage, can't I?'

Oh come on, thought Millie. We're not actually talking pubs here. Nevertheless she quite liked the idea of having David along, providing he understood that nothing had changed since that time in the loft when she'd turned him down.

'What about Helena? Will she mind?'

'I'm often in London.'

'But not with me,' Millie pointed out. Put on the spot, David became a bit embarrassed.

'We're only going to a pub together,' he reminded her.

'Uhuh,' said Millie. 'Long as you're sure of that. I mean, like, as long as it's worth your while staying on in London just to look at a pub with me.'

'Oh no,' David replied, recovering some of his composure. 'I believe there are some very interesting pubs in London.'

'Oh *yeah*,' said Millie with a grin. 'Fascinating.'

So that was it. Back at the house David went straight into his billiard room office and rang Design Block at TV Centre. He got through to the inevitable answerphone. The entire BBC was usually away from its desk these days. The cool, calm woman on the machine told him that if he wished to leave a message for Keith, Patrice or Anita he should speak after the tone. *'If you wish to get back to the switchboard: Press Zero. Now. If you wish your call to camp on to an available member of the History team: Press Button One. Now. If you wish to send a fax—'*

'Oh for Christ's sake,' David muttered but the answerphone was droning on with its own self-important verbiage. If he had rung to order a copy of the brochure that accompanied the series they were currently being reprinted and please to leave an address with postcode and credit card number. If he wished to register an interest in the advisory panel . . . This Patrice or Anita woman had clearly gone into the BBC hoping for a career as an on-air announcer.

'If you are just ringing up to arrange a bogus alibi . . .' said David, mimicking her air of self-importance, *'please press your erogenous zones against the receiver. Now.'*

'Hello?' said a voice. It was Keith. Christ! How much had he heard?

Five minutes later and a conversation at total cross purposes, because Keith thought David was that *other* David at first, the deal was done. Keith had a 6.30 screening so David was booked in at 5pm.

'Look forward to it,' said Keith.

'So will I,' said David. Yes he would. He would be *so much* looking forward to it.

On Thursday Helena finally had the phone call from Gareth that had been threatening to come all week. Of course, it came when she was least expecting it.

'Helena,' said the voice as she wrapped a towel round herself. 'It's Gareth. Is this a good time?'

It wasn't a good time in as much as Helena rarely took baths during the day. And that the pleasure of doing so made her feel so guilty that, when the phone rang, she'd leapt out and run to the bedroom, convinced that it was one of the children injured at school or David dying at the wheel of his little red car.

But no, it was Gareth Box.

Wet and steaming, Helena clambered into the Mosfords' carved and heavily upholstered bed.

'No,' she said. 'Not really. I'm collecting the children shortly.' Helena still kept up the fiction that it was the children's needs rather than David's hostility that made it difficult for her to speak to him.

'I'm in Cardiff,' Gareth announced. Helena nearly yelped. How could Gareth possibly be in Cardiff and she not have noticed? She should have been able to tell.

'Will you have lunch with me tomorrow?'

'When's tomorrow?'

'Friday.'

She hadn't thought about this. She hadn't been expecting Gareth to just turn up, particularly when David was going to be away. She really wasn't happy about this.

'Have you applied for the Chair?' she asked. It seemed suddenly important to know.

'Does that make a difference?' he asked.

'Yes, it does,' she replied.

'Has David?' he asked. The truth of the matter was she didn't know. He had been in the billiard room a lot this week but he had hardly talked to her about the job at all. She didn't even know when the closing date was.

'Look, Gareth,' she said and her voice was not the calm maternal voice of a thirty-seven-year-old woman who has put all that behind her. It was the voice of that Helena Moreton of seventeen years ago, the one who used to say 'Look, Gareth' in that particularly unimpressive way and who was now saying it again now.

'Look, if you and David are both going to be in for this, you've got to know I'm on his side.'

Gareth was silent for a moment as he digested her reply. His voice, when he spoke again, was quieter and gentler still.

'I'm only asking you to have lunch with me.' He sounded *so* reasonable, Helena couldn't see what the problem was. Lunch in a public place with a man who meant nothing to her. That was fine. The only arguments against were if David were against it, or if Gareth did mean something to her still. The former was likely. Was the latter? She did hope not.

'Ring me tomorrow morning,' she said and she wanted to put the phone down straight away.

'What time?' she heard him ask, his voice getting quieter and gentler by the minute. The assignation trap again. Him and her against the world. She would not be lured into it.

'Give me your number. I'll ring you,' Helena told him.

That afternoon at the school gate Crispin noticed that Helena looked as if she had spent a long time in a hot bath. She was still slightly damp about the hair and her face was pink. She also looked preoccupied while waiting for the children. He mentioned this to Millie when cooking the children's supper.

'Don't think things are too good with her and Dave,' said Millie.

'Really?' Crispin hadn't got that impression. It wasn't *that* kind of preoccupied look. He knew *that* kind of look. He knew how that look feels on the inside.

'You should invite her round here,' said Millie. 'While I'm in London.'

'Oh, I don't know,' said Crispin

'Why not?'

'Well, um . . .' Crispin was at a loss. 'She may have other arrangements.'

'She'll be putting Emma and Nick to bed, Crisp! How can she have other arrangements?'

Millie was not going to be gainsayed.' You two get on really well. So do the kids. It makes sense while Dave and me are in London.'

'I would feel embarrassed,' said Crispin, and he used the word in a very precise way. 'I would feel embarrassed presuming on Helena for yet another weekend.'

'Your problem, Crisp, is that you are miles too easily embarrassed.' Millie picked up the portable phone which was lying beside her. 'You go out looking for problems, for reasons not to do things.'

'No!' said Crispin as she pressed the buttons.

'Don't be stupid,' Millie replied and she had connected before he could think of anything else to say. Crispin, in acute discomfort, went up to his study.

'*Hi, is that Helena?*'

When he came down ten minutes later, Millie was very pleased with herself.

'She really likes the idea. She wasn't looking forward to being on her own and she's actually invited you over there, with the kids as it's their turn.'

'Is it?' Crispin asked.

'Some of us are counting even if you're not!' Millie poked him with the unretracted aerial. 'I think you should be grateful, Boo.'

The next morning Helena and Millie actually met walking their children in. Crispin had been out late after supper. Or late by his standards. From time to time he talked to a group of theology students at St Michael's College about his research although Millie could not believe these apprenctice vicars wanted to hear all that sick stuff that Crispin was into.

'We went on for a drink,' Crispin mumbled as he got into bed.

'It's half eleven,' said Millie in surprise.

'Two drinks,' he agreed.

Millie laughed. 'Oh Boo Boo, are you a little bit drunk?'

'Just tired.'

'Well, we've got a cure for that,' said Millie, making to clamber on top of him.

'It's all right,' said Crispin.

'Don't be daft,' said Millie, pulling up his night shirt.

'No, Millie,' said Crispin.

'Why not?' she asked finding his hands on her wrists and struggling to loose them. 'Why not then?'

'I'm *tired*,' said Crispin trying to turn over. Millie tugged up as much of his clothing as she could and aimed to kiss his stomach.

'Stop it, Millie,' said Crispin.

'Just a little nibble,' she insisted, knowing best and working her way down.

'No! Oh for goodness sake!' Crispin pushed her off him and Millie fell sideways. She was shocked. As was he. He could see the look in her face, illuminated by the street lighting. Her face shocked, her body fallen at a strange angle and tangled up in the bedclothes.

'There have to be times,' he told her. 'Times when No can mean that.' Millie slowly pulled the duvet up around her, covering her nakedness. Her eyes were still shocked.

'You don't know when you're well off,' she said finding her voice at last.

'I do,' said Crispin. 'I am very lucky to have you. It's just that tonight I am *tired*.'

And to prove it Crispin turned over to go to sleep. He didn't manage it immediately. For a while he could feel Millie's anger rising in the room as she threw aside the bedclothes, pulled on a T-shirt and then threw herself into a chair. Perhaps she got back into bed eventually but Crispin didn't notice. He slept surprisingly deeply and actually overslept his usual 5 am start. He was still asleep in fact when Millie, very resentfully, found herself awake at 7am. So it was Jonathan and Katrin's mother who, most unusually, took them into school that morning. But Millie, being Millie, had rallied by the time she found herself at the crossing with Helena.

'How's Dave?' she asked.

'Gone to London already. He's very excited.'

'About London?' Millie asked.

'Oh, about meeting this producer. And about going to this pub with you.'

The lollipop man waved them over. Katrin and Emma did their usual running up the drive and disappearing act leaving Jonathan scuffing behind slowly in the hope of meeting some mates and Nick holding on to Helena's hand.

'You know, um,' Millie felt herself sounding foolishly like Crispin. 'You know, er, Dave's . . . quite safe with me.' This was something she really felt she should say. And walking alongside each other up the drive to St Dyfrig's seemed a good and suitably insignificant place to say it.

'Oh,' said Helena, stopping and checking Millie's face and then moving on when she'd got the gist. 'Oh no. Don't worry about *that*!' And then she smiled. 'Yes I'm sure he's safe,' she said.

Helena's was a sad smile but Millie found herself smiling too. Sure it was daft getting bothered about her and Dave staying in London for a night. They weren't even going to be bedding down in the same postcode.

'And I'm sure you're OK with Crispin,' Millie added.

'Oh yes,' Helena agreed, and she laughed. For her the subject of Crispin was clearly a less problematic one. 'Oh yes,' said Helena. 'He looks like the kind who'll take no for an answer.'

But Helena wasn't laughing when she met Gareth in Garlands Coffee House later that day. She felt far from happy. As if to make herself less happy still she was concerned that she hadn't *actually* asked David how he felt about her going out to lunch with Gareth. He had disappeared hurriedly after breakfast because he wanted to call in at the University en route to the station. It wasn't until she heard the ridiculous car reverse and drive off that Helena remembered she had been going to broach the subject. They could have spoken about it last night but David had been unusually difficult, ever since this London thing came up.

Gareth was already sitting at a corner table in Garlands. In the mock-Viennese decor of the coffee house he looked like a fin de siècle poet. But of course. With his lock of hair falling forward he was the archetypal pseudo Viennese poet in a pseudo Viennese coffee house. Helena knew that Gareth would have preferred some wine bar. Here the tables were too close together, the staff were too cheerful and the menu didn't run to champagne. But she had to admire his equanimity in these surroundings. David would have made it clear he was not comfortable without a wine list and he would have thrown up his hands in horror at the serried lines of tooled leather spines that were impersonating a two-dimensional bookcase. Gareth, however, made it clear that wherever Helena was he wished to be. She was his favourite venue. *The old smoothie.*

'You look wonderful,' he said, standing as she approached the table. This was something that David did, she remembered. Something that David's father did too. It was supposed to be an English custom but it always felt very Welsh to Helena.

'And this is the second time you haven't been late,' she pointed out. They sat down.

'The place hasn't changed,' Gareth said simply.

'Cardiff? Garlands? Or are you referring to the fish dish?' she asked.

'Wales,' he said and his accent was suddenly very pronounced.

'Oh stop that, Gareth.' She really could be quite harsh with his sentimentality. These feelings surprised her. 'I'm English, remember. It doesn't wash with me.'

'You've no idea,' he said. 'What it means to be back.'

'No, I haven't. All it means to me is that I'm living further from my family than I want to, amongst people I don't know, in a house that we took on because it fell into our laps.'

'I thought you liked living in Cardiff,' he replied, passing her a menu.

'We live a life that has been determined by the fact that David's parents died when he was looking for a better job and everything seemed to point here. Just a salad, please.'

Gareth absorbed all this and tried to attract the attention of a jolly round waiter who was involved in some horseplay at the till.

'So,' said Helena putting down her menu, 'please don't talk to me about Wales. Let's talk about what we've come here to talk about.'

Was this a council of war or were they in fact on the same

side? Oh dear, she was sounding very strident again. Why was she being so hard on him?

'OK,' he said. 'Let's talk.'

'You first,' she told him, giving nothing away.

So he did. And when Helena came out of Garlands the situation was, if anything, one to make her yet more unhappy.

8 ∫

Getting Off

David Mosford had a routine when in London. Usually he would stay at the Oxford and Cambridge Club where he would always feel an outsider, but a comfortable outsider nonetheless. Then he would choose a restaurant in St James's for the evening and window shop either side of Piccadilly before taking tea somewhere smartish. This was being 'out for the day' as Davy's father called it. On such occasions he carried the old man around with him in his head showing him things, reminding him of places they 'd been together, pointing out places they would never visit together now.

Old Mr Mosford was never a member of any London club and rarely had he travelled to the capital without Davy's mother. But once or twice David and his Dad had been out to dinner in the West End like a pair of gents. As Welshmen they did not feel any compunction about going into the smartest restaurants, or the most expensive shops and ordering what the hell they liked. But they never felt they belonged either.

'You see, there are only two classes in Wales,' old Mr Mosford had once explained to Helena. 'Peasants and Doctors. We don't quite understand the English class system with all its substratae and social distinctions. You all look the same to us, isn't that right, Davy?'

David smiled at the memory. His father had charmed Helena

in a way that he couldn't and never would. This was a man of the old Welsh school. Clever, accomplished, courteous, curious, yet devoid of any real ambition. A man who could have done more but who limited his horizons, happy in the confidence that comes from knowing his own world very well. He was not a man given to displays of wit or learning, a man whose very antitype was Gareth Box. Was Gareth a Welshman of the new school? And what kind of school was that? Davy wondered. *History and Archaeology*? God, and our cunning, preserve us from that.

And it was in pursuit of such preservation that David was having to go over to the BBC in White City. A very ungentlemanly pursuit indeed. But of course the BBC was also a cover for his pursuit of Millie Kemp. It therefore had to be done.

As the taxi lurched from log-jam to log-jam, on its tedious way through Holland Park, David thought about Millie. The prospect of unbuttoning her clothing and unleashing the full wonder of that chest was currently obsessing him, obsessing him to the exclusion of much else, and yet it was beginning to bore him too, like one of those memory tape loops that plays too often. Already he was also thinking of Helena and her weary sanction. He knew this was not what she had meant. He knew that this was putting their friendship with Crispin at risk. Presuming Millie told Crispin and he told Helena, of course. Perhaps it could all be left ambiguous. Perhaps Helena wouldn't need to know, just as she wasn't supposed to know about Lyn from Leeds.

'*Yes?*' said the woman on reception as Davy approached in tandem with two enormous bikers. The boys in leather were in no great hurry so he identified himself ahead of them.

'David Mosford. I'm looking for Keith Brabant. He's in the Design Block.'

'David who?' asked the woman. She was one of those dragons the BBC hired for their total unflappability rather than their charm.

'Mosford,' said David. The woman consulted a long list of names before her.

'There's no David Mosford here,' she explained in a weary but satisfied way.

'No *I'm* David Mosford,' he explained ... 'I'm looking for Keith Brabant.' The unflappable basilisk returned to her list of names without any indication of amusement, embarrassment or irritation.

'Keith Brabant?' she checked.

'Yes.'

'He's in Design Block,' she told him, satisfied that her duties were now fully discharged.

'But can you tell me where Design Block is?' asked David.

The Dragon stifled a sigh. 'Do you want me to ring his PA?' she challenged, making it sound as though she was being so sorely pressed she might actually contemplate this rash act, just to get rid of him. David expressed his enthusiasm and gratitude for such an undertaking without sounding, he hoped, too ironic.

'Take a seat,' he was told.

Becoming famous was not fun. David reminded himself of this fact several times as he looked at the display boards featuring a Summer of Sport on BBC2. Then he watched the sunlight stream down endlessly through two storeys of dusty window. Endless sun, endless wait, endless murmuring of forgotten visitors wondering when their turn would come. 'David Mostyn!' called the voice of his tormentor and she held up a scorched telephone receiver in her talons.

Interestingly, the very nice, rather hesitant PA on the other end also seemed to be under the misapprehension that his name was Mostyn but she was, nevertheless, quite sure that Mr Brabant was keen to see him.

'The only thing is, he's got to go to a screening this afternoon.'

'Yes, I know that,' said David.

'But he says could he meet you in Red Assembly before the screening. If you're free now.'

David decided not to ask the young woman what she thought he was doing in London at 5pm on a Friday afternoon. He simply asked where Red Assembly was.

'Oh,' said the PA at a complete loss. 'Um, I'm only here for today.'

'Don't worry,' said David. The Dragon would know and he would risk being fried by her breath as she pointed him in the right direction.

Red Assembly was a blue-collar coffee bar full of under-paid

ethnic minorities and presided over by a trio of noisy matrons who
seemed to have been hired for the express purpose of providing
cockney repartee. They laughed noisily as they served and cashed
up and cleared the little plastic tables, so loudly in fact that most
customers felt as if they were intruding on a private party.

'Hello, Dr Mosford,' said Keith Brabant sitting himself down
suddenly out of the blue. Away from the terrors of three hours
in the Severn Tunnel, the producer of Sunday's débâcle was
a much calmer and more confident man. He wasn't going
to have a coffee or tea as he had to be at a screening
at 6.30.

'Did Kate tell you that?'

'Yes she did,' said David with a smile.

'So . . . you're doing some other show today, are you?' Keith
asked. 'I hope you didn't come up specially.'

'Not at all,' David lied.

'I thought you were very good last weekend,' said Keith.

'Thank you.'

'The other two were awful. Fortunately Vincent is such a
trouper he really pulled the whole thing together.'

David was pleased that Keith thought him a cut above the
average Welsh studio guest but this was flattery, not the leg up
he'd been hoping for

'That director girl was a bit hysterical,' Keith continued. 'Have
you worked with her much?'

Davy was beginning to realise that his patron had totally
forgotten their career-development conversation in Cardiff. He
seemed to be under the impression that he, Mosford, was already
on television a lot.

Time to move the conversation forward.

'How's the right-wing/left-wing historian programme looking?' David asked.

'Oh God,' came the apocalyptic reply. '*God*. No-one will do it!
Half the profs I rang are barking mad and the other half refuse
point blank!'

I'll do it, thought Davy.

'It's a good idea for a programme isn't it?' Keith asked. David
nodded. 'But all the big names are running scared.'

'So you're not doing it?'

'Oh, *God,*' Keith scratched his head and looked despairingly at David the would-be media star. 'Oh, *some time* I suppose,' he admitted 'But never mind about me. What about you? What are you up to these days?'

The man had clearly completely forgotten what Davy was doing there. Was this time to say 'Thank you for wasting my time' and catch the next train back to Cardiff?

Davy decided that making Keith feel justifiably guilty wouldn't actually help matters.' 'Oh this and that. I'm keen to do more general shows though. Controversy, moral dilemmas, you know the kind of thing. Not just history.'

'Oh you should,' his increasingly useless friend replied. 'You were very good on Sunday.'

Keith waved at someone who had just come in through the double swing doors of Red Assembly.

'So who do you think I should try?' Davy tried to keep them on the subject.

'I don't know. I suppose the thing is you don't have much time in your line of business.'

'No, no, my time's pretty flexible.'

'Well . . .' Brabant thought long and hard. 'You could write in suggesting your own series. Infotainment. Retrodoc. That kind of thing.'

'I don't think I've had enough exposure,' Davy replied sensibly.

'I tell you what, Simon Rees is putting up a programme about the Welsh something or other centenary. Isn't it a hundred years since they discovered coal down there?'

'No I don't think so.' David tried not to sound as if Brabant was a first-year student who might be better off studying Forestry.

'Mind you he's not going to get it through. Michael hates the Welsh. No point attaching yourself to that really. Look, next time you're up let's have lunch, talk about this properly. I'm afraid I've got a screening now. Did Kate tell you about that?'

David told Millie about his brush with stardom when they met late the following morning in Camden Town. She laughed. One of the great things about Millie was that she could laugh about that kind of thing and make you see that this whole silly business was just a whole silly business and little else.

'No fame without pain!' she grinned.

'No fame at all at this rate,' he told her. They were at what had been Millie's local in the days when she and Crispin lived off Chalk Farm Road. The pub had dark corners and a billiard table that looked like it might be coming free soon.

'Why d'you want to become famous?' Millie asked, finishing her half. She had driven up that morning, parked with some friends and come straight to the pub in her usual jeans and T-shirt. Davy, by comparison, was even more overdressed than usual.

'I don't really want fame,' he replied. 'In all likelihood I'm trapped in this job at a level that no longer challenges me. And television offers a kind of alternative.'

'I thought you were going to be Professor of History.'

'But if I'm not, I have to look elsewhere.'

'Like the box?' She seemed sceptical. 'So why don't I see loads of failed profs every time I switch on?'

'Oh but you do.' David put down his glass to better make the point.

'Just getting interviewed once in a blue moon about your subject isn't difficult. It's getting on with any regularity that's hard. That takes ability. And luck. Telling jokes to your students all day may make you feel like God but it doesn't necessarily make you a good TV presenter.'

'But you are?' It was a good question. Davy rubbed his extensive forehead with the palm of one hand.

'I'm better than most.' Up until now he had been staring in an abstracted way at his glass of wine but now he turned to face her.

'I've just got to find *something*. I know I'm not going to be happy just to draw a good salary till I die. If I can't get the Chair I'll probably need to get out. But there aren't many sideways moves in my world and I'm not fit for anything else, apart from teaching.'

'You don't want to do that,' said Millie.

David was looking at his wine glass again.

'What about writing?' she asked.

'Doesn't pay,' he told the wine glass.

'Journalism?'

'None of it pays unless you're a celebrity. And that's where TV comes in,' he insisted. 'Oh God!' David leaned back in his chair and stared at the ceiling. 'Most people would say I have everything, wouldn't they? Flash car, good salary, safe job long as I keep my hands off the students and my thoughts to myself—'

'Beautiful wife,' Millie added.

'Oh yes. Beautiful wife, lovely house, wonderful children,' Davy agreed. 'But I am stuck now until I retire. Stuck. This is the pattern that my existence will repeat ad nauseam and beyond. Beyond nauseam! What a thought.'

He abandoned the ceiling and looked at her again in case she happened to have the answer to hand. 'I've got to get out, got to change something.'

Millie nodded towards the billiards. 'Table's free,' she said. Davy smiled. He really did value her company.

'Best of three,' he replied.

They went their separate ways after Millie won two games outright. The arrangement was to meet at eight in this pub she was going to look out. Afterwards they'd have dinner somewhere. David kissed Millie then headed back to town. Why did he not feel attracted to her today?

Millie watched him go, stepping over the piles of uncollected rubbish. She did enjoy his company and suddenly she felt very sorry for him. And for Helena. But not because of the University. Millie reckonned she had a good idea what David needed. And it wasn't his own chat show. It was pretty much what Crispin needed when they first met.

She rolled up her sleeves to catch the afternoon sun and wondered if David would try it on again this evening. And if he did, was there really any harm? She was free. Crispin was free. David had this sort of arrangement. Helena didn't seem to care. Of course she'd have to tell Crisp. But that might put him on his mettle. A bit of a mutual Self Help Group all round. Well, why not? Millie Bountiful Crispin had once called her in their Aberystwyth days. She remembered that afternoon was for shopping with her friend Gail. Better get some fresh underwear, she supposed.

*   *   *

Helena was watching Nick and Emma play up and down the Cross on Llandaff Green. She had quite missed David that Saturday. Every time she ran out of something in fact, which was even more often than usual. This was her third expedition that day to the Spar with the children in tow and each visit was taking longer because the children felt entitled to more and more fun on the way.

'Nick . . . Emma . . .' said Helena in that weary, impotent way she so often heard issuing from other pathetic parents. 'Please, I've got cooking to do.' It was very hot, surely they would tire out soon? But, no, the Mosford children continued to run up and down those blocks of sand-stone where once, if you believed the historians, departing crusaders had bent the knee in prayer. Helena didn't. Historians would say anything to get on television. Even in the thirteenth century.

She was still annoyed by the way David had been tempted towards a little notoriety. The pursuit of sex was something she could try and tolerate. She could certainly understand it. But it was a *private* folly. Television wasn't. Television was a very public folly. That was the whole point of it. Sitting on that sturdy wooden commemorative bench while her children cheerfully ignored her, Helena found herself getting very annoyed. With them, with David and with God. God, who took such a passive role in all of this. God, who let the Crusaders go off and butcher in his name. God, who allowed the Church to say just about any old nonsense in his name. God, who made such stupid suggestions when it came to saving her marriage. God, who hadn't warned her about Gareth Box.

She had been brooding about Gareth ever since yesterday. In fact, one of the reasons why there had been so many trips to the Spar was that Helena just wasn't able to plan ahead. She could work out that she needed parsley for the parsley sauce but didn't realise, until they were home, that of course she also needed milk. That was what Gareth did to you. Ruined your recipes and, given half a chance, your entire life as well. He'd found a way in again. That was the terrible truth.

'I'm forty-five, Helena,' Gareth had said across the little wooden table. 'My Dad was sixty when he died. That means I may only have another fifteen years.'

She hadn't intended to be moved by this. 'Your father died of coal dust, Gareth. It isn't inherited and there's not much of it to be found in American universities.'

He shook his head. 'My Dad was in the accounts department. He was a clerk. He never went below ground more than five or six times in his whole life.'

Helena looked at him in amazement. She could remember arguments in student pubs and the middle common room in which Gareth Box had won the day by throwing his father's martyrdom in the face of all-comers.

'He died of pancreatitis,' said Gareth.

'You lied all those years—' she began.

'You knew I lied.'

'Yes but not about that. I believed you about that. That was your platform.'

Gareth played with a striation mark down one of his finger nails. 'Phoney,' he said. 'So much of my life has been posturing. You know that. You always knew that. That was why it was stupid of me to lose you.'

Helena had wanted him to stop there and then but she didn't know how to.

'But now I've decided that I want to live out what remains of my life honestly. Espousing what I really believe in, fighting for what I value.'

She really didn't want him to say any more. He might be a different Gareth Box now but his way of advancing an argument hadn't changed. Gareth always went from the general to the personal. Like the night when he had talked to her about the need for spiritual and intellectual freedom, the relentless and unfettered quest of the academic mind, and then ended up by telling her he'd found someone else to sleep with. That was how Gareth approached subjects of real import and she really did not want to be the conclusion to this particular peregrination about the things he truly valued.

'Hello!' sang out a voice that was bound to be Sarah John. Well that's what comes of dwelling on such matters. Your children turn delinquent on Llandaff Green and you don't notice the approach of Sarah, out in force and determinedly good-hearted. Helena got up smiling and feeling guilty. 'Hello,' she said and hello again when she noticed that Sarah had Katie with her.

'This one was in need of some fresh air,' said Sarah, holding up her daughter's sleeve. 'Too much late night revision!' Emma ran over to Katie and gave her a big hug.

'Oh? No *David*?' asked Sarah with her unerring ability to notice that which should not have seemed significant, but on this occasion was.

'London,' said Helena.

'With his girlfriend,' added Nick, taking hold of his mother's legs. Helena saw Katie glimpse across at her mother before Sarah burst out laughing, as if that was a very funny idea indeed. Helena laughed too. 'He's seeing some television people,' she explained.

'In a *pub*,' Nick added in his very definite way. Sarah gave a slightly less jolly laugh and wiped the perspiration from her brow. 'Well, television people do a lot of that, I believe, Nicky!'

'Oh dear, I've got to get on,' said Helena. 'I'm cooking dinner tonight and we're right out of . . .' She had been so concerned to get out her excuses for leaving that she had blundered right into that one. 'Of *things*, you know.' Helena could see the interest flicker in Sarah's eyes.

'Cooking things to er, cook with . . . you know.'

'Milk,' said Emma helpfully.

'Oh, so David's back tonight then?' Sarah asked.

Damn and blast! thought Helena. I am thirty-seven. I am not going to make up excuses like a teenager.

'No, he's back tomorrow,' she explained.

'Well you don't want to cook for *one*,' said Sarah, good-hearted still and yet also keen. 'Why don't you come round to us. Katie would look after the children for you.'

'Thanks, that's nice of you,' said Helena. 'But I've . . . I've got someone coming for dinner.'

There it was. Out.

'Oh right you are!' Sarah announced magnanimously. She seemed sorry but satisfied with that. Helena breathed a sigh of relief and silently prayed that Nick wouldn't say a word. It was to Nick that she had described Crispin as . . . what was it? *the man who lives with Daddy's friend*.

'Time to go,' she said, squeezing Nick's shoulder.

'Jonathan and Katrin are coming to our house tonight,' Nick announced to Sarah.

'That's nice,' said Sarah, but without the same enthusiasm. She knew whose children they were.

'We're all going to sleep in the same bed.'

'– room,' Helena added. 'They all sleep in the same bedroom. Well, the boys in one and the girls in another.'

'That's nice,' said Sarah once again, and she exhaled heavily.

'Do you know who Jonathan's daddy is?' asked Nick.

'Come on darling!' Helena laughed as she took a step back.

'Do you know who Jonathan's daddy is?!' Nick repeated in his loud boy's voice. Helena had begun to move off but Nick was stubbornly standing his ground which meant that he and she were now at arm's length from each other, their limbs like two lengths of taut rope, knotted at the hand. Sarah crouched down to him.

'You tell me who,' she said pretending it was all great fun.

'Crrrrispin,' said Nick with due emphasis.

'Well!' said Sarah feigning to be impressed 'Crispin indeed!'

'Time to go!' cried Helena again. Fortunately Nick had said his piece by now and so he dutifully moved to her side.

'Come on Emma!' Emma detached herself from Katie but not before adding, 'Crispin's Katrin's dad too.'

'Ooh,' said Katie pretending there were matters of great import in all that. Helena took hold of her daughter's hand. 'But they're not married,' Emma continued matter-of-factly.

'Emma! Please!'

As the Mosford family made their way across the Green Helena told Emma off.

'You should come when I ask you.'

'I did come,' Emma grumbled 'You didn't have to pull *me* away like you did Nick.'

Helena felt guilty. Emma had been the final straw whereas Nicholas had been a complete bale of indiscretion. Oh, she was allowing herself to become overpreoccupied with these Gareth thoughts when what she really needed to do was lock them away in a box. Safe and sound. A Gareth Box in fact.

'I'm sorry,' said Helena to Emma.

'You always pick on me,' her daughter replied without a scrap of magnanimity.

David had spent the afternoon in moments of intermittent lust at the back of the British Library's reading room. On the hour, or so it seemed, his mind would run the Kemp cleavage clip just to remind him of his destination, to keep primitive Mosford on the coital target. But Davy was so familiar with that particular reel by now that thoughts of Millie hardly distracted him. This had been both disappointing and reassuring. As had the fact that in London, and in the fetid heat of a London pub, and particularly in her travelling clothes, Millie had seemed much less exotic than in Cardiff. All this week David had been prey to many demons: in meetings, in the car, in the marriage bed. It had been good to actually have a holiday from them this afternoon.

At five-thirty he went back to the Club, had a long bath and watched highlights of the cricket on TV. For a moment it seemed rather absurd to be on his own in a London room while his wife and family were in Cardiff. Why was he here? Because of his interest in pub architecture? Because he had hopes of getting off with the woman who turned him down a few weeks ago? Did he *really* believe that some sophisticated ménage à quatre could help save his marriage? Was Millie the one? Or was this all so much folly? If only sex meant as little to him as it did to Helena.

David decided to get dressed and send for some sandwiches. He imagined that there would be nothing worth eating at Millie's dive and he didn't want to be seen to be turning his nose up. This was her pub. Her art. Her part of the evening.

Millie was actually taking off her clothes about the time Davy was putting his on. Her friend Gail had poured her a large glass of sparkling wine and run a bath full of bubbles.

'I'm only going to look at a pub,' said Millie as she was bundled upstairs.

'With a man!' Gail reminded her.

'I do that all the time, it's part of my job,' Millie insisted.

'You don't always buy fresh knick-knacks first, though, do you?'

Gail was insistent and before she shut Millie in she gave her the half empty bottle to finish off. It was all a bit of an adventure for Gail who had always felt that if her friend was going to settle down and have children it should have been with someone who had a bit more fun about them. Not 'the mad monk' as she called him. That afternoon's shopping had been a very silly girly giggly time with Gail trying to find out more about this man that Millie had come to meet and Millie denying it all but letting bits of information slip.

Suddenly alone, Millie sat down on the side of the bath and poured herself what remained of the fizz. She had caught sight of her body in a mirror that one of Gail's exes had fixed to the ceiling. Viewed from above she looked squat, more like her granny than her mum.

Millie had never thought herself a great beauty but she had had plenty of boyfriends and always attributed her successes to the fact that she was good company down the pub and fun in bed. 'It's going to take one hell of a lot of exuberance to overcome that,' thought Millie looking balefully up at her bottom.

Crispin had arrived at 7.30 with his two and a bit on edge. He reproached himself several times for having forgotten to bring wine and then left Katrin and Jonathan with the Mosford pair while he nipped back to High Street. Helena had no trouble with the girls who disappeared conspiratorially upstairs, so close and so fast that it looked as if they were running a three-legged race. Nick had become tired and already put himself to bed so Helena let Jonathan watch TV in the play room.

'Will you be all right in here?' she asked, making a show of tidying a few odd things nowhere in particular.

'Orright,' said Jonathan.

When Crispin came back Helena had changed into something with white leggings.

'Um . . .' said Crispin.

'Jonathan's watching TV, is that all right?'

'Er, yes,' said Crispin, trying not to be distracted by Helena's legs. 'I like the . . . er.' but here words failed him and Helena felt convinced that he didn't.

'*Wine*?' she asked.

'Thank you,' said Crispin. They were standing in the kitchen which was quite a big space in Ty Escob. Its tall ceiling and wide-tiled floor did make it ideal for a crush of servants preparing dinner, or for a noisy departmental drinks party, or even for several children painting merrily on the kitchen table. But it did seem rather empty with just Crispin and Helena in it.

'Very quiet without them,' said Helena when she'd been to the fridge and brought out a bottle.

'Yes,' said Crispin. They stood either side of the table, seemingly awaiting their cue.

'I mean David and Millie,' she added, in case he thought she meant the children. But he didn't.

'We'll just have to cope the best we can,' he replied. Helena felt rather put out by that remark until she noticed the tiny smile at the corner of Crispin's mouth. With David the jokes were signalled clearly and he always delivered a punch line exactly where you wanted it but Crispin took some listening to.

'Yes,' she agreed. 'I just hope they aren't too worried about us.'

Crispin looked at Helena's long, pale face. Its beauty was losing that effortless bloom of early womanhood. It was a face for looking at, he thought.

'Joke,' said Helena.

'Yes, well at least we know we needn't worry about *them*,' he agreed.

'Yes, I'm sure David's safe with Millie,' she laughed, in search of reassurance.

'Oh, I'm sure David's safe with any woman,' Crispin replied with a smile. 'He's, er, devoted to you.'

That's nice, thought Helena. Nice of him to say it anyway.

David had been surprised to find that Millie's pub was near the Oval. The big roomy taxi bounced him past roads he'd walked along as a Wisden-infested student and he rather wished he was going to watch a game that bright and summery evening. Certainly rather that than sit in a pub with Millie Kemp. Why was he feeling so perverse? Why on earth was he behaving like this? The likelihood was that, even if he tried it on, she'd say No. So why was he getting so hot under the collar about this very vague possibility? Had he gone off her? Only yesterday in a big roomy taxi, very like this big roomy taxi, he was having to tell himself to run another clip through the subconscious projector gate, so frequently was she in his thoughts. But today he'd been in two minds about this assignation. Two? Three. At lunchtime. Four by now. His resolve, that resolve which on Monday had set him on a precipitate course towards Millie's body was weakening. It was growing confused. It was frightened.

There was the time in Leeds. He hadn't forgotten the time in Leeds with that postgraduate called Lyn (or Lynn) (or was it Lynne?). Lyn Something from Leeds. She had been involved in a conference at which he had been speaking. They had already corresponded a few times because her subject was Unemployment Between The Wars. Lyn from Leeds had even seen him on the television on one occasion. And she had written him a note to say that she would be at the conference as one of the co-opted organisers and how nice it would be to meet him after all this time. There was an agenda set between them. Even though these conferences were legendary for academics getting their many legs over and under each other, no conclusion between David and Lyn was actually intended. They were each other's Any Other Business to be explored if a time arose that was mutually convenient. Either party could opt out of discussions at any stage, without the other feeling compromised.

He very much regretted Lyn from Leeds. He wished he could forget everything about her and not just how she spelt her name. They had got on fine after the mutual shock of being a little disappointed at the sight of each other. Why Lyn was disappointed in him he couldn't understand because she had seen him on TV. Perhaps he was even less impressive in the flesh than on camera. She, on the other hand, was much more striking in appearance than he had expected, ash blonde hair, long nose, strong jaw. As ever, with the women who wrote to him, she was not, in the flesh, his type. That was an inviolable rule. Mosford's type of woman did not write to him.

But as the two days of endless coffee wore on they shared a few jokes and on the last night Davy stayed on late at the obligatory drink. He usually paid his dues by buying a round and then leaving because of his early start back to Wales the next morning. But for once he decided to see it through to the end. Things had got to a significantly bad level at home. It was rare for David to hang around a bar until everyone decided to call it a night, but that time he did. And it was as dull as he imagined it to be. The repartee slowed down just as the sense of achievement in what had occurred over the last few days soared. After a while Lyn sought him out. She was slightly drunk, greatly relieved it had gone off well and surprised to find he was still there. Lyn had clearly recognised David as a *one round and back for A Welcome In The Hillsides* kind of man.

'Hi,' she said. 'Thanks ever so much for coming.' Later on she said, 'You're really funny, do you know that?' and later on still she asked him if he wanted to go on to somewhere they were all going on to. It was that kind of evening.

'Why don't you come back to my room?' David asked. 'It's much nearer.'

Even today he wondered why he had made the suggestion. It came easily because, in all honesty, he didn't much mind if she said No.

True, things between him and Helena were not at all good. True he was feeling uncommonly frustrated. And true, he had been given virtual carte blanche by Helena some months previous, in the days when they used to talk about such things. The gist of Linna's weary dispensation was that, while she just didn't want to have sex, she wouldn't stop him getting it elsewhere as long as she didn't know about it, as long as it wasn't with someone they both knew and as long as he stopped moaning on at her.

But why he acted this time David didn't really know.

Of course he didn't tell Lyn any of this, neither about his marriage problems nor about the arbitrary nature of this decision to proposition her. What he did tell her was that he didn't want to mislead her, that he was married and wouldn't do anything to endanger his marriage but that he did find her attractive. He was going to ask her if that seemed a reasonable basis on which to have invited her in to his room but Lyn started to kiss him. David Mosford would dearly liked to have paused to make the distinction between inviting someone into your room and into your life but Lyn had just come to the end of three weeks of anxiety about this conference and she seemed to have a great need to get her tongue into David's mouth.

So this is the Great Conference Legover, thought David as they went about it, or rather as Lyn went about it. There was surprisingly little for him to do. He always expected he might be drunk when something like this happened but in fact he was hardly under the influence. The euphoria, such as it was, was purely sexual.

Afterwards David felt very pleased and grateful to have had sex with someone. Lyn, on the other hand, seemed fonder of him and to have grown suddenly sober. He didn't like that look in her eye but that didn't stop him responding when she encouraged him to do it again. And the next time he looked at her she was looking distinctly, if sadly, appreciative of him. This was the critical distinction. He was grateful, she was growing fond.

She had been an odd shape, Lyn from Leeds. He remembered thinking that evening, as they rolled around, that in future he should spend less time lamenting the recent change in Helena's body. Lyn had no Emma and Nick to blame for the bits that were no longer the size or shape they ought to be.

Afterwards he stroked her ash blonde hair which was even paler in the pale moonlight and she talked to him until he fell asleep. David slept warm and physically satisfied and when he woke she had gone. It was like a dream. How nice, he thought.

But it wasn't. In the weeks that followed Lyn phoned and faxed him frequently at the University and David vowed never ever to get involved with someone in his own line of work ever again. He thought he had been fair. He had as good as told her beforehand that nothing could come of this but she seemed to hold this very fairness against him.

'You're so calculating,' she moaned down the phone.

'Did you want me to mislead you?' he asked as a seminar group sat waiting for him outside in the corridor.

'You could have. You could have led me on and then dumped me. At least I might have expected that.'

At that moment Big Meg had opened David's door and frowned meaningfully at him. Meg was new in the department in those days and David was shocked by her intrusion.

'There are students out here,' she said. '*All over* the corridor.'

'One minute!' David replied, incredulous at her intrusion. 'I've got to go,' he told Lyn.

'We've got to meet,' Lyn told him.

'That's not a good idea.'

It was a very sensible thing that he said to her at that moment. But, unfortunately, instead of sensibly slamming the receiver down or sensibly shouting at him, Lyn started to sound all choked and in her incoherent silence David gave in. And he did meet her and it was awful and he tried to talk to Helena about it and she wouldn't and generally it was awful, awful, awful and he decided never ever, ever again.

David paid the taxi off and took a look at the pub. It was a bleak-looking 1960s brick rectangle with about as much atmosphere as a small air traffic control tower.

'Oh no,' he thought.

Helena and Crispin were coping very well without their partners. They had spent some time indecisively wondering whether to eat in the great long dining room or the great tall kitchen of Ty Escob but eventually they'd settled for the kitchen which was convenient because Jonathan came in twice asking for cans of Coke and the two girls came down looking for ice cream.

'Is this a dinner or a takeaway?!' Helena asked as they finally got to finish their first course.

'Good job David isn't here,' said Crispin and they talked about the theatricality of David's hospitality. Crispin made Helena laugh by suggesting that when the Mosfords staged a dinner party David looked upon such infant interruptions as heckling. Then he asked how Nick was these days. Funny, thought Helena, funny how he can introduce the subject of Nick and David can't. Crispin notices so much. Crispin is so sympathetic. Crispin understands. Suddenly, and guiltily, she realised that being together with Crispin at a corner of the large kitchen table felt comfortable in a way that being with David didn't.

David really did not like The Middle Wicket as a pub, as a name for a pub or as a pub in which to meet Millie. Fortunately he did like Millie when she turned up in a brightly coloured jacket she'd bought that afternoon.

'*Please* take me away from all this,' he muttered as they exchanged kisses.

'This is my job,' she said.

'You deserve danger money.'

Millie wasn't too taken with The Middle Wicket either but for her there was a pleasure to be had from seeing how the plans she had been studying translated into reality. She had thought she could have predicted where people would congregate around the bar. She could usually spot all the nodal points but in fact one area which should have been a transit zone was unexpectedly congested because there was somewhere to put down your pint while gazing up at the TV.

'I can think of a very nice restaurant miles away,' said David.

'Well, you keep thinking about it,' she replied replenishing his glass of reddish wine and going off to look at the garden. This, thought David, is worse than the station coffee bar in Leeds. There the decor was Coffee Bean Braziliana with chrome fittings. It had a sort of inappropriate panache. But here there was nothing to redeem the place except the likelihood that it was flimsily built and would probably demolish in an hour. Preferably tonight. Still Millie was looking very nice and she wasn't calling him a calculating sod or telling him *Lynfashion* that that was it, she'd had it with men. These were ameliorating factors.

In Cardiff, Helena and Crispin were comparing backgrounds in the drawing room. Both had been rather shocked not to have even finished the one bottle of wine that Helena had got from the fridge.

'What will they say?' Crispin laughed when Helena held it up.

Now they were having coffee and had left the subject of David and Millie far behind. Crispin was asking questions about a past life of Helena's that she had almost forgotten. But it was all still there, and seemingly important when unearthed. Why had she chosen a paper on the Oxford movement as her special subject? For that matter why did Crispin know so much about Cardinal

Newman? Helena couldn't help wondering how many of these interests he actually shared with Millie.

'So why was it that David became the academic, and not you?'

'Oh,' she said and, for no conscious reason, she began to unpin her hair. 'Well, David always meant to be. His father encouraged him too. That's where men so often have the advantage. Boys have this irresponsible childhood, followed by focused adulthood and career. We get distracted.' Musn't let that happen to Emma, she thought.

'And why were you?' he asked.

'What? Distracted? Well, I was thinking of research, at the time, and my degree *was* good enough. But it was all bound in with this man. That's the mistake girls make. When the man went, I decided to jettison the research as well. Do something "real" and demonstrate an independence which . . .' She looked into the grate at where the fire would be, come wintertime.

'Which I think really wasn't necessary. At the time I couldn't see, I didn't recognise, that actually the research might have meant more to me than the man.'

'And the man obviously wasn't David.'

'No.'

It sounded for a moment as if the conversation had ended there but it shouldn't. Really that wasn't fair on David.

'He . . . he came shortly afterwards,' she added loyally. Was she going to tell Crispin about Gareth? Share the contents of that Pandora's box? Surely not.

'Do you, are you able to help David with his work?' he asked.

So, that was it. She wasn't going to after all. Good.

Helena agreed that she had always enjoyed helping David with his work. 'Yes. That's definitely been one of the things that has kept us together,' she added.

Crispin smiled as if he often wondered what kept relationships together.

'So, what did you do that was "real?"' he asked, playing with a hole in his pullover.

'I worked for a charity for a while. I believed in the cause but not the work.'

He looked up, interested.

'I mean I think I did it well enough, but no more. It wasn't much more than a gesture really. So since the children I haven't done anything.'

It had grown so gradually dark that she could hardly see his face now. She should put on a lamp or something.

'What about you?' she asked, reaching the impossible distance towards a switch. 'Will you go back to something when your children are bigger?'

Crispin's smile suggested he could not imagine such a time. Bigger children? Would a bigger Jonathan mean less time spent worrying?

'Oh er, back to something, I suppose. The thing is what I miss is not the work, or the money, it's the people. If it weren't for my days seeming so empty at times I could enjoy being a parent full time. I think . . . I've, um, I've got into it. It's messy and irritating. And nobody seems to know how it's done. But I feel I should try. My own family were so distant. They knew more about livestock than they did about children . . . this is . . .'

'Your second chance?' she asked.

'Yes. Having missed out on families when I was first supposed to be in one!' he smiled. 'I do sometimes wonder how they're surviving it, though.'

He wanted her to say they were growing up well. He would have taken her word when he wouldn't take Millie's but Helena was staring at the grate again. It would have been good to have some flickering flames to gaze into, she thought. Summer evenings don't provide the eye with such necessary distractions, unless the waves are lapping, the sun is setting or the birds are swooping overhead. But none of these were currently visible in the Mosfords' dark drawing room.

'Tell me,' she asked, 'how did you come to be working for this American?'

'Dave, this is Neville,' said Millie returning through the melée with a thickset young man carrying a briefcase.

Who the hell is Neville? David thought as he stood up to shake hands.

'Nev, this is David Mosford,' Millie continued.

'Good to meet you, Mr Mosford. Can I buy you a drink?' said Neville. His hand had a very self conscious grip about it. This young Nev person was keen to let his strength be known.

'I'm fine,' said David, alluding to his half empty glass. 'The wine's *dreadful*. But I'm fine.'

He must have been looking at Millie in a particular way because once Neville had dived back into the bar Millie asked him what the matter was.

'Who's *Nev*?' Davy replied putting the name into heavily inverted commas.

'Ah,' said Millie with a grin.

'Just idle curiosity. Just interested to know if our Nev's the real reason you are here.'

'Certainly is,' said Millie.

'Ah.'

'Nev's the best there is,' Millie continued. She was teasing him. But what with?

'And you've known him long?'

'We met in Somerset. On the Taunton job.'

'Ah,' said Davy. 'He's your *foreman*.'

'That's right,' Millie told him. 'Nice eyes, nice body. Good with his hands. What did you think he was?'

'Oh I thought he was your . . . foreman. It's obvious.' They seemed to grin at each other. David and Millie: the old team. This was the first time there had been any kind of return to their usual sparkle. 'And how long is dear Neville going to be with us in this proto-fun zone of yours?' Millie told him that she and Nev had some ideas to go through. A good foreman should be able to help you cost the ideas as you go along. At that point Neville returned with two pints.

'You sure, Mr Mosford?' he asked jerking his thumb to the bar.

'Oh. Another glass of this curious red thing,' conceded David. 'You're very kind.'

One had to show willing but, really, he was spending the night in one of the world's great capital cities. This evening thousands of tourists would be out looking at the thousands of things that are worth seeing, and drinking the many things that were worth drinking, while he would be languishing (there was no other word for it) in a pub so execrable it might have been Dorkin's local.

Helena *was* telling Crispin about Gareth.

Or rather *almost* telling Crispin about Gareth. Helena was very much wanting to tell Crispin about Gareth. What held her back was the knowledge that she would feel guilty afterwards. If she told Crispin as much as David knew, she would end up telling him more and that wasn't fair. It was pitch black outside now and the problem was that, despite her best endeavour, whatever question Crispin seemed to ask the answer always led her back to Gareth Box: why she wanted to do research, why she gave up, how she met David, whether David would get the chair, whether they would stay in Cardiff. The lid was definitely being prised off.

And yet, en route, at some stage during her evasions and hesitations, Helena had let slip the fact that she had done counselling work when they were first living in Canterbury. She had actually forgotten this stage in her career and it intrigued Crispin.

'Is this the work you said you didn't believe in?' he asked. 'The work you didn't want to go back to?'

'D'you think I should have?'

If that was a thorny question it was only so because she'd wondered it herself. Here she was, wasting a good degree and even that little training course, in all its perfunctory unimpressiveness, was going unused.

'It depends,' he replied. 'You said a few weeks ago that you were looking to find a role.'

The thing about Crispin, thought Helena, is that he not only *listens* to what you say to him, he remembers too. Of course probably not with Millie. She wasn't so naive as to think that any man is a hero to his wife. But it was nice to throw these ideas in and to see how they bounced off this new receptive surface and to find them returned to you with a different spin.

'It was just like the charity work really. Something I thought I ought to do rather than something that I wanted to do or thought I would be really good at. The thing is,' she said, lifting herself back up on to a sofa, 'the thing is, I haven't really had to address the question of what it is I want to do because the children have taken up so much of my time.'

'And because you've been a good mother,' Crispin pointed out. 'I can say that because I'm a mother too.'

'I shout at them,' Helena confessed.

'You think I don't?' he asked. 'But listen, I think that now the children are . . . what is it?'

'Emma's nearly eight and Nick's six.'

'OK, now they're so much older and Nick is well and they don't need you so much . . .'

'Yes,' said Helena. She knew what he was getting at.

'You should think about it. Think what you really want to do.'

David had had enough of Listening with Neville. He was on his fourth glass of wine now and feeling sorry that so many grapes had died in vain. After more than half a bottle of this disgusting stuff, and nothing to eat, Millie's views on the optimum use of space, the provision of themed areas and all this cubic cost effective nonsense sounded like so much Carys Rees. Neville was nodding and making notes. This, after all, was his bread and butter, translating what Millie thought the brewery believed the customers would stomach into breeze blocks and mortar.

'Excuse me,' David suddenly found himself demanding, 'but wouldn't it be cheaper to knock the whole bloody thing down and put up something half way decent?' It had been a rather rude and abrupt interruption so Millie paused a moment before continuing.

'*Maybe*,' said David, who wasn't used to being ignored. '*Maybe* some people like it this way.'

'Can we come to your ideas later?' Millie asked with a smile. She was trying not to sound heavy.

'No,' said Davy. 'Because if you adopt my ideas, you don't have to go through all this cost-cutting cubic-fun-units per square-customer-lavatoryseat nonsense. You can just say: it's an awful botched little abortion of a place and it ought to have been pulled down years ago.'

Poor Neville looked quite thrown by this and decided to keep his head down. Having been a soldier, this was something he did quite literally by hunching forward and dodging the bullets.

'I don't think the brewery would buy that,' said Millie as flatly as she could.

David felt irritated by her response. It reminded him of Helena's mood swings, of the sudden and disastrous shift in Lyn from Leeds. What was he doing here with this woman?

'Well, I'd like to know what the customers think of your ideas,' Davy challenged her.

'I don't work for the customers,' Millie said, abandoning all pretence of not being heavy now.

'OK. I'll ask them,' said David, sitting forward and turning in the direction of another table.

'Don't you dare!' said Millie. 'This visit is strictly low key.'

'Oh is it?' David had got to the stage now where he would argue about anything just to divest himself of this dreadful sense of irritation and misplaced anger. 'Then why are we, or rather why are you, sitting here openly discussing these changes in front of the poor sods who'll have to live with them!'

'This is my job,' said Millie in a challenging way.

'So you keep saying. But don't you ever question what you're doing? This pub is awful but at least the people who come here must like it. Presumably the brewery want *more* people coming here so they send you in. And what is your job? To prepare the place for a coterie of camp window dressers. And their job? What's their job? To tart the place up so it fools the missing element, *the families*, into thinking this is a kid-friendly zone while, of course, not driving out the regulars.'

'It's as good a way of earning a living as any,' Millie retorted.

'Oh is it?'

'Yes and it's a bit rich,' she added. 'You with your tenure and a house that just dropped into your lap, it's a bit rich you turning up your nose at the way I support my family!'

People at the next table had started to listen.

'But don't you see!' David insisted. 'Don't you see that what you're doing is turning everywhere you go into a *phoney theme park*, a series of meaningless tawdry icons instead of a, a part of real life – of, of social reality, of community!'

Davy wanted to stop himself. He was going seriously over the top. Somehow he'd hit the wrong note and, because for Millie this was work, she hadn't come back at him with her usual level of banter. There was nothing to cap his excess.

'And, apart from all that, apart from all that, what's *really* wrong is that these family pubs are just *kennels* where children get abandoned, with a clear conscience, in some roped off hyperactive play area, while the parents can stagger off and get pissed. You and your brewery are returning us to the morality of Gin Lane!'

He could see that she was hurt by what he'd said. He could see that she was compromised between how she normally behaved with her colleague and how she misbehaved with her boozy friend. But he only saw it for a moment, just one moment before he was aware of being pulled into the air and of finding Neville's face in unusual proximity to his.

'You are out of order,' said Neville stabbing a finger dangerously close to David's nose. 'You don't talk to Mrs Kemp like that.' Out of the corner of his eye Davy was aware of Millie looking despairingly as if this was all she needed.

'You are absolutely right,' said David, surrendering out of guilt and the desire for self-preservation. 'I do not speak to Mrs Kemp like that.'

'It's all right, Neville,' said Millie, trying to get them both to sit down and looking over her shoulder. The bar was going quiet.

'Too fucking right you don't,' said Neville, still jabbing a mean finger which by now was in range of David's eye.

'All right, Nev,' said Millie firmly. 'Sit down.' She had stood up and was between them now with one hand on Neville's shoulder and the other on David's.

'I'm telling you straight—' Neville began again but Millie swung round on him in a fierce but perfectly audible whisper. 'If you don't sit down this minute you are going to find yourself one arsehole out of a fucking job!'

Neville could always respond well to that kind of reasoning and down he sat. The bar began to sense that the alarm was over and started muttering to itself again. Millie sat down and found David's glasses which had landed on the table when Neville had seized him. She passed them up to him.

'You too, Dave,' she said quietly. 'Will you please sit down?'

David felt very foolish. He also felt very violated by Neville's attack. It was as if he had lost not just his spectacles but also his dignity.

'Please sit down,' Millie repeated. 'This visit is supposed to be low key.'

'If it's that low key, I think I'd better leave you to it,' David announced pointedly.

'Don't be silly,' said Millie.

'I think it might be better,' David insisted, straightening his tie which had also gone adrift in the ruck.

'Look,' said Neville from where he now sat which, from David's perspective, appeared to be somewhere under Millie's thumb. 'Look, I don't want to spoil your evening, Mr Mosford. I mean sorry for the rough stuff but, like, you and Mrs Kemp are going out to dinner.'

'We *were*,' said David and there was a cold anger in him now. 'Yes we were but I think that's probably not a very good idea now.' Why was he doing this? Why was he letting himself slide into this pit of malice? 'Good night,' he said. Too late to be sensible now.

Once out in the road David felt very silly and very tempted to go back in and apologise. But he also felt it best to draw a line under this whole business. To put it *Lynfashion* he had had it with women.

'I wonder if they're having a good time,' said Helena. Crispin smiled. The conversation had dipped. There was a different rhythm to the way the two of them talked. Without David or Millie around there was no seamless continuum of chatter. That very catholic ragbag of profound, bitchy, scatalogical, controversial and flirtatious badinage was replaced by Crispin and Helena discovering interesting moments that led to more ideas which then suddenly ground to a halt when those ideas had been stated and exchanged. Crispin, like God, was silent at times. Helena found his pauses restful.

In one of the recent ones she had been thinking about why she hadn't told Crispin about Gareth when the opportunity arose. He was such good company that she was tempted to believe she could tell him anything. But more than that, she was now feeling a frisson of excitement at the prospect of confessional. It was like being a teenager again.

'Actually—' she said in a decisive way but Crispin was suddenly looking at his watch.

'Erm, Helena this is terrible,' he said. 'I said I'd meet some students at half-past ten. That was before Millie arranged tonight. I haven't been able to get in touch with them. Will you excuse me if I just pop down to the Black Lion?'

Helena was having trouble catching up with this. Crispin hadn't mentioned students before. She knew he had some dealings with St Michael's College but she couldn't believe that the ordinands' timetable included tutorials in the Lion, especially at closing time.

The deal about the four children was that if they hadn't woken they would sleep over at Ty Escob. The deal about the adults, somewhat unspoken, was, of course, that Crispin would go back to his house. Millie had teased him a lot about this. Indeed it did seem odd, as Helena and Crispin got to their feet now, that he was going off and leaving his children with her. Crispin was such an easy presence in the house that his staying over would have been an entirely natural and even rather comforting thing. Still, Helena thought to herself by way of consolation, it avoided the daily risk of Nick saying something deeply embarrassing in front of someone like Sarah John.

'Please leave the washing up for tomorrow morning,' Crispin asked. 'I'll be over first thing.'

'It's not a problem,' Helena insisted. 'I did most of it before you came.'

'Well, thank you. It's been a splendid evening.' Crispin sounded suddenly like several of Helena's old uncles. 'We must do it again.'

'Next time our spouses go off somewhere together!' Helena added. Crispin laughed.

But David and Millie were not off together. David was off on his own, and he had had to walk some way down Kennington Lane before finding a taxi. During that time he became very disheartened. Why did these things go so wrong? Why had he arrived in a state and then got worse? Why had he let that silly incident happen? It wasn't the bad wine, although that hadn't helped. And it wasn't the pub, although that hadn't helped either. There was a time earlier in the evening when he and Millie had been bound for the same destination and yet for some reason he had deliberately stopped the bus and got off. Why? Was he unwilling to wait for her attention? Was he jealous of Neville? David really didn't know but none of the possible answers to these questions made him feel at all happy about himself.

Finally finding a cab he took comfort, the way he always did in London, cutting himself off from the city, rocked to and fro inside this well-upholstered box. He couldn't help but be amused at the thought that despite his best endeavours, no, *because* of his best endeavours he and Millie would be drinking their Horlicks in separate beds tonight and so, he assumed, would Helena and Crispin. So much for the sophisticated ménage!

Helena went to bed after checking all the the children and putting some things to soak in the sink. It seemed strange to have Crispin going off like that. This prohibition about his staying in her house, it was odd really. She would have liked him to have come back, after seeing the students. They might have finished their several conversations over a drink and gone to separate bedrooms under the same roof. That would have been friendly. But Crispin was having to return to his own house because the assumption that would greet his remaining in Ty Escob with his children was that he and she were having sex. What an absurd idea: they hardly knew each other . . .

Crispin moved at some speed across the Green. He was not fit but he'd always been light and could walk at a pace. He sped down Llandaff High Street, past the Llandaff Pharmacy, its lights bright with deterrence, and quickly past the Bishop's Tea Rooms. Then he crossed by the Cathedral Cleaners, and made it to the Black Lion, just as the last customers were being herded out.

'I am most terribly sorry,' he said to Sue whose face lifted with relief.

9

Just the Two of Us

Crispin's relationship with Sue had started imperceptibly. This serious, rather censorious, young girl was often to be found in her sensible coat listening to the theological students in the Black Lion. Occasionally she would join in their arguments in a voice that was quiet, all too definite but not entirely happy. Crispin recognised the mid-Welsh accent and the fact that she was seeking to articulate her ideas in a second language.

'Are you by any chance from Aberystwyth?' he asked one night when she had joined a coterie at the bar but was receiving scant attention.

'Devil's Bridge,' she replied but, other than that qualified agreement, told him nothing else.

'I was in college in Aber,' Crispin explained.

Sue's head gave a little nod as if she could well believe it. Crispin presumed that was the end of their conversation and he was just going to ask her if she would like another drink when Sue chimed in, 'I suppose it's the way I speak.' She said this in such a challenging way that Crispin's instinct was to sidestep the issue.

'What are you doing in Cardiff?' he asked and so the conversation was resumed.

'Teacher training.'

'Ah,' said Crispin.

'With Divinity,' said Sue.

Now he looked at her properly he could see that she was younger than he'd first thought. Her features, long – sharp even – were those of an older woman. In a few years' time she would have matured enough to be able to carry off a face like that. Sue didn't look directly at him but she stood close, as if she didn't want to let go in case no-one spoke to her again.

'Do you . . . um . . . miss Aberystwyth?' Crispin asked. 'I mean Devil's Bridge.'

'Oh yes,' she replied with great feeling. 'I don't like Cardiff.'

For the rest of that evening Sue stayed by Crispin and listened while he talked to the young men from St Michael's. She knew one of them, Ieuan, from home and it was he who had been responsible for introducing Sue to this rowdy, convivial group of would-be clerics. They mostly took no notice of her but were never hostile.

When everyone went back noisily across the road to college, Crispin and Sue found themselves standing together outside the Lion. As the students shook hands and said goodbye to Crispin there almost seemed to be an assumption that she had come as his guest so he did her the courtesy of asking if he should walk her to her bus stop.

'I live in Ely Road,' Sue announced and pointed the direction to her student bedsit. She seemed to be assuming that Crispin would walk her back, so he did. It was Friday evening which meant Millie was home and so there was no pressing need to get back. It was a cold dark night for a young girl to be out alone.

'Do you want to come in?' said Sue at the door of a tall, very neglected-looking house.

'I'd better get back,' said Crispin. He felt very sorry, leaving her in this place on such an unfriendly evening. The house felt damp, even from the outside. He wouldn't like to think of his own daughter marooned in such a place. 'You're staying here?' he asked hoping that she could tell him she was moving into hall next week.

'I thought I would rather not live in the city centre,' said Sue. Everything she said was like a statement. It was as if she daren't actually have a conversation in case she gave away too much.

'Do you live here with friends?' he asked.

'They're mainly English girls but there are two I like.' For Crispin it seemed awful that within less than half a mile of his own house, so warm and noisy, there was this terrible place where the children of good-hearted people languished, alone in a deep and dark city. The next time Sue invited him in he went. And the time after that, although visiting was an uncomfortable experience and student coffee had lost none of its scalding bitterness.

At the end of that term Sue gave him an Easter egg. This was to be the last Friday night he walked her home before the vacation. It came as something of a shock to Crispin to realise that he had been doing so for six weeks now. She also gave him a book on Dietrich Bonhoeffer which he'd already got but it was kind of her.

'I'm afraid I, er, haven't got you anything,' said Crispin. Although he had begun to enjoy his late-night chats with Sue, it hadn't occurred to him that here was a relationship to be commemorated by the exchange of gifts.

'It doesn't matter,' said Sue with a shrug. 'I liked your company.'

Their evenings had been pleasant enough although there was a limited number of subjects that interested Sue. She disliked University and would often complain about the kind of people who went to such self-indulgent places. She liked to talk about her family, about animals, about a school trip she had been on to, of all places, Tunisia and about the young men from St Michael's, many of whom she disapproved of and two she seemed to like. She also talked a bit about her two college friends but both had now got boyfriends, leaving Sue somewhat out of things. To Crispin it was like being nineteen all over again – except that Sue had none of the deliberate exuberance of students as he remembered them.

'And my Mam sent this,' said Sue. She looked under her bed and brought out a small box which contained something wrapped in straw. Sue laughed mischievously as she passed it over.

'It's, er . . . it's not a mouse is it?' asked Crispin. He was wary of small animals and she knew this. To his surprise the box contained a 500ml bottle of whisky.

'She said that's for walking me home at night.' Crispin was taken aback.

'It was a pleasure,' he said, shocked to realise that he must be a subject of conversation when Sue rang home once a week from the payphone outside her room. He felt moved by the loneliness of her existence but Sue was still laughing about his fear that she was handing him a mouse.

Crispin hadn't kissed Sue goodnight before but he felt he had to do something in recognition of all the emotional investment she was putting into him. So when it was time to go that night he did. She seemed shocked by the touch of his beard against her face and so he withdrew.

'Like a sheep,' she said, holding her cheek.

'I'm sorry,' he said but to his surprise she stroked the rough hair on his cheek with the back of her knuckles.

'Like an old sheep,' she repeated. Crispin thanked her for his presents and made to leave.

'Will you miss me?' she asked him out of the blue.

If she had asked him that before she had caressed his cheek he would have been falteringly gallant and tried to make light of it all.

'Yes, he said. 'I think I will.' There was something extraordinary about that caress. It had an innocence and yet also a sensuality that had entranced him.

'Thought so,' she said. 'If I give you my address will you write to me?'

'I will certainly write and thank your mother for this,' he said, holding up the whisky and backing politely towards the door.

'I can't write to you so you'll have to write to me,' she said and she held a piece of paper towards him. On it she had already written:

> *Miss Siwsan Coity*
> *Cae Rhiw Farm*
> *Cae Rhiw Y Ffynhonnell*
> *nr. Devils Bridge*
> *Dyfed.*

The image of Sue standing in that desolate room holding a piece of paper towards him stayed with Crispin all Easter. He sent Sue two postcards of Llandaff Cathedral. He also wondered about her declaration that she could not write to him. That was not true. The truth was she chose not to. Was that because she felt constrained by the fact that he lived with Millie or that she disapproved of the fact that he lived with Millie? With Sue it could be either. She was so young.

After the vacation when Crispin returned to her room his postcards were up there on the mantelpiece.

Crispin had been thinking of his visits to Ely Road and decided that he really should not take advantage of Sue, nor spoil her chances with the college boys by seeming to have some long-term relationship with her. Seeing those postcards given such prominence, he suggested she came round and met his family. Millie would be very friendly, he imagined, and quite overwhelming. Sue would cease to see him just as someone who walked her home and listened to her thoughts. But when Sue did call Millie was in the West of England and the children in school. He wondered if she had chosen that time of day deliberately.

Sue only stayed for coffee but she did ask to see Crispin's study and was pleased to notice that one shelf displayed her mother's small bottle of whisky. She loved all the books and asked to borrow one. She returned it three days later wrapped up in a brown paper parcel when he was working at the bookshop. On an instinct Crispin didn't unwrap it there but took the book back to his study at lunchtime. There he opened it carefully. Tucked inside the book was something he half expected, half dreaded, a letter in Sue's long, neat handwriting. Crispin hadn't seen a girl's handwriting for years. It had a self-conscious grace to it. This was not the writing of a woman with a hundred things to do. This was the handwriting of a teenager who has sat all evening in her room crafting that letter while listening to music on her battery-powered cassette player.

He sat down to read, feeling for all the world as if he had discovered a secret passageway in his office that led who knows where. The letter was full of Sue trying to impress Crispin with her thoughts about the book she had borrowed. It also thanked him for sending the postcards at Easter and justified this letter on the basis that it was time she replied to those, and would he now reply to her? She asked him to send her another book to read and she ended the letter with a drawing she had done of a mouse in a dress with a little placard that read 'Hello Crispin'.

It was really rather well drawn.

He should have said No at that point. Or even sooner. No to books and letters and everything. But when he looked at some of the titles above him on those shelves, Crispin knew there were one or two that she really should read. So he did parcel one up and dropped it in through her letter box later in the week and Sue did return it, with another letter, to the bookshop and gradually this clandestine correspondence grew until Crispin began to doubt she read the books at all. The letters were only about herself, little insignificant things and yet things she felt she could not say to him. He wrote too, advice and ideas he might have been too cautious to voice face to face. Ideas about the value of study, the value of people and why she should fear neither. Sometimes he joked about his fear of mice. And still they met on Friday nights when Millie was back home and the theological students were ensconced in the Lion.

If he was being seduced it was a most unusual seduction. Crispin could remember his first sexual experience in Aberystwyth with the fearsome Belinda. She was the kind of well-heeled Englishwoman he had set out to avoid by coming to Wales. As soon as they met she made it abundantly clear that she wanted him to come back to her room for a shag. With Millie, on the other hand, he could remember the fun that led very easily, very naturally to bed. But nothing was easy with Sue. She was forever summoning up the courage to ask him directly for what she wanted. 'Will you put your arm around me?' she asked as they walked back one evening in the early Spring. Crispin had declined. 'Would you take me to this film I want to see?' He'd declined that as well. He was happy to be her friend. He enjoyed discovering her mind. He recognised an affection for her even but he would not do these things that were tokens of a deeper relationship. He wanted to help her find a boyfriend for that was obviously what she was craving. Whenever Sue began to inveigh against the omnipresence of sex in student life and the squalor of the times in which they lived, he knew that she was bemoaning the lack of it in her own life. Sex if not squalor. In the silence of her room, with just the roar of the relentless A48 outside, Crispin often wanted to put his arms round Miss Siwsan Coity and tell her it would be all right. That one day she too would meet someone like Millie who would make it all seem so simple and good. But when he finally did put his arms round her – and he could still remember the sensation – his arms around her slender shoulders and her lips so suddenly on his, then he forgot all about Millie. Afterwards he could not believe it but he did forget entirely about her. There he was rolling around with this young girl on her narrow student bed, aroused and yet frenzied because she had forbidden intercourse. And she was frenzied too. She wouldn't have sex with him, nor at first would she let him remove any of her clothing, but she was as driven as he by the potent frustrations of near delight.

It became a regular thing on Friday nights although the evening that Millie went with David to Rock Point was a notable exception. Normally Millie would return and make a great fuss of the children. Then after their supper he would go and meet the theological students for what was now just a social drink, no longer much to do with the Anatomy of Martyrdom. He had begun these talks as an opportunity to get out and meet people, much as he had begun working at the bookshop, but now both ventures served a different, clandestine, purpose. Now, usually at some late stage in the evening, Sue would turn up and take her seat quietly. Then at closing time he would walk her home. These days they rarely talked as they crossed Cardiff Road, Western Avenue and Ely Road. They would go silently to her room and then once the door was closed all the embracing, pushing, kissing, dishevelling and grinding, all the near violence of their unconsummated coupling would begin again.

It was a strange relationship. Sue still wrote letters when she returned his books. Increasingly, though, she began to call at the house to do this. On one occasion she'd actually arrived during that little dinner party with David and Helena. Crispin had taken her to his study with an overpowering sense of his own outrage. This was too much daring on her part and his. They should not even touch, he had decided. They must not. She would hand him the brown paper parcel and then take the book he had chosen for her, his letter enclosed within and they must not even brush against each other. Fortunately Sue felt the same, although she trembled all the time they were in that tiny room.

'Will you read my letter?' she had asked He told her 'Later.'

When he returned to the office it was still there, Sue's letter, folded inside the book (a dubious text on the eroticism of crucifixion). He looked at where the letter now lay and found that he feared its significance over all the others he had received. Never before had Sue alluded to the presence of a letter within. Never before had she checked that he read them. Crispin opened the folded pages with a mixture of fascination and dread.

Sue had never spoken of any feelings for him although this by no means reassured Crispin that she had none. He recognised her silence on this subject for what it was. Now her letter spoke of *wanting* to tell him of her feelings and yet, by the bottom of page one, it had not. He could see that the second page ended half way down. What significance could lie in what remained? At that moment his peripheral vision caught the word 'night' somewhere ahead of the paragraph he was reading. He skipped down and isolated the sentence. It was as if his subconscious had speed-read the entire letter in an instant and now his conscious mind was catching up.

I would like it if there was a night when the two of us could be together and I could tell you.

Crispin sat back, cold with the shock. He had known that this was coming. Despite his more honest endeavours to wean Sue away from him, he had known from weeks ago, maybe months ago, that this was coming. He was unaware of whether it was something he wanted. It was just something that had been going to happen and now seemed to be happening. He didn't know what to do. But, to be honest, he felt there was little he had to do. Just find a time when Millie was away with the children and inform Sue. That was all.

Very slowly he got up and took down from the bookcase an old cash box which had been his hiding place at school. It was covered in dents and scratches from when other boys had tried to break it open. Crispin still had the key. He had always known where that key was to be found. Retrieving it now, Crispin opened the box and put into it all Sue's juvenile letters which had hitherto lain undisturbed in a desk drawer. Then he folded this latest letter into the box. Finally he took down the half bottle of whisky from the shelf. It just fitted alongside the letters. He locked it in, threw away the original packaging and hid the cash box in his drawer.

Had Crispin and Helena ever had that conversation about Gareth, he would have understood exactly what she meant about boxes in which to lock away the danger. But he would never have told her that he actually had one. These boxes were metaphorical, too. Crispin had, over the years, developed silences within himself that not even Millie knew about. His arrangements with Sue were one such silence. All evening at dinner in Ty Escob Crispin had been aware of the memory of sitting down that Saturday four weeks ago and selecting a book at random from the shelves, then of picking up a postcard and writing:

There is no obvious time at the present. I will let you know.

But he did not revisit these memories, not even as Helena talked. He just knew they were there.

That night he had parcelled the book and postcard up, walked the quarter of a mile to Sue's house and posted it through the letter box. When he got to bed at one o'clock Millie was asleep.

But within what seemed no time at all Millie had to be in London and was arranging for the Williams children to sleep over at Ty Escob. 'Of course you'll have to come back here, I suppose,' she'd laughed. He hadn't.

'Poor Crissybag kicked out and sleeping on his own round the corner.'

Still he hadn't laughed. He had simply dropped another note in to Sue. *Next Saturday may well be possible. If it is I will come to the Lion just before closing time. If you're not there I'll assume it isn't possible for you. If I don't turn up it is because something has prevented me.*

Then he thought no more about it. Or as little as he might given that Millie would keep trying to fix him up with Helena Mosford for the weekend. Any thoughts Crispin had about Sue were silences, locked within that old cash box. He tried not to explore them or even admit them although he found that his irritation with Millie grew. The lazy relentlessness of her sexuality seemed insensitive and an affront given the extraordinary bravery of Sue's gesture and the pressing reality of her need. He had heard no more from Sue until the Friday David went to London. When Crispin called in at Halls Peter told him that a young woman had returned a book he had lent her. Inside his study Crispin opened the parcel and found no letter, just a little drawing. It was another mouse in a dress. Maybe that was all that Sue could draw. Mice in dresses. This time the mouse held up a placard that read. *Mice like Lions on Saturday*. He locked it away.

That Sunday morning Crispin woke at his usual five o'clock. He was surprised to find he was lying against a wall and that sunlight was streaming in from the wrong side of the room. Then he remembered he was in the guest room. Last night it had seemed wrong to take Sue into the room he shared with Millie. Then he remembered: *Sue*. And there she was, amazingly, her head on the pillow next to him. They had not had sex although both Crispin and Sue had arrived at this assignation with condoms. The reason that their strange passion had not been consummated was that Sue was so obviously scared when things seemed to be going that way. Crispin had desisted but now, at five in the morning, he was exhausted. The signal advantage of having sex over not having sex, from a male point of view, was that at least you get to sleep afterwards. By stopping short of consummation they had continued kissing and writhing around until gone three o'clock. And now it was five in the morning and he was awake. He had dozed for no more than two hours last night and this was definitely what sleep deprivation felt like.

Crispin looked fondly at the sleeping girl beside him. Her body was so exotic because it was so unlike Millie's, so long because it was so thin, so white, so undeveloped in some ways. Crispin now had as great a wish to penetrate her body as he had her mind but he knew that something sensible had to be done. She must leave now before there was any danger of the children returning or Helena telephoning, or them starting all over again.

He made some tea, woke her and said she must leave. 'I have to go and do some washing up,' he said, kneeling there by the bed. It was an incongruous aubade but Sue nodded and got out. Crispin cupped his hands over her small pointed breasts and kissed her once on the forehead.

'If there is another time, shall I tell you?' he asked. Sue nodded again. Later he could not recall whether she had spoken to him at all that morning.

By six o'clock she had left the house. Sue didn't want to be seen leaving by the front door so early in the morning, the house on High Street being so very exposed. So Crispin took her down the garden, through the garage, and out into the back lane. Then he took a bath until it seemed reasonable to go and fetch his children. In the bathroom he thought, inevitably, of Millie. Well, that was all right, he could think of Millie again now.

What Crispin didn't think about was the curiosity and disapproval of his neighbours. Several of them in Back Lane had heard the garage doors creak open and observed Sue's departure from behind their curtains. *That House* would once again be talked about for days.

David Mosford, having raided the minibar in a state of profound nocturnal irritation, did not wake until half past eight. And when he did awake he no longer felt irritated, or profound, just very very stupid and possessed of a headache. Realising that he didn't have Millie's number in London, David rang Helena to ask for Crispin's but, at that moment, Millie's chap was actually sitting opposite her, having breakfast in their kitchen.

'Oh good,' said David, 'mind if I have a word?' This really was very cosy. It harkened back to their jovial ménage, to the time before he had been so foolish. How very innocent life was in Llandaff, he thought.

'Hi there,' said Crispin.

David was honest. He explained that he and Millie had had a bit of an argument last night although as he did he wondered why he was actually doing so. Mind you, there was always something to be said for pointing out to your friend that you haven't slept with his wife.

'I'm afraid I haven't got Gail's number with me,' said Crispin. 'I'll ring you back when I'm home.'

Millie was in the bath when Gail brought the telephone. It

was on a long extension lead from the landing. 'It's your fellah,' she said, nudging the door open with her shoulder and sliding in the phone.

'Is he grovelling?' asked Millie. 'He'd better be grovelling.' But David had already heard this.

'He's grovelling,' Gail relayed.

'Tell him it'll cost him,' said Millie.

'He suggests the Savoy,' said Gail.

'Ten Pin Bowling,' said Millie with the beginnings of a grin.

'He says you're a hard woman.'

It wasn't easy to stand in the lobby of Millie's favourite Maida Vale bowling alley with a large bunch of flowers but David Mosford did it. He also made a good show of joining in Millie's favourite Sunday lunchtime game and, as she pointed out, he had not for once dressed like a complete prat.

They had cola and burgers for lunch.

'Scrummy,' said Millie as he let her have his sachet of tomato ketchup.

'Yes indeed,' said David with only token enthusiasm.

'OK, you can stop trying now,' Millie conceded. 'I appreciate the gesture but you're not going to convince me this is your scene, Dave.'

'No,' he replied with a smile. They ate in silence for a while.

'So do you want to tell me what it's all about?' Millie asked. 'Last night, I mean. It wasn't the booze, was it?'

'Not entirely, no. Isn't it easier to say I made a complete prat of myself?'

'Uhuh,' said Millie and she took another mouthful. 'Won't help to get it off your chest though.'

David took off his glasses with a sigh and squeezed his eyes. They felt warm enough for tears to be forming and he didn't want her to see that.

'What if I say I'm under a lot of pressure at the moment?'

Millie nodded. 'Do you want that burger?'

'No, not really.' So she took it from him. 'What kind of pressure?'

'Work . . . Family . . .' he said.

Millie munched for a while in silence. 'You know, for a skilled communicator . . .' she began.

'Yes I know,' said David. 'I think . . . I think it comes down to two problems really. One is I'm not sure what I want and two is . . . whatever it is I'm pretty certain I'm not getting it.'

'*And* you're forty,' she reminded him.

'I don't mind being forty,' he insisted. 'I just feel I'm not where I should be at that age. If I'm forty I should be up there.' Millie was about to ask where where actually was but she could see David was getting into his stride now. 'There's this fellow who's almost definitely in for the job I'm going for. He was a professor in his mid-thirties. In America. They're all professors over there but he's brash, lowbrow, flash in the pan, full of self regard, totally unscrupulous. Everything the University is looking for.'

Millie smiled at him.

'But there are personal reasons too. Reasons why I couldn't stay in the department if he gets the chair. So you see suddenly, or not so suddenly perhaps, you look round, you're over forty, your career seems blocked, your marriage is, well it's got problems and, and . . .'

Millie nodded 'You think well, why the hell not,' she agreed.

David's thoughts had rather run ahead of himself. He was shocked by the way in which Millie had completed that sentence. There was a momentary pause.

'I'm sorry?' David put his glasses back on.

'You thought, with all these problems, why not have a bit of fun for the hell of it,' she chided him. 'Meaning me . . . mm?'

Well, there was a sort of sense in that. It came close to something he could recognise.

'I'm sorry,' he said.

Millie laughed but she laughed kindly. 'Well, I didn't think you were head over heels in love with me, Dave!' He blinked at her through his glasses.

'I'm sorry,' he said again, unsure whether it was wise to explain himself further. 'I think I did feel something like that, yes. I mean I think that was why I stayed up in London. Do you mind?' Millie would have laughed again but she resisted.

'Nothing wrong with temptation, Dave.'

'It's just that last night I just felt that it was wrong, all wrong. I felt annoyed with myself for having gone that far. That was the problem last night, I think.'

'Yes, you think too much,' she told him with a wink.

'D'you mean . . .?' He didn't know how to complete that question. What *did* she mean . . .?

'But that was last night,' she reminded him, finishing his burger and wiping her lips. David was shocked. But pleasantly so. Was that really what Millie was saying . . .?

'So you're not offended, then?' he asked.

She shook her head. 'I'm still sorry we didn't have that meal but if you mean am I upset you thought twice about trying it on? No. Mind you,' she said, 'if you're going to do the decent thing, Dave, there are better ways of going about it.'

He had tried to tell her the truth. He'd come close to it. But that wasn't really the reason, was it? It wasn't really that he had felt guilty or judgemental about the subtext to last night's rendezvous. The problem was he had objected to being in thrall to sex at all. That was what it was. He had gone to London and wasted his time with that ridiculous BBC producer, and in Camden Town, and at the British Library, and in that awful, awful pub just in the hope of getting off with Millie Kemp. And he was angry about all that. He had spent an entire weekend doing things he didn't want to do and all for sex. Why was sex such a problem in his life?

These were David's thoughts as he and Millie travelled back in her car. They were friends again. For Millie sex was simple. For David it was anything but. But they were friends again and that was good.

Helena was very pleased to see her husband and he gave her a long hug while Emma looked to see what he'd brought. 'I've missed you,' said David. Helena was worried by the length of that embrace and when she looked into his eyes she feared that she'd see a certain uncertain look of his, a look that might follow her round the house, but, no, it wasn't there. He seemed sure of her and of himself. There was nothing in his look to suggest he must hide things from her or, worse, that he must reveal things to her.

'It's nice to be home,' he said. She was still looking at his face. 'Why don't we go out to dinner tomorrow night? Just the two of us.'

'I thought it was nice to be home!' she chided him.

'Let's go out properly and talk properly.'

'What about?'

'About how nice it is to go out and talk properly. About us. It's an important subject.'

He kissed her. She kissed him back. They might have said more but Emma asked, 'Haven't you bought anything for me?'

Millie was very pleased to be home too. Weekends were usually for her children even if weekends with Millie left her children in no fit state to face the coming week. 'Who wants to go to Burger King?!' she shouted as she grabbed them both. An argument ensued between Jonathan and Katrin over the respective merits of Burger King, Wimpy and McDonald's.

'How was Helena?' she asked Crispin who was picking up her luggage from where it lay in the hall.

'Fine.'

'Did you stay over?' Crispin looked at her and raised an eyebrow, as if he thought she was trying to provoke him.

'Only asking,' she teased and she stroked his beard. With the flat of her hand, not the knuckles, just the palm.

'You are such a virtuous old bone-bag, aren't you?' Crispin took her case to the stairs.

'Oh we didn't either!' Millie called after him and she laughed. 'In case you were wondering. Right then kids! What's it to be?'

On Monday David came out of a meeting with several heads and acting heads of department which had actually been called to look into the possibility that too much time was being taken up in meetings. After lunch they were scheduled to meet again and discuss Links with Industry. How the hell could History have Links with Industry? Reinvent the Spinning Jenny? Reimpose the Corn Laws? Thankfully there was a message with Meg for him to ring Clare Mankiewicz.

Good, thought David. Wales and Vichy France. And about time too. But in fact Clare was in a bit of a state.

'David, I don't know how to say this really. I don't know if you know but one of your department, Alun Taylor, has written the most horrible letter and is insisting I publish it.'

'Ah,' said David. He really wanted to sit on the fence about this one. Unequivocal responses like 'Has he really?' or 'First I knew about it.' might not be easy to justify in due course.

'It's completely *ad hominem*. He's attacking Professor Box from the Mosiman Institute.'

'Yes,' said David.

'You know about it?'

David backtracked. 'No. I know he's from Vermont, this Box fellow.' But Clare wasn't going to be distracted by his hasty clarifications.

'The thing is, I could publish this and it would be good for circulation. People love this kind of gross pettiness but I'm giving you the chance to have a word with Alun Taylor. To see if he'll withdraw the letter.'

'Right. Good. And when do you want an answer?'

By the sound of her tone Clare clearly felt exasperated that David was taking such a relaxed approach to all this.

'I'm doing you a *favour*, David. This is going to look very bad for Cardiff.'

'I appreciate it, Clare.' He kept his response muted. If she wanted to fly off the handle and publish before he'd had a chance to talk to Alun well that would just have to be unfortunate . . .

Crispin and Millie were having lunch which she had prepared. It was hot in the garden. Ideally she would have eaten out of doors but in deference to Crispin she had laid the kitchen table.

'You still haven't asked me how it went with David,' Millie pointed out over some grapes.

'I imagine it went well.'

'Don't you want to know if he tried it on?' Millie smirked. She was feeling keen again. What was it about the old scarecrow that always got her going?

'But I know you didn't,' Crispin replied. 'Because you told me.'

'Doesn't mean he didn't ask me though.'

'No, it doesn't,' Crispin agreed. 'Did he?'

'No.'

'Well,' said Crispin. 'There we are.' He was peeling an orange and finding the very Milliness of Millie very irritating today. If only they would start her on this London job.

'Aren't you interested?' Millie asked, breaking off some more grapes.

'In what? In the fact that David Mosford didn't ask you to have sex with him? No, no I'm not. There must be some men in this world who don't want to have sex with you. Their existence is not going to shake my belief in a rational Universe!' Crispin pointedly set the pith aside.

'Why are you being so unpleasant?'

It was a fair question. The fact of the matter was that Millie on her own terms he could accept, enjoy, love even. There was a lot of her. You couldn't live with Millie unless you were happy to be submerged by what she was and that was something he had happily settled for. But Millie judged from the perspective of Sue: that was another matter entirely. Crispin did not want to think about Sue when Millie was around. He had been able not to think of Millie when he was in bed with Sue. Surely he could return the compliment now she was home? In the days when he believed he had left Belinda for Millie, and Belinda didn't, it hadn't been a problem to differentiate. To keep the two worlds separate, at least inside his head.

'I'm sorry if I'm being unpleasant. I'm . . . preoccupied. I think I need to get on and do some work.'

Millie felt that Crispin was deliberately frustrating her.

'The kids won't be back for another two hours . . .' she pointed out.

'Yes, well,' Crispin hadn't quite got an answer for that. Or the answers he might give were not the kind she wanted to hear. Millie got up and walked round to his side of the table.

'You spend too much time reading those books, Boo,' she told him. 'All those bodies being pulled apart and burnt and God knows what.' She put her arms round him. 'There are much nicer things that bodies can do to each other.'

. Crispin felt trapped by her arms but he kept himself calm.

'Millie, you know there is *more* to a relationship than sex.'

'Uhuh, but this is the fun bit. You know that we haven't since I came back from London . . .'

Crispin looked at her with compassion. Even if there was something to tell her this was not the time.

'I'm sorry, I really must get on,' he explained, explaining nothing. Get on? What did he mean? Oh, it was all so difficult. Crispin stood up in order to change the subject and tactfully loose her embrace.

'Oh, your father rang while you were away.'

Millie swore.

'He said your mother was disappointed that she hadn't been able to see the children last weekend.'

Millie slumped visibly in a way that Crispin found endearingly childlike. She was always the same when the subject of her family came up.

Crispin wandered to the kitchen door to check on the weather.

'He asked if you would like to go up to Montgomery soon?'

Millie sighed.

'And if you don't want to stay with them they wouldn't mind if you stayed at Lyme.'

'*Oh*,' said Millie. She would like to see Lyme and her friend, Alyson, who was restoring it. 'I suppose we could take David and Helena.'

'Can't we do *anything* these days without the Mosfords?' Crispin asked from the patio.

'You know,' said Millie, 'if I didn't know you better I'd say you and Helena did on Saturday!'

Crispin smiled sympathetically but he couldn't join in her laughter. This was not the time.

On Monday evening David and Helena went for a Chinese meal at the Happy Gathering. Monday had been declared an evening when they would not talk about children or the University. This was David's idea and it left a pretty well limitless horizon before them but not one to be explored indefinitely, because Katie John was babysitting and she still had one GCSE to take.

Nevertheless Katie seemed relieved to be doing her revising in another house and when last seen was talking happily to Emma.

It seemed odd to be inside a restaurant on such a bright evening, especially as The Gathering was a spacious windowless box, divorced from the elements. It could easily by spring, summer or winter outside. Equally it could be Fukyiing province itself as far as the customers could tell.

They felt exposed in the restaurant. Eating so early, and in such isolation amongst the empty tables and watching the pianist unpack, was not easy.

'Funny it's so empty,' said David for the second time. He had his back to the wall, facing out, which meant that he was very aware of the lack of ambience tonight.

'It's the bright summer nights,' Helena explained. 'Crispin told me. The same thing happened with them when they went to Le Monde. Most people turn up later.'

'We're out of practice,' he admitted. 'Still, it's nice to be out and not talking about the children and the University.'

'Yes,' she agreed.

'Right! House white,' said David, putting the wine list aside. 'Near freezing point. It's the only thing worth drinking with Chinese food.'

'You say that every time we come here,' Helena reminded him.

'Oh.' He looked saddened. 'It is true, though. Unless you want saki. Do you want saki?' She shook her head. A large fish was swimming in the adjacent aquarium and mouthing obscenities through the glass at them. 'Do I also always make the joke about ordering from the fish tank?' David asked.

Helena thought about that. 'Not always,' she replied. 'But to be on the safe side I think not tonight, please.'

There was a silence, the almost inevitable result of David and Helena abandoning their two main topics of conversation. But David wasn't going to be deterred.

'So what else did Crispin say?' he asked. 'On Saturday. I haven't asked you about it really.'

'Oh he was very good company. He listens a lot . . . he's a good listener.'

'Very commendable,' David agreed. 'And what did you say then?'

Helena looked slightly thrown by that question, so he expanded on it. 'I mean you say he was listening a lot . . .'

'He *was* listening a lot.'

'Then you must have been *talking* a lot. Or were you both listening? To the silence?' She took this as a joke which, fortunately, was how it had been intended. They still had that.

'No, I talked.'

'Good.'

'Mostly about the children and the University, I suppose.'

'Ah.' He could see the funny side.

'And about you and me.' She saw his eyes light up.

'You talked about Us?' he asked.

'Yes.'

'What conclusions did you come to?'

'I wasn't expecting to come to any conclusions,' she said, turning her attention to the menu.

'Oh come on, Linna, we're just getting to the interesting bit.'

'Meaning you?' She smiled at him despite herself. The idea that even when he was away from home the subject of David Mosford would still be talked about in Ty Escob appealed to David. His egoism, at its most naive, could be childishly attractive.

'All right then. Let's talk about Crispin, shall we?'

'Do we have to have an agenda?'

'I'm just keeping off the subjects of University, the children and me.' He was getting cocky now.

'I don't see why we had to outlaw those in the first place.'

'Because I want to talk about Us,' said David. Helena sighed within the pages of the menu. She wanted to talk about Us too. Us was a big subject but how did one get into it? Not by cutting a ribbon and declaring the subject officially open. Where did one start? Were there confessions to confess? Reproaches to reproach with?

David was uncomfortable with silence. 'I would be interested to know about Crispin, honestly.' Helena put down the menu.

'What about him?' she asked, conceding ground

'Well, for Godsake.' David was losing his patience. 'What's so interesting about this man apart from the fact that he *listens*?

I mean, there are giant telescopes at Long Mynd that listen to pulsars millions of miles away but that doesn't make them great dinner guests!'

Helena smiled to herself. She could sense the hyperbole, the outrage. She knew he couldn't keep these discreet enquiries up forever.

'He remembers things.'

'What kind of things?'

'The things I say to him.'

'Ah,' said David as if Helena had scored a home run there. 'So: he listens, and he remembers and, presumably, he also talks interestingly.'

'Yes, listens, remembers and talks.'

'Talks on those occasions when he isn't too busy just listening and remembering?'

Helena agreed that Crispin did talk interestingly. Very interestingly at times.

'Right, fine, but is he *attractive*?' David produced this question as if he was delivering the coup de grace.

'Yes,' said Helena. They were playing games. A preliminary tussle before getting down to whatever was going to be the meat of this discussion.

'Oh.' He was surprised but he pretended to look hurt. 'Are you *sure*?' She pretended to consider her answer.

'Yes, I think I'm sure,' she concluded.

'Well, bugger me,' said David hoarsely. Initially this seemed an over-reaction on his part but Helena could tell from David's face that he had seen something over her shoulder. She could also tell that whatever it was had suddenly taken the buoyancy out of him.

'What is it?' asked Helena starting to turn around.

'Hello!!!!' said someone with a familiar giggle in her voice. Helena knew it was Pippa before she even saw her.

'What are you doing *here*?!' The pixie wasn't gushing tonight but she did sound pleased to see them both. So why was David looking so pale at the prospect of the Arnsteins? Helena was still turning round in her chair as these thoughts occurred to her. Yes, Anders had his drawbacks but he would hardly cast a dampener over the Mosfords' night out.

'Well, isn't this *fortunate*!' Pip continued. 'You must come and join us. This is Gareth, who's been in meetings all day with Anders, the poor thing.'

And at that moment Helena finished turning. And as she finished turning she saw Pippa in something fluffy and non-existent and Anders in his expensively cut suit, and some other woman of indistinct appearance and a man who could only be Professor Gareth Box.

'Hi, David! Helena! Great to see you.'

Women in Tears

What happened next surprised Helena. From the look that had first passed across David's face, she would not have been surprised if he had insisted they walked out. In fact he stood up with great alacrity and advanced on Pippa's party, his hand outstretched.

'Anders,' he boomed. 'Good to see you! Hello *Gareth*,' he added in what might be taken as a friendly, if less enthusiastic, manner which was followed by '*Pip!*' and a kiss on the pixie's cheek.

Helena wasn't certain what she should do but it felt wrong to remain seated, especially as she was currently twisted backwards in her chair. As she rose she noticed that Gareth had dropped back in her direction.

'Hello, Helena,' he said, pitching it *not quite* as if they hadn't met for over a year. Pitching it as if they might have met in the last few months, or even weeks, but not pitching it as if it was only four days ago. Gareth was clearly practised at many kinds of Hello.

'Hello, Gar,' she replied noncommittally. 'What's going on?'

'I didn't know you knew Anders Arnstein,' he replied for want of an explanation.

'Didn't know you did either.' They were watching on the sidelines as David was being introduced to the fourth member of Anders' contingent.

'Actually I know his wife,' Helena added.

'Philippa?'

'Pippa, yes. She's very nice.'

'The wives usually are,' said Gareth. Helena glanced across at him. If she had had a fan to hand she would have rapped him with it to signal her disapproval of this raffishness. That was what her great aunts would have done. But any rebuke was forestalled by David and Anders who seemed to have agreed that the six of them should share a table together.

'Is that all right, Linna?' David called.

What's happened to the big discussion about Us? thought Helena but by then she was being introduced to the tall middle-aged woman with bobbed blonde hair who seemed to be Gareth's partner for the evening.

'This is Menna,' said Gareth.

'I work with Anders,' said Menna very quickly. She was clearly concerned to establish her pretext for being there.

'Helena,' said Helena.

'What's that?' said Menna, looking over her shoulder anxiously.

'Me,' said Helena. 'I'm Helena.'

David was arranging the seating while waiters hovered and Anders had a dark and subtle word with Gareth. He was that kind of person. Though only a little over thirty, he had the girth and manner of a mediaeval intriguer, his manner effortlessly conspiratorial even when all he was doing was explaining how the Arnsteins came to know the Mosfords.

'Pip, you sit by me,' said David. 'Gareth sits next to Megan . . .'

'Menna,' said Menna. 'Oh sorry,' said David, losing his train of thought for a moment.

'No, Menna will sit by me,' Anders announced with finality and he guided her round to the seat between himself and David. This left Helena on the other side of Anders and one chair between her and Pip into which Gareth slipped. David was still standing and not looking at all happy.

'Well done,' said Gareth, with self-conscious subtlety.

'Nothing to do with me,' Helena told him. Gareth nodded. He took the point.

David had sat down now, his seating plan defeated. He frowned and Pippa was frowning too. What was the problem?

'I don't see what all the difficulty is about, do you?' Helena asked. Gareth nodded.

'Anders and Menna,' he said, pouring her a glass of water. And so quietly did Gareth say those words that for a moment Helena thought they had formed directly in her head and not been spoken at all.

'What?'

'I think Philippa's only just found out,' Gareth murmured. Helena was stunned. So she was right. And yet she was stunned. In fact the fact that she was right stunned her more than the sorry fact about Anders and Menna.

'How do you know?' she asked.

'It's obvious,' he replied.

'Is it?'

'Sounded like it in the taxi down.'

'Cheers, everyone!' David announced rallying his spirits and raising a glass. 'What a happy coincidence. Gareth, *Croeso i Gaerdydd.*'

'Translation please!' demanded Pip from his side and with a glimmer of her old sparkle.

'Welcome to Cardiff,' David explained. 'Been back long, Gar?'

'A few days or so,' said Gareth, sweeping that lock of hair out of his eyes. Helena was well placed to kick him under the table but she was unused to this kind of subterfuge and missed. The wine glasses shook as Helena's foot hit the table leg instead.

'You should have given us a ring,' said David insincerely.

'Oh, I'll take you up on that,' said Gareth, gently returning Helena's kick with equal insincerity. 'It's good to be back.'

What a pair of hypocritical bastards, thought Helena. And the only other man around the table was sitting next to her, talking sotto voce to Menna. No, make that a trio of bastards.

David was still recovering, and recovering surprisingly well in the circumstances, from two very unpleasant shocks. Firstly he had no idea that Gareth Box was in Cardiff. It made sense that the man would come down and look around if he was applying for the job but to see his hateful face wander into a Cardiff restaurant just like that, especially at a time when he and Helena had come out to talk about difficulties in their relationship! It was a monstrous intrusion and a dreadful coincidence of the kind that any sensible divinity, or half decent head waiter, should have been able to prevent. But at least it was the kind of coincidence that might happen within a cruel, yet sane, Universe. But what happened immediately *afterwards* had almost made his heart stop. There, behind Gareth, was Pippa Arnstein. It was like a dream. Or a nightmare. The one person who knew how despicably he might have behaved towards Gareth Box was dining out with him tonight. At first he couldn't believe it. He'd tried to reassure himself that he'd only mentioned the name 'Gareth' once and that had been several courses into a boozy dinner. Certainly he'd never got round to mentioning Gareth's name last Monday in her *office*, had he? Unless he'd forgotten doing so . . .

It was at this point that David's imagination really took flight and a fantasy formed in his mind that, after he'd left Seattle Credit last week, Pippa must have telephoned Gareth in the Mossywhatsit Institute and told him that there was a Welsh academic trying to dig up the dirt on him. Professor Box was so outraged he had flown over, denounced David to Stella Price and now here he was, going out to dinner with Pip to celebrate the demise of David Mosford's career. It was the only sane and reasonable answer.

When two more people wandered in behind Gareth, David quite expected them to turn out to be Stella Price and Alun Taylor. That would have been his worst nightmare confirmed.

But in fact it wasn't a dream. It was a tall woman with blonde hair and Anders Arnstein. At the sight of Anders, who was too dark and earthy a character ever to find himself in anyone's dream, David knew that this was just a dreadful coincidence. Gareth was having dinner with Anders, as people did. As everyone did. And it was just unfortunate that Anders' wife was someone David had tried to recruit as his spy. And, more unfortunate still, someone who was also Helena's friend. But that was all it was. As long as Pippa was not starting to put the right two and two together, there was no possibility of her completing that particular sum and taking it round to Ty Escob for Helena's edification – and his mortification. No chance. All he'd said to her was *Gareth* and there were lots of Gareths in the academic world, most of them in Cardiff. The chances of Pippa connecting last week's *one-word-over-the-dinner-table* Gareth with this one were minute. But if she did then any chance of putting matters right between him and Helena would be gone for good . . .

In this not entirely sane frame of mind David had swung into action on the seating plan. He had hoped to get Pippa to himself and away from Gareth. He had to find out what, if anything, she remembered, and to effect what damage limitation was still possible. Unfortunately Anders had skewed David's subtle plans by placing Menna next to him and leaving Pippa dangerously close to Gareth. And now, before David had the chance to suggest they all moved round again, Pippa stood up and pointedly suggested that she and Helena withdrew to the Ladies. No reference was made to Menna.

'Where are you going?' he asked Helena as the two of them made to leave.

'To the lavatory,' said Helena in a tone that suggested she shouldn't have to answer that kind of question but if it made him feel better on this one occasion she would.

'Why?' asked David, convinced that Pippa must have indicated to Helena that she had something important to talk about. Helena was looking at him as if he were cuckoo. 'I mean, um why together?' asked David.

'Maybe we have something to talk about,' said Pippa with an incipient sniff and a glance at Anders.

Oh Christ, thought David. Suddenly the idea of people talking about him when he wasn't there lost all its attraction.

'Let them go, David!' laughed Anders, who seemed quite content to be mumbling into Menna's hair. Menna laughed to cover her embarrassment at being excluded by Pippa and Helena and Gareth said, 'Menna, tell me, how long have you been working with Anders?'

In the small, far from oriental, and badly tiled Ladies, Pippa burst into tears. Helena was half expecting this.

'How could he?' snivelled Pip, not caring to make any obvious sense.

'Anders?' Helena asked helpfully

'And that woman!' wailed Pip.

'Megan?'

'Menna,' said Pip, pausing between the tears.

'Oh yes, sorry.'

'It's his way of telling me,' she continued. 'I always arrange who is going to make up the numbers. He *knows* that. But yesterday he came over all heavy and said it had to be Menna. And when I asked him why he wouldn't tell me.' Pippa looked at Helena with her big red eyes and nodded her head significantly.

'You mean he's having an affair?' asked Helena.

Pip nodded again. 'It's obvious,' she said.

'But has he admitted it?'

'Oh no,' said Pippa, shuddering in a very definite way about that.

'Did you ask him?' Pippa nodded silently and tears burst out of her eyes again. Helena put her arms round the girl. 'And what did he say?' she asked.

'He just laughed.'

'He laughed?'

Pip nodded.

'He didn't actually say anything?'

Another nod.

'Well . . .' said Helena.

'He treats me as if I'm a Silly Little Thing!' declared Pippa indignantly.

'And what about Menna?' asked Helena. 'Have you spoken to her?'

Pippa looked angry. 'I wouldn't even let her come in the back of the taxi with us. She had to sit in the front.'

Oh dear, thought Helena. There may well be something in this. On the other hand, what Gareth picked up on might just have been Anders' vindictive sense of humour.

'Have you got any cotton wool?' she asked. It was time to repair Pippa's make-up and restore her self esteem.

'They are a very long time in there,' said Anders, gazing over the leathertex menu with a certain grim satisfaction.

'Yes,' said Gareth, glancing round the table. 'Does anyone fancy sharing Peking Duck?'

But Menna and David were feeling too uncomfortable to reply, each of them convinced that they were the subject of that conversation amidst the ablutions.

That bright and hazy evening Millie and Crispin had been working in the garden which was beginning to look more like the kind of thing that people usually have behind their houses and less like a home for abandoned packing cases. Katrin had placed herself in charge of deciding which plant should be grown where and she was not happy to be told that it simply wasn't possible to plant tulips in the height of summer. Katrin Williams believed most things were possible if you were sufficiently determined and spoke in the right tone of voice. Crispin was growing very irritated by the sound of that voice. Usually the noise of his children, happy or sad, was like water. It could either refresh him or wash over him. Never before had he felt he might drown in it. But tonight he dearly wished that someone would seize hold of that dripping tap called Katrin Abigail Williams and turn it off.

'Isn't it time for your bath?' he asked, as Jonathan helped him tie up yet another black bag of refuse.

'*No,*' said Katrin. Millie re-emerged from the house with a tray.

'Millie,' said Crispin wearily. 'Isn't it bath-time for these two?'

'I've just got us all drinks and crisps,' said Millie. 'You said yourself they need some fresh air. All that time watching telly—'

'Makes Katrin Williams fat and smelly,' added Jonathan. Crispin blinked. His first reaction was to be impressed at this sudden verbal flourish from his son.

'Pig,' said Katrin who was less impressed and proved it by lashing out with her foot.

'Oink, oink!' shouted Jonathan. Crispin sighed.

'Why don't you go off and have a walk or something?' Millie asked as a fight broke out in the geraniums. Crispin was surprised by that suggestion. 'It's probably all this heat,' said Millie. 'It's oppressive. We need a burst of thunder.'

'Um, well. That's very nice of you,' said Crispin.

'Go on then,' said Millie stroking his beard. 'I'll put them to bed.'

'OK,' said Crispin. He wished she wouldn't do that. It was awful, but he really wished Millie wouldn't stroke his beard.

'One of the advantages of having me at home,' she said, this constant partner of his.

'Right, I'll go and get a book then,' he said and headed towards the house.

'Why a book?' asked Millie

Crispin stopped in his tracks. 'Oh you never know,' he said.

It wasn't a lie, and Millie didn't ask him to explain further, and besides she was now demanding of Jonathan whether he wanted this cider or not. As Crispin selected a book from his study and picked up an envelope into which it might fit he wondered if he was wrong not to tell Millie more. He was trying to keep the two worlds separate but it was difficult. He selected an old postcard on which he might, if the need arose, write something.

He might have to. He really might. In the garden that evening he had felt *invaded* by a very real sense of Sue. There was no other word for it. His body had been invaded by the desire for hers. A desire which was hugely frustrated by the fact that unless Harry and Selwyn got their act together, Crispin's normally absent partner was going to be at home and omnipresent for the foreseeable future. He had needed to ignore this feeling but couldn't. This had made the noise and grind of family life suddenly quite unbearable.

As he headed up the High Street and across the Green Crispin hoped that he was not going to be foolish. There always was a turning back. He knew it was one of the fallacies of martyrdom that we have no choice.

The cathedral was locked but he sat quite happily by the Romanesque arch of the little south door and studied the detail of its geometric masonry. When had it started, he wondered. When did he reach a point with Sue which meant that something inescapable had been set in motion? The fact was that that point had already been passed when she gave him the letter which said '*I would like to to think there would be a time . . .*'

How then, he wondered, how might he have escaped? And yet he found himself acknowledging that he didn't want to. As a student in Aberystwyth, Crispin had seen a play in which the heroine, exulting in the hero's arms, had rejoiced that she was damned. It had made little sense to him at the age of twenty but now it did. That was this feeling. He could go back now, replace the book, return the postcard to where he usually stacked them, tear up the envelope and make love to Millie. Or he could go round to Sue's house. He had no message to give her. There was no date when Millie and the children might be away again. So if he wrote to her now, as he wished to, all he would be doing was upping the stakes. But the problem was he *had* the book, the envelope and the postcard. He *had* the time to write, and to walk round to Sue's sad lodgings. He *had* the need and inclination. And the damning fact was it was easier to write to her now than not to write to her. In fact it was *possible* to write to her and, he seriously wondered, maybe it was now impossible not to.

Crispin took out his pen. Birds wheeled in the dusk. When he looked up at them he could see a buttressed gargoyle, with the devil's forked-tongue. From this perspective the little monster seemed to be blowing a raspberry at the cathedral's belfry.

Dear Sue, he wrote. *Here is another book. There is no obvious time at the moment but I hope that there will be soon. When does your term end?*

David was managing to keep Pippa from talking to Gareth. This wasn't difficult, because Gareth was talking to Helena, something David couldn't prevent unless he engineered it so Gareth talked to Pippa. Still, given the two of them hadn't met for over a year, it wasn't surprising that they had much to catch up on. Furthermore, given that Anders had come out of his shell for once and was engaging Menna in relentless conversation, the whole strange arrangement was working remarkably well. David and Pippa, Gareth and Helena, Anders and Menna. Of course this wasn't how the dynamics of a dinner party normally resolve but everyone seemed happy with their own tête à tête although Pippa did glance unhappily at Anders from time to time. And Menna did look rather uncomfortable every time Anders put his long arm around her shoulder. And Helena did look uncertainly at all three men from time to time. But those considerations aside everyone was happy. Well the men anyway.

He wasn't having much success with Pippa tonight. She was being deliberately discreet about the topic they had discussed in her office.

'I don't think we should talk about it here,' she said in a brave and wounded voice. 'If that's all right with you, David.'

'Of course,' he replied. Her eyes were looking narrow and red.

'Anders may choose to mix business and *pleasure*,' said Pippa with a sudden burst of distaste. 'But I don't.'

'No,' said David, 'er, how, how do you come to know . . .' this might well be the moment of truth . . . 'come to know . . . um, Professor Box?'

'Oh he's just someone Anders is trying to *impress*,' said Pippa meaningfully. 'Anders is always trying to impress. It really doesn't matter *whom*.'

Once again a barbed comment and this time Pippa flickered an eyelid in her husband's direction. David was at a loss with this conversation but he little cared. It did seem pretty likely that Pippa had not connected last week's *one-word-over-the-dinner-table* Gareth with the Professor Box who was currently spooning sauce on to his aromatic pancake. All in all things were looking positive. David just had to get the evening over as quickly as possible.

'Have some more,' he said rotating the serving rostrum and keeping her occupied. The sooner everyone was wrapped in their own safe little beds the better.

'There are five kinds of Chinese restaurant in Montpelier,' said Gareth, and he recited their names with the conviction of a food critic.

'Wonderful,' said Helena who was currently coping with noodles of positively spaghettoid proportions.

'But the Cardiff Cantonese take some beating,' Gareth added. Helena turned to look at him and her noodles slid off her chopsticks one by one and curled up again in the bowl.

'Gareth. I'm not the University. You don't have to convince me,' she said.

'And of course the company's so good in Cardiff,' he told her.

'Stop it,' she said. He really just couldn't help trying it on. That was Gareth.

'I told you, Helena,' he insisted. 'I am in earnest; I told you that in Garlands.'

This was heady stuff although there were flashes of the old

Gareth too: the facility for words, the wonderful air of bogus sincerity. It was possible to laugh some of this off. But Helena couldn't just tell him not to be ridiculous this time. She was too confused between the old Gareth, the new Gareth and the return of the new Gareth to the habits of the old.

'Have you applied for the job?' she asked.

'On Saturday,' he said and then, thinking he could put it better, he added, 'On Friday afternoon, in fact, as soon as I left Garlands.'

'I thought you said Saturday,' she said.

'Friday and Saturday,' he conceded. 'It's a long application form.'

Crispin stood outside Sue's awful flat. The orange street lights had just burst into life. He could smell the traffic fumes from the A48 hanging in the air and see two bicycles collapsed, or rather crashed, wheels drunkenly splayed, in the porch. Sue should not have made the mistake of living here. This might once have been a nice house except that it was too tall and too thin, too near a major road and so badly built. Probably no owner-occupier had ever lived in this house. Maybe the entire terrace had been converted to flats as soon as the shabby building work was completed and everyone realised what they'd got. How sad that these houses were here at all, so close to the serenity of Llandaff Green. How sad that Sue should live here. He was tempted to ring the bell and ask after her, to hand the book over personally, maybe go in. But no. He had been foolish enough for one night. He prised open the letter box to deliver the envelope and in doing so he imagined his hand prising open her thighs.

Her white virginal thighs.

'Oh good grief,' said Crispin. He wasn't going to hang around any place where delivering the mail took on sexual connotations. He walked swiftly away and didn't even turn back to see if her face was peeping out from between the grey lace curtains. It wasn't. But he didn't want to know either way. He had to keep this under control.

Anders was puffing a cigar, pleased to have provoked a debate between David and Gareth about student numbers.

'You cannot ultimately educate everyone to University level,' David insisted. 'The basis of a University education has to be selection. It's a vital principle as far as standards are concerned.'

Gareth silently shook his head. David had always hated the way he did that. It presumed such a level of superior knowledge that a discussion shouldn't be necessary. On this particular point Helena would also have disagreed with her husband but at this particular moment, and in these particular circumstances, it seemed disloyal.

'Coffee or tea?' asked the waiter.

'Just the bill,' said Anders before anyone had had time to consider. 'Professor Box,' he prompted, as if the table had elected him as moderator of this discussion. Gareth flicked the hair from his eyes.

'We have to remember that until recently the only selection that has operated in Britain has been on the basis of wealth,' Gareth declared. 'Selection on income is no basis for setting *standards*.'

'At least it's selection,' David argued. 'You'd let anyone come.'

'Let them come,' Gareth insisted. 'They'll go away if they're not getting anything out of it.'

David feigned outrage. 'Meanwhile the good students suffer from those who aren't up to it!'

'Just like Oxford when we were there,' Gareth insisted. He spoke with passion, and yet with no malice. 'Except when we were at University, the real under-achievers were inbred English middle-class fools.' Anders laughed but Helena saw David scowl at that. Why did he object to Gareth speaking slightingly of their contemporaries? The remark was certainly justified.

'Tea or coffee?' asked a second waiter who hadn't got the message but who'd brought the bill.

'Coffee at our place,' Anders announced, producing his wallet. 'David! Helena! This is on me.'

'Well, thank you very much,' said David, losing interest in the debate but relieved that the evening was over. Helena was still thinking about what an enthusiastic teacher Gareth had been twenty years ago, his enthusiasm had even extended to those students with whom he wasn't currently sleeping.

'My pleasure,' Anders announced to everyone. 'It's been a great evening.'

Helena noticed how Pippa flashed Anders one of her looks but Anders was determined not to notice.

'We'd better get back,' she told their host. 'But thank you for the meal.'

'Why?' David asked his wife across the table.

'Katie,' Helena explained, also across the table.

'Professor Gareth, you'll come and have a nightcap with us,' Anders boomed.

'Thank you,' Gareth replied. Now Helena saw David's face register alarm. What *was* going on here?

To David it was simple. He really didn't want Pip and Gareth left together making smalltalk over the brandy when there was the smallest possibility that on home territory she would start back on the primary mathematics. Two plus two equals disaster.

'Look, Linna, how about I go on with Pippa and Gareth and you relieve Katie,' he suggested. 'Would that be OK?'

'It *could* be OK,' said Helena. This kind of thing had happened before. So much for their romantic evening together.

'Menna, you'll come, won't you?' said Anders to his employee. Helena could see the look in Pippa's eye which was reaching incandescence now.

'Perhaps I ought to be getting back,' said Menna but Anders was having none of that. He put one of his large hairy paws over her hand. 'But we're all having such fun. Aren't we Philippa?' Anders turned to look at his wife with a vulpine smile at which point Pippa stood up and very obviously burst into tears.

'What is the matter?' Anders asked, spreading his hands wide. But Pippa was already on her way out to the lavatory again. Helena had had enough and up she stood too. 'What are you playing at?' she asked across the table. 'This is the woman you are supposed to love.' Anders' hands went wider still and he looked helplessly at David as if to ask what on earth was going on with these preposterous women.

But Helena was livid. And there just happened to be a glass of wine to hand. So she flung it across the table. It was a gesture as much in anger against David, for being so ineffectual, as Anders. Not much of the wine hit its target but, as the rest spattered across the restaurant, several more diminutive waiters suddenly appeared from nowhere, surrounding the table on a state of high alert.

Helena had already gone to find Pippa. Menna was in tears. David was looking left and right, totally out of his depth, and Gareth was offering a napkin to Anders.

'Is there a problem, gentlemen?' asked a senior waiter.

'It was a joke,' said Anders and he rocked with what seemed to be genuine laughter. 'A joke she doesn't understand!'

'I'm terribly sorry,' said David, looking left and right again. 'She's never done anything like that before.'

Gareth suggested they should order a taxi. Anders gave the head waiter a generous tip and David asked Menna if she were all right. He had only just noticed that the woman sitting on the other side of him now had her face in her hands.

'Will you take me home, please?' asked Menna.

'Oh right,' said David glancing up at what Gareth was doing.

'Let me,' said Gareth, assuming this was a hint. 'I'll catch up with you folks later.'

'We'll take a taxi together!' Anders announced but Menna couldn't face that idea.

'No! Thank you,' she cried. Clearly any more time with the Finn that evening was going to finish her off.

'I'll do it,' said David, reverting to Plan A. After all, he had neglected Menna all evening. It was the least he could do. Suddenly everything seemed to have got a lot more serious than a question of keeping Gareth and Pippa apart.

When Crispin got back Jonathan was watching the TV and Katrin was in bed. Millie was sitting on the stairs and just finishing a conversation on the portable phone. She clicked the hand-set off and smiled up at him.

'Bun's in bed,' she said. 'Jon'll go after they slice up the policeman, so he tells me. You were a long time.'

'I did a round trip,' he explained. Crispin felt uncomfortable standing there in front of her.

'Supper?' she said and stood up to kiss him. There seemed to be no space between them. Millie crowded in on him again. He felt ridiculously trapped.

'I'm not really hungry.'

She looked disappointed. 'Let's have a glass of wine anyway.'

'Yes, um, OK,' said Crispin. He really didn't want Millie's body pressing against him again.

'You do make it very hard for me to get round you, you know,' said Millie. This irritated Crispin, the relentless omnipresence of sex in their relationship. He decided to put her on the spot.

'Why do you want to get round me?'

'Because they've asked me to go up again. To London.' She glanced at the phone and gave him a look which confessed that she really was an awful woman, pushing his legendary tolerance beyond endurance.

'How soon?'

'Tomorrow.'

'You'll have to stay over?' he asked.

Millie nodded and put her arms round his waist. 'Just the one night.'

'I've, er, got this *sort of commitment* tomorrow evening,' said Crispin suddenly. 'Student thing. Perhaps I could get a babysitter . . .'

'I'll arrange something now,' said Millie. 'It's my job, my responsibility. I am sorry, Crisp. I'm not being a selfish cow, honest.'

'No, you're not,' said Crispin and he kissed her. 'Not at all.'

When David got back from dropping off Menna, Helena was trying to work out how much she owed for the evening.

'Oh hi, David,' said Katie. 'Menna back OK?' There were times when Katie John seemed so au fait with their lives that she could have been one of the family

'What happened with Pippa?' asked David of his wife, as she hung up her handbag.

'She went back with Anders in the end.'

'What on earth's going on there?' he asked following her into the kitchen.

'Would you walk Katie back please?' Helena didn't seem particularly disposed to talk. So David did as requested and he answered Katie's various questions on automatic pilot.

'Have they advertised Professor Dorkin's job?' It was a starry night on the Green.

'Yes.'

'Is Pippa Arnstein's cat better?' Was Dorkin looking down on them tonight?

'Er, I'm afraid I don't know.'

'Is Mrs Kemp not working anymore?' They were at the gate of her parents' house by now. 'It's just that I've seen her around a lot more recently.'

'Yes,' said David. 'Her latest project's hit a snag.'

It never occurred to him for a moment why Katie would expect him to know about Millie's domestic arrangements. He was too busy thinking about the evening he had just been through and Helena's uncommunicative attitude to him back at the house.

Crispin had suggested they had an Indian takeaway for a change. He had even been out in Millie's car to pick it up while she rang Sarah John, to see if Katie would be free tomorrow night, and rang Helena about the trip to Lyme. He was such an accommodating man to have about the house, even if he was a grumpy bag of bones at time. Millie decided that she would be a good housewife in return and made herself a mental list of things she'd do before setting off tomorrow. She laid the kitchen table and then started on the monstrous pile of clothes in their bedroom. Most of these would go to wash and some old bits of underwear could just go altogether. God, some of this stuff stank. She was going to change the sheets on the bed too but Crispin should be back any moment and she didn't want their bed half stripped at the end of the evening. Particularly as she would soon be 'unavailable' again. She'd do the bed in the morning.

Crispin was a bit later than expected but then the Indian on Cowbridge Road was incurably optimistic about how soon food would be ready and, of course, he had stopped off, unbeknownst to Millie and dropped in another card into Sue. A card which superseded the previous one. Millie, for understandable reasons, blamed the Bangladeshis when her dupiaza was cold, not the girl from Devil's Bridge.

'I don't think they can say anything but *Ready in fifteen minutes,*' she laughed. 'If there was a queue half way round the block it would still be *"Ready in fifteen minutes".'* Crispin smiled at her good humour but said nothing. How much longer Millie could be deceived by her own blithe assumptions he didn't know. He felt bad for letting these misapprehensions by. These were lies of some sort. Never mind. Perhaps, unexpectedly, something would happen that would mean he didn't have to deceive her at all. Maybe Sue would refuse to see him on Tuesday night. A part of Crispin dearly wished that his plans for tomorrow would be frustrated. But if they were not, and it happened, he would not overtly lie to Millie. That was the awful truth of it. He would do everything he could to keep these two worlds apart but if they collided he wouldn't lie. He couldn't.

Don't be a martyr, Crispin thought.

When David got back Helena wasn't in the kitchen. She must have gone straight to the dressing room off their bedroom. David wandered in and slipped off his shoes. She was wearing a dressing gown and brushing her hair in a very deliberate way. It was never a good sign when Helena brushed her hair like that.

'Well, quite impressive that,' he said.

'What?'

'Your christening Anders with the house white.'

Silence.

'I feel sorry for Menna,' he said. Helena seemed not to have heard that either. 'She's from Swansea you know. Not that that's *necessarily* a reason to feel sorry for her.' He was talking nonsense. He wasn't even aware if she was listening to him. David sat down by the door and looked for his stretcher bars. Helena tugged at her hair.

'Is there anything between her and Anders, d'you think?' he asked.

'You're a man.' Helena put down her brush angrily. 'You should know about these things.'

David got the feeling that, in a perverse way, he was being blamed for Anders' behaviour.

'I'm going to bed,' Helena fumed. 'If you want to talk we can talk there.'

'You need a break Linna,' he said, standing up and putting his arms around her.

'Oh stop staying that!' she positively snapped. David was surprised.

'Well, excuse my stating the obvious but it's not normal behaviour chucking a wine glass over your host.'

'He deserved it.'

'Yes he did deserve it and a lot more,' David reasoned. 'But nevertheless people don't normally *do* it. That's what I'm saying.'

'Stop talking about normal for Christ's sake!' David took half a step to the side in case she was going to follow up her stated intention of marching off to bed. 'And stop backing off all the time!' she challenged, and she actually pursued him that half-step.

'I am not backing off,' he replied, although the force of her language was worrying. 'I am just waiting for you tell me what this is all about.'

'What what's about?'

'All this anger.'

'Don't you think I'm justified in being angry when, throughout the entire evening, I watch my friend being made miserable by her *toad* of a husband, trying to make her jealous, and you and Gareth do nothing about it.'

'What was I supposed to do about it?' said David, caught off guard. Then, rapidly revisiting his conduct for that evening he added, 'In any case I *was* doing something about it. I was talking to her, wasn't I?'

'Yes,' Helena replied. 'Funny, I thought we were supposed to be talking about *Us* tonight.'

It was one of those arguments that defy logic because the real battle was going on at an unspoken level. But if they were being wholly unreasonable David was not to be outdone.

'You didn't seem to mind,' he riposted. 'Not once you'd got all that attention from Gareth.'

Helena looked to heaven in her despair.

'Oh, you are so *puerile* in your jealousy, aren't you?'

'I agree it has a certain youthful quality,' he replied.

Helena took hold of David's arms and shook him. This contact was a shock. 'What have you got against Gareth?' she demanded.

'Gareth? Well it's obvious. The way he treated you.'

'That was a long time ago and I forgave him. Years ago. You know all that!'

Gareth was not a good subject to bring up at the moment. Not only was Helena currently confused about her feelings for him, she had just spent an entire evening in his company, something that was unlikely to engender reasonable responses in her. Why were these men either horrible or useless, she wondered.

After David had departed with Menna, and Pippa had assured Helena she was OK, Helena decided a walk back would do her good. It hadn't taken long for Gareth to catch up with her and tell her how splendid she had been.

'Anders was way out of line,' he explained as Helena strode along Cowbridge Road.

'So why—' Helena asked stopping and looking him directly in the face. '*Why* didn't you do something about it?'

'I offered to take Menna home,' said Gareth.

Helena was unimpressed. 'And now you're going back to coffee with him, are you?' she challenged.

'No, we've agreed not to have coffee in the circumstances—'

'In the circumstances!' Helena was outraged. 'That man was being a complete and utter toad and yet you would have gone back with him for coffee. While his wife cried herself to sleep upstairs no doubt!'

Changing her mind, Helena tried to flag down what she thought might be a taxi.

'Look,' said Gareth. 'I was their guest. It wasn't for me to be judgemental.'

'Well sometimes, Gar, some things *cry out* to be judged. And that is when you have to be judgemental. Things like cruelty for instance, things like reducing that poor silly girl to tears! Those things require judgement.'

'Well, there you have the advantage over me,' Gareth replied, rising to her anger. 'I had never met these people before. As far as I knew this was what normally happened when one went out to dinner with Anders Arnstein. I looked to you and David for the lead.'

'To us?' she asked. But she could already see his point. And Gareth was developing it in his own defence.

'I'm at a business dinner with people I have only just met. I can't just march in and sort out my host's marital problems. Who the hell am I to do that? I offered to take Menna home. I kept the ball rolling as best I could. I don't think it's for me to chuck wine in Anders' face.'

'Because of this wretched job?' she asked, still angry but uncertain of what to say. A taxi that must have seen Helena's wild gesture pulled up.

'Do you want to take this?' Gareth asked. Helena was feeling she had been a bit unfair on him and yet she was still too wound up to apologise. In her confusion she just didn't reply. 'You are amazing,' Gareth said and he took one step towards her. 'You know I am in love with you, don't you?'

'Oh stop it, Gareth,' said Helena, feeling both worn down and yet quite out of control. Her emotions were so confused. She was feeling so many things and none of them calmly.

'But I mean it,' he said. 'More than I ever was seventeen years ago.'

'I'm sure you mean it but you've got to realise two things. One is I may not *like* you meaning it! And the other is . . . is that even if I did I probably wouldn't want to hear about it now. Not tonight. Oh I don't know!'

She looked away as the taxi driver leaned over and asked if either of them had any interest in getting in.

'I must see you again,' he told her.

'No,' she replied. 'Maybe,' she added. He kissed her. She didn't stop him. What was happening? Then she realised and pushed him away. Why had there been no sense of outrage? Why hadn't she even noticed it happening? Had she been *expecting* that kiss? Did the mood she was currently in *need* someone to kiss her? This was definitely the time to get into that taxi.

'I have never loved anyone as I love you,' Gareth explained. His hands were holding her arms now and still she wasn't in the taxi. Why wasn't she in?

'Please! Not now,' she insisted.

'When?' She had to get in the taxi. She was amazed to think she wasn't already inside.

'It, it isn't possible,' she said then finally she got in. 'Just not possible.'

The taxi driver had his radio on. She asked him if he'd turn it down and so definite was that request that he turned it off completely and never spoke again for the entire journey. Helena felt disturbed. She certainly did not get back home in the best mood to calculate how much the babysitter should be paid, nor for conducting a cosy post-mortem on the evening with her husband.

As he undressed David was unsure what to make of Helena grabbing hold of him like that. She often got physically angry but usually only with inanimate objects. Mops, buckets, the occasional wedding present. Was she really so annoyed about his attitude to Gareth? And if so why? As he came to bed he could hear her tossing and turning.

'What's the matter?' he asked, although he feared he wouldn't want to hear the answer.

'I don't know,' she replied, although she feared she knew.

They lay together in silence for a while and then David put his arm around her.

'I need to get away,' she said. It felt like suffocation.

'Yes, you need to get away,' he agreed.

Helena exhaled heavily. 'Shall I go to Dad's? I could go on Wednesday. If I don't it'll be school holidays soon and if I go off then it means you having the children all day or putting them into playcare.'

'You go soon as you like,' he said. 'I'll be as wonderful as a man can be.'

'Will you hold me?' she said.

'I am.'

'Tighter.' He did.

'Tighter,' she said. David was pulling her hard against his flank. 'I don't want to squash you,' he said.

'Tighter. *Please*.' She was shuddering, almost crying, but he didn't notice. She was in such a state, angry and aroused in equal measure. Whether it was David she loved and Gareth she hated or Gareth she loved and David she hated she no longer knew and for that moment she didn't care. She was just prey to this strange powerful feeling and she knew she had to give in to it as completely and utterly as possible.

'Do it to me!' she whispered. 'Please do it to me.'

Later that night, Crispin and David were both awake and both thinking about sex. Crispin had got out of bed and, by the light of the street lamp outside, was watching Millie sleep. There was something sadly over-familiar about their love-making, he thought. Tonight, because he'd suddenly felt very sorry and fond of her, Cripsin had hoped that it would be better than it usually was, but no.

In fact, apart from that time in the stable loft, their sex life of late had become almost routine. Millie, marvellously boisterous at twenty-two, was no longer exciting. Like the avant garde she had become passé overnight and nothing had changed in twenty years, despite the fact that he had. It seemed ungallant to think this of her but Millie's very boisterousness now lacked vitality. It followed an overfamiliar pattern which she wouldn't break or simply had no interest in varying. Crispin could never tell her this but that night of unconsummated, even anxious, caresses with Sue had been his most sensual experience for many years.

David Mosford was in bed. He was staring at the ceiling but not as he usually did. Nor did it seem the same ceiling. Extraordinary, he thought. *That* had been *extraordinary*. What was it that had happened that had made the two of them so different? He had found himself making love to this wild sexual creature, this person that his wife used to be many years ago. She was so different and so, therefore, was he. But what had changed? He almost wished he'd stopped her in the middle of it all and asked what the answer was. What was it that had thrown the switch? And now that Helena had, seemingly, found it would she remember where she kept it for future use? Why *now*? She had been annoyed with him. Irritated. This was nothing new. And then she had needed him. It was, as they say, very nice to be needed but this went beyond need even. There had been a desperation, a craving to experience him that had been exhausting, painful even. He felt wiped out. Wonderfully so.

On Tuesday Crispin was at his sick books as early as ever but he got little done. Those tall shelves seemed to be nothing but reminders of Sue and warnings about the forthcoming assignation. Millie didn't actually leave Cardiff until mid-morning, having uncharacteristically chosen to busy herself with changing sheets and other household jobs. At coffee time they checked child-care arrangements or rather the *lack* of arrangements, given that she hadn't had much luck last night. Katie John had proved unavailable to sit. In fact Helena's friend Sarah had been quiet but firm on the subject.

'You'd think I was asking if we could involve Katie in some immoral act!' Millie joked.

Crispin smiled in an uncomfortable way. Well, that was one way of putting it.

What was he *doing* with this young student?

Mind you, what was he doing with Millie?

'How long do you need tonight?' she asked, this long-standing helpmeet of his, as she poured milk into her coffee. It seemed an extraordinary question.

'For this Student Bash you're going to,' Millie added.

Oh, of course, yes.

'Um, well. The longer the better I suppose.'

'If it was just a short affair we could try Siân again.' He really wished Millie would leave the subject alone.

'An hour or two, d'you reckon?' Mind you, she was only trying to be helpful but that only made matters worse.

'I can't be sure. It, er, doesn't matter.'

'How about David and Helena?'

'We can't ask them again.' But Millie liked the idea. 'The kids could stay overnight. It's a real godsend having found them, you know. You should ask. Honestly, Crisp. Then you can stay out all night if you wanted to.'

'Why would I want to do that?'

Millie took her first sip of coffee. 'You never know,' she smirked. 'You might get lucky.'

It was a joke but it made him very uncomfortable. 'Shall I give them a ring now?' Crispin just wished Millie would go back to being as unconcerned as she normally was about how he lived his life. All this unprompted solicitude was unwelcome. He would feel caddish if he grew angry with her now but, really, if she didn't leave him alone soon . . .

'Oh, I wouldn't bother them,' he muttered.

'It's OK,' said Millie. 'I've got to check with Helena about Lyme. David's keen and Alyson says we could have the stable block.'

Crispin stood up. He had had enough. Why couldn't Millie just fuck off to London? Fortunately the phone forestalled any eruptions of irritation. It was David ringing from work and explaining that Helena was going off to visit her father for a few days. This meant that it was going to be his responsibility to arrange the taking in and picking up from school. So was it possible to come to some arrangement with her and Crispin?

'I was thinking of a kind of Child Share, if that doesn't seem too awful.'

'Sounds fine, Dave,' said Millie. 'The only thing is, I'm going to be away as well so we've got a favour to ask you.'

'It really doesn't matter,' muttered Crispin, sitting down, defeated.

'Fire away,' said David.

And so that was how it was arranged. On Tuesday afternoon Crispin would collect David's children from school so David could give a seminar on the Munich Crisis and, in return, David and Helena would have Crispin's children overnight so he could relieve Siwsan Coity of her virginity. Everyone apart from Crispin seemed very pleased with the arrangement. Crispin alone found it difficult. But then he was the only one who actually knew what was going on.

David phoned Helena from work later on to discover that she had just received a large bunch of flowers from Anders.

'And there's a card congratulating me. Honestly!' said Helena.

'I presume he's commenting on your rectitude rather than your aim.'

'What a strange thing to say,' Helena grumbled. '*With my congratulations.*'

'He's foreign,' said David. 'It's probably a literal translation of what they always say over there. Everytime someone flings a smorgasbord across the restaurant. How's Pip?'

'Oh he's sent her flowers as well. She's going to stay with her mother for a few days to punish him.'

'She rang you.'

'She rang me.'

'And Menna?'

'It seems it was all a tease. There's nothing going on there. What a sod that man is!'

'Poor Menna,' said David. 'You have to feel sorry for her.'

'I'd feel even more sorry for her if she *was* having an affair with Anders.'

They left it pretty much at that because David suddenly remembered he was supposed to see Alun Taylor but then he found that Alun was at an examiners' meeting in Oakhampton.

'Is there a University in Oakhampton?' he asked Helena who laughed. He remembered it seemed to be one of the ways to cope with Helena, make her laugh.

At 7 o'clock Crispin brought the Williams' children round to David and Helena. They welcomed him in generously.

'You know I would have come and babysat,' Helena offered. 'Trust David and Millie to arrange all this disruption for you.'

'No, it's fine,' said Crispin. But given that Katrin and Emma seemed to be perversely and suddenly at odds over something, perhaps that would have been a better idea.

'Look, do you want to stay over as well?' David offered from where he was scanning the fridge for wine. 'There's plenty of room.' Crispin thanked him but pointed out that his usual 5am start would mean disrupting everyone by getting up in the middle of their night.

'Have a nice time in Gloucestershire,' he told Helena at the kitchen door. Suddenly he felt absurdly sad. These are nice people, he thought.

'Hey!' said David, happily reunited with a bottle of chilled something. 'How about *I* take your two in tomorrow? With ours. Start this child share thing off properly. Then you can even have a lie in.'

'He begins work at five,' Helena pointed out.

'Oh yes,' said David.

'But it's a generous idea,' Crispin conceded with alacrity. 'I'd appreciate having the morning wholly to myself.'

'Done,' said David.

So Crispin Williams left the house of his friends with the prospect of a whole evening and even a morning lie-in ahead of him. And the prospect of sharing those hours with Sue.

'Odd fellow,' said David giving Helena her glass.

'No he's not.'

'Permanently distracted.'

'That was just tonight.'

'But why?' David asked. Helena didn't know.

'And you reckon women find him attractive?' David continued, taking a sip from his glass.

'Oh yes. Some. I'm sure some women find him very attractive,' she replied. She was definitely teasing him this time.

David smiled at Helena. He was only just beginning to lose the memory of last night. Sadly, recollection of all that physical pleasure would fade far sooner than the purple imprint of Helena's teeth on his shoulder. That was still surprisingly painful. Nevertheless he had hopes that there would be more from where that had, inexplicably, come.

It was a bright and wonderful summer evening on the green but when Crispin arrived at the door of 27 High Street he found Sue posting a book through the letter box. This was not what he expected. Neither did Sue Coity expect Crispin to suddenly come up behind her.

'Come in,' he suggested, improvising arrangements. His note to her hadn't suggested meeting until nine, and then initially at The Lion to decide where to go. Sue looked unsure. 'What's the matter?' he asked.

'It's difficult,' she said.

'Come in anyway.'

His heart had leapt at the sight of her. Then, when he saw the indecision, even the discomfort in her face, he had been moved simultaneously to relief and disappointment. *So*. She had changed her mind. *So* this bright summer's evening – which held Such Hopes – would be the occasion of Such Relief instead. He was stood down from his terrible destiny. And yet already there was such sadness too.

'Come on,' said Crispin, keen to get the door closed. He felt she should exclude the neighbours from their discussion.

Sue stood in the hall, still holding in front of her the envelope in which she was returning his book. For Crispin it was a novel experience to find a woman at a loss in his presence. Most women, his mother, Belinda and Millie in fact, had always known exactly what to do with him.

'Is that for me?' he asked.

'I was saying I couldn't come tonight.'

'Oh.' He was standing by the door. She was standing by the stairs. There was sufficient distance between them for this to emphasise the difficulty of their conversation. She seemed to want to say more but didn't.

'Have you changed your mind?'

Sue shook her head. Crispin was not finding this easy but she seemed so unhappy that he felt he had to ask more.

'Have you, um . . . Have you decided it's wrong?' She shook her head again and after a moment tears began to roll down her cheeks. He felt that he had to put his arms around her.

To cross that short distance unbidden was another novel experience. His mother had insisted on her two kisses a day, Belinda had seized him by the buttocks as soon as they met – and not relinquished her grip until Millie had displaced her – and Millie was forever hugging on to him. Aware of his own curious features, and always reluctant to chance rejection, Crispin had never before felt he had the *choice* to embrace a woman. The choice had always seemed to be theirs. But now it was his and he took it. He placed his hands on her shoulders. He could feel them shaking. The sensation of Sue beneath his fingers seemed to tell him so much about her. It was like osmosis. He seemed to absorb the essence of her and yet he still didn't understand what on earth was going on. Sue spoke to him in Welsh.

'What's that?' he asked, trying to look at her face.

'I love you,' she said, looking up with such simplicity, such pain.

'You must teach me to say it.' She nodded.

'Rwy'n dy garu di.'

'Rwy'n dy garu di,' he repeated and at the sound of his mangled Welsh she hung on to him as if for dear life.

'What's the matter?' Crispin asked. 'I'm out of my depth here, Sue. You say you want to stay, that you don't think it's wrong. That you love me. Have you written me a note in the book? Shall I read that?'

'It just says it's not convenient after all,' Sue admitted, formally and unhappily, into his chest. 'Well that doesn't tell me much,' said Crispin squeezing her affectionately. Then it all made sense.

'Have you got your period?' he asked. Her big wet eyes looked up at him, and looked up in such relief.

'Oh Sue, why didn't you say? You couldn't, could you?' She blinked and a tear flew into the air.

'But what would I have thought? If I hadn't met you outside, if you hadn't come in . . .' He was so sorry for her. He was moved beyond his native tongue. 'Oh Siwsanfach, rwy'n dy garu di.'

They went upstairs and lay together on the guest bed, Sue curled up against him and Crispin kissing her head. It was eight o'clock. Whatever did they do till ten-thirty when Crispin made them both supper? Or, later still, till 2 am which was the last time that Crispin saw the clock before finally falling asleep?

Millie had rung while he was cooking supper. Sue was having a bath at that time. Millie had sounded very jolly, very positive about being in work again, very fond of him and very happy to be in touch.

'I wasn't sure you'd be back this early,' she said.

'Oh yes,' he replied.

'What are you doing?'

'Making supper.' And at that point she went on to talk about her day and the new project which looked to be definitely on. Crispin thought he should tell her about Sue at that very moment but it was unfair to do so on the telephone and, besides, last orders had just been called in London and Millie had promised to get them in for Nev and Harry.

'See you tomorrow, Baggy,' Millie called into the phone. When Crispin switched the receiver off he saw Sue standing in the kitchen doorway. She looked so fresh and young in his paisley dressing gown. 'Millie,' said Crispin. Sue didn't make any comment but held out her arms to him for another kiss. And another, and another. They had kisses until the early hours of the morning.

When Crispin woke up he could see Sue getting dressed in the gentler light of dawn.

'It's only six o'clock,' he said.

'I'll go out the back way,' she told him and then, in her half-dressed state, she jumped on to the bed and started kissing him again. 'Can we do this properly?' she asked. 'By the end of the week?'

'Is that when your term ends?'

'Yes.' She was nuzzling his neck.

'And you're going home then?'

'My mam expects me,' said Sue and she laughed. 'But I don't want to go back *as I was.*'

'You won't,' he assured her. He dearly hoped she wouldn't. These nights of non-penetrative sex were quite exhausting. 'Millie's back tonight. I'm not sure when I can get away. I suppose I could come round to your flat but I couldn't stay the night.'

'I want you to stay the night,' she said.

'I want to stay the night,' he said and they rolled around in bed together, seemingly unable to let go of each other. When they finally ground to a halt Sue started to laugh for the second time because she had to find her underwear and get dressed all over again. She saw him admiring her body and looked up smiling. Crispin felt as if he had never seen such happiness. As he gazed down at the wonder of her pale skin, and the relaxed affectionate glow in her eyes, he realised that Sue wasn't at all as he had first thought of her. She wasn't angular and awkward in the slightest. Or rather she needn't be. With the right clothes and a genuine belief in her attractiveness she could be quite beautiful.

'I do want to be done properly,' she said gazing up at him.

'You will be,' he promised.

He took her only to the kitchen door this time. Sue was very concerned that he should get some rest. The garage being open, there was no need for him to accompany her down the garden path. By the time they had had kissed their last it was seven o'clock. Crispin went back to the guest bed and didn't wake until eleven and even then he could still smell Sue on the sheets so he lay in bed working out what he should tell Millie and how he might meet Sue again. How unfortunate that by the time Millie's new job started, Sue would be on the long vacation.

David was in late that morning because he hadn't realised how difficult it was to ensure four children were ready and dressed for school. He and Helena had agreed that Tuesday morning would be a dry run for the two days when she was away with her father so at seven o'clock David made her tea and insisted she stayed in bed while he proved himself an exemplary father.

Half an hour later he told Helena, 'The girls have locked their room and won't come out. But don't worry. This can't possibly happen while you're away because I'm going to make sure that dreadful little Katrin Williams isn't even going to set foot across our threshold. However in the meantime . . . do you think you could come and have a word with them?'

At 8.30 he had marched them all into school and come back to take Helena to the station. Despite the fact that they had two cars, Helena had to leave her estate behind because David would not be able to transport both his children in the ridiculous sports car. There was, unusually, a parking space free in front of Cardiff Central so David had slipped into it and offered to come up on to the platform.

'I'd rather you didn't,' said Helena. 'If you don't mind.'

'I do mind,' he replied. 'I mind that you mind about my seeing you off.'

'It isn't you,' said Helena. 'It's just me. I like to be on my own when I'm going somewhere.'

Had last night been like Monday night, David wouldn't have minded in the slightest. He would have happily accepted a few more bites and scratches as proof that his wife loved him. But Tuesday night had been domestic, with child after child coming down for drinks, cuddles, stories and Big Jonathan asking if he could watch this film that had a man whose head comes off and all this stuff shoots out. When they had got to bed Helena had finished her packing and settled down to sleep. There had been no time to talk and argue and then have a repeat performance of Monday's passion.

'I'm sorry, David,' she said when she saw that look in his eye. So he had stared at the ceiling again and it had seemed the same ceiling as before. As it always was.

Not surprisingly David had not been in his best frame of mind on arriving at work, a state exacerbated by the fact that he couldn't find a parking space at this late hour because of all the sodding professorial Volvos everywhere. And by Megan, looking cheerfully at the clock when he got in. And by the way the entire morning seemed to be scheduled with Head of Department nonsense. And by the fact that this day, of all days, was the day that Stella Price's office rang up to arrange the interview and open lecture for Dorkin's sodding job!

'That's soon,' he told Stella's secretary. 'Oh it's to do with the availability of other candidates from abroad,' she replied with no tact or discretion whatsoever. I bet it is, thought David.

Crispin was picking up the Mosford children that afternoon so when David had parked the ridiculous car he walked back across the Green. It was yet another fine summer's Wednesday afternoon but at 27 High Street all four children were watching TV stiffly in the front room. David was not very empathetic when it came to atmospheres but even he could see that the way they all sat, upright and unspeaking, signalled something was up.

'Hi kids,' said David, adopting Millie's greeting in Millie's house. Emma rushed over and held on to him. 'Can we go?' she asked. He was about to reassure her that of course they could when Millie came down the stairs.

'Hello, you're back early,' he announced.

'Yes,' said Millie looking very strangely at him, her eyes small and angrily red. 'David, can I come round and see you tonight?'

'Yes,' he replied. What had he done now? Crispin was nowhere to be seen so David asked if he could pass on his thanks via Millie and he pointed out that tomorrow Crispin was doing the taking in so he, David, would drop the Mosford two off at about 8.30 before heading into work. Millie didn't seem to be taking any of this in. Something was definitely up.

The thing that was up was that at some time around 3pm that afternoon Millie had got home just as Crispin was going out to pick up all four children. She was pleased to have got out of Chiswick so early. Selwyn had had them all in a meeting at ten and had opened with the words 'If any fucker here has got a good reason why we don't do this fucking pub pronto I want to fucking know it now.' Faced with such a persuasive chair the meeting had quickly found consensus in favour and moved on to specifics. Millie was in the car park by midday.

'Remember,' said Harry. 'Any problems at all, whatever they are, however small . . .'

'I'm on my own,' said Millie.

'Too right,' said Harry.

She had driven back simply happy to be working again and bought all manner of unnecessary things for Katrin and Jonathan from the M4 services at Leigh Delamere. She had parked with equal happiness in the lane and hugged Crispin very happily as they met at the front door, him going out, her coming in. Great to be working. Great to be home. Great to have someone like Crisp to come back to. She hadn't really noticed his attitude to her. The Old Bones usually took a bit of warming up but what Millie did notice, as she went to put her overnight bag away like a good little girl, was their bed. She had intended to surprise Crispin by putting her spare sweatshirt back in its drawer and her knickers in the washing basket but instead he surprised her, by seeming not to have slept in their bed. She knew he hadn't because it looked exactly as she had left it yesterday morning.

And yet he was there cooking supper last night at 10.30 when she rang. So where had he gone afterwards? Millie was not normally a jealous – or even suspicious – person but she was intuitive and she knew that there was something that was more than odd about this. She really hoped that Crispin had fallen asleep last night over his blessed books. But she also knew that was not the case. She just knew it.

When Crispin finally got all four children back he started giving them tea. Millie marched into the kitchen with an armful of presents and then announced that she wanted to speak to Crispin upstairs when he was ready.

'Fine,' said Crispin, seemingly not at all unnerved by this. Millie made a fuss of Jonathan and Katrin and talked a bit to Emma Mosford while Nick glowered at his food and ignored everyone. Then, once the food had gone, Millie took the children into the front room and was very quick indeed gaining an agreement on which video they wanted to watch.

'I don't want any of you fighting or shouting or leaving this room, OK?' She raised a finger threateningly and they all promised to behave. Even little Nick.

'Our bed wasn't slept in last night,' said Millie to Crispin when he joined her upstairs.

'No,' he said. He looked surprised but he didn't prevaricate about responding to the accusation.

'Do you want to know how I know that?' she asked.

'No,' he replied. 'I was going to tell you about it in any case.'

'Tell me what?' she asked, still on the offensive but feeling the ground move, slipping away beneath her, being lost to him.

'I slept in a different bed last night,' said Crispin.

'With somebody else?'

'Yes.'

'Here?'

'In the guest room.' He was being very calm about it or seemed to be. With a sudden flush of anger she knew she hated him for being so calm about all this.

'Who?'

'Sue. Susan Coity.'

Millie sat down on the bed. She was staggered. Had it been someone like Helena that would have been dangerous but rather sexy. Had it been someone like Gail that would have been silly but such fun. Had it been another Belinda that would have been extraordinary but at least not a surprise. But Sue . . .

'That miserable looking girl who comes round here, the student?'

'Yes.'

Millie was glad she had sat down.

'Why?' she asked.

Crispin replied that that was a difficult question to answer. Millie told him he'd better answer it and soon. And so he did. And it was that answer that David had interrupted when he came to pick up his children at five o'clock. And it was that answer that Millie relayed to David when she eventually went to see him at nine o'clock that evening. But not at first. At first she asked him if he still wanted to have sex with her.

Some Things to
Tell Each Other

Wednesday had been a difficult day for David with Helena away. On top of all the usual single-parent balancing acts, to which he was spectacularly unaccustomed, Stella Price had called him in for a sherry at six and he'd had to decline.

'Pressure of family,' he'd explained on the telephone. 'Helena's away.'

'Ah yes, I'd forgotten you have children,' Stella observed.

'That's what my wife says too.'

'Well,' conceded the Head of School,' this *is* a family university.'

More corporate-speak, thought David. Why Stella, normally a very sensible woman, regurgitated the University's PR so shamelessly he never really understood. In the early days of their acquaintance he used to think she was basically a sensible person who had some odd ideological quirks. Just as his wife was basically a very sensible person who went slightly mad once a month. But now he suspected, and suspected increasingly, that talking, writing and preaching bollocks was the price that you had to pay for a position of power in the University. Maybe even Dorkin had started off sane. Once upon a time.

Coming home, of course, he had walked into something strange at Millie's and then in the kitchen he'd had trouble with Nick who was clearly worried that his father was going to poison him while Helena was away.

'Your mother has left me a list. Look,' said David indicating all the things that Nick could eat.

'Mummy's left you a list, *honestly*,' echoed Emma but Nick was not convinced. David knew Nick was not convinced. Nick knew him too well. He was happy enough to rub shoulders with David but only because he knew Helena was in change of important things like life, death and nutrition. Without a doubt Nick was possessed of the knowledge that his father had been no use when he was ill. David had no proof of this but he somehow felt certain of it. Nick as an ailing baby had absorbed Helena's disillusionment.

It was a warm and oppressive evening. Dense clouds rolled over Cardiff Bay, sealing in the heat and muttering to themselves darkly. By nine o'clock David had got the children to sleep and some whisky out of its bottle. He had decided to take a look at these statistics on inter-war street violence and was just about to decide whether his findings would be best suited to a tabloid or broadsheet article when Millie turned up and asked if he still wanted to have sex with her.

She didn't put it *quite* like that but it didn't take her long to get to the subject. David gripped the whisky bottle more firmly.

'Why have you changed your mind?' he asked. They were sitting in his office and, as dusk fell outside, the screen of his computer was beginning to bathe the room in blue light. Millie held out her glass in the darkness.

'You said there'd be no problems your end,' she told him as he topped her up. 'And that's what I want.'

'Sex with no problems,' he repeated, stalling for time. 'What about Crispin?'

'Stuff Crispin.'

'You're annoyed with him?'

David wasn't brilliant on human motivation but even he could tell that something significant was wrong. She kept making these little movements, hand gestures that cancelled themselves out, shrugs that came from nowhere and subsided into nothing, as if while she was talking to David she was having another conversation elsewhere.

'Look, are we going to do it or not?' asked Millie after a while. Her voice was no longer husky but hoarse. Her eyes simply no longer looked like those that had captivated him in the park, at Rock Point and in the loft at 27 High Street.

'Er, I don't think we should here,' said David. He didn't know what Helena would think of all this but he certainly couldn't imagine her accepting an encounter between him and Millie while the children slept upstairs.

There ought to be a moral imperative, he thought. This situation ought to be simple to resolve. He was married, after all, but Millie looked so unhappy. David felt for her looking so unhappy. He wanted to help although sadness didn't make her look in the slightest bit sexy. He got up from his chair and put his arm around her. She leaned into his embrace.

'What's the matter?' he asked. Millie didn't reply but took his right hand and placed it on her left breast. Perversely, David wished she hadn't, but he was not immune to that kind of thing. Never had been. Indeed it didn't actually take him long to overcome his initial wish that she hadn't done that. It was a contact he had been craving for nearly two months now. Although he had had that one amazing night with Helena recently, David had not entirely forgotten how much he had lusted after Millie Kemp. To touch her thus was heavenly and they were bound to kiss, definitely bound to kiss, but at that moment Nick's stumpy footfall became audible on the stairs. David drew back.

Later, when Nick had come and gone, David again asked Millie what the problem was. He had watched her talking to Nick and thought how brave she was, the way she overcame her obvious unhappiness to be jolly with his curious son.

'I'd better go,' said Millie standing suddenly. 'You've got kids. This is wrong. I'm sorry.'

'No don't go,' said David and he caught hold of her by the wrist, her warm and freckled wrist.

They were in the hallway by now. 'Let's talk about it tomorrow. I'll meet you. Somewhere.'

Millie looked sulky and indecisive, like a teenager. 'It's daft,' she said. 'I shouldn't be here.'

David felt so sorry for her. He put his hand on her head and felt the strength of her hair, her warm and wonderful hair, and then of course he kissed her. And of course Millie kissed him back. It was like the kiss they had had in the loft at 27 High Street but it went on longer. It was one of those kisses that, once begun standing up, longs to be horizontal and, as a result of this, Millie and David soon crashed backwards into the coatstand. An old Cardiff College boater which had been placed there for decorative effect snapped. The straw rim detached itself almost completely from the crown as it became impaled on the wall.

'I'm sorry,' said Millie breaking from the kiss. 'I'll get you another one.'

'It doesn't matter,' said David, moving after her. She had stepped back out of his reach but only slowly. She wanted to go. He wanted her to go. But their bodies wanted them to stay. The next kiss crashed them on to the inner door leading out to the porch and Millie got the large enamel door handle firmly in the small of her back. She was so enjoying his kisses on her neck that she really tried not to notice the discomfort pressing into her spine but, when she tried to move them both over, David lost his footing as an Indian rug slipped on the polished floor. He fell sideways on to an old oak settle that had come from his grandmother's house in Llandeilo. It gave an ominous creak.

'I'm sorry,' said Millie.

'Doesn't matter,' said David, getting breathlessly to his feet and putting his arms round her neck. 'Two hundred years old . . . really mustn't think of getting me another one.'

He was kissing her again. And again. She had to go. This was all so silly. Why had she come? With her free hand Millie reached back to the enamel knob and opened the lobby door. Yet while her left hand was trying to leave, her right hand was staying in touch with David's bottom and pulling him hard against her.

'OK,' she said, between kisses. 'Meet you tomorrow.' Her denim shirt had buttons. Millie's T-shirts always had buttons and David's hand seemed to be releasing them. 'My place or your place?' she murmured.

David wasn't listening. 'Or some hotel?'

Not listening at all. 'I don't care. Mmm, yes that's *good*,' she said but then he stopped.

'This isn't right,' he said, yet dearly wishing he wasn't so scrupulous.

'What d'you mean?' she asked. It had just been getting very right indeed.

'It's all the wrong reason, isn't it?' said David, removing his hand. 'This is revenge, isn't it?'

She looked away, nodded and started to cry.

David and Millie stood in the open doorway for some time. He asked her what the matter was. Millie did up a few buttons and then talked about Crispin and a few more buttons were done up. David listened in a mixture of guilt, for taking advantage of her, and frustration, for not taking advantage. He also felt such compassion. Then he invited her back inside for coffee and they closed the inner door, completely unaware of the fact that for the last ten minutes both of them would have been visible to anyone who might have been coming down the path to Ty Escob in the dark. Anyone who was calling at the house, knowing Helena was away, and who would have seen her husband talking to another woman who happened to be adjusting her cleavage in front of him.

Helena did like waking up in Barrington. She liked the birdsong and the lack of traffic. She could forgive the occasional RAF jet that silenced the morning chorus with one belligerent roar because here there was no hum, no relentless, dehumanising traffic hum. All those vans from West Wales heading east along the M4 and all those vans from England heading west along the A48. And all those Cardiff people relentlessly pumping their cars round and round the capital city, adding to the constant noise of urban life. But here in her father's house, a somewhat rundown property owned by her great uncle, Helena felt at home.

Everywhere she looked she was assailed by the colour green. Dark green hedges, bright green lawns and sycamore trees whose green against the sky was almost black. It was the summer green of England.

Although Helena's father had money, the Moretons had never owned a house. In her family one only bought for dynastic purposes and the Moretons had never been that wealthy.

As a grand niece of Barrington House, it would not have

occurred to Helena's mother to set up home in the suburbs of Cirencester, as other solicitors' wives might do. Fortunately this had never been necessary. Great Uncle John had always managed to find Helena's mother a home somewhere among the properties that he owned. Consequently Helena and her brother had grown up in a variety of old Cotswold houses, all referred to as cottages but mostly quite huge. Whenever a more immediate member of the family was found to have a more immediate need the Moretons were moved elsewhere but Uncle John and his descendants always looked after his niece's family. And now that Ted Moreton was widowed he had been put into a little two-bedroom coach house next to the main building.

On Thursday morning Helena woke early, which was a shame because there was no need. She woke missing David and her children. There wasn't room at her father's cottage for all four of them and, as David's parents were dead, there was no-one to have the children for a few days were the two of them to come on their own. But what woke Helena was not David's absence but the guest room curtains, so light and flimsy, too flimsy for a bright summer's morning. It was six o'clock. The choice was to stay in bed, to try and sleep, or to get up. Helena chose the latter. Ever since she was a child she had loved having the big garden at Barrington to herself. She left a note for her father on the kitchen table and went out across the tiny lane that separated the coach house from the kitchen wing.

'I could live here,' she said to herself. The great lawn was so wide that in Cardiff they would build a housing estate on it. 'Oh yes, I could live here,' she said.

Why was she in Wales? She loved the mellow stone of Gloucestershire. She loved the space that affluence can create around a life. Space that will help it develop. She loved the time her cousins and aunts had for each other. Cardiff had its points. Cardiff was a good city to live in if you liked Victorian architecture, the thrust of capital city life, the world of night clubs and money, the sense of an emergent nationhood even.

The problem was that Helena didn't.

'I could live here,' she said again to the morning air. Except of course she couldn't. This was not where the life of Helena

Mosford was. And, were Barrington not so lovely on a summer's morning, that fact would have made her truly sad.

All things considered, it was not a good day for Gareth Box to turn up and offer to take Helena away from it all. Which is what he did just after lunch.

'Darling,' said her father who was just going out to look at a blocked sink for one of the aunts. 'Darling, look who's here.'

Helena's father had cultivated vagueness since his retirement. He enjoyed pottering, doing little jobs to justify his status as a Barrington pensioner, and preferred to pretend that life was a bit of a joke. But he was a good listener, old Mr Moreton. When things were obviously bad between his lovely daughter and her husband, he had listened to all her complaints and written the cheque for a large sum of money so they could take a holiday. But he hadn't offered his opinion. Maybe, as a solicitor, he felt he had spent enough of his life taking money and dishing out advice. Now he preferred to give, and to keep quiet. If his lovely daughter chose to get away from her husband and children for a few days then so she should. If one of her old boyfriends turned up the next day then it was probably best to pretend there was a funny side to all this.

'Hello Helena,' said Gareth in the kitchen doorway. Helena was shocked to see him. Then pleased, then angry that Gareth's intrusion would cause her father to assume she had arranged this assignation.

'Gerald, isn't it?' said Mr Moreton.

'Gareth, sir,' said Gareth with his engaging freshman's smile.

'That's right!' chuckled old Mr Morteon. 'Oxford!'

'Indeed,' Gareth agreed. 'I introduced David and Helena.'

'Oh well done,' said Mr Moreton. 'Well I'm just off to take my plunger round to Hester. Helena will make you welcome, I'm sure.'

'We'll go out for a walk,' she announced firmly.

'Excellent,' said her father and Helena caught his eye. He knows, she thought. He knows why this man is here. He's as worried as I am. 'Excellent,' Mr Moreton repeated as he pulled the door to behind the three of them.

It was a hot, oppressive afternoon as they walked down the lane. The birds were keeping quiet in all this heat and so was

Helena. But as soon as Mr Moreton had turned off for her aunt's she demanded to know what Gareth thought he was doing there, how he knew that she was there, and how he had found out the address. Gareth was able to explain that she'd told him at the Happy Gathering that she was planning to visit her father. The address he'd remembered from when she was a student. 'You gave it to me in case I was going to cancel our first meeting in London,' he reminded her. Helena was touched to think that even then she must have had Gareth pretty well sized up.

'I think I thought you would cancel,' she told him.

'I was crazy about you,' he insisted. No, I was the crazy one thought Helena. I was so in love with you. Mind you, she was being pretty crazy now.

'And you kept my home address?' she asked. She shouldn't ask that kind of question because it got the kind of answer Gareth liked to give.

'Would I forget it?'

'Barrington House, Barrington,' said Helena. 'Not too difficult, I suppose.' She took them through a gap in the garden wall. 'OK. So tell me, what are you doing here?' she asked.

'I had to see you.'

'Why?'

Gareth stopped walking because he wanted her to turn and look at him. This made it impossible for Helena not to stop slowly in her tracks but she kept her eyes on the distant lake and waited for his words to come. Whatever they were, she felt she'd only be sucked in further. Gareth's words: they seemed to form on the lake and to rise towards her. She knew they were on their way.

'Because we never finished our conversation at the restaurant and because I've never apologised properly for the fact that seventeen years ago I made the greatest mistake in my life when I told you to go. I should have begged you to marry me instead of David.'

'You did,' she said, determined not to be affected by him. 'The night before we were married in fact. You asked me to run away and marry you instead. Have you forgotten that?'

'No. No, I haven't.' He seemed to pause, as if she had caught him off guard. 'But I didn't try hard enough. Helena—'

She wasn't looking at him. She feared that if she did she might laugh at the look of deep sincerity on his face. Or, worse, she might be convinced.

'That's why I'm asking you now,' he said. His voice betrayed that same depth of feeling, that unaffected gaucherie, that unexpected note of sincerity she had heard at Fortnum's and in Garlands.

'Gareth, you must stop saying that.' Now she could hear the tenderness in her own voice, that dangerous fondness that led to beds and a lifetime of mistakes. She was staring very hard at the lake. She wanted so much to say 'Oh look, a mallard!' or 'Did you see that fish jump right out of the water!' but nothing happened to break the surface or the moment. Her family, all of whom could use the garden at any time, were nowhere to be seen. No aircraft cut across the blue, no shadows were cast by passing clouds. It was a still summer afternoon. Perfect and silent with only the weight of all that sky bearing down upon them.

'You're not happy with David,' said Gareth moving closer. Not a bird or a leaf stirred. 'I could make you happy. And, if you'd forgive me for what I did, you could make me happy too.'

It was like finding yourself in a familiar landscape and seeing it for the first time. Helena was standing on the lawn that had been a backdrop to so much of her childhood. She was looking at a skyline that she had seen all her life. And yet suddenly she was a person seeing it all for the first time. And finding it so silent too. The world had gone as silent as it had in Piccadilly three weeks ago.

'I think,' she said after a deep breath, 'that we should have tea.' This was what her great aunts would have said. 'Tea is what people usually do in the circumstances, don't you think?'

Barrington no longer ran to full-time domestics but Mrs Dorrell, who was a housekeeper in Helena's childhood, sat every afternoon slowly polishing silver in the kitchen. She fussed about getting tea for the pair of them but Gareth insisted on carrying it into the garden. They sat on two wicker chairs near an enormous sycamore.

'Can I assume,' Helena began, 'that despite all evidence to the contrary, your intentions are honourable?'

'Never more so,' Gareth agreed. The sun throbbed in her forehead like a migraine.

'So you're asking me to leave David and marry you?' It felt like a monumental utterance but this was the kind of thing she could say to Gareth. She had never shocked him as she could shock David.

'Of course,' he replied. 'If that's what you want. I hadn't thought of marriage but it's not a problem. If you'd be willing to be married to me then I'd be delighted.'

'Well, that is the problem,' she agreed. 'Marrying you means *being* married to you, Gareth. And you are not the kind of person who can successfully be married, are you?'

'I've never tried before.'

'I thought you'd been engaged.'

'It's not the same. I would try. Helena, you're not happy with David. I think you could be happier with me.'

She thought about this for a long time, looking at the sycamore and the wide, wide lawns. Barrington always gave her space to think about difficult questions.

'I wonder,' she said. 'I wonder if I could be happier with you. And if I could . . . is it worth the risk?'

'We only have this one life,' he reminded her. 'I may be dead in fifteen years' time. In fact I'm sure I will be. Please, I'm not asking you to feel sorry for me,' he insisted. 'I'm just telling you the truth. I believe I have only a quarter of my life left and I don't want to spend it without you. I have to ask you to do this. To make me this happy.'

'Where would we live?'

'Wherever you want.'

'Tell me about Vermont.'

Gareth was surprised to be asked that question but he gave Helena a picture of life in his part of America. She seemed determined to understand its history and the sense of space. She wanted to grasp the beauty of its landscape, feel the cold, cold mornings of winter. Helena also asked him about his colleagues and for the first time she began to understand something of the world where he had made his home. Fortunately Gareth had always found her attention the greatest encouragement. He talked for far longer than he intended about his bachelor house in the hills, its wooden porch, the stream where he swam in the summer. He even had a photograph of it.

'Do you really want to see this?' he asked.

She looked at the picture for a long time, even though it was clear that Gareth was growing uncomfortable at her silence. But he, unlike David, didn't rush in to fill it.

'Are the winters long?' she asked.

He agreed they were. 'Sometimes the snow is beautiful. The British have no idea how many kinds of snow you can get. But you're always glad to see it go.'

'What do you do in the winter?' she asked.

'Keep warm, visit, work and go to New York. It's not far away. But look we don't need to talk about Vermont. I may get the chair over here and then you won't have to move.'

'No,' said Helena. 'If I say yes to you it's because we'll leave Cardiff. I might consider going with you back to America. But if I leave David I'm not leaving him with nothing, Gar. If you want me you've got to withdraw from the job.'

That same Thursday afternoon Crispin went to see Sue. A lot had happened in the last twenty-four hours.

When Millie had come back from wherever it was she'd stormed out to on Wednesday night, Crispin was in his study. She had gone out in a state and by the sound of the banging door downstairs had come back in a state too.

What Crispin didn't know was that by the end of her chat with David, Millie was actually feeling quite good about herself and the situation. She knew there was a calm way to handle all this but as soon as she got back to the house where *He* had secretly had *Her* (never mind all this non-penetrative crap) she was livid again.

'I want to talk to you,' said Millie, flinging open the door of his study. It smashed against the bookshelves.

'Oh. Right,' said Crispin, as if this was a new idea on her part. 'Do you want me to come downstairs or are you going to shout at me up here?' Millie was about to hit him again but she resisted. In her attempts to understand better, Millie had struck Crispin several times that day and it wasn't doing either of them any good. Her hand was definitely hurting far more than he seemed to be.

When they got downstairs Crispin asked if he could have the first say this time.

'Uh huh,' said Millie grimly and she hoiked a bottle of wine out of the fridge. Crispin found his usual position resting against the sink.

'Before we say anything else, um, I think you should appreciate that Katrin is asleep but that Jonathan isn't. They're in the same room tonight and obviously know something is up and, er, I really think we should try to keep our voices down.'

'You should have thought of that *Before*, shouldn't you?' said Millie blackly.

'The other thing I wanted to say,' Crispin continued, undeterred, 'is that throughout our relationship you have always maintained that we were free to explore other relationships. This fact rather slipped my mind when we were having our first and second arguments this afternoon. It's, it's something worth bearing in mind when you are pondering the basis of my shitty conduct. That is, as I recall it, your term for the relationship I've been having with Sue.'

'Do you want a drink?' Millie asked belligerently.

'No. Thank you.'

'OK. Let's get some things straight,' she said, resting on the open fridge door. 'We are not married but we did commit ourselves to Something, right?' Crispin nodded. 'And part of that Something was that we were free to have other relationships. Right?'

'I've just told you that,' Crispin pointed out.

'But the *important thing*!' Here Millie checked herself. 'The important thing – which I thought you understood – was that we didn't deceive each other. That we told each other.'

Crispin could see that Millie was trying very hard to hold on to a reasonable discussion of these issues. He let her continue. 'Like if I'd screwed one of the foremen I would have told you. Or if you'd had it off with Helena when you went round there the other night you would have told me. That was the arrangement, right?'

'Right,' Crispin agreed.

'Not that I ever have. Have you?'

'No,' said Crispin.

'Until now,' said Millie. 'So. Why didn't you tell me when I got back from London last week?'

'I'm sorry,' said Crispin. 'I should have told you. I would have.'

'You didn't, though.' Her breathing was accelerating.

'I was at fault, I'm sorry.'

'But *why* didn't you tell me?' She was being tenacious about this. Although even to Millie the reasons for her tenacity were unclear.

Crispin wiped his hand across his forehead. 'I, er, I was going to tell you. It's really . . . well to be honest it's crept up on me really. I didn't realise at first what was happening, that it was becoming a relationship.'

Millie stared blackly at him over her wine glass. 'You mean you didn't realise something was happening even though you went to bed with her twice. Oh come on, Crisp! She didn't just turn up here and you just ended up in bed by mistake, did you?'

'No,' he admitted.

'You arranged it, didn't you?'

'Yes,' he agreed. Millie slammed the fridge door shut. The bottles clattered alarmingly.

'And that's what I think is so shitty about this. It wasn't a mistake because you were both too pissed to realise. You set out to seduce that kid.'

Crispin shook his head. 'That's not true,' he said. 'It was something we both wanted.'

'You're still taking advantage though. And that's pretty shitty. In fact it's worse: it's very very shitty.'

'I am not taking advantage!' Crispin looked very definite about that.

'Not taking advantage,' Millie echoed with mock incredulity. 'You chose the one virgin at Cardiff University—' Crispin tried to interrupt but she shouted him down. 'You chose some poor desperate kid and exploited her!'

'That is not so!' Crispin felt an unaccustomed anger surge through him. The force of his words took the wind out of Millie's sails for a moment. 'You know me better than that.'

'Oh,' she said. Yet she couldn't get her head round the alternative. 'You mean this happened because you genuinely liked her?'

'Yes,' said Crispin. He felt quite amazed at her attitude. *'Of course* I liked her!'

'You like her . . .' Millie repeated. 'You *fancy* her?'

Crispin looked away. He was finding this distasteful and yet he was obliged to answer.

'Yes, if it makes any difference, I fancy her, I did *fancy* her, yes. That's true.'

'I don't believe you,' said Millie.

'I found her attractive,' he insisted. 'I still do. Probably.'

Millie shook her head. She really was finding it very hard to credit this.

'OK. So if you do find her attractive – which I don't believe – but if you do, if you did – why didn't you tell me? That's all you had to do.'

Crispin was beginning to wish he'd had that glass of wine.

'Well, to be honest, I didn't think you would understand.'

'Well I don't!' said Millie. 'But would that matter? I think I'd say there was something pretty cock-eyed about your tastes. Something a bit fucking male menopausal, perhaps. I mean there would be but, well, we could have talked about it, I suppose.'

Crispin picked up a glass and filled it from the tap. 'And that is precisely why I didn't want to talk about it,' he told the draining board quietly. 'Because of what you've just said. I wanted to keep her out of all that!'

'Out of all what?'

'All your *easy-come-easy-go*, petty, catty, lazy, *get-the-sex-right-and-the-relationship-will-sort-itself-out*, foul-mouthed clap trap.' He took a gulp from the water and Millie watched as a stray globule flowed down his beard and hung there for a moment. She was stunned.

'Christ, Crisp,' she said. 'You love her, don't you?'

Which conversation was the reason why, on that Wednesday afternoon, Crispin went to find Sue, while David collected all four of the children from school. Millie had said that he had to find out, or take time to decide, whether this was screwing or love. If it was just a screw that hadn't quite happened then it was a mistake and he was in the wrong for exploiting Sue but that would be the end of it as long as he didn't intend to continue the relationship. Of course he would have to end the relationship responsibly but, as long as he did, things could go back to how they were. But if he was in love with her then that was the end of everything.

'What do you mean?' Crispin had asked sipping from his water. His throat was dry, not exactly with fear but with slow dark realisation.

'You and me,' said Millie. 'The end of us.'

'But what does that mean? Are you asking me to move out?' Millie looked into the wine she had poured herself. There were two of them studying the glassware now. She didn't want to say these things but they were already there in her mind waiting to be said.

'If you don't love me, I don't want you living here.'

Those thoughts might be in her mind but they took her heart by surprise when she heard them voiced. And they hurt her so much. So much so that Millie wanted to ask him again why he had done this. But that would mean starting all over again with the recriminations, anger and tears.

'I've never said I don't love you,' Crispin pointed out quietly but he was only pointing it out. He wasn't proclaiming it from the rooftops, or even from the kitchen sink. Millie just wanted to get away from him. When he'd gone she poured herself another glass of wine and tried to think of someone to phone. In the end she could think of no-one. Not Gail, not Alyson, not David, not even Harry. She felt so alone. She remembered hearing her father say that, years ago, and her mother shouting at him, 'How can you feel alone in Montgomery? You've got family here and children and friends!' Well, Millie had got her family and friends here too but today she felt so alone. Utterly, utterly alone.

At the same time that Crispin went to see Sue, Gareth was on the spot in Gloucestershire.

'But if I got the chair in Cardiff,' he was saying, 'nothing in your life would have to change. You would keep your friends, your children wouldn't have to move school . . .'

Helena shook her head. 'If I leave David I want to leave him with his dignity. If you got the chair that would leave him nothing.'

Gareth got up. 'I hadn't realised,' he said. 'You're saying it's a choice between you and the job?' And Helena had to agree, simply and firmly, that yes, it was. But she didn't want to. She didn't want to be disappointed in Gareth again. And yet she had to know.

'Don't you like Wales?' he asked.

'No,' she replied.

'I thought you did.'

'I don't know why you thought that.' Helena stood up too. 'You've clearly never listened to what I've said.' Gareth could see that now she was standing she could walk away. He tried to keep her there.

'I had hopes that I could return to Wales and be with you and live out my days in the place and with the person who means most to me—'

'Well, you'd have to choose, Gareth. It would be Wales or me. I hope that wouldn't be a difficult decision . . .'

'And if I choose you . . . will you choose me?'

She didn't want to be hard on him. In all likelihood she loved him and wanted his happiness but the Gareth Box of old had to make way for a man she could respect if anything was going to come of this.

'Gar, it's not a simple question of rewarding you for making the effort. I will not consider leaving David while you are trying to take this job off him.' Gareth sat down again. 'You've got to choose. What do you want most? His wife or his job?'

Crispin had left a note at Sue's flat the previous evening after his third big talk with Millie. *Can I come and see you at 3pm tomorrow (Thursday)?* it said. He had not heard back from her, neither at the house nor via Halls. So at 2.45 he set off for Ely Road unsure of whether she would be in. It was another hot day. They were having so many. Crispin wished this foul weather would break and he kept to the shadows as best he could.

An envelope was pinned to the front door which read *Mr Crispin Williams*. Inside it he found the front door key. Crispin was alarmed at the naivety of such an action. When he got to the door of her room he was further alarmed to find it on the latch and a note which read '*Back at 4*'. Crispin had both envelopes in his hand now. Two matter of fact communications in Sue's big neat schoolgirl handwriting.

He sat on her bed and found himself pondering the fact that in his life three women had given him their keys. At Aberystwyth, when he was a first-year student, Belinda had given him her room key in the Union Bar at their second meeting. 'I've got some things to do, see you there in an hour, OK?' she'd said. Her voice was effortlessly commanding. She sounded like his sisters' friends. Crispin was staggered but he was only nineteen and very keen to have sex with someone, anyone. So he went along to Belinda's room and studied the necromantic exotica while he waited. When she came back Belinda hadn't taken much notice of him. She'd prepared something which they'd both smoked and then she had had sex with him. It was all surprisingly impersonal. Afterwards she had said to him, 'Normally what I do now is tell the blokes to fuck off but you're a sweetie.' Thereafter she didn't leave him alone and succeeded in detaching him entirely from his other friends. She was a big girl, Belinda, and both her size and class gave her the expectation of getting her own way. After a month or so of being commandeered continually for sex Crispin was beginning to form the opinion that he didn't actually like the woman he was servicing but he found it very difficult to communicate this fact to her. Mostly she avoided all eye contact with him and seemed to dislike even speaking to him in her room. It was altogether an increasingly unpleasant experience but Belinda was not to be gainsaid. One weekend she had gone home to see her father and told Crispin that if she found he'd been at it with anyone else while she was away she would cut his dick off. He more than half believed her.

After Belinda, Millie was a breath of fresh air. She was a designer working for a touring theatre group that had visited Aberystwyth. Crispin's theatre studies group had been encouraged to meet the company and he had taken an immediate shine to Millie Kemp. After Belinda in her thick black cloak, thick black tights and overtight black dresses, Millie had seemed like sunlight itself. But Crispin had remained frightened of the Black Widow Spider. One spring morning he'd been having coffee with Millie down by the pier when Belinda had walked in on them. Crispin and Millie had met a few times during the last few weeks and he had always dreaded this might happen.

'I want to see you outside,' Belinda hissed, avoiding all eye contact with Millie. '*Now.*'

'No,' said Millie who knew something of Crispin's curious and unhappy life. 'No, you want to see me.' And up she stood.

Belinda had seemed to evaporate at that point. She just went. He couldn't believe it. It was so easy. 'Sorry about that,' said Millie with a grin. 'I don't suppose you'll be getting any oats from now on.' Crispin had told her with some relief that he thought he'd cope. Millie slid the keys to the company van across the table.

'I think I owe you one,' she joked. 'You want to wait for me outside?'

Crispin felt very fond of that memory. He felt very fond of Millie too. They had had some good years following that trip down to the sand dunes at Ynyslas. His praying mantis had always insisted on blacking out any room in which they had sex. But Millie liked doing it in the open air. It was all so easy with Millie, apart from the grains of sand which seemed to get into every bodily crevice.

Yes, Crispin Williams, sitting on Sue's bed, had once felt very fond of Millie Kemp. So what had happened? What was he doing here? He didn't understand it himself. The only sense Crispin could make of it was an obvious one. Sue was the only woman in his life with whom he had been the more sexually experienced partner. But that seemed an unlikely reason to get involved with her. Maybe he wasn't involved with her. Maybe it was all an illusion. It had certainly seemed so last night, talking to Millie. He had felt, as they argued to and fro, that Sue was an imaginary friend of the kind he had had as a child and that Millie had found out about her and was trying to chase her out of his mind. He found it difficult to believe that Sue Coity was real and that he had twice shared a bed with her.

But when Sue returned at five past four she seemed so real and so sure of everything as she called him *cariad* and sat on his lap and told him that she thought she would be 'ready' tomorrow, and wasn't that just in time?

'I think you ought to know,' said Crispin, 'that Millie has found out about us and has told me I must choose between you.' Sue called him a poor dear and stroked his face but she seemed nevertheless delighted. 'You must leave her straight away and we can get married,' she said and she kissed him joyfully but in that kiss something stabbed at Crispin. Something harsh, like a realisation. What was she talking about? It had never occurred to him that Sue might think of marriage. He could not marry Sue. He loved her, yes that was probably so, but he could not marry her. If he married anyone it would have to be the mother of his children.

'Sue,' he said '*Rwy'n dy garu di*, you know that don't you?' She nodded and kissed him. 'But I have to look after Jonathan and Katrin.' Sue clearly hadn't thought of this. She had never ever mentioned his children. She seemed to be unaware of their existence, in fact.

'Oh, they can live with us,' she said.

But you couldn't be a mother to them, thought Crispin. You are only ten years older than Jonathan. With you in the house I would have three children and besides Katrin would hate you and you couldn't cope with that. And who would earn the money to keep us all?

He felt dreadfully responsible. Somehow something absurd and unexpected had happened. Susan Coity had decided to marry him. She must realise this was not possible.

'Sue,' he said '*O Cariad fach, rwy'n dy garu di*, but I don't think I can marry you.' Her big eyes filled with tears.

'But you're not married to her,' she replied. 'Why can't you marry me? If you love me?'

'Oh, I do love you,' he assured her. 'I'm sure I do. But I can't see how we would make it work. And when you're older I think you'll see I'm right.'

Millie was thinking about her parents and how her Dad had looked so old when she first came back from college. When she'd gone to London he'd said to her, 'You've no idea how much I'll miss you, lovely girl.' Then he'd told her to come back soon.

But when she did come back for Christmas her mother had found out and already it was over. Even today Millie wasn't sure who this other woman had been. Her name was never mentioned and at the age of eighteen Millie was determined not to care. It was all over anyway but on Christmas Eve she'd heard him say those words, as she'd passed her parents' bedroom: 'I'm so alone.' Millie repeated the words in her head. He'd never recovered, her Dad. What a way to be married. Millie felt paralysed. Yet she must do something. What must she do?

Crispin didn't remember crossing the ferocious A48 but he assumed that he must have obeyed the pedestrian lights because he got to the other side in one piece. He didn't remember crossing Cardiff Road either, nor walking up the High Street. What he did recall was seeing Millie when he came in. She looked up at him from the kitchen oven where she was, of all things, cooking their supper.

'Can we go and sit down?' Crispin asked. They went into the front room with its old, sagging comfortable furniture. He felt so sad, so completely sad.

'What did you tell her?' asked Millie. She looked worried and old sitting on the settee opposite him.

'I told her that it's over,' said Crispin. Millie's eyes seemed to melt with relief. 'But there's more,' said Crispin. This was the moment when martyrs see the instruments of torture or realise how hot the flames will really be, he thought. This was the last moment to recant, the final chance of escape. Why don't we take it? he wondered. 'She er, . . . she wanted to marry me. I told her that it can't work out, that I cannot marry her . . .'

Millie nodded. She was bracing herself and hoping that she knew what he was going to say.

'I'm afraid, Millie, I told her a lie. I told her that I do love her. I, er, think at the time I believed it.'

Millie nodded again. This time more slowly. She could forgive him. She knew she could.

Oh God, *please*, thought Crispin, but he knew the reason we don't take the option to escape from the mutilations, the agony and the flames is that because, really, we know the option is *illusory*. Put to the question, many people recant but then, incredibly, change their minds. Joan of Arc renounced her voices but then, knowing truly that she could not give them up, she had insisted on going to the stake and being burned to death. She had had no choice. Similarly he was not *choosing* now to tell Millie what he had to say. It was just that he had hitherto made the mistake of believing he *had* a choice in the first place. Now he knew he didn't. Hadn't. Never had.

'I now know that I don't love Sue but I'm afraid I don't love you either. I'm sorry.'

On Friday morning David had a meeting with Stella Price for which he was late because, with Helena away, Emma couldn't find her painting overalls.

'Where do you normally keep them?' David asked her. After shepherding four children yesterday, his patience was no longer what it was.

'I don't normally keep them,' said Emma looking unhappy at the tone of implied criticism in his voice. 'Mummy keeps them.'

'Well *where* does she keep them?'

'I don't know!'

Then, when he got into the department, Megan was typing up a list that she wanted him to have.

'This morning everybody wants you to call them back.'

'I've got a meeting,' said David.

'Won't take long!' sang out Megan cheerily but waiting for her took long enough for him to be really late for Stella.

'I thought you should know I had sherry with Alun last night,' said the lady, munching on the corner of her mouth. 'As you were busy with your family.'

I thought we were a family university, said David to himself.

'Alun's very down on this professor from Vermont,' said Stella. 'Gareth Box. Do you know him?'

Christ! thought David. I haven't done a thing about Clare Mankiewicz and the poisoned pen mail. He could see Stella was expecting a reply from him.

'I – er – I knew him at Oxford. Long time ago.'

'Alun seems to think him unsound.' Now this was difficult territory.

'I don't know if I could take a view on that,' David replied. He was in at least three minds. Part of him wanted to damage Gareth's candidature as much as possible for all the old reasons.

Part of him wanted very much to play the decent man, to show admirable restraint (particularly if there was a chance that the full nature of his relationship with Gareth was going to become known in the next few weeks). But part of him was also suddenly, foolishly and inexplicably worried about the phonecall that he'd had from Helena last night. The Mosfords didn't speak much on the telephone. It was one area of their lives where words played a very small part. But on Thursday evening she had rung him up just after he'd taken Jonathan and Katrin home. At 6pm his wife had rung and told him that she loved him. This was an unexpected, if welcome, reminder of one of the reasons why they stayed together. But it was not the kind of thing that David and Helena said to each other on the telephone. Why was she ringing up from Barrington to tell him this? And why did he suddenly feel it had something to do with Gareth Box? There was no reason and yet in Stella's office he found himself suddenly connecting the two.

Stella was disappointed at his noncommittal response. 'I need to know if you think it possible that the appointment of Professor Box would cause dissent. What, in your opinion, is the basis of Alun's antagonism?'

'Oh, probably a misunderstanding,' said David lightly. 'You know what Alun's like.'

What an opportunity he was passing up here to do some real constructive damage! But David was into self preservation now. He felt sure that he had got to get out of this meeting and throw Alun off that particular scent, preferably within the next few minutes. And *whatever* Alun said, he must ring Clare and ask her to stall publishing that letter. And then he had to get to the station and meet Helena from the train. He needed to pluck up the courage to ask her why she had rung him last night. He had an awful, awful feeling that somehow he already knew. Stella Price was staring at him, unaccustomed to his obvious introspection.

Millie was at home and supposed to be working. She had plans in front of her but all morning they had just meant so many lines, figures and squiggles. Nothing more. And now it was lunch time and she was supposed to ring Harry in Chiswick to give him a series of estimates. But she had done nothing all morning. This was not like her. She felt as if she had been shouting and crying for two days now. Tuesday 3.45 pm she had begun. Since then it had all been unbelievably awful and totally beyond her comprehension apart from that hour with David when surprisingly he had talked a lot of sense. Apart from that her world had just disintegrated around her in the last forty-eight hours. She thought of her mother. Her mother had known something of this. Her mother had known a man who said he didn't love her. Millie understood. Millie felt she was her mother now. Millie couldn't cope.

Crisp was at Halls the Bookshop where he was supposed to be behind the counter but Peter hadn't gone out after all so he and Crispin were discussing rooms to let.

'It's just a room, is it?'

'Yes,' said Crispin.

'Just for a while?'

'Yes.'

'And you want it in the High Street?'

'Um,' said Crispin looking at the greeting-card counter. 'Yes I do really. As close to home as possible.'

'But not actually *in* your home?' Peter smiled to cover his embarrassment. He was having to tease this out bit by bit though of course he had heard rumours. Number 27 occupied a prominent position in the village and its owners behaved as if they hadn't noticed this fact.

'I think as close as possible without actually being in. That's the sort of thing.'

Peter said he'd ask around.

Crispin wondered how things had got like this and how strange it was that having got like this life simply carried on. He and Millie weren't doing very much, the children had been totally neglected. But bills still expected to be paid and, amazingly, the same things still came out of the taps and the radio as they ever did. He wished that Helena was not away. Since moving to Cardiff she was the only real friend he had made. Unless you counted Sue which, alas, he couldn't now. He had left her very upset. It hurt him to think of her distress. And Millie's. Wherever he went at the moment he seemed to leave to the sounds of women crying. No doubt if Helena were here she would be in tears by the time he reached the door.

'Are you all right?' asked Peter Hall.

'Um,' said Crispin. 'Yes . . . Sorry, what was the question?'

David should have picked up Helena from the station but in fact he had had a particularly difficult day. First of all he'd failed to find Alun Taylor and then, deciding to take executive action as acting Head of Department and withdraw Alun's letter unilaterally, he had failed to reach Clare Mankiewicz. Then when he did find Alun the little man stuck to his guns and accused David of backtracking just because this Bot fellow had had the nerve to apply for Dorkin's chair and might be wielding unwarranted influence as the new professor of Political History. Finally when David did get through to Clare she was sorry but as he hadn't got back to her last week the piece had gone to press.

David threw several things across the room and several more when he realised that he'd also missed Helena's train. How could he have done that?

'Mrs Mosford on line A,' said Megan. 'Personal call, I assume.'

'Yes,' David replied heavily. 'I doubt if she's inviting me to a symposium in Helsinki.

'Oh,' said Helena's voice. 'You're *there*.' She sounded as if she was having to project over the noise of Cardiff Central's concourse.

'Yes,' he replied. 'And you're *There* too I assume.'

'Yes, not the same *There* though is it?'

'No, sorry about that. Problems. *Here*.'

'Ah. I'll get a taxi. Where are the children?'

'With Millie and Crispin again,' he replied.

'Oh *David*.' She was embarrassed, 'What about Sarah?' she asked.

'Yes. That's what I always say,' he replied and then her money ran out. He wished he'd been there to meet her, to ask her why on earth she had rung him up to say she loved him. Something must be very wrong.

Helena was no sooner home and taking in her luggage when

Sarah herself, unruffled and benign on the surface, but clearly suffering a substantial inner flap, arrived at the garden gate.

'Oh Helena,' she said. 'Do you have a moment?' Sarah was breathing hard. There was deep significance in what she had to say.

'Well,' said Helena. 'Actually I was just going to pick up Nick and Emma.'

'Are they at 27 High Street?' Sarah asked with a show of deep anxiety. Don't tell me it's burned down, Helena thought, in a spasm of maternal anguish.

'Yes they are . . .' she replied cautiously.

'Can we go inside?' Sarah asked. So they stepped into the drawing room.

'Oh my dear,' said Sarah as she joined Helena on the settee. 'You know, Helena, that I try not to judge and I would certainly be loth to criticise Your Friends.' Helena knew that Sarah wasn't entirely happy about the recent omnipresence of Millie and Crispin at Ty Escob. This had manifested itself in many ways, one of which was the fact that despite having been introduced to both Millie *and* Crispin Sarah still scrupulously referred to them as *Your Friends*.

'Helena, I'm worried. Some of my oldest, dearest friends on the Green live in Back Lane, behind 27 High Street, and they have seen such carryings on.'

'Does this affect Nick and Emma?' asked Helena. She felt uncomfortable to have one friend of hers denouncing another. A threat to her children, real or imaginary, was the only criterion she could accept for gossip about close friends.

'No,' said Sarah. 'Or at least not directly. Please let me continue. As I say, my friends the Vernons, at number 5 – they're such nice people – Helena, they have seen and heard such things.'

'What things?' asked Helena. This was the Sarah John who was usually so jolly, the Sarah who enjoyed a chuckle about other people's foibles. Helena felt herself being drawn in to the portentousness of this conversation.

'You know I wouldn't normally tell you this kind of thing . . .' Sarah began and then she got going. The initial evidence against Crispin and Millie was fairly innocent stuff which Sarah herself could forgive. Topless sunbathing, plying children (well

Jonathan) with alcohol, having stable block sex during daylight hours which actually proved audible in the lane.

'There's more,' said Sarah as she noticed that Helena was trying not to smile.' I know this may seem silly but . . .'

'What?' Helena asked.

'Young women coming and going at all hours.'

'Really?' Helena could not imagine what this meant. A *multiple* ménage à trois?

'By the back gate,' Sarah added significantly. 'But all this is nothing,' she said again, 'if they were not influencing *David*.'

'Are they?' This Helena did not believe. Sarah nodded. 'We know how easily influenced he is,' she reminded Helena. 'David has been seen in the Castle Grounds with *Her*.'

'By whom?' asked Helena.

'By Katie.'

'What were they doing?'

'They were only talking, but please Helena, let me give you the fuller picture. David has also been seen in the garden at 27 High Street when *She* has been sunbathing. He has even been seen going upstairs into that "loft" with her late at night.'

'He did that while we were round there for dinner,' Helena protested. 'I was in the house.'

'But all this is nothing,' said Sarah. Well please get to something that *is* something, thought Helena. 'All this is gossip were it not for the fact that on Wednesday night, while you were away, I called on David to see if he needed anything at all, and the porch light was on, so I went round to the front of the house . . . and, I'm afraid I must be indiscreet here, Helena, but what I saw shocked me. *She* was here and, as far as I could see, she was unbuttoning her clothing in front of him.'

Sarah paused to await Helena's reaction. Helena was indeed shocked.

'Her clothing?'

'Her blouse.'

'She was unbuttoning her blouse in our porch?'

'She might have been buttoning it up.'

Helena still found this bizarre. 'In the porch? With the light on?' Sarah nodded significantly. 'Why should she be unbuttoning or buttoning her blouse in front of David in the *porch*?'

Sarah shrugged her shoulders, breathed in deeply and shook her head as if her failure to understand this action made it all the more portentous.

'But the *porch*,' Helena repeated. Variegated terracotta quarry tiles are so chill on the back, even in summer time. It was bizarre. There was a silence which Sarah couldn't leave unfilled.

'Maybe she was buttoning her blouse up again,' she suggested. 'Before leaving.'

'Did she leave?'

'No, she went back inside.'

'So she wasn't buttoning up her blouse prior to leaving, she was buttoning – or unbuttoning – her blouse prior to coming in,' Helena reasoned.

'Yes, I'm afraid I do think so,' said Sarah as if this was all damning evidence rather than just damn confusing.

'And what was David doing while she was buttoning up or buttoning down?'

'I don't know,' Sarah replied. 'He seemed to be looking at her and talking.'

'Well, people do do that,' Helena admitted, determined to see the funny side, because there was a funny side to all this, even if it were a side to which Sarah was totally immune.

'He wasn't *helping* with the buttons was he?'

Sarah shook her head.

'Did she stay long?' Helena asked.

'Oh, Helena, I wouldn't know *that*.' Sarah fairly bristled at the thought that she might have been spying on such an intimate exchange.

'Well thanks for telling me,' said Helena, wondering what on earth it was she'd actually been told.

'I felt I had no choice,' Sarah admitted sadly. 'You know I am not one to judge but David is so easily led. And well, Your Friends . . .'

Yes, indeed, thought Helena. What had been going on? Yet of one thing she was certain. It was probably, almost definitely, *not* what Sarah believed. Clearly it was something. But when Helena was at the point of fundamental decisions about the future of her life she could not really bother herself about 27 High Street and the identity of nymphets who sneak in and out of it. As she set off to pick up her children from Crispin's, Helena decided that whatever happened to the rest of her life she was not going to let it be influenced by however many women had flaunted their decolletage in front of her husband. Particularly on a quarry-tiled floor.

Crispin opened the door to 27 High Street. 'Oh Helena,' he said, looking surprised, relieved but also distressed.

A very large bang was heard from the kitchen. 'Do come in,' said Crispin. 'Millie and I were just having a talk in the kitchen.' Another bang was heard. It sounded like a cupboard door that was being repeatedly slammed to create the maximum noise. Which was what it was. The Mosford children appeared from nowhere and clung on to Helena.

'Please, we don't want to come here again!' said Emma.

'That's not a very nice thing to say,' Helena replied, trying to keep to the proprieties.

A sound of breaking crockery was heard from the kitchen closely followed by a mouthful of bilingual abuse. Millie appeared at the kitchen door. 'I've just broken the second milk jug so you'll have to buy yourself another one, and serves you bloody right!' Sighting Helena, Millie checked herself.

'Oh sorry. I'm afraid your kids have had a rotten time this afternoon and it's all my fault. I'm sorry. Mine and *his*.' This did not look like the temptress of Ty Escob, the woman who began a strip-tease on the terracotta threshold. This was a very angry, middle-aged housewife.

'Mummy—' said Emma gripping Helena.

'Millie and I are, um, we're . . . er—' Crispin didn't quite know how to complete this particular sentence.

'Splitting up,' said Big Jon from the staircase. Helena looked up to see both Jonathan and his sister sitting glumly on the stairs. Helena looked at Millie.

'Temporarily,' she said. 'Perhaps. *Christ*, I don't know.'

'Mum . . .!' said Katrin from the stairs.

'Mummy . . .' said Emma from somewhere round Helena's waist. What was going on?

When David got back the Mosford children were doing

schoolwork on the kitchen table and Helena was cooking. It looked a perfect domestic scene to walk in on.

'Good time?' he asked kissing his wife.

'Good time,' she replied. Emma jumped up and hugged him.

'Katrin's mummy was calling Crispin a bustard *all afternoon,'* she complained.

'Bastard,' Helena corrected automatically.

'A bustard is a large, funny-looking bird that runs very fast on the ground,' David explained.

'Why is Crispin *runnering* very fast on the ground?' asked Nick, not looking up from his drawing pad. Both David and Helena smiled.

'Can we talk later?' Helena asked.

'Later,' he agreed.

Helena had made crisis food but David didn't particularly notice. He was pleased to be cooked for. He was pleased to see his wife again. He was pleased to feel his family all around him again and he felt relieved to think that whatever awful things were going on with Millie and Crispin, nothing like that was happening here, nor could ever happen here. While the children were having their bath David opened a good bottle of claret and let it breathe. By the time he and Helena were sitting down at their dining room table the wine was good, the food smelled good and to see her was as good as it got.

'Can I ask you something?' said Helena, serving them both. 'This thing with Crispin and Millie . . . it isn't anything to do with you?'

'No,' said David.

'Good. I'm glad,' she said.

'Why? Did you think it was?'

Helena slid the bowl to one side. 'Well, you and Millie . . .' she said.

'But nothing came of that. You know that.' She nodded. He felt uneasy.

'You don't believe me?'

'No, I believe you if you tell me that.' David felt he should explain. 'The Millie-Crispin thing has come about because he's involved with some student. It's nothing to do with me.'

'Crispin is?' She was shocked by this but it explained why Millie was so much on the offensive this afternoon. Totally offensive in fact. How sad. How disappointing. Poor Millie. Poor Crispin. Poor everyone.

'How do you know?' she asked. 'Has he told you this? Has she?'

'I always check my sources,' said David, picking up his fork. 'She came round on Wednesday night.'

Ah, thought Helena, she came round on Wednesday night, unbuttoned her blouse at the door and said Crispin is having an affair with a student. No, somehow it still didn't sound right.

'You didn't tell me on the phone.'

'No,' he replied.

But then he wouldn't. Would he? They didn't talk about that kind of thing on the phone.

'And was Millie in a state?' she asked. She didn't want to fish too deeply on this one.

'Oh she was a bit upset. I comforted her.'

'A bit?'

'I'm sorry?' he asked.

'She was upset and you comforted her a bit?'

'Yes a bit. In equal measure to her distress.'

'Not a lot?' Helena asked with half a smile.

'Not a lot, no,' he replied with a full understanding of what she was asking. David had woken on Thursday morning almost sorry he had not taken advantage of Millie on the settle. Now he was grateful that he hadn't.

'Makes you feel . . . lucky, doesn't it?' said David sliding his hand across the table and taking hers. 'For what you've got.'

Yes . . .' she said. Maybe this was the time to tell him.

'I've missed you,' he said. *Well, maybe it wasn't the time.*

'Oh and I've got the date for the interview and the formal lecture setting out *my* vision of Political History. It all came through today.'

No, this definitely wasn't the right time. She should wait until he'd been through all the selection rigmarole. This was not the time to mention the fact that Gareth Box had asked her to leave David. Nor the fact that Gareth had actually offered to withdraw from the chair if she would marry him.

'They're seeing Alun too,' said David. 'And Gareth. Of course.'

A shadow passed across David's face as it always did when he talked of Gareth Box. He squeezed her hand. She squeezed it back.

'Is everything all right?' he asked.

'Yes.'

'When you rang up last night you . . . said you loved me,' he reminded her.

'Yes I did, didn't I?' she agreed in a pleasant, noncommittal way.

'Bit unexpected,' he admitted. 'On the phone like that.'

'On the phone,' she joked. 'Very.'

'I love you too,' he said. 'In case you're wondering.'

'Yes . . .' she said. It was definitely not the best time to say anything, to anyone, about anything.

12 ∫

Distracted Mothers

Helena drifted. Drifted like she had in pregnancy. The day-to-day details of life seemed to be happening somewhere else and not to her.

She was distracted by Gareth and all that he personified.

Fortunately, and fortunately was probably the right word, she had not gone to bed with him that Thursday afternoon. This had not been an easy decision but it had definitely been the right one.

In purely practical terms, to which bed might she and he have gone? This kind of question had to be addressed. There were any number of *actual* beds around Barrington House belonging to her family but all of them were in rooms leased out to distant relatives. The only one that Helena had any access to, any right to, was in her father's guest room. Not only would it seem an act of impropriety to abuse Mr Moreton's hospitality thus, but he would be returning at any moment with a plunger from Aunt Hester's. That would not do.

The other option was the garden which was warm and inviting and had a number of suitably shady spots but old Mr So-and-So was bound to wander by on his way to the potting shed. Or Mrs Dorrell would stagger down with a plate of biscuits and seek them out doggedly from bower to bower. Or her cousin Mark's St Bernards, of course. Their cold noses had disturbed one or two adolescent clinches in the past. Besides which, she wasn't a teenager now. She was a married woman of thirty-seven who was being asked to leave her husband and marry someone else instead. This needed thought, not impulse.

Back in Cardiff, Helena suddenly found herself wondering if Gareth had had a room booked nearby. How strange she hadn't thought of that at the time. How strange he hadn't mentioned it. He was losing his touch. So was she.

How on earth had things gone so far? And now, suddenly, it was the last day of term and she had to collect Nick and Emma early. Helena wanted to get their bedrooms tidy so the holiday could start as David wanted it to go on. Downstairs her husband was having to prepare his personal vision of Political History for next week's open lecture and he simply couldn't do that if he was continually crunching plastic figurines underfoot.

And yet she could have been tempted to go off, that Thursday night, to a hotel with Gareth Box. She, Helena Mosford, previously Moreton, previously – seventeen years ago – the mistress of Gareth Box, could easily have been tempted to go off with him. For one night. Just the one. As Helena stacked away the Playmobil in its different plastic containers she was overwhelmed again by the sensation of Gareth. His physical presence seemed so acute, so real, she could have believed he was in the room.

Pirates/Campervan/Cowboys. She sorted Nick's Playmobil into the three plastic biscuit tins. Keeping order by segregation. Pirates/Campervan/Cowboys. That was how Gareth used to do it, she knew. When he was with her he had loved her. That was Helena's box. When he was with Miss America in Jermyn Street he loved her. And that was her box. But Helena knew she couldn't live like that. It wasn't so easy for women. She had tried to have her Gareth box but the moment he had kissed her outside the Happy Gathering it had fallen apart. And the moment she had kissed him in the garden at Barrington she knew she was running an almighty big risk.

There was no box that would keep Gareth contained. He either was in her life or he wasn't. That was the decision she had to make. The Pirates were getting in the Campervan and the Cowboys were everywhere. When he had thrown her out seventeen years ago she had taught herself to believe that he could never come back. And now he had. And more than that, he had said Yes, she meant so much to him he would withdraw from the job, if that was what she wanted. And then they had kissed, hadn't they? That kiss had gone on for a long time, the one in the garden. It was not a husband-and-wife kiss. It was a kiss of two hungry souls discovering something desperately, and deliciously, important on each other's lips. There was a lot to discover. That was why it went on for so long. There was a lot that was delicious. That also was why it went on for so long. And it was a hot sensuous summer afternoon. That was yet another reason. And no gardeners, cousins, domestics or dogs interrupted it, as they absolutely should have done. These were all reasons for that kiss to endure. Indeed, there were so many reasons for it to go on for so long and no valid reasons to stop, none apart from the needs of respiration. But they did. Eventually. For her hair had become entangled in their lips.

'We should go somewhere,' said Gareth as she moved away from his shoulder and brushed the rest of her hair back. How strange he didn't mention the room he must have had booked somewhere nearby. Helena shook her head. 'But you want to?' he asked. She paused and thought.

'You want to,' Gareth repeated, not mentioning the room, the champagne, the lifetime of broken promises that lay ahead. 'And we should. To be *sure*. It's been a very long time.'

'Oh, I'm sure,' said Helena. 'I know what it would be like.'

'You can remember?' he asked, clearly intrigued by the idea.

'Can't you?' she asked in turn. Gareth tried to backtrack on that. She wouldn't let him.

'Don't say you've never forgotten how wonderful it was and that no other woman has been as good for you.' He smiled, pleased that she knew him so well and that she forgave him for being what he was.

That was last week. And this was now. And suddenly it was the last day of term and Helena Mosford was sitting in Nick's bedroom with the Playmobil around her. The Pirates were marauding unsorted and somewhere downstairs her husband wanted her to listen to his vision of Political History. But Helena was remembering the temptation of last week and thinking about the future.

Whatever Gareth said, there would always be other women.

She knew that. Each of them in a box. The best she could hope for was that hers would be Box Number One. Would that be enough? Anyone who married Gareth would have to be a pragmatist. Helena gazed at the carpet. Yes, she could do that. She could do that now. At twenty she had been an idealist, foolishly believing that she could be everything to this man. He could never have married a woman like that. But now . . . A sensation overcame Helena that left her cold. It was the realisation that Gareth really needed her and, worse, that she would be good for him.

Helena rocked forward on the floor. She was aching now. It was unbearable. What did she do with such feelings? Did she go with them? Did she leave the Playmobil unsorted for the rest of her life? No, there had to be lists. There had to be decisions. She would say and do nothing until the interviews were over. That was next Thursday. Then they were going away for the weekend with Millie and Crispin. So she would not say anything then either. And then the next week David would know. And then she would know too, and when they both knew she could tell him.

Millie and Crispin. Were they going away with Millie and Crispin? In the midst of all this upheaval she had quite forgotten there were problems there. She must seek out Crispin and find out if it was all still on.

Stella Price was not happy with *Radical History*, with Alun Taylor or with David. At the moment she had the magazine on her desk and David on the carpet.

'This University respects intellectual freedom, as you know, but this—' Stella tapped the publication with the back of her hand. 'But this is an abuse of that freedom.' As her knuckles tap-tap-tapped the pages David noticed that Stella's skin was acquiring those brown patches he associated with age, not just with loss of youth but with age and decay. 'I just don't know what Alun was playing at!'

He did not enjoy being in the presence of angry women, particularly women who held his future in their mottled hands. Tap, tap, tap. 'And you say you encouraged this letter?'

'I drew the original article to Alun's attention. I was concerned for the department. Subsequently, when I realised what lengths

Alun was prepared to go to, I tried to suggest he withdrew the piece from publication.'

'And when you drew Alun's attention to this did you *know* that Gareth Box was applying for the chair of Political History?' This was the crunch question. He did not wish to lie. Truth was a potent thing and yet also a fragile thing. It could be broken easily but should never be broken lightly. Yet at the same time David did not wish to flush the chain on his own professional prospects either.

'I had heard rumours about Box but I didn't actually know until last Monday night when by chance I met him in Cardiff. The following day I tried again to ask Alun to withdraw the piece and I rang Clare Mankiewicz.'

'Who's she?'

'The editor. Of *Radical History*. I rang and asked if the letter could be held over. She was a former student of mine and I thought as a favour . . .'

Stella snorted and glowered at the pages before her.

Phew. Yes, he had managed to put himself in a reasonable light. He had omitted that it was all his idea but, that aside, he had kept within striking distance of veracity without actually yanking on the old professional lavatory chain. It dangled there, though, still within reach. Stella was staring out of the window for a moment, collecting her thoughts and giving the folds of her mouth a hard time.

'You do realise what this means . . .' she said. Her tone was grim. Oh God, thought David. He was over forty and yet he felt as if he were at school again. 'This means you have no option but to withdraw your candidacy for the chair.' He was waiting for the words to fall from the sky and with them his career. One big sploosh and Mosford down the pan forever.

'You realise that it is going to be very difficult to have Box and Alun in the same department?'

Ah, thank you God. Thank you so much. *You don't know what this means to me.*

'Yes,' said David with a nod of the head that was over-emphatic. Perhaps it made him look pleased at the prospect. As if sensing this, Stella continued, 'But that doesn't mean it can't happen. And if it does I will be looking to you to be the peacemaker.'

'Of course,' David agreed.

'We'd better not discuss this any further now. I'll see you at the interview.'

'Yes, indeed,' David agreed. He was in agreeing mode at the moment. After all, he might well have escaped with his professional life intact. David headed for the door and hoped to make it before Stella started reaching for the chain again.

'Oh David, would you do something for me?' she asked apropos of nothing. *Shit.*

David paused in the knowledge that whatever it was he had no choice but to agree.

'Wendy Dorkin,' said Stella. 'She's back in Cardiff now. This is going to be a difficult time for her. Would you go and see her, look after her a bit? Can I ask that of you?'

'Of course.'

'She rang me. She knows the chair has been advertised and we're interviewing next week.' Stella's eyes betrayed the compassion that David knew lurked beneath all that corporate nonsense. He liked her for her wisdom and her compassion. And he knew full well that he would be seeing the latter if she had to tell him he hadn't got the chair. 'I think she'd appreciate it. She knows how close you and Peter were.'

Well, even Stella had to get some things wrong.

The school holidays came as a total shock to Millie Kemp. That morning Crispin had left her a note before he went off to Halls.

Millie, if you're collecting J&K don't forget they're out early today 2pm (last day of term)

Millie's first reaction was to take this very personally. If the bastard was moving out, what did he expect her to do during the seven weeks lock-out that St Dyfrig's was unreasonably imposing on all parents? Why hadn't Crispin told her about this before? Mind you, had she put this to him, Millie could guess what his reply would have been. He hadn't told her because she wasn't speaking to him at the moment. He was devious like that. Bastard. She had found the note when she came down for breakfast at 10am. Life was hard at 27 High Street but Millie still slept in late.

She rang him at Halls.

'It's *me*,' she said. 'Have you arranged anything for the holidays?'

'I'm serving at the moment. Um, look, can I ring you back?'

When he did, Crispin explained that there were various Cardiff child care schemes he had found out about but things had been so up and down recently he hadn't got round to booking anything.

'You do realise I start in London next week?' Millie asked.

'It had slipped my mind with everything else that's going on.'

'And whose fault's that?' Millie asked with due venom. She was beginning to hate sounding like a fish-wife. Crispin didn't reply for a moment. He refused to acknowledge his role of fish-husband. He felt sorry for her, he had apologised but he drew the line at any more arguments, particularly when he was supposed to be taking the money for a copy of *Tomos Y Tanc*. After a moment for them both to draw breath, Crispin offered to ring the playcare schemes when he got back. Millie told him he was useless and not to bother coming back at all and put the phone down.

Oh God, she sounded like her mother. Millie had no sooner started crying when the phone chirruped. It seemed so uncannily instantaneous that for a moment Millie thought this just had to be Crispin who had changed his mind and was ringing home to say he loved her after all.

It was Helena. 'How are things?' she said.

'Oh . . .' said Millie wondering where you began.

'Can I come round?' Helena asked. 'Or would you like to come here?'

'Oh,' said Millie 'Thanks.' She was quite surprised at this offer. 'I'm waiting for a call from London. Can you come round to us?'

At lunchtime Crispin would normally have gone home but as Millie had told him to bugger off – and given every impression that she meant it – he didn't. In any case, there was something he had to do. When he had arrived at Halls that morning Peter had pointed out a parcel of books that a young lady had returned the day before. Of course today was the end of Sue's term! Crispin felt he had to go and say goodbye. Or at least leave her a note. He set off feeling very unsure of himself. What did he say when he saw Sue? What proprieties govern such situations as these?

He walked down the High Street and crossed Cardiff Road with its relentless stream of anxious, skewed traffic. Some cars were holding up the flow by attempting to turn right into Ely Road while others held it up as they tried, simultaneously, to go left into the High Street. Meanwhile every other vehicle continued to barge past in a hurry. Traffic was a metaphor for life, thought Crispin. A foolish mess in which people collide because they are too busy seeking out their own destinations and ignoring each other. By the time he reached the A48 the traffic had grown angrier and more determined still. Intent on speeding east and west it was particularly resentful of the pedestrian crossing. Lorries heaved and snorted with pent-up fury as they waited for Crispin to get to the other side.

An old saloon car was outside Sue's flat. Somebody must be loading or unloading but this meant the front door was open. Crispin went up the dark, unlovely, uncared-for stairs. As he approached Sue's room he realised that there was movement and noise within and, before he could turn back, Crispin had come face to face with a merry middle-aged woman carrying one end of something large and box-like. At the other end of the something large was a slight man with a red face and white neck, the kind of wiry agricultural man who keeps his clothing buttoned up in all weathers and beats his dog. Helping him just a little was Sue. Crispin saw all these people in an instant and realised, as quickly as realisations come, that he was face to face with the complete Coity family.

Her face absolutely fell. Crispin was blocking the landing so the merry mother and the sourfaced father put the trunk down.

'Um, I've come to say goodbye,' said Crispin. Sue nodded. That might well have been enough said but Sue's mother was a woman of great curiosity.

'Well, do come in!' she said and she spoke to her daughter in Welsh. It must have been a request for introduction because immediately afterwards Sue said, with no grace whatsoever:

'This is Crispin Williams that I told you of. Crispin, this is my mother and father, Mr and Mrs Coity.'

'Pleased to meet you,' said Crispin, shaking hands and being ushered into her room.

This was difficult.

Sue retreated to a corner. Crispin noticed that for the first time since he'd known her she was wearing trousers and a pullover. He also noticed that Sue's sad room was now stripped of its pictures. The mantelpiece was empty. As he took this in, Crispin could hear Mrs Coity expressing her gratitude for the way he had looked after Siwsann.

'Er, well, it was a pleasure,' said Crispin.

'And you live locally?' asked Mrs Coity. She was so unlike her daughter, thought Crispin. Sue, her back against the wall, looked as quiet, as thin and as dissatisfied with life as her father.

'Yes, off the High Street,' said Crispin. 'Near the cathedral.'

'Oh, very nice,' said Sue's mum. 'We been up there, haven't we Sue? She always takes us for a little walk round.' Clearly Mrs Coity did the talking in this family. Although Crispin had recognised immediate similarities between Sue and her father, he could now also recognise the happiness that showed in Mrs Coity's face. That merriment (or was it really joy?) was what he had seen in Sue's face on the two occasions that they had been in bed together.

He looked at Sue and felt his heart go out to her as she stood glumly against the wall. If only he could love her . . . Sue looked back, neither angry nor resentful. She seemed withdrawn into herself.

'Thank you for the whisky,' Crispin told Mrs Coity.

'Well, thank you for looking after our girl here,' said Sue's mum.

'Pleasure,' said Crispin again. He was repeating himself. He had to go.

'Teacher, are you?' Sue's father suddenly demanded from where he stood by the door. Crispin got the feeling that Mr Coity used his voice rarely. It was a quiet voice but all the more menacing for that. Sue's father was probably only in his mid-forties but his weatherbeaten face and old-fashioned clothes made him look like the relict of some older generation.

When he spoke it was probably always to a point, if not directly so.

'No, I research, mainly. And, um, work in a bookshop and, er, I look after my children the rest of the time.'

'Oh,' said Mrs Coity. 'You're married then?' She seemed to look simultaneously delighted about the state of matrimony in general and yet disappointed that this specific male was offering no scope for her daughter to enter upon it.

'Er, not exactly,' said Crispin, confusing things further.

'Oh,' said Mrs Coity, unable to disguise the fact that her happy round face was brightening up again at this news. Sue addressed her mother in Welsh. Her words formed a short quiet request for Mrs Coity to desist from something. Crispin recognised *paed*, the 'don't' form in Welsh. She was probably asking for there to be no more questions.

'I'll, er, I'll leave you to get on,' said Crispin. 'I hope you have a good vacation, Sue.'

'Well, say thank you!' scolded Sue's mother, happily.

'Thank you,' said Sue. Crispin could tell that Sue was getting increasingly uncomfortable about this. He wanted to say something positive, but what? He could hardly say in front of her parents that he valued her and hoped that one day she would be happy. If he offered to write to her she might think he intended to revive their relationship. What did he say?

Mrs Coity was obviously one of these people who cannot abide a moment's silence. Now she was telling Crispin that Sue had been terribly lonely when she first came to Cardiff and how she had really valued his friendship.

'You're in all her letters,' she added hopefully.

Oh God, thought Crispin. He looked at Sue, who was concentrating hard on the floor.

'Well, I've very much enjoyed her friendship too,' said Crispin. Any minute now he was going to say it had been a pleasure again. He had to go. If only these parents would take that trunk downstairs and leave him one moment with Sue. But it seemed not to occur to them. And it didn't occur to Crispin to suggest it. Or to ask her to come down to the road for a moment. Or anything. His mind was simply blank with impotent compassion.

'Well, perhaps I'll see you next year,' he said to Sue, who was still looking at her feet.

'Well, say goodbye!' said Mrs Coity.

When Crispin got back to 27 High Street he felt worse than when he had left Halls. He didn't love Millie. He didn't love Sue. He felt sorry for both of them. He could at least have made one of them happy by lying. What was wrong with him? He was begining to feel sorry for himself now too. What was so important about the truth?

Millie was looking for her mobile and swearing.

'I'm going to pick up the kids,' she said. 'We've got to talk.' Crispin nodded. Millie looked at him. She didn't want to speak any of the things that were in her heart.

'I've had lunch with Helena,' she said.

'Oh that's nice,' he replied.

'She says if you want to go and . . . talk to her . . .' Millie felt the words trailing off. She couldn't stop them.

'That's, er, that's very nice of her,' said Crispin.

'Yes. And we need to talk too,' Millie repeated then she put her hands, and her cards, on the table. 'Look,' she said. 'I'm working in London next week.'

'Oh yes.' Crispin nodded to show that he remembered.

'So we need to discuss arrangements. Have you found anywhere to live?' Crispin shook his head.

'Well, I'm not going to be here and, well, the kids will need looking after so Helena's suggested you could take it in turns to have them. One day here, one day there, that sort of thing—'

'Good idea,' said Crispin. Millie bridled. She wasn't looking for his endorsement.

'So . . . if you want to stay on during the week until you get something sorted . . .'

'It would seem the best idea,' Crispin agreed. 'Thank you.'

'But I want you away at the weekends,' she reminded him with a sudden flash of hatred. 'Completely away.'

'I'll do my best.'

Silence. Crispin was having a lot of these awkward, valedictory scenes at the moment. Millie, however, was not one to hang around when the words came with difficulty.

'I'll go and pick up the kids,' she said and she headed towards the door. Crispin sat down on a kitchen chair. 'Oh, one other thing,' said Millie. 'I've arranged with Helena that I'll take Jonathan and Katrin on the trip to Lyme next weekend. Just the three of us. It wouldn't really be right if you came too.'

'No indeed,' said Crispin. His voice betrayed the absence of any real feeling.

'But I'd rather you didn't stay here while I was away either.'

'Right.'

'So that's OK?'

'That's OK.' He felt so tired. So sad.

'*Right,*' she said and she was gone. Crispin wished he'd said something to ease her unhappiness. He used to love this woman, he still cared for her. He didn't want Millie to suffer as she was suffering and yet at some stage, as the children were growing up, he'd ceased to love her. This was the simple truth. But what comfort in the world can ease the pain of someone we no longer love? It was all so horribly sad.

That night the Mosford children were wild. The pretext for all their noise and hilarity was the end of term but this euphoria was exacerbated by the lack of attention they were getting from David and Helena.

'Nick! Come on *in*!' shouted David from the kitchen door but Nick had got his clothes off and was cavorting, there was no other word for it, round and round the garden.

David sighed. 'I blame his parents,' he told Helena, who was hoping to dish up supper.

'Absolutely,' she replied. 'They spend too much time talking about themselves and the children just get ignored.' From upstairs came the noise of Emma doing her 'exercises' which sounded very like the noise made by a seven-year-old girl jumping on and off her parents' bed.

'Emma! Stop that!' shouted David from the bottom of the stairs.

The kitchen phone rang. 'Oh, can you deal with that while I get Nick?' David asked and he went into the garden. He just wasn't up to phones tonight. Helena picked up the receiver.

'It's Gareth,' said a voice, that voice. The one that wanted her to leave her husband.

'It's not convenient,' she replied. Helena had gone beyond trying to be fair to David now. She knew she had to speak to Gareth. That was important and she wouldn't pretend otherwise. But after that primary need the *secondary* consideration was that she mustn't upset David's equilibrium at this important time.

'When?' he asked, this man with the voice that wanted her to leave her husband.

'Give me your number. I'll ring you some time tomorrow.' She reached for a pen. She was arranging an assignation behind her husband's back, something she had thought she would never do. These days it was the lesser of two necessary evils.

'Well, actually, I'm not certain where I'll be tomorrow.'

Oh, for goodness sake! This was ridiculous. She tried to think quickly. First day of the holidays: David would probably take the children out after breakfast . . . But even now she could hear him returning up the garden path with Nick.

'Ring me at eleven,' she said and put the phone down. Instantly in came David with Nick, a squirming, giggling pink bundle in his hands. He was going to ask her who was that and she had the choice of lying or seeing the whole evening, and even her marriage, unravel.

Why does Gareth want to speak to you?
Have you seen him since last Monday?
Where did you see him?
Why did he come to Barrington of all places? Did you invite him?

It would all be too awful. David's morale before the interview would totally crumble. She would have to lie to him and she had never done that. Even when it had hurt. He was her husband and he trusted her.

'Who was that?' asked David. No, she couldn't lie. She wished she could. But just at the moment she opened her mouth there came the most enormous crash and cry from upstairs as Emma, in leaping off her parents' bed, hit something hard. David looked momentarily at Helena, put down Nick and ran up the stairs. Helena followed and Nick, after a while, took himself back out into the garden.

That night Helena couldn't sleep, yet again. They had spent

the evening talking about his lecture and about some piece David was writing for the *Daily Mail*. Helena found it difficult to focus even on one subject at a time at the moment, and she made the mistake of asking why the *Mail* wanted to hear David's views about the future of Political History. Then David got on to the subject of Millie and Crispin which was one that currently obsessed them both. Helena passed on what Millie had said at lunchtime. Things were so bad that Crispin wouldn't be coming to Montgomery the following weekend. David had genuinely seemed upset about his friends' unhappiness.

'Now it's happened to them, I feel it could happen to any of us.' And he reached out to hold her hand. She hated the irony of this situation. On one side of the table, David was thinking about saving their marriage. But on her side, she wondered if it was all too late. It was the same when he got on to talking about the interview. To his side of the table it meant one thing. To hers another.

'What about you?' he asked. 'How would you feel about being the Professor's wife?'

He had meant it as a joke but she didn't take it well. Couldn't take it well. Helena could produce nothing more than a weak, and – *if he knew it* – guilty, smile. David looked at her the way he did when he knew he had said something wrong.

'Tell me about it,' he asked. 'I thought we were supposed to be making things better between us.'

Helena stood up to stack their plates on the trolley. She was growing unjustifiably irritated. 'Last time we did that you spent the evening talking to Pippa and left me with Gareth,' she replied. Oh, to reproach *him* with Gareth when she was actually considering going off with the man! Helena felt desperately guilty. David felt guilty too but in his case it was for all the reasons that had caused him to monopolise Pippa that night.

'Linna,' he began.

'I'm sorry,' said Helena, leaving the trolley unstacked. 'I've got a headache, I think it must be the weather. Do you mind if I lie down?'

'No,' he replied, minding hugely.

'I'll look in on Nick,' she said.

'Yes,' he replied, minding more and more. In fact he had half a mind to follow her upstairs and sit on the bed and ask her again what the matter was. But David had always dreaded asking such a question of her sudden annoyances, not because he feared to ask but because he feared the reply.

Fifteen years ago on their honeymoon he had asked Helena what the matter was. They were in Siena and feeling very grown up. She was twenty-two but in the last few days she had ceased to look like a student, more like her cousin Ming and the Barrington aunts, in fact. Long she looked and elegant. The pearls had definitely done it. A present from one of her great aunts. Before their honeymoon Helena had never worn pearls. Now she wore them during the day and he helped her put them on, securing the catch behind her neck and losing himself in all her wonderful hair. It could take them hours to put those pearls on.

One lunch time they had been laughing about some dreadful drunken tenor who wandered round every table singing tunelessly a series of operatic flourishes, no song, no words, no notes really, just one rallentando fusing into the next. Then David had begun to talk about the importance of truth and how, presumably, on one occasion this poor Tuscan had been told he had a good voice and no-one since had dared correct such a terrible mistake.

'Do you think lies are more powerful than the truth?' Helena had asked.

'Well, they can be. After, all, *anything* can be a lie. Very few things are true. When you lie you have the infinity of your imagination to draw on. When you tell the truth there is nothing to draw on but your honesty. I think it can feel very lonely sometimes. Being honest.'

'I will always tell you the truth,' said Helena, reaching out for his hand.

'Except for my voice,' said David. 'You may lie as often as you like about my wonderful singing voice.' To his surprise he saw her laughter disappear, no, he saw it never really rise, it lay stillborn on her face.

'What's the matter?' he asked.

'There's something I feel I ought to tell you,' Helena explained. 'It's been bothering me ever since Saturday.' Saturday had been their wedding day at Barrington. Everything at that stage in their lives divided simply: Before or After *Saturday*.

'You *don't* like my singing?' David asked.

'Will you forgive me?' she asked, her hand still reaching for his.

'Anything,' said David, taking her hand, yet feeling that perhaps this was not so.

Surely, in her heart, Helena knew how much he loved her. She *must* know how much he could forgive. Not that there was anything to forgive. But David knew that if she was asking for forgiveness then there must be something else. Something major. Something awful, awful, too terrible to have been spoken of before.

'You didn't get a first in the end?' he feebly joked. She was looking into his eyes trying to know the person behind them. 'What is it?'

'The night before, last Friday night. Gareth rang me.'

'Gareth rang you at Barrington?'

David was shocked because, by joint consent, there had been no question of inviting to the wedding the man who had abandoned Helena four weeks before Schools. It was over a year ago that he had done this but David still chose not to speak his name.

'He wanted to talk,' said Helena. 'I said he could come round.'

David held on to the table as if the whole world was spinning out of control. She could see the logistics of all this defeated him.

'But Gareth's in America, isn't he?'

'He was staying in Cirencester,' Helena explained. 'He asked if he could come round and I said he could. We talked. I actually took him for a walk round the garden because I didn't want my mother to know he was there.'

'I thought you were having a "do" with your cousins, Minky, Pinky and the other one.'

'I was. I did; later. But first I went round the garden with Gareth.'

'Oh, I see.'

David was wiping his forehead. Already, at the age of twenty-five, the hair was beginning to retreat rapidly from his scalp, leaving him with a lot more brow to furrow than the average newly married man.

'And that's all?' he asked.

Helena took his hand and kissed it. 'That's all we did. We talked. And he asked me to reconsider.'

'Reconsider?'

'To reconsider marrying you and marry him instead,' she explained.

David looked as if his hatred of Gareth would actually get the better of him. At any moment it seemed possible he might die of a heart attack. He didn't even look like David anymore. Now Helena was in tears.

'I said no to him,' she insisted. Surely this was his consolation.

'You must have,' said David, completely lost in introspection. 'Or else you wouldn't be here.'

She hoped he would leave it at that.

'I'm sorry,' she said. Miserable, most miserable.

She had really wished that he would leave it at that, but David was no-one's fool – although she would have wished him so that day.

'How long did it take you to say No?'

That was the killer question for Helena. The one she had dreaded. David had seen it in her eyes. And fifteen years later it still hurt him.

'We talked for half an hour.'

Half an hour. Half an hour during the time that he was with his parents at a restaurant in Cirencester and promising them all the great things that he and Helena would do together. While he was planning the rest of his life with her, she was having second thoughts.

'I *wasn't*,' Helena insisted.

'But you couldn't tell him straight away? It took you half an hour to tell him to go.'

That question hung in the air while a waiter brought fresh bright glasses and some local wine.

'I chose you,' she said. 'Can you forgive me for hesitating?'

Could he?

Since Italy they had hardly ever stayed in a hotel. David could not abide them. Neither hotels nor pasta nor even tenor arias.

Fifteen years later, while Helena lay upstairs in bed, unable to sleep, David found himself thinking of Siena. He had recognised again the old old reason why he did not ask her such questions. *He feared the answer.* He had never asked her why it took so long. Never why she had chosen to marry him in the end, because the answers could well be more cruel than he could ever bear. Angrily he got out again his piece on inter-war street violence. It was time to knock it about a bit.

Helena did not know why David came to bed so late that Friday night and why he made such careful movements in the hope of not waking her, even though she was awake. But his tactful distance suited her tonight. Tonight she, too, was overwhelmed with her own old questions, questions she had never expected to consider again. She knew tomorrow Gareth would ask if she was willing to leave David. He would have to withdraw his candidacy soon if he was going to do so with any professional integrity. He needed to know. Helena felt locked inside her own feelings. She simply could not engage with the question. How on *earth* did she come to be in this situation?

On Saturday morning Millie took her children to the fairground at Barry Island while Crispin went out flat-hunting. And David took his children to the Maritime Museum while Helena waited in for Gareth's phone call. The Maritime Museum was always a great favourite because Nick liked to play on the steam engines, leaving Emma free to talk to her father. Unfortunately for Helena on today, of all days, David had persisted in suggesting that they all went down to the docks together.

'I've got things to do,' said Helena.

'It's the first day of the school holiday. We ought to celebrate. The four of us together.'

'We can celebrate when I've got the house straight.'

David insisted they could have lunch at the Norwegian Church.

'No, you get out,' she insisted. 'Just leave me in peace!'

She felt bad about saying that. In fact she felt bad about the whole business. By the time Gareth rang, she felt absolutely *dreadful* and yet the sound of him saying her name reminded her of why things had got to the stage they had.

'I need to see you, Helena.'

'Not now,' she said.' It isn't fair.' *And yet she wanted to put her arms around him.*

'It's fair on us,' he argued.

'Gareth, you've got to understand that I'm very confused at the moment. I need time to think. Seeing you would just make it more difficult to decide.' *And yet she also wanted his arms around her.*

'I've got to wait until they've decided on the job,' she told him. 'I can't tell David before.'

'So you *are* thinking of leaving him?'

'I don't know what I'm thinking. It's all too much. I'm sorry.'

'You realise I will have to go for the interview.'

'Yes,' she said.

'And if they offer it to me?'

If they turn David down, she thought. If they give the job he's always wanted to the man he hates.

'Yes,' she said. 'I'll know by then. So you can decide. If I'm staying with David, you'll have the job and if I'm leaving him, well . . . then you'll have to decide.'

'It's no contest, Helena,' he said, sounding just like the Gareth Box she always loved and never trusted.

'I don't believe you,' she replied but her tone was tender. Her whole body was tender and starting to ache for him again. Could there be any contest in this?

The door bell went. 'I've got to go,' she said.

'I love you,' he said. She wanted to tell him that she loved him too but someone in this world had to be sensible.

'I care for you,' she said. 'So much.'

The bell went again.

'There's someone at the door,' she told him. It was true. It was Pippa. And Pippa was wearing something long in leather, with quilted this and that which Anders had bought her.

'Isn't it wonderful?' she trilled. 'It was waiting for me when I got back.'

Pippa seemed very pleased with herself. 'And he's going to pay for you and me to have lunch on Friday!'

'Friday?' asked Helena, quite unable to keep up. Oh yes, that day that usually cropped up towards the end of the week. The day after David's interview. What *was* Pippa talking about?

'The fascia place north of Brecon,' Pippa insisted cheerily. 'Don't say you've forgotten.'

'Er, no,' said Helena, remembering their long promised girls' day.

'But best of all,' said Pippa. 'He's sacked that Menna person.'

'What?'

Pippa sat down in the hope of coffee. 'Well, she's resigned. Asked to be moved to a different job in the firm. Says she can't work so closely with him in the future. Too right she can't. So—' Pippa gave Helena a great big preening smile. 'So things are looking up all round, aren't they?'

The morning of the interview was one of the few days when David Mosford felt at a disadvantage for having so little hair. The bathroom mirror confirmed his belief that just about every other candidate was bound to appear much, much shaggier than the pink bespectacled fellow who was facing him in the mirror. Did that matter? Could this even be in his favour? No. Professors were no longer chosen because of their eccentric demeanour and polished crania. Profs were salesmen and university status symbols. He looked like neither.

David had woken early and shaved scrupulously. It was important to be well shaven. A professor of Political History was always well shaven. He dressed slowly and rejected one shirt because the cuffs, on closer inspection, were beginning to fray. Any half-way decent professor of history invariably shot perfect cuffs. This was well known. And he had breakfast wearing an apron because academics of professorial rank never, ever, looked as if they'd had to scrape something off their tie. Finally, on his way into the university, he took the ridiculous car through a multi-programme car wash because these things mattered. Or at least they mattered to Davy. He did not want to go into that interview with grimy hubcaps.

David was due in after eleven and Alun at 10.30.

Little Alun had found it rather odd that David had applied for the chair. Everyone knew that David was only caretaking. That was Alun's view anyway. Fortunately when the list of interviewees was first made known David had joked about only being in there to make up the numbers and Alun had rather taken a shine to this idea.

'They've given themselves a very tight schedule,' he told David when they collided in Dorkin's outer office. 'I thought the field was rather poor.'

'Oh, I don't think so,' said David as he tried to make head or tail of something about costing centres that Carys Bloody Rees had sent him.

'I mean, with people like you coming forward for form's sake,' Alun continued. 'Now the day's so crowded I'd have thought Stella would have asked you to stand down.'

'No,' said David. 'No, she hasn't . . .'

'Ah well,' said Alun. 'On their heads be it. They're the ones who've got to sit through it all.'

Hooper popped his head through the door.

'Good luck, both,' he said. 'Heard about the Crumpet?' David looked round to check that Megan hadn't come back in.

'What's that?' he asked. Hooper likewise checked in the corridor to make sure there were no students in earshot. 'She's no more than thirty. Been something impressive over in New York State. Glyn saw Stella showing her around yesterday. Dragged me down to her lecture for a once-over. You haven't seen anything like it.' Mike was clearly in seventh heaven at the prospect of his department's improving academic profile.

'A *woman*!' snorted Alun who had only just caught up

'Very much,' Mike grinned. 'So sorry, boys, if I cast my vote elsewhere.'

'What *are* they playing at?' Alun Taylor exclaimed. Eccentric as it was to interview David Mosford, fetching a woman over from New York was pure folly. 'How old did he say?'

'Thirty, possibly younger,' said David.

'Now I've heard everything!' said Alun and out he walked.

A *woman*, thought David. A young woman at that. The University was, amongst everything else, an equal opportunities employer. The University did not regard such candidates as Crumpet. The University did not stalk out when such people offered to occupy the professorial chair. As far as David was concerned a woman of any age, even Sarah John, even *Katie* John, was preferable to Gareth Box.

Helena knew that David was being interviewed some time after eleven and she knew she wouldn't be able to settle so she rang Crispin and asked if they could pool children for a few hours.

'Well, Jonathan's gone down to see his friend Maxy,' said Crispin. 'But Katrin's here.'

Helena could hear Katrin objecting to having that awful Emma Mosford *again* but Crispin insisted they came round anyway. It was ironic that, just when the two families were going away together, Katrin and Emma had fallen out. Helena said as much to Crispin when he was filling the kettle for their coffee.

'Even more embarrassing that Millie and I have "fallen out",' said Crispin darkly. Nick, who was playing on the kitchen table, looked up.

'Grown ups fall out!' he scoffed, as if Crispin's lack of understanding appalled him.

Helena and Crispin smiled at each other.

'One of us had to mention it,' said Crispin to Helena. She thanked him and suggested that they walked around the garden. She wanted some time alone with Crispin. She wanted to say she thought she understood what he was going through. After all, he was thinking of leaving Millie, wasn't he? That was a scenario that had certain resonances for her.

After a few paces she asked him if he'd like to tell her about it.

'I think I'd like you to *know*,' he replied. 'I don't imagine I would enjoy telling you but you're bound to hear a version from Millie or the children.' Crispin sat himself down on a garden seat that Millie had begun building two weeks ago, a garden seat that had remained unfinished ever since all this started happening.

'The main thing is . . . the main thing is . . . I have realised that I no longer love Millie. This is a very sad confession to make. Millie, understandably, doesn't want to live with me any more. I have told her I don't want us to do something silly like selling the house and splitting the proceeds. That wouldn't be fair on the children. So the simplest thing is, we have agreed that I move out, although I shall look after the children during the week.'

Helena felt it would be presumptuous to sit down beside Crispin so she squatted alongside him, as she might with one of her children.

'And you've realised that you love someone else?' she prompted. Crispin shook his head.

'No,' he said. 'That's sad too, isn't it?'

'Yes,' she agreed. This was not what David had explained, nor what Millie had hinted at.

'Some people find they love two people,' she said. 'They don't know why but they know they have to choose . . .'

'Yes,' said Crispin. 'I believe that is more normally the case.' He looked so sad, so tired and worn. As Millie had looked tired and worn. What an awful business to withdraw your love, thought Helena.

'I'm sorry you're not coming to Montgomery. It's going to be a difficult time if David hasn't got the job.'

'Yes,' said Crispin. He had often seemed distracted but now he was continually focused somewhere else. 'I don't think Millie's going to be in much of a state to cheer him up.'

The sound of the kettle boiling and Emma shouting at Katrin silenced Helena's reply and drew them back to the kitchen.

Neville had brewed up for Millie down at the Middle Wicket. She had been giving him a hard time this morning and he'd been passing it on, blow by blow, to the boys.

'Thanks, Nev,' she said cupping her hands round the drink. 'Sorry I'm being such a bitch.'

Neville shrugged. He kept his head down on such occasions.

'You all right though, Mrs Kemp?' he asked kindly. Millie stretched out in the sun. Her knees were a wonderful colour now but she didn't care any more.

'No,' she said. 'No, I'm not OK. No in fact I'm bloody miserable, Nev, and anything I say you should take with a pinch of salt.'

Neville nodded. 'Well, anything I can do, you know . . .' Millie smiled at him. Actually she wanted him to put his arm round her. She *so* wanted someone to do that.

'Well, you can promise to buy me a drink tonight,' she said. Nev nodded. Yeah, he could do that.

'You not heading back to Cardiff then? You normally pop back one night a week don't you?'

'No, I'll clear off early on Friday instead. We're going away for the weekend with some friends. I'll see plenty of the kids then. I may stay up all through the week on this job.'

'Right,' said Nev. *Go on,* thought Millie. Ask me why. I'd tell you. I really would. She hadn't told Gail yet for obvious reasons. Gail would want to throw a party and get all her exes round for Millie to have the pick of them. But Nev might offer to do Crispin over. That would be nice. Or even put his arm round her. That would be nicer still.

'Right, well, see you for a pint then,' said Nev.

'Uhuh,' said Millie. *Uh-bloody-huh.*

David had rung up and said very little. Part of what he did say was that he'd phoned once before but she hadn't been in. Helena explained she must have still been walking back from Crispin's at the very time he came out of the interview. She felt bad not to have been in. But she felt bad all the time at present.

'So how did it go?'

'Straight down the line,' said David. 'They didn't ask me anything remarkable. And I didn't say anything remarkable. We were very fair with each other. It was, I think, a mutually unimpressive experience. We're not going out tonight, are we?'

'Of course not,' said Helena, feeling all fond of his inability to speak on the phone, his fussy but lovable intelligence.

When she had put the phone down, and when she had fed the children and sent them out to play, and when she had dealt with the fact they *realised* their playing was for her benefit, not theirs, Helena sat down and tried to marshal her thoughts. She should start the packing for Montgomery if they were heading off tomorrow but somehow she didn't want to until she knew more about the job. It seemed as if there would be different clothes to pack depending on whether or not he had got the chair, or whether or not he knew that someone else had. So, instead of writing an inventory of necessary socks and underwear, she took the pad from her coat and began a very different kind of list.

[1] I think I love Gareth and want to be with him.
[2] I hope I love David and want to be with him.
[3] What about the children? How would this affect them?

She tried not to think about Emma's enmity, how Emma would take David's side and hate her for a while. She had to think of the long term. It was odd wasn't it, how little she had considered the children in all this? Did that mean she was a bad mother – or simply a distracted one? Instead of addressing that issue, Helena continued with her list.

[4] David is not very helpful with the children but Gareth would be worse. He would be kind but physically and emotionally absent whereas David is only emotionally.

She didn't like the repetition and almost replaced that second 'emotionally' with 'the latter' but this was not an essay she was writing. Style was not a consideration.

[5] I can cope basically on my own with the children.

Yes, after all, that was how it had been with David on occasions, especially over Nick. With Gareth it would just be like that all the time. So if the children did not sway this issue one way or the other what did it come down to?

[6] I must look to my own happiness.

What would make her happy? She had to be completely frank and honest with herself here. She must not second guess which way this little document was heading:

[7] I am not convinced being married to Gareth would make me happy

She chewed the end of her pencil. What followed now seemed very obvious. Unanswerable but obvious.

[8] So: i) do I love Gareth?
       ii) do I love David?
      iii) do I love both?
      iv) either? neither?

She didn't like the last. She didn't care for the Crispin option. This was all terribly uncomfortable, even painful, stuff but she would rather have the misery of loving too many people than the misery of loving none.

'Outrageous,' said Alun Taylor. He had said it several times already. David was actually on the telephone to the *Daily Mail* about his street crime piece and speaking to someone who was being very heavy about its exclusivity. 'Outrageous!' said Alun with greater emphasis. David couldn't agree more. Part of Megan's duties in the outer office involved keeping the likes of Alun Taylor out there until the likes of David wanted him in. Particularly when David was on the phone to someone who was quibbling about his byline.

'They asked me about this new American Thing!' said Alun without any preamble whatsoever.

David thought he knew what this was about.

'At the interview?'

'Yes. They asked me what my view would be if the practice arose in this country of regarding university education as a form of educational fucking contract!'

'Yes, they asked me that,' David agreed. Alun, who up until that moment had been pacing away from David, swung round in mid-footstep.

'What did you say, then?'

'Oh, I trotted out the usual bollocks.'

'What bollocks?' asked Alun as if some essential part of his collegiate in-service training had been omitted.

'Well, you know how Stella likes us to be aware of the ongoing re-evaluation of tertiary education's obligations to the community.' Alun looked aghast.

'But this is saying that if a student fails his degree he can sue us because the education we've provided isn't good enough to get him through?' David nodded. Alun felt he just couldn't have made his point clearly enough.

'But, David, it's turning us into a service industry. God knows, we have little or no quality control over which students we take because it's always the blessed *numbers* that have to be kept up. But at least at the moment we can fail a few of the more obvious halfwits. But if we're obliged to *guarantee* all these dimbos and slackers a degree, those degrees – *our degrees* – are going to become worthless. And if our degrees are worthless, what is the point of working for such a crappy institution!'

'Is this what you said to Stella?' David asked from Dorkin's desk.

'In as many words,' Alun replied with a swagger that was fast losing its confidence.

Well, thought David, whoever is getting Dorkin's chair, it obviously isn't going to be Dr Taylor.

'I mean, was I wrong?'

David felt his heart unexpectedly go out to the man. 'No. You were absolutely right, old fellow. There are a lot of people who'd agree with you on that around here. But not many who'd have the courage to say it.'

'Well then!' Alun declared with a purposeful nod and he let that flourish be his last word on the subject. He left Dorkin's office fairly transported with his own moral courage. David went home soon after, unconvinced of his own.

As he parked the ridiculous car and looked up at his parents' great dark house David found himself thinking about Gareth. How would Professor Box have acquitted himself today? Would he have known when diplomacy was required? When it was best not to have a view? Would he have sailed through the little political correctness traps? He certainly would have recognised some that he, David, might have missed. But would he have *shone*? David feared that, yes, Gareth Box would have shone, like a beacon in fact, like his father's bloody lamp the time he was trapped below ground and the pumps failed. That's how he would have shone. 'Some of these Oxford girls,' Gareth had said to him. 'They'll believe anything. They like a bit of the old priapic pit pony, David. You should try it.' Helena tried it, didn't she? Helena believed it. Maybe she still did. For some reason he didn't entirely understand David felt even more depressed now he had arrived home.

Emma came running out full of glee at the sight of his return. I love you so, said David through the windscreen of his car.

At nine o'clock Millie was fed up of drowning her sorrows with Neville. He was a good-hearted chap, old Nev, and he knew his trade pretty well but he was dull and she didn't really fancy him. She had tried this evening. Really tried. On the face of it, there was every reason to fancy Nev. He was tanned and fit, muscular and easy-going. He even had what Gail would have judged the right kind of *butt*. OK he was married but lots of people coped with that one, didn't they? The problem was, Millie didn't want Nev's butt or any other part of him, not really. Millie wanted Crispin who was pasty and stringy, lop-sided and tight-arsed. Crispin who was unable to love her any more. Why didn't he love her? Millie wondered, as she stared into the bottom of a glass that had until recently contained her third pint of the evening. He said he didn't love Sue. Or anybody else for that matter. So why couldn't he love her? Why couldn't he just *try*?

Sometimes you just had to try.

'You all right, Mrs K?' asked Neville yet again.

'Oh for God's sake call me *Millie*,' said Millie. Nev took this on the chin. She wasn't being very good company, was she? Millie put down her glass.

'Fancy another?' said Neville. It was one of his two conversational gambits tonight. *Fancy another* and You *all right Mrs Kemp?* Millie declined as graciously as she could manage.

'Nev, you're married aren't you?' Neville shrugged his agreement.

'What's your wife think of you being here?'

'Here?'

'With me.' Neville shrugged more slowly this time, a bigger shrug. Not such an easy question.

'Work, isn't it? She puts up with that.'

'And what if I say let's go on to a club somewhere?' Neville nodded his head like a big slow boxer dodging some unexpected blow. 'Well, still work, isn't it? I mean, I give her the money, she has to let me get on with the work.'

'And if I say why not come back to my place?'

'What? After?' asked Neville.

'Uhuh.'

'You having me on, Mrs K?'

Up until that moment Millie wasn't sure what she was doing. Was she making a pass at this allegedly attractive man? Was she teasing him? Was she just trying to find out if she was still attractive to men? But at Nev's reply Millie started to shake with silent mirth. She couldn't help it. The idea of Neville humping away in Gail's box room unable to stop calling her Mrs Kemp was too funny for words.

Oh God Mrs K you got a lovely body. Millie sniggered

Oh God, yes, yes, Mrs Kemp that's lovely that is. Millie positively tittered.

Oh Christ, I love you, I love you, Mrs K!

Millie was laughing out loud now and Neville was smirking too. 'You were pulling my leg, weren't you? Christ, you nearly had me fooled there.'

Millie was still laughing in her taxi home and only when she got back to Gail's and faced the prospect of that empty bed did she begin to feel really sad again. She helped herself to a gin and tonic and Gail's telephone.

'It's *me*,' she challenged.

'Oh,' said Crispin, many miles and a large part of her life away.

'What were you doing?'

'Reading.'

'Where?'

'In the kitchen.' *In her kitchen.*

'How are the kids?'

'Still fine,' his voice said.

Why didn't he love her? It didn't make sense.

'I hate you, you know,' she said in a very quiet voice, hardly her own and almost devoid of malice.

'I know,' said Crispin. 'I wish it wasn't like this, Millie.' There was a silence.

'I'm so sorry,' said Crispin.

'Then why not . . .' Millie began but she couldn't go on. Now there was a long silence between them. The line ticked and surged in that silence. '*Oh,*' said Millie finally. 'Oh, just fuck off out of my life.' She put the phone down and, after a moment, began to howl with grief. It was a long dark bestial moan that issued out of her, as ugly as the pain within.

'Oh, Pippa called in today,' said Helena. They were both in bed and had just had sex in such a mild, polite but comforting sort of way that it seemed quite normal just to resume previous conversations and catch up with the gossip. Helena had suggested sex at the end of their meal. It was not the kind of suggestion she usually made over dinner but David had looked terribly tense.

'I must admit I doubt my ability to rise to the occasion,' he had told her, folding his napkin resignedly but she had promised to give him every encouragement and indeed they both put up a creditable performance. Nevertheless Helena had felt detached from it all, and guilty at her detachment. Afterwards he had thanked her. 'My pleasure,' she had assured him. 'No it wasn't,' he replied. 'It was all mine but I am grateful.'

It was ten o'clock and they were going away tomorrow with Millie. Helena got up, put on her nightdress and went to clean her teeth. David watched for her return and his eyes followed her as she moved around the bedroom packing clothes into piles like the long white ghost of an Edwardian chambermaid. He felt pleasured but lonely. When she got back into bed he felt happier and they talked of this and that and David even told Helena of Alun's stand for political unorthodoxy.

'Poor thing,' said Helena but she knew that David didn't want to say any more about the interview. They'd been through it question by answer. He hadn't done badly, Helena thought, but then again he was right: it didn't sound as if he'd done well. It was best to keep off the subject which was why Pippa was a useful diversion. Her feminine absurdity always cheered David up.

'She's in a tiz about this thing in Brecon tomorrow. You remember I said I'd go with her to that mill that sells walnut veneer.' David gave a snigger, he had his arm around her now and she could feel the deeper notes of that merriment vibrating in his chest.

'Walnut *what*?'

'Dashboards, table tops, you know the kind of thing. It was in the Sundays. They're exporting fascias all over the world.'

'Are they really?'

'Well, obviously we're going in her car . . .'

'. . . because she wants them to measure up her dash?'

'Yes.'

David laughed now.

Helena felt that had it been Anders or Mostyn John who was tempted by a walnut dashboard the subject would not have been half as funny to David but she was more concerned to establish tomorrow's arrangements.

'And then we're going to Llangoed Hall for lunch . . .'

'This all sounds vaguely familiar,' David admitted.

'But,' said Helena, 'the thing is: now Anders is joining her up there. Just for the evening.'

'Oh right,' said David, beginning to relish the prospect of distracting himself with the logistics of Pippa Arnstein's wonderful life.

'So you mean how are you going to get back to Cardiff to pick up the children and me, ready to go up to Montgomery?'

'Yes.'

'Well, the answer's simple,' said David, pulling the duvet around them. 'Where are the children tomorrow?'

'Crispin's got all four. You're supposed to be helping.'

'OK, so you stay on at Llangoed and I'll drive up in the ridiculous car to collect you while Millie brings all the children in hers. She and I can go in convoy as soon as she gets back from London.'

'What a pity we can't stay in Llangoed,' said Helena. 'Like Pippa and Anders.'

'Pippa and Anders don't have two children,' he replied. 'Damn!'

'What?'

He sat up. 'What if I get a call tomorrow to go in and see Stella Price?' He looked at her as if he genuinely feared bad news.

'Crispin's in charge,' Helena reassured him. 'You're just helping out while he's flat-hunting. And anyway, Stella Price isn't going to call you in tomorrow. She isn't going to call in anyone. That's my instinct anyway.'

David settled down to sleep. He liked Helena's instincts. They were wrong, however.

13 ∫

Men in Tears

Llangoed was heavenly.

Its long panelled hall reminded Helena of the house at Barrington. Its sofas were deep, the North American periodicals irresistible. She even found Pippa's chatter, irritating in the car and increasingly bitchy at the fascia warehouse, now simply distracting.

All through the morning Helena had found herself veering between simple frustration and a distress that bordered on anger. Away from her home, she immediately started to think about Gareth and all the things that had come tumbling out of the Gareth box. Beyond the constraints of Llandaff, there seemed to be nothing to stop her. Here she was, incredibly, as attracted to Gareth as she had been twenty years ago and yet she still didn't know why. And yet there was no outlet for thoughts like these. They overwhelmed her at times, the way that grief overwhelms, but then they would pass, the way a headache passes. And in the silence that was left it was good to be alongside little Pippa Arnstein, listening to her spend forty minutes deciding that walnut was after all the wrong kind of wood.

They were in Llangoed's drawing room now and Pippa was flirting with the waiters who seemed very young to Helena. Funny at thirty-seven to realise you are an older woman and yet to see Pippa, at thirty, quite oblivious to it.

'Would you like to see the wine list?' a new waiter asked.

'No,' said Pippa with a little laugh. 'I'd just like champagne.'

'The house champagne?'

'Lovely,' said Pip. She turned to Helena. 'Or do you think I ought to sting Anders for Bollinger?'

'I'm sure he's suffering enough,' Helena assured her.

The lunch had been very good but Helena's mood shifted once again. At the table she had found herself growing irritated by all this Pippa *noise*, all these shared confidences about who was clearly keen on her and who was holding himself in check. They were just reminders of the Gareth box and all its contents, so liberally scattered throughout her life. Would she ever manage to tidy them up now? Or would she just have to close the door on this mess that was her current life and walk away? She *so* needed to talk about this! If only she were here with Crispin, or her father, or one of her cousins or her London friends. Helena could really have opened up about the dilemma she found herself in to them. But in Pippa's presence she couldn't even ponder the matter in silence.

'Let's have some more of this, shall we?' asked the Pixie with a giggle.

When David arrived at four o'clock Helena was uncomfortably half asleep by the large redundant fireplace. Pip, who had been spark out for the last hour woke up instantly, as if her feminine wiles had never slept but only shut down until a suitable male came past.

'Hello, David,' said Pippa, simultaneously yawning, stretching and offering her hand to Helena's husband. He helped her up gallantly. Helena was left to get to her feet unaided. That was the price you paid for Pippa's company.

'Where's Millie?' Helena asked.

'I'll tell you in the car,' said David as he kissed Mrs Arnstein goodbye.

'I think I'll get some rest,' she told him. 'Have a bath. Anders is coming up this evening.'

'He's a lucky man,' said David. Pippa liked that and she gave him her totally ravishing look from the top of the staircase.

'Bye!'

In David's little red car he began to tell her something about his day.

'Millie rang to say she wouldn't be leaving London till three. She's having to have her gasket fixed first.'

'Is that serious?' Helena asked.

'I don't know,' David replied, overtaking as the road narrowed north.

'Don't they blow?' Helena suggested. 'Gaskets? Isn't that what they do?'

'Yes, I think that's what this one has done.'

'Oh dear.'

David tucked his car quickly back into the side of the road as a lorry bounced past.

'In what direction?' Helena asked. 'In or out?'

David didn't honestly know and he had something more important to tell her. 'Actually . . . I'd only just come off the phone to Crispin when, of all people, Stella rang.'

'Oh God,' said Helena quietly

'Exactly.' This was the big stuff. 'She wanted me to go in.'

'Why didn't you ring me?' Helena asked, not quite looking at him. She felt so bad to have been chewing his ear about gaskets. And to have been away at lunch when Stella had rung. She had been sure Stella would not ring.

'I only thought I'd ring you if she'd had anything to say,' he replied.

'And she hadn't?'

'She hadn't. She thought I'd want to know that no decision was going to be made until Monday.'

'Oh *God*,' said Helena. David slowed down behind a short convoy that was following a very self-possessed little tractor all the way to Builth Wells.

'God indeed,' said David.

'Are they taking up references or something?'

He changed gear rather than stall. 'I don't know but, whatever it is they're doing, it has to involve someone from outside the University.'

Gareth, thought Helena.

Gareth, thought David.

'You ought to get that job,' said Helena fiercely. 'You're the best person in for it.'

'Thank you,' said David. 'I think that has been my opinion too. Of course I'm notoriously partial on the subject of who should sit in the chair of Political History. Somehow what was always most wrong about Dorkin was that he so much wasn't *me*. I think I never could forgive him for that.'

It was one of David's jokes.

'I love you,' said Helena staring at the tailgate of the lorry in front. It did all seem so very wrong. Would David really fail twice to get the job his father always wanted for him?

But over the engine noise David had failed to hear her declaration.

'However, the good news is I seem to be published in the *Daily Mail*.' David couldn't resist laughing as he announced this. 'There is an article which appears to advocate a return to 1930s capital punishment with my byline and a photograph of Mosford looking for all the world like a would-be chief hangman.' Helena glanced across at him.

'Are you joking?' she asked.

'Not at all. It's on the back shelf somewhere. You'll see – if you actually read the article – that what I say is that during a time of flat caps and capital punishment street crime was at its lowest level for one hundred years. The poor benighted sub at Derry Street has of course extracted that bit and assumed hanging kept crime off the streets.'

'That's dreadful,' said Helena. *History confirms that capital punishment kept crime off the streets, says Dr David Mosford, Reader in History at the University of Cardiff.*

David laughed again but without merriment. 'Of course, causality has never been the *Mail*'s strongest suit. They seem to think that because two things happen simultaneously one must have caused the other. We're quite lucky they don't claim I'm advocating a return to flat caps!'

Helena could recognise that the joke was a painful one for David. She scanned the article.

'You don't say any of that,' she agreed. 'You should have let me read this.'

David nodded. 'I thought I was too political, too clever to get misinterpreted like that.'

Helena gazed at the article.

'Is this why Stella called you in?' she asked.

'Yes. Don't worry. She thinks it's shoddy and of course it does bugger all for our Impact Factors but evidently the Vice Chancellor loved it. Just what the University's signalling to Westminster at the moment. Well done, Mosford. I think she wanted to tell me about the VC in person so I could share the joke.'

'But it's not true,' said Helena.

'No,' said David.

'And doesn't that matter?' she asked. David looked at Helena and she at him. He nodded. It did. It mattered and it hurt but then they started to laugh at the silly sadness of it all.

That afternoon Crispin had hoped to be going to see a room over the estate agents which sounded ideal. He had been warned by John Cavendish Williams that there was a lot of interest so when David rang to say he had to go into college, Crispin decided he could wait no longer.

'I want you four to go out and play in the garden till I get back OK? Don't touch anything, or do anything. Just play. OK?'

Unfortunately Nick Mosford was not happy with going into the garden.

'What's wrong with it?' Crispin asked as they stood either side of the kitchen table.

'I don't like the plants,' said Nick.

'Is there anything else you'd like to do?' Crispin asked.

'Is there a piano, Crispin?' the boy replied.

'No,' said Crispin. 'Do you play?'

'No,' said Nick darkly as if he'd like to do something rather awful to a piano if he could only get his hands on one.

'Come on,' said Crispin and they wandered hand in hand into the garden. The girls were no longer playing together but Jonathan seemed to have befriended Emma Mosford who was burying his feet in the dusty soil.

'Why don't you play with Katrin?' said Crispin.

'Oh I want to come with *you*,' Katrin moaned. She was very clinging at the moment.

'All right,' said Crispin. 'OK. You two come with me and Emma and Jon stay here.'

Nick did not look impressed. 'I will like to stay with Emma and Jonathan Willums,' he announced.

Oh, God, thought Crispin who could see this room being let by the time he arrived.

'OK, OK. I'll be back in ten minutes. Emma, Jonathan, you look after Nick. Nick, you stay with them. OK? Jonathan I said OK?'

'Oink, oink,' said Jonathan Willums.

Katrin kept close to Crispin these days. Sometimes he could almost feel the hurt within her. Nevertheless several girls in her class had separated parents, so this was a new club for Katrin to belong to.

'It isn't a legal separation,' Crispin explained as they waited in the downstairs reception for a key. 'We're just living more separately.'

'Is it a divorcement then?' Katrin asked.

'No it's just informal. We'll still share the same money.'

'Oh that's good,' said Katrin. 'I don't suppose you could live on what you earn.'

'Good point,' said Crispin. Worryingly good.

The key and an estate agent carrying it turned up at that point. The flat was attractive enough and it had the great advantage of being nearby. Moreover Katrin clearly liked the idea of visiting Crispin in it. The problem was that it was a flat, not a room, and it was being offered at the kind of rates flats commanded in Llandaff. John Cavendish had no fears that he could let it twice over that very afternoon. Crispin felt depressed. He couldn't afford this and yet how could he expect Millie to finance his inability to love her?

'Never mind, you can still live with us,' said Katrin as they left.

When they got back to number 27 the hall telephone was ringing. Emma was lying on her back with her legs in the air and making pig noises while Jonathan stared at the receiver and did nothing. Crispin wondered about Jonathan, he really did.

The call was from David who was ringing from the University in a bit of a state. Finding that Millie wasn't back from London yet, David told Crispin he'd go on direct to Llangoed Hall and collect Helena, if that was all right. Crispin watched Nick Mosford run past without any clothes on and agreed that, probably, that was fine. The girls were chasing Nick now.

'I was going to drive up with Millie in convoy but really it's not a good idea,' David explained, 'and I do need to speak to Helena this afternoon.'

'Er, right,' said Crispin. Really, he could do with some male solidarity at the moment. Or just *person* solidarity to be honest. He could do with someone, anyone, to help police these children but he also remembered that David might be hearing about the job today. In fact David had muttered as much when he said he was having to go into the University. Presumably that was what David had to talk to Helena about. This was not the time for Crispin to declare that he wasn't coping, that Nick was naked, the girls hysterical and Jonathan's brain apparently dismantled for the day. David spoke briefly on the phone to Emma and Nick to tell them he'd see them at Lyme. Then he was gone.

'Oh where is *Millie*?' Crispin said to himself. She had a new gasket on her car. What more did she need?

Lyme Hall had clearly been something and, by the amount of building work going on, it was clearly going to be something again in the not too distant future. At the moment, however, most of the parkland looked as if some giant child had scattered his toy tipper trucks all over it, and then broke several of them.

By the time David and Helena found the estate they felt they had travelled a very long way, from Cardiff, from the University, from Gareth Box and what he privately, and even secretly, meant to each of them. The old hall was very much as Millie had described to them except that it was coated with fine grey builders' dust on the outside. Inside was cleaner but neglected. Old oak ran everywhere but stopped – as if in horror – alongside a very inappropriate 1960s reception desk, quilted in what seemed to be faded orange plastic. A harassed, sweating woman called Alyson appeared from nowhere. She had copious amounts of grey hair. Or was its hue due to builders' dust? Alyson told them she was the owner's wife, that the owner was an idle sod and that David and Helena were in the stable block.

'You're in Vernon. Millie's in Herbert. They're the furthest from all this awful mess.'

'Why didn't you close down while all this was going on?' David asked as he brushed some more dust from the visitors' book.

'That's what I want to ask my husband,' said Alyson. 'When I've finished kicking him. Shall I get someone to bring your bags over?'

David thought it would take forever for someone to be unearthed from inside the hall, besides which most of their luggage was coming up with Millie Kemp. David and Helena walked to the stable block acutely aware of how much they were on their own. They were the only two people in the world. The silence of mid-Wales hung in the air. David could almost hear Helena's dress flapping as she walked. Silence. The silence of his forefathers, of Owain Glyndwr and Lywelyn The Last. All of a sudden David felt very Welsh. Silence. It was timeless, leaving time itself hanging, like the afternoon sun, suspended forever in the sky.

'We should do this more often,' he said.

The stable block was properly converted. Six apartments, two up four down, looking on to a quiet little swimming pool. Two apartments didn't have windows in yet. Two more were unfurnished. Only the Mosford/Kemp pair, either side of the archway, were finished although one of those had a ladder abandoned against it. David stepped over the encumbrance. 'Actually it's an heraldic device,' he said. 'Builders use them wherever they go. At college, the day work was supposed to start when they came round, dumped two pallets of bricks and then buggered off. Marks out the territory, you see, like a flag, or a cat peeing on the furniture. Builders always leave a ladder so you know the site is still theirs.'

Helena had taken off her shoes. 'Do you think anyone's around now?' she asked.

'No,' said David trying the key in their lock. 'Isn't that a wonderful view?'

Indeed the Severn Valley, bathed in the beginnings of a golden sunset was entrancing.

'Where is it?' asked Helena. The view reminded her of the calm, patchwork fields of her childhood.

'Wales,' said David. 'You know what Wales is, don't you? The bits your lot didn't want when they galloped into Gloucestershire.'

'1089,' she replied. 'Before my time.'

Helena dipped her toe in the water. 'I could live here you know,' she said. David had the door open by now. 'Quicker to commute from Barrington,' he grumbled. Helena sat by the pool and slid her legs in. The water was just cool, but not too cool. From inside their flat she could hear David laugh.

'Compliments of Mrs Kemp!' he cried as he emerged with a bottle of gin. 'Isn't that wonderful? I'll see if she's got them to put any tonic in the fridge.'

They sat on some garden furniture that hadn't been fully unwrapped yet. Man and wife, drinking in the sun whilst drinking in the gin.

'Needs a slice of lemon,' David observed for the second time.

'Oh, do shut up,' she asked, but not without affection.

David reached across and took her hand. 'I don't care about the University,' he said.

'Neither do I,' Helena replied. 'Fancy a swim?'

'I think all our stuff's in Millie's boot at the moment.'

Helena stood up and looked at him as if he was being obtuse. Then she unbuttoned her dress.

'Come on,' she said.

'Here?' said David.

'This is where the water is,' she replied, stepping out of her dress.

'But,' said David as his wife released the catch on her bra. Before he could say much more, Helena had all her clothes off and was wincing as the water slid up over her waist. To be a vision totally out of David's sexual fantasies she would have dived in head first, rising through the water like an Arthur Rackham Rhinemaiden, her long hair coiling down over pubescent breasts. Neither the action nor the figure was *absolutely* perfect but he wasn't complaining.

'Come on,' she laughed. He wished he could but somehow moments of spontaneous naked sensuality were beyond him that evening. To abandon oneself to the moment it is best not to have spent the previous eight hours worrying about jobs, outrageously subbed newspaper articles and congestion on the Builth to Brecon throughfare.

'What if Millie turned up now?' he called as Helena struck out along the pool.

'I'm sure she'd join in!' Helena replied.

'Yes!' he agreed. Helena completed her modest length and stood up, less modestly.

'Then you'd have two of us,' she told him.

'The mind is boggling,' said David with an appreciative smile. 'But there would also be four children, don't forget. I think that pool would be getting rather crowded.' As soon as Helena remembered the children she ceased to look like an unusually tall water nymph and more like a mum with no clothes on.

'Shouldn't they be here by now?' she asked.

'I'll go and check. Ring Crispin. See what time they set off.' David stood up. 'I'll also see if I can borrow you a towel, Mrs Mosford.'

At the very moment Helena Mosford resumed her swimming, and David wandered across the dusty lawns to where the orange plastic reception desk remained hideous and unmanned, Millie Kemp was swearing at her car. It was in the lane at the back of 27 High Street and surrounded by four children with absurd amounts of vital luggage: roller blades, tape recorders, portable TV etc.

'I thought you'd had the gasket fixed,' said Crispin unhelpfully.

'Bastard Thing,' Millie swore. 'I asked Nev to give it the once over before I set off but he's about as much use as a spare dick on a whatsit.'

'A spare *Nick*?' said Nick. Katrin whispered a giggle into Emma's ear.

Crispin was aware that one or two censorious neighbours had congregated to watch this scene and others were opening their doors. He felt that, in public, Millie's household should try and look constructively on the problem.

'Should I ring the AA?' he asked helpfully.

'Oh, great idea,' Millie shouted at him. 'If only we were *in* the fucking AA!' A tut ran round the neighbours who clearly felt that the failure of Millie's car to move was a divine judgement on the low life at 27 High Street. The little man with the stick pointedly turned his back and walked away. At that point someone heard the telephone ringing inside.

'I'll get it,' shouted Katrin and she put down her Walkman, trainers and velcro bats.

'That's probably bloody David,' said Millie to Crispin. 'We should be half way there by now.'

Helena had enjoyed her swim but was getting a bit cold now. She had felt no hesitation responding to the unexpected sensuality of their afternoon together but she had been in the pool for ten minutes now and the sun was beginning to dip. Uninhibited as she had been when she stepped into the water, and when she had let it swallow up her nakedness, she was now *distinctly* inhibited by the prospect of climbing out and re-exposing that nakedness to what remained of the sun, and even what remained of the builders, should she be really unlucky. One of them might well be coming back for that ladder. Helena heard footsteps and was about to crouch down in the water when David emerged from underneath the arch with several large white towels.

'Everyone all right?' Helena asked as he opened one up to embrace her.

'They're fine but Millie's car has had problems again.' He wrapped the towel around her.

'Where are they?' she asked with a shiver.

'Still in Cardiff. Crispin's going to try and get a garage to come out. Whatever happens they won't be here for another four, possibly five hours.'

'Oh dear,' said Helena.

'There's nothing we can do.' David sat down on one of the unwrapped chairs again and held out his arms to her. 'Let's have a think,' he said.

Helena sat on David's lap. She felt strange to be disconnected from her children like this.

'They're all right?' she asked.

'They're fine,' he said and he stroked her hair. It had all come loose now, great black coils over the soft white towel. There was so much hair, he thought, and it was thicker now than it had been for years. How strange. He could lose himself in her hair, like he did on their honeymoon.

This is nice, thought Helena. David's hands in her hair, endlessly teasing out the strands. This is like it was that time that Nick was conceived. This is what it was like a lifetime ago, a lifetime of struggles and doubt. She put her head into his neck, burying her face. She liked the feel of his hands, the smell of his skin.

'Is there a bed inside?' she asked. 'As well as a bottle of gin and some mixers, has Mrs Kemp managed to lay on a bed?'

'I think so,' said David. And yet he sounded sad.

'I love you, you know,' Helena said into David's neck. Everytime she thought of Gareth these days she found herself telling David that she loved him. And it was easier to do so if she spoke into his neck. Easier than to look at the unhappiness in his eyes.

'I love you too,' he replied. 'But I don't know if I'm up to doing anything about it.'

'Sod the University,' said Helena and she sat up on his lap decisively.

'Yes,' said David. 'Sod the University.'

They went upstairs to the little double room which was off the little narrow staircase. Because all the new bedrooms were under the eaves these rooms were very warm from all the sunshine that had beaten down upon the grant-approved Welsh slates. Helena lay down on the bed and David stroked her stomach. The wait for this job was making him feel terribly vulnerable. Almost physically so.

'Sod them,' said Helena after a while.

'Yes, sod them,' said David and he unloosened the laces of his shoes before slipping them off. They were no stretcher bars, of course. Millie hadn't been able to run to those. Helena held out her arms to him. He seemed so tense, so sad, she wanted to take all that from him. She felt enormously strong lying naked in front of him. David moved to get on the bed but then stopped and took off his trousers. All the time he was watching her.

'I love you,' he said.

'Come on,' said Helena. 'Come to me.'

David got on the bed beside her. She took hold of his shirt and pulled him on top of her.

'Sod the University,' she said.

'Sod the University,' he replied and they kept repeating that until she had aroused him and pulled him inside her.

Afterwards David fell asleep his head between her breasts. The room was totally silent. No hum of traffic, not even bird song as the sun dipped. Somewhere perhaps a fridge was whirring as it chilled the necessary tonic. Helena stared at the ceiling and thought about how much she loved David. As sex went that had gone pretty quickly, and yet she had never felt so happy making love before, with anyone. With Gareth sex was more enjoyable. Exciting but never intimate. The intimacy had always been on her side, she felt, never on his. And afterwards he could make you feel like the best there was. But she had never felt like *this* with Gareth. This warm sensation of being needed, and being happy to be needed. She was fulfilled by it. She liked the sense of David finding that home between her legs. He needed her. But he'd needed her in the past, hadn't he? When Nick was young, he'd needed her a lot but at that time his need had just worn her down. So why did she love him and his need for her now? And how could she love Gareth when she was with Gareth and David when she was with David?

What was happening to her?

'Fuck, fuck and fuckit!' said Millie. 'I'm going to have a bath.' Every garage that Crispin tried at half past five on a Friday night promised to be out first thing. Which was, as everyone knew, no fucking use if Millie was supposed to be fucking driving up on fucking Friday night. Even Selwyn of Chiswick would have admired her eloquence on this subject.

'Um,' said Crispin from the bottom of the stairs.

'*What*?!' said Millie from the top.

'Um, I'm supposed to be going now. You asked me to stay on until you got back but not to stay over the weekend . . . so er, I've arranged to go to this place near Glastonbury.'

Millie looked hugely let down.

'Oh Crisp, you can't leave me here with four kids marauding round!'

'Do you want me to stay over, then?'

'Just stay for supper, please. Oh, and if David rings, tell him we'll be up by midday.'

She disappeared, then popped back.

'Could you put some wine in the fridge?'

When David woke it must have been nearly six thirty. He could make out the time on his wrist-watch as he nuzzled her breasts. He lay there like a baby and Helena stroked his head. The time was six-thirty but the time was also standing still. David gazed down, with sad admiration, at the marks that pregnancy had made on Helena's waist and when he looked up there were the creases round her eyes. Yet when he saw those eyes, looking into his, none of the other stuff really mattered.

'That was very good,' he said. He wondered why it was so good. 'Shall we do it again?'

Helena was also wondering why it had been so good. She had wanted to. That was definitely part of it. Now he wanted to she was less relaxed. David began to kiss her breasts. 'No,' she said. David was heading towards her left nipple. He always went for that one first. She found herself disliking the predictability almost as much as the trespass. He stopped and looked up at her.

'I don't understand,' he said. Helena wrestled with what she should say.

'I think we ought to get some food.'

It was a quarter to seven now. All the provisions that Helena had bought were at 27 High Street.

'I could go into Montgomery or Newtown,' said David trying to be reasonable. 'See what I can get.'

'That would be nice,' said Helena and she sat up in a very definite way. 'Where are my clothes?' she asked.

'I think we left them by the pool. Don't get dressed,' he asked her. 'Have a bath or something and I'll be back as soon as I can.'

It was odd this feeling inside her. It was like anger. A quarter on an hour ago she had been so fond of him, so fulfilled, and yet once he was awake she seemed to actually hate him. She had never felt that before. However, watching David dress in his usual careful manner, Helena found herself growing fonder again. And then she ran a bath. What was happening to her?

Millie's bath was beginning to grow cold. Fortunately Katrin had wandered in and been sent down to get a glass of wine for her mother. This had been some consolation but generally it was a pretty shitty start to the weekend.

Crispin walked in as Millie was finishing her drink. 'Oh, I– um– I'm sorry,' he faltered.

'Don't be daft,' said Millie. She had enough to bother her at the moment. Who cared if her estranged common-law husband saw her in the bath?

'Just getting my things,' said Crispin.

'Where is it you're going?' Millie asked putting her glass down on the window ledge.

'Oh, um, it's a sort of monastic thing,' he explained. 'A retreat. I thought it would help.'

'Uhuh. No women then?'

'There might be,' he explained. 'The community is male but, er, but I don't think there's a bar on women going on retreat, as such.'

'So *she* isn't joining you?' Millie asked, pointedly. She couldn't help it. And the daft thing was she knew she didn't suspect that at all.

'If you mean Sue,' said Crispin, '*no.*'

Millie sat up. It was time to get out.

'Are you gay, d'you think?' she asked Crispin. He smiled an unseen smile as he zipped up his toilet bag. 'No more than any other boy who had my kind of education.'

'You're aroused by women?'

'Yes.'

'Not men?'

'No.'

Millie stood up in the water. She could be inside his trousers and down on top of him in an instant, they both knew that.

'I'm sorry,' said Crispin and he put his hands lightly on her shoulders. 'I'm sorry. It wouldn't be fair on either of us.'

'Fuck fair,' she said stepping out of the bath.

'I'm sorry.'

Millie hit him on the shoulder. She hit him and hit him. 'You queer bastard,' she said. 'I hate you!' Crispin stood there. Every time she hit him he rocked on his feet but he didn't move. He seemed to feel that his role was to absorb the blows. Millie hated him and hated herself. She hadn't intended this to happen. She thought she was over him but every time she saw Crispin the hope seemed to rise physically within her.

'I hate you so much,' she cried.

Crispin tried to embrace her, to calm the anger as he might calm a child, but the gesture was fumbled. She avoided his touch.

'*Bastard.*' They were both hurting so much.

'I'd better go,' he replied.

David had rung and said goodnight to Nick and Emma, bought a bottle of the most expensive wine he could find in the Montgomery Spar and come back with bread, cheese and fruit. They ate in the tiny bedroom with flakes of french bread dropping onto the sheets. He was sorry she had put her dress back on but intrigued by the knowledge that she wore nothing else underneath. How perverse that a nightdress of similar proportions would be far less arousing.

'Odd without the children,' said Helena.

There was something unreal and yet wonderfully simple about being there without Emma and Nick. When you were hungry you just bought food and ate it. Why was family life so complicated?

'We should go for a walk tomorrow,' said David. The children hated walks. Helena nodded.

'And I should spend more time with Nick,' David continued. 'Emma's got to an age now when she'll be wanting to talk to you. I should try harder with Nick.'

Helena nodded again.

'You know,' said David. 'I really did admire the way you campaigned for Nick. You really saved his life.'

Helena nodded. 'Me and Sarah John.'

'I should have said that before,' he admitted, finishing his bread. She nodded yet again. 'I do want to get on better with him, you know. It's finding the time. I don't know—'

Helena had suddenly got up. She had swept the bread crumbs

up with her hand and thrown them into the bin. Angrily she tugged her dress off. Helena's irritations had often manifested themselves in sudden unexpected movements, but never before in stripping. She paced the tiny room (an activity which didn't take long) as he struggled to remove his shoes again. Then Helena threw herself on the bed. She seemed angry or aroused beyond endurance and rolled from side to side. David was just undoing his trousers when she leant forward and grabbed him by the shoulders and pulled him on top of her. He fell awkwardly and found her mouth on his, kissing him repeatedly as he struggled to kick off his trousers.

'I love you,' he said, his lips somewhere between her collarbone and chest.

'I hate you,' she replied. These were words she had not expected to say. He looked stunned by that statement.

'Why?' he asked.

'Because you left me alone with Nick,' she said.

'When?' In his compassion he was going to stroke the stray hair that lay on her face, she could feel his hands coming towards her. 'Linna?' he said. Angrily she pushed his hands away, and him away. David lost his balance and fell to one side.

'I hate you!' said Helena and she started to hit him.

'What are you doing?' shouted David, lying on his back and lifting his fists to ward off the blows. Helena climbed up over him.

'You selfish, selfish bastard,' she shouted. 'You left me alone with Nick when he was dying!'

'I never left you!' he cried.

'Oh not in the house,' she said. 'Not in bed. But here!' She hit him on the chest. 'And here!' She hit him again. 'Or wherever it is your heart is, you selfish, selfish bastard.'

To David this was a glimpse into the pit of madness. Or rather, given his current position spread-eagled on the bed, it was the vision of a devilish, raven-haired avenger, astride him like an incubus. Frightening yet demonically arousing.

Recently, when they had made love Helena had bitten his shoulder, but that was during intercourse and women were, by all accounts, strange things after penetration. But this was sheer hatred mixed with sexual fury. He was alarmed and yet excited. David reached up and put his hands on her breasts which now hung irresistibly in front of him. Helena wrestled his hands away.

'I never left you alone,' he insisted, grabbing hold of her a second time. Again she pulled his hands away and the fight became his hands grappling with her hands.

'You bastard, bastard, bastard!' she shouted. Somehow in all the tussling he had come inside her. They looked at each other in surprise, Helena glaring at him for the intrusion. Then she held his hands down hard by his side and started to move up and down on top of him.

It was only after Crispin had left that Millie realised no-one had told her parents of the day's events and the delay. She wondered about asking Katrin to ring but Bunny had suddenly been very upset about Crispin leaving and Millie couldn't face her again at the moment. So she sat in the kitchen with what remained of the wine and dialled. She was going to keep it businesslike but when her father answered, and sounded so grateful to hear from her, Millie found herself unable to speak.

'Dad,' she wanted to say. 'You stopped loving Mum once. Did you ever find a way of loving her again?'

'Is everything all right?' Millie's father asked.

'Uhuh,' said Millie. Everything's fine. The kids are fine, the job's going fine, I'm fine.'

'And Crispin?'

'He– um– he won't be coming with us. Got himself double booked, the silly twit,' she almost choked.

Tell me, Dad, tell me he'll find a way of loving me again.

Crispin just managed to catch the last bus out from Bath and he watched the sun turn pink from its dusty windows. The bus was almost empty, save for a young mother and her four-year-old son sitting down by the driver. As they wound on their way over the Mendips, the whole world was flooded by a burst of rosy sunset from the west. Crispin saw the boy fall asleep and his mother put her arm around him. He thought of Sue, and of Millie and of himself and he felt that he might cry. He hadn't been dwelling on his his research but suddenly the words of St Paul came to him. 'Though I give my body to be burned, and have not Love, it profiteth me nothing.' We are here such a short time, Crispin thought. If we cannot love, what point is there?

The next morning Millie was woken by Nick Mosford and Katrin.

'He wants his Mum,' said Katrin holding the hand of a very red-faced boy. 'I've tried waking Emma but she's asleep.'

'It's OK,' said Millie 'We're going to see her soon as the car is fixed. Get me a Coke, will you, Rabbit?'

'Sure,' said Katrin, happy to abandon the miserable looking boy to Millie

'What time is it?' she asked.

'Six o'clock.'

Millie was *never* awake at six o'clock on a Saturday morning.

'I want Mum,' said Nick unhappily.

Helena actually awoke at about this time not because she knew her boy needed her but because David fell out of bed. They had spent a strange night making love compulsively, talking and, in between the bouts of sex and confessional, sleeping close to each other. As day made itself clear through the undrawn curtains, David had stirred from where he was lying on top of her and then it was that he finally overbalanced and crashed on to the floor. After a moment of confusion he dopily crawled back into bed, and into her.

'Oh we can't again,' moaned Helena stroking the back of his head. She was so tired that she had lost count of how often they had done it. While they were having sex extra resources of energy came from nowhere but afterwards she was doubly shattered.

'You'll hardly notice,' said David. 'I promise if you get even an inkling that I'm doing this I'll stop.'

'Doing what?' she asked, her arms around his shoulders now.

'This,' he said.

'Oh that,' she said.

'Yes this,' he said. 'And this, and this.'

'And this,' she joined in.

'Oh yes, definitely that,' he replied. And they started repeating it like a mantra, enjoying the simulated frenzy, until the real thing interposed itself briefly and everything was over yet again.

Millie found breakfast hell but she had to be up to check the garage mechanic arrived. She was on the phone at half past eight just to make really sure someone was sent out. It was only after she had put the receiver down with an aggressive flourish that Millie noticed Jonathan was wearing one of her dresses.

'Jon, why are you wearing that?' she asked. Jonathan grinned and said moo. Emma tittered.

Millie sighed. 'Well, you'll have to change when the car's repaired.'

'Oink, oink!' said Jonathan.

'Oh shut up,' Millie retorted as she went to the fridge.

'Oinkkk!' shouted Nick Mosford in a very loud voice.

Give me strength, thought Millie.

Crispin had woken early too. He had been given a small undecorated guest room which was painted white. Last night he had unpacked nothing from his suitcase apart from a nightshirt and the photograph that Millie had given him some months ago. It showed Crispin with Jonathan and Katrin. He had spent a long time looking at that last night. It was ironic that Millie was the one who took the family photos. Apart from a few of Katrin's accidental skyscapes which, if you were lucky, might just have just caught the heads of Crispin and Millie, there were no photos of the two of them. Crispin looked at his children. He loved them so, of that much he was sure. He knew that he was not a good father by instinct but he had learned to be concerned for them, learned to anticipate their needs, learned to be around when they wanted him. And part of that learning had meant that he now *had* an instinct, albeit a learned instinct, to be with them. He missed them. He wondered what they were doing.

'I wonder what they're doing?' asked Helena of David as they sat by the swimming pool. David had come back with a jar of instant coffee last night so breakfast was possible, after a fashion.

'I'll ring later,' said David. He also said that last night had been wonderful.

'Mm,' said Helena. She was looking at the view and smelling the coffee before she drank it.

'I'm sorry I hit you,' she said. David took her hand. 'I'm discovering a lot of things about you,' he said. 'I really didn't realise how badly you felt.'

'No,' she said.

'But you feel better now?' he asked.

'At the moment, yes. I don't think it's over yet. I think I'm coming to terms with it still.'

David was unsure of her meaning. 'The Nick business?'

Helena nodded and studied the view.

'I really had no idea you felt like that,' he said again.

'I think,' said Helena. 'I think I loved you less for not loving Nick when he was ill.' David tried to protest, he had loved Nick, he loved him now.

'You withdrew,' she insisted. 'I felt it.'

David wasn't used to this kind of discussion. This wasn't a David and Helena conversation.

'I, er, I did feel inadequate,' he admitted. 'That he was unwell, that I'd fathered such a sickly child. I did feel that it was my fault, that another man . . .'

She was looking at him with such compassion

'It wasn't anybody's *fault*.'

'No,' said David. 'I can see that.' Her hand was towards him and he took it. She had dry hands, long and dry. He could still remember holding her hand for the first time in Oxford.

'Please, I want to make love,' he said and he said it in such a simple way that Helena laughed. It was like Nick asking if he could go on the slide again.

'You need a mistress,' she told him.

David shook his head. 'I'm monogamous at heart.'

'A highly sexed monogamist,' she pointed out.

'I need you, Linna.'

'You've got me,' she said and she moved over to sit on his lap. 'Only some time soon, we're going to have two children again. And then if you want this to continue, you're going to have to start coming to bed earlier in the evening.'

'No problem,' said David, lifting her dress and sliding his hand inside her welcoming thigh.

Some heavy footsteps announced grey Alyson who looked as tired as David and Helena ought, given the small amount of sleep they'd had.

'Telephone for you, Dr Mosford,' she announced from the archway. 'You haven't seen my sod of a husband, have you?'

David and Helena looked at each other. *Dr* Mosford sounded ominously like the University. Stella had said there would be no decisions made over the weekend.

But it wasn't Stella, or Carys Bloody Rees, it was Millie whose fucking car had just been given the once over by a useless spotty teenager who wanted to tow it in.

'So I'm hiring,' she announced. 'Bugger the expense, I'm coming up. Be with you some time after lunch.'

'How are the children?' David asked.

'Oh, your friend Sarah's got them.'

'Sarah has?'

'Can you believe it?' said Millie. 'I went to the chemist's to get some Tampax and those four were being such little sods with the loofahs and what not that I thought we were going to be asked to leave. I really lost my rag and that was when Linna's friend Sarah Thingy appeared from nowhere and offered to take them off to the park.'

'And where are they now?'

'She's got them running relay races or something. It's amazing what she can do with kids.'

'She's pretty effective with adults,' added David.

When he got back Helena was sitting holding a swimming costume that she'd been lent by Alyson. She glanced up. She was convinced that David had the news. And there, hovering over his shoulder, was the spectre of Gareth, poised to come between them.

'*Millie*,' said David. 'They'll be here this afternoon.' Helena felt she couldn't bear it any more. It had been over a week now since she last spoke to Gareth, over a week that she had been struggling to choose between a man who would promise her the world and a man who could only give her Llandaff. The question had resolved in her mind last night. Now she felt sure.

'David, there's something I want to tell you,' she said, taking a deep breath.

He wished she hadn't said that. He had an ominous feeling about the way those words came out and it was a feeling that recalled a terrible time. The restaurant in Siena. This was how he felt on their honeymoon.

'Shall we go for a walk?' he asked. They had talked about a walk, through the redwoods perhaps. There was a place from which you could get a view of the castle, distant, in Montgomery.

'This will do, won't it?' she continued. 'It doesn't amount to many words.'

David sat down. He had known as soon as she had asked if they might talk that the subject would be him and her, the two of them. He also knew that somehow, strangely, all that wonderful sex last night might just be Helena's way of saying goodbye.

'Are you sure you want to say this?' he asked. 'You know what happened last time.' Did she know he was talking about Siena? The subject they never spoke of . . .

'Not everything needs to be said you know,' he told her. He would have begged her if he could.

Helena didn't understand. This wasn't like David.

'I wanted to talk to you about Gareth,' she began.

'That's what you said on our honeymoon,' he interrupted.

'Yes,' she said, surprised at that remark. Where had it come from?

David got up and looked at the view. He had a horrible sense of déjà-vu about this. He knew what she was going to say. He was going to ask her if she'd seen Gareth and she was going to say yes she had.

'You've seen Gareth since the Chinese meal with Anders and Pip?' he began.

'Yes.'

'I see. At our house?'

'No.'

'Where then?' he asked. Helena wished the conversation hadn't gone this way. It seemed to have slipped out of her control and become something that it should never have been.

'At Barrington,' she said

'*What*?!' She knew he was not a violent man but if anything was going to make David lash out, this clearly was it.

'You saw Gareth at Barrington, when you were staying there?'

Helena tried to say yes because that was the truth and still she believed that the truth could not hurt. The truth ought to be good.

'He, er, came to see me.'

To David this was more than déjà-vu, this was the nightmare from which there is no escape. This was the same random cruelty that had broken into their honeymoon, replayed all over again. This was turning around fifteen years later to find that however hard you ran, the wolf was still there waiting, slavering, ready to devour. He had not escaped. He had never hoped to defeat these monsters entirely, they would always be in his head, but he didn't think they would break in from outside again. But no, there they were.

Helena was looking up at him in such acute concern.

'It isn't what you think,' she said but he wasn't listening to her.

'What did he want?'

She really didn't want to reply but her not replying only fuelled his anguish. What was happening? she asked herself.

David was also asking that question. Only last night they were so much in love, she with him and he with her. This was the nightmare breaking into their life and splitting it apart. Completely apart.

'He wanted you to go away with him?'

She nodded.

'And what did you say?' Helena tried to find her voice. Suddenly her decision to keep all this to herself seemed monstrously wrong. She no longer felt like the person who was torn between two men.

'You said you *would*?' he asked.

No, she was the person who loved David and wanted to be with him for the rest of their lives. *Why hadn't she told Gareth that?*

Well, at least she could put David's mind at rest about that.

'I said I would have to think about it,' she replied. But hearing her indecision spoken out loud suddenly made it seem worse, much worse to both of them.

'You've been thinking about leaving me for over a week?!' Now she thought he *was* going to hit her. 'Christ almighty, Helena, last time it only took you half an hour!'

She knew that they had reached a point of total crisis. Dreadful things might happen, dreadful things were happening. She leapt up and took him by the arms.

'You know things have been bad between us!' she said and she said it angrily. 'What was all that last night about if not about rebuilding?'

'Yes! Bit bloody ironic that!' snapped David.

'No it wasn't ironic,' she countered, her desperation angry and eloquent. 'Last night helped me see there was a future for us. That there *was*. Because I'd really begun to wonder—'

'You had?' he asked.

'Yes I bloody had and if you hadn't wondered that yourself then you're pretty bloody stupid!' Helena didn't normally swear. The shock of this language threw him momentarily.

'But for over a *week!*' He looked desolate. It sounded awful and yet Helena realised that in her own panic she had missed the point.

'I told Gareth I wouldn't decide *until the job was decided*. That it wasn't fair on you to know he'd even suggested it until you'd had the interview and been told who'd got it.' David was still concerned.

'You couldn't tell him straight away though? You had to keep your options open.' He was sounding now more miserable than angry.

'Things haven't been good between us,' she repeated and she shook him. 'Have they?' David shook his head.

'But why did you tell me this now?' he asked. 'Why didn't you wait till after we heard from Stella?'

'Because I know now,' Helena insisted.

'Know what?' He was so confused by this stage that it was having to be spelt out.

'That it's you I want. If you still love me, you are the one I want.'

David tried to take this on board. 'Why?' he asked. 'Is it because of the children?'

'In a way.'

His pride was hurt. 'You mustn't stay with me just for the children.'

'No, listen.' She tried to move closer to him, to put his arms around her.

'Listen, it's because it's taken me till now to realise what it is that I've been valuing when I've spoken to Gareth, when I've been with him. It's that we've always been *without the children*. It was such a release. I couldn't understand why it was so important to me. But last night we were together, you and me, and we were without the children and I felt the same . . .' she struggled for the word. 'The same freedom with you. Only more so because I love you.'

'It's not . . .' he began to say and then he turned away because the tears that had been imminent for so long had started.

'What?' she asked.

'It's not that you're, that . . . It's not that you're doing the decent thing?'

She had her arms tight around him now. 'The decent thing?' she asked.

'I always felt, after you told me in Siena about Gareth coming to visit you the night before we were married . . . I always felt that you took half an hour to decide because you were very tempted but you decided in the end to do the decent thing. Not to let your family down. To stand by me.'

Helena was stunned. She had been married to this man for fifteen years and she had had no idea. Never, ever, that he had attributed these motives to her. She knew he meant it because David was not trying to hide his tears any more. He doggedly repeated his fear to her and as he did he found himself breaking down into sobs.

'I always thought that you would have preferred to marry Gareth . . . but you stuck with me . . . in front of your family . . . because you didn't want to behave in a scandalous manner. Not in Barrington.' He sniffed. 'And of course because you felt a bit sorry for me.'

Helena held on to him more tightly than she had ever done before. 'But we've had so many good times,' she insisted.

'Yes,' he agreed. 'But in the bad times, when they came, like with Nick, I always felt that maybe you might have preferred to be married to Gareth.'

'I married you because you were the man I loved.' She shook him in the hope that these words would sink in.

'Yes, but didn't you think that if Gareth had been the father, Nick would have been OK?'

'Never,' she said. 'It never occurred to me.'

'It occurred to me,' said David. 'When I saw you with him and he was so ill.'

'David,' she said, and she was tearful too

'Oh God, please hold me, Linna.'

She did and they stood for a long time by the edge of the pool, swaying dangerously close to the edge in that embrace.

'Let's go inside,' Helena whispered to him. David nodded. 'Please,' he said.

At that point footsteps announced Alyson of the dusty hair.

'Sorry to bother,' she called from the archway. 'Mrs Kemp on the phone again!' David sighed.

'Oh dear,' Helena shouted back. 'Would you mind telling her we're still in bed!'

Later that morning Alyson stuck a message on the apartment door. It read *Mrs Kemp says maximum lie-in time five hours.* and in brackets was a little PS *(ETA:3pm)*

David and Helena went to visit Powys Castle and had lunch within the cold stone bastion. They talked about all the things that neither of them had realised and there seemed to be a lot. They also talked about Lyn from Leeds and why there had been a Lyn from Leeds and David was surprised how much Helena had realised about this episode. He was also surprised that she minded so little about what had or had not happened; it was the loss of his support that had hurt. They also talked of how things would be better in future. That Helena must tell David what help she needed from him and not just cope. And that David must believe she loved him and stop looking to sex to prove it.

'Even though it has,' said David.' Proved it very much.'

'Even though it has,' she agreed. 'Very much indeed.'

'And can I touch your breasts again?' David asked because her denying him had had such an effect on them last night.

'Not over lunch,' said Helena. So David proposed a toast to Helena's breasts but he proposed it in Welsh. For Welsh was a very poetic language for such things and the fourteenth century flowering of *cywyddau* had addressed itself to little else. So they toasted all of Helena's attributes with the chilled Welsh water, which was all they had to hand, and then Helena proposed a toast to Millie's car.

'To its wonderful gaskets,' David agreed. 'Long may they blow.'

Sarah John saw off Millie, the children and her hired car feeling strangely pleased with herself. She was a reasonable woman and she never judged. She had had her reservations about Millie Kemp but then she had been told so much about that woman which was worrying. Yet Millie had been looking after David and Helena's children while they had a long-earned break. This was admirable. Sarah had offered many times to have Emma and Nick while their parents went to a hotel but David and Helena had never taken her up on that. Well, she was not proud. She knew that these things could only be done the way they had to be done. And the four darlings had definitely benefited from a spot of calming down, and some cleaning up, at Sarah's hands. When Millie arrived with the hired car Sarah felt that she and her flannel had done some good in the world.

Sarah decided to take some flowers round to David and Helena. She had a back door key that was Mrs Morgan's spare in case of emergencies. Here it was she met the handsome man with an endearing lock of hair. He was coming from the front of Ty Escob and looked preoccupied.

'They've gone away,' Sarah called out. He swung round to see where her voice was coming from.

'David and Helena, they're in mid Wales.'

'Oh, thank you,' he replied. Sarah was very happy to talk if he was but he seemed most uncomfortable.

'You were looking for the Mosfords?' she asked cheerily.

'Well, Helena, actually. I'd rung but there was no answer.'

'That's because they're away,' she repeated.

'Yes.'

'Shall I give her a message?' Sarah asked.

'Oh no. Thanks all the same.'

And with that he was gone. 'I think Helena may have a secret admirer,' said Sarah John to Mostyn over a good cup of tea later that day and then she laughed. Mostyn laughed too but then he always did.

'Mossy, what did I just say?' Sarah asked in a moment of intuition. Mostyn looked up from the book he was reading. 'No idea. But it was funny at the time. Very funny indeed.'

'Dear old Mossy,' said Sarah and she thought about baking a cake.

The End

David didn't get the job. Stella was, of course, very compassionate over coffee. But David was less concerned about her high opinion of him. He wanted to know who had got it.

'Karen Gombrich,' said Stella. 'Did you hear her lecture?'

Oh the Crumpet, thought David and he smiled. Gareth Box vanquished by the Crumpet.

He almost laughed.

David and Helena coped with this disappointing news by sodding the University greatly. And then within that week Karen Gombrich got a better offer and declined the proffered chair and the Mosfords had to go through all that waiting and doubt again. One hot evening, while Stella and the VC were presumably chewing over the also-rans, David decided he had had enough and wrote out his resignation from an academic body that was at such pains to minimise the importance they placed on him.

'Sod the University,' he said.

'You've taken three pages to say that?' Helena enquired.

'I didn't want to leave Stella in any doubt as to my motives.'

Helena told him she was very impressed but she also wondered what they might live on in future.

'Well,' said David, 'we have no mortgage and no private education, even the car's paid for and what I make from TV and journalism should easily,' here he paused, 'should easily pay for us to go and spend one night in a really good hotel.'

'Who needs money?' said Helena. 'I suppose I could do something while you have a think.'

'Then again I could just tear this up,' David suggested, waving his resignation letter. The telephone rang.

'Gareth,' said David. They had been waiting for a response to the letter Helena sent him, declining his offer of bed and board in Vermont. But now they also feared the news that Professor Box had been invited to occupy the chair which had never even borne the imprint of Professor Gombrich's illustrious rear. This presumably was Gareth, or news of Gareth's triumphant return to Wales, and a very real possibility of David sending that letter. But it wasn't Gareth, or news thereof. It was Stella Price.

'David, can you come and see me?'

'It's nearly ten o'clock,' he replied.

'Never too late to be Professor of Political History,' said Stella.

He nearly dropped the phone. 'Is that a joke?' he asked.

'It's the best I can manage at this time of night,' Stella replied. 'But the chair is yours. Congratulations.'

Now David did drop the phone and Helena finished the conversation for him.

'I want to tell her to stuff it,' said David as he looked for his car keys. 'I want to tell her I'm not having a job that neither Karen Gombrich nor Gareth Box wanted.'

'You don't know it was offered to Gareth,' Helena pointed out as she found his keys for him. 'Besides, the important thing is now you know they want you.'

'In the end they want me.' He looked at her. Tonight she looked plain, tired, almost ordinary. He wanted her to look again as she did at Lyme.

'I want to tell her to stuff the job,' he declared.

'But you won't,' she replied.

'But I won't,' he agreed. And he didn't.

David never did know if the chair had been offered first to Gareth. Or whether, in fact, Helena's letter had been the thing that decided Professor Box to turn it down. But did that matter? In the last ten days he and Helena might had gone over every inch of her two decisions to stay with him. And still he realised that, in the end, he would have to trust that she wanted him. The time for a leap of faith in her direction had come and yet he couldn't make it. Not yet.

Helena didn't know about Gareth and the chair either because, when Gareth replied to her letter, he never referred to the job. She preferred to think that either Gareth had not been offered the chair – because the University thought David a better candidate or that Gareth had been offered it but declined the job because he did not want to be the one to hurt her or David. Either way, she was left thinking well of somebody: her former lover or her husband's employer. One or other had behaved well.

What Gareth did say was that he going to get married. He was sure he hadn't many years left and he wanted to live out those years with a wife and children. Helena didn't show this part of the letter to David. She wished him well when she replied. She doubted that Gareth Box would find happiness in matrimony but she hoped he would. And this was the sentiment, rather than any doubt, that she expressed to him.

Millie Kemp found the life of a single parent very difficult even when she only had the weekends to cope with it. By the time Crispin was handing the kids over on Friday night, Millie needed to restore her own batteries and be fun. But at weekends Katrin and Jonathan were emotionally draining and demanding. Moreover, they no longer looked to Millie for the simple things she could best provide. One afternoon at the end of the holidays Jonathan, Maxy and Katrin wandered off on their own while Millie was asleep. They were going to Barry Island or to find Crispin – they hadn't decided which. Fortunately Sarah John found the three of them at a bus stop and brought them back. Millie had a long soul-searching session with David and Helena, and a bottle of wine, that night after which she suggested that Crispin took over the children full time and she just visited every weekend.

Crispin had been spending his weekends in Sue's old room which the landlord was pleased to rent out. But with autumn approaching, he was happy to surrender it. Once Millie was convinced that Crispin could not be persuaded to use this new arrangement as an opportunity for them to reconcile she found herself an expensive modern pied à terre just off the A48 where she entertained the kids on Friday nights and Saturday afternoons. After a while Millie started coming down to Cardiff with her new chap who was more the kind of person Gail would have chosen for her, partly because Gail had. This new chap was the first of several. Millie never found another bag of bones quite like Crispin and she never quite gave up hope of getting him back. Unfortunately.

Crispin and Helena became firm friends and he encouraged her to take up research after all this time. It was the only way for the wife of a professor to avoid becoming Wendy Dorkin. She had to have her own life. Crispin did not begin his relationship with Sue again when the autumn term commenced. This had not been his intention and she never responded to his letters.

He was pleased one day to catch a glimpse of her walking around the green with a big-hearted theological student who wore a multi-coloured college scarf and never took his arm from her shoulder. Pleased but saddened too. He would have liked to have had Sue Coity as his lover for a little while. He was sorry to lose that. But he could never have married her and that was what she wanted. Whereas this jolly fat vicar-in-the-making would marry her. And Crispin could tell that already the mysteries of sex were no longer a mystery for Sue. The man of God had helped her with that.

Crispin never embraced celibacy as a matter of policy but, unlike Millie, he didn't set out to find someone else. Helena told him that looking after children and going on religious retreats was no way to find another lover. But Crispin wanted to bide his time. He felt he was slow to love and that the women in his life had always rushed him.

'I'm worried about Crispin on his own,' said Helena looking up from her notebook one evening.

But David was not. 'Oh, plenty of women fancy him,' he replied, *'so I've been told.'*

Katie John did well enough in her GCSEs so Sarah was happy. She and Mostyn had two very good weeks touring the Gower that summer and when she discovered a postcard he was writing to his young receptionist concealed within the gazetteer Sarah decided to treat it as something of a joke. But not a joke she could share with Helena.

Helena's friend Pip continued to have a rocky relationship with Anders who continued to look at other women. In the autumn she stopped work altogether, in the hope of provoking a baby, and Anders stopped looking at other potential mothers long enough to play his part in the scheme. And indeed, by November Pip was pregnant and convinced that henceforth everything with Anders would be perfect. Neither David nor Helena openly agreed with this statement, though they toasted the imminence of Baby Arnstein with champagne. Pip was going out with some friends later that night for more celebrations and she invited David and Helena along. David declined as he had some work to do. 'In a weak and sentimental moment I made the mistake of inaugurating a Peter Dorkin Memorial Lecture,' he explained. 'And now I've got to find some fool who'll be willing to give it!'

But after two fruitless phone calls David came to the conclusion that in this respect he was probably better placed than anyone. 'I think I am the fool I was looking for,' he told Helena with a kiss.

'Me too,' she replied fondly. 'I haven't started supper. What do you want to do?'

Inevitably they started talking about Pip again. It was one of their better days. They still had good days and bad days but at least they talked about them now which meant that David was sent less often to the Spar and Martha Morgan was left to beat the carpets on her own.

'She does worry me,' said Helena for the second or third time that evening. 'It's too soon.'

'It's always too soon to have children,' he replied. They were standing, both of them, Crispin-like, at the sink.

'But you've got to start off with something strong when you have kids,' she told him. 'If not, what are you going to have left by the time they're seven or eight?'

David kissed her.

'Nearly scuppered us,' she reminded him.

'I'm sure they'll cope.'

'Are you sure you're sure?'

'No,' he admitted. 'Not really.'

Released from David's night of the long phone calls, they wondered what to do that evening. Katie John was letting it be known that homework was very light for sixth formers which probably meant that Katie either had a new boyfriend or a pressing need for babysitting money. Or both. As supper wasn't cooked, they could always catch up with Pippa . . .

'Or there's that film that's supposed to be better than anyone who's seen it thinks,' Helena suggested.

David shook his head.

She tried another idea. 'Crispin said to call round any night this week.'

'No,' said David. He found too many diversions tedious these days. 'Let's just stay in tonight. The Two Of Us.'

And although that was what he said so often these days Helena still treated it as a novel idea and one well worthy of consideration.

'Yes,' she said. 'The Two Of Us.'